WICKED'S SCANDAL

KATHLEEN AYERS

.

LONDON, 1832

"I have arranged a marriage for you."

The words thundered in Alexandra Dunforth's head, echoing so loudly they made her teeth ache. Her uncle's breath, smelling of port and ill humor, wafted over her cheek. Try as she might, she could not stop cringing in disgust from the man. Oliver Burke squeezed her upper arm and shook it, as a cat would do to a mouse in its jaws.

"Stay here." One fat, ham like hand pushed Alexandra against the wall. "Don't try anything." His moonlike visage resembling a wedge of cheese sweating in the sun, leered over her. "If you do not, your precious friends at Helmsby Abbey will all be out on the street with no references."

Alexandra's back bumped against the smooth paneling that covered the walls of Lady Dobson's ballroom. She took a deep breath to calm herself and nodded mutely.

Lord Burke snorted, smiling in approval at her compliance. He waddled away towards the gaming tables.

Alexandra sighed in relief. She squeezed her eyes tight, wishing the noisy, crowded ballroom could be nothing more than the result of eating too much treacle the night before. Cautiously, she opened her eyes. Dozens of the titled *ton* swirled about Lady Dobson's parquet ballroom. This was no dream.

"Bloody hell." The words flew out in a whisper. She looked around to see if anyone noticed her language, but no one was paying the least attention to her.

Invisibility suited Alexandra well. Left alone in Hampshire since Aunt Eloise's death, she ran the family estate, Helmsby Abbey, blissfully forgotten by Odious Oliver. Lord Oliver Burke steadfastly ignored his wife and niece, much too busy with spending the vast Dunforth fortune as fast as he could. She'd only actually seen her uncle a handful of times since her one and only Season several years ago. How she detested Odious Oliver.

"Miss Dunforth!" The shriek came from behind her left ear.

Alexandra turned to face her erstwhile chaperone, Lady Agnes Dobson.

"Stand up straight. Try to look attractive."

Lady Dobson reminded Alexandra of a praying mantis. Tall and thin, her arms overlong, she looked about to pounce on unsuspecting prey. Namely, Alexandra. For tonight's festivities, Lady Dobson wore an enormous purple turban, a spray of feathers anchored to the center held firmly in the middle with a large ruby. She looked down her thin pointed nose at Alexandra and gave a sniff as if Alexandra were spoiled pudding.

"Stop slouching! Attempt to look demure." A boney finger wagged at Alexandra. Lady Dobson's lip curled. Her duty done, she dismissed Alexandra. Lady Dobson spun in a neat semi-circle, her purple skirts fluttering around her sticklike figure and faded back into the glittering crowd.

Alexandra clasped her hands in front of her and pressed herself deeper into an alcove, wishing fervently she could simply disappear. Dread, suffocating and thick, rose up in her breast. The insane notion to run as fast as she could for the front door and hail a passing hackney made her legs twitch. Lady Dobson's home nearly burst with the glittering *ton*; surely no one would notice one slight spinster from Hampshire running for her life. She chuckled ruefully. *I am very neatly trapped. Outsmarted and outmaneuvered by a man who has all the intelligence of a turnip.*

"A green dragon tattoo? How positively scandalous!"

Alexandra looked to her left. A beautiful brunette, introduced to Alexandra earlier as Lady Martin, waved her fan and gestured towards the ballroom. Lady Martin licked her lips as if she had just eaten a sugar biscuit. She didn't look the least scandalized. She looked...*hungry*.

"Richard has seen *it* at the club. Lord Cambourne took off his shirt after a fencing match. His opponent scratched him, *accidentally*." The buxom blonde standing next to Lady Martin wiggled her eyebrows as she relayed the information. "Then his opponent had the unfortunate notion to make an observation about Lord Cambourne's mother. His *real* mother."

Lady Martin gave a small gasp. "What type of idiot would insult the Marquess of Cambourne? The very wealthy and powerful Marquess of Cambourne?"

The blonde shrugged. "Lord Cambourne nearly beat the man to death. Some baron's son. He's now recuperating at his father's country estate."

Intrigued, Alexandra took a step out of the alcove that sheltered her. She loved lurid gothic novels when not running Helmsby Abbey and avoiding her uncle. The hero of her favorite series, Lord Thurston, sported a tattoo and he often

3

engaged in swordplay with unsavory characters. Listening to gossip was much better than worrying about when her uncle would arrive with her unwanted suitor.

"Richard says the tattoo is actually quite beautiful. The dragon's head takes up the whole of Lord Cambourne's back. The tail," the blonde paused dramatically, "winds around his *navel*," she whispered.

Lady Martin twittered behind her fan.

Alexandra stood on tiptoe. Her height kept her from all but a peek of a tall man with glossy blue-black hair making his way across the ballroom. The aristocrats parted as if they were the Red Sea and the dark-haired man were Moses. She doubted, though, that Moses had sported a tattoo.

"He's this season's biggest catch in spite of his rather dubious character. Do you remember that business with Lord Ranson's wife? I'm told Cambourne did the honorable thing by firing into the air and allowing Ranson the opportunity for a clear shot. Ranson, the idiot, became so startled by Cambourne's actions that he put his gun down and shot his own toe off."

Alexandra rolled her eyes. Duels sounded very romantic, but they rarely turned out well. She found it a stupid way to settle an argument. Aunt Eloise instructed Alexandra that the honor of men, particularly a titled gentleman, was questionable at best. *'Just look at the man I married with his immaculate pedigree,'* Aunt Eloise sighed as if in pain, *'for an example of how perfect breeding can equal a foul nature.'* Alexandra agreed with Aunt Eloise on that point.

"Satan Reynolds—"

"Watch your tongue, Lady Norris!" Lady Martin looked around, saw Alexandra, and dismissed her. "It would not do well to run afoul of the Dowager Marchioness. She does not care for her grandson to be called *Satan* Reynolds or for the reputation he has garnered."

4

What a ridiculous nickname! Alexandra gave a small snort. Oh, she supposed it sounded very deadly and all but really, she mused, Lord Cambourne likely came up with the moniker for its seductive quality on women. Lady Martin practically salivated as she studied the man.

Alexandra's eyes flicked over the blonde. In addition to being stuffed into her dress, an annoying spray of ostrich feathers rose from the side of Lady Norris's head. She resembled an overstuffed capon.

Lady Norris sniffed and lowered her voice. "Of course, you know all about him living in Macao with the heathen Chinese. He went native, smoking opium and keeping a *harem* like a Chinese warlord." The words dangled in the air above Lady Martin, waiting for her to take the bait.

Macao? Chinese harems? Alexandra moved as close as she could to the two women. Having never really left the safety of Hampshire, and certainly having never been any farther than London, Alexandra adored tales of faraway places and exotic locales. Many nights she would sit in the Helmsby Abbey library with a cup of tea, brought by the aged butler Jameson, and read an entire book on geography in one sitting.

"Oh, *my*! He *is* something, isn't he?" Lady Martin clutched one hand to her breast as if she were about to swoon.

Alexandra's attention snapped back to Lady Martin. She tilted her head in an effort to hear. The women of the *ton* were incredibly silly. Alexandra never found any man to be worth swooning over—even if he *did* have a tattoo. She stood on her toes to try to catch a better look at the man who'd caused such dramatic behavior.

Satan Reynolds burst through the crowded mass of dandified gentlemen and preening ladies into Alexandra's line of vision. She gaped, realized her mouth hung open, and quickly shut it. The man striding through the ballroom did indeed resemble the name he had been given, for after all, wasn't Satan supposed to be the most beautiful angel of all?

Lord Cambourne was tall and lithe with broad shoulders that stretched the limits of his perfectly tailored coat. He walked slowly through the crowd, never acknowledging the stares of the men and women who stood aside to let him pass. Nervous whispers and gestures followed in his wake. The long, dark hair danced above the top of his expertly tied cravat, in defiance of the current fashion. He looked down his patrician nose and across his elegantly carved cheekbones to survey his surroundings with bored arrogance.

Alexandra thought him the most stunning creature she had ever seen. The lads in Hampshire weren't even the same *species* as the man sauntering across the ballroom.

A tall voluptuous redhead in black silk pushed her way through the crowd, blocking his path. Satan Reynolds quirked his full mouth in amusement but gave the woman his attention.

The woman dipped into a curtsy so deep that even Alexandra could see directly down the woman's bodice. No doubt Satan Reynolds could as well. He smiled and brushed a kiss across the redhead's hand.

"Lucky Lady Fellowes." Lady Martin opened her fan. "How convenient for her that Lord Fellowes's heart finally gave out last year. The man was eighty if he was a day. She looks quite stunning in her black, doesn't she?"

Alexandra had to agree. The black of Lady Fellowes's dress set off her red hair and creamy skin to perfection.

Lord Cambourne leaned into the redhead, cocking his head to listen to something she said, while his fingers glided over her arm.

"Did I ever tell you that Richard attended Eton with Lord Cambourne and the other Wickeds?" Lady Norris said sotto voce.

Lady Martin shook her head. "No."

"Cambourne, the son of the Mad Countess and Viscount Lindley were roommates and teased by the other lads. Lord Cambourne for his possible illegitimacy, though it's never been proven," Lady Norris added carefully. "The insanity of the earl's mother and Viscount Lindley..." She snapped her fan shut. "Well, I think we all know about *his* family, don't we? Even I am not bold enough to discuss him *openly*."

Lord Cambourne nodded politely again to Lady Fellowes, brushing her knuckles against his lips before moving again through the mass of the ton. He likely knew he was the subject of much speculation by the number of whispers and hands over mouths, but he never slowed or even spoke to anyone else. Alexandra wondered if it bothered him—to be on display. He had to be. His looks alone, regardless of his reputation, would garner attention wherever he went.

Lady Norris nodded towards Lord Cambourne. "The three lads visited a gypsy in the woods—a woman who could see the future. The lads wished to learn their fates."

Lady Martin gave her friend a skeptical look and pursed her plum colored lips into a perfect rosette.

"The old lady said they were cursed with wickedness and gave them each a terrible fate. Ever after, the three were always called The Wickeds. The other boys gave them a wide berth."

"Really? What rubbish! Was the 'curse' of Satan Reynolds to be the most sought-after rake in London?" Lady Martin mocked her friend.

"All I know is that he lived up to his name. Richard's sisters were never allowed to visit him at school when Satan Reynolds was in residence for fear they'd be ruined." Lady Norris seemed quite sure of her story. "He even seduced the headmaster's wife! The elder Lord Cambourne sent for his immoral son, dragging him back to London. A few years later,

Satan Reynolds just disappeared into the jungles of Macao, which I'm told is much more primitive than India. We all thought he was dead. His grandmother, the Dowager, sent ten men—*ten men*—to fetch Lord Cambourne back to England. He didn't wish to come back, you see. *Ever*."

The two women exchanged a look of confusion as if not understanding why anyone, let alone a man who had the title and wealth of Lord Cambourne, wouldn't wish to be in England amongst the *ton*.

Alexandra felt a pang of sympathy for the handsome, tattooed marquess. Of course, he hadn't wished to come back. Who would want to be the object of so much scrutiny? Or to have your parentage questioned? She wondered why he chose Macao for his escape. How she would love to ask him. Now that would be a true scandal, having the biggest rake in London at her disposal to answer the questions of a bluestocking. He would make a most inspiring Lord Thurston.

Lord Cambourne reached the far end of the ballroom. He nodded in greeting to several gentlemen and their overly adorned wives. The women twittered, shooting him buttery glances from beneath their lashes while their husbands regarded Lord Cambourne with trepidation.

Alexandra thought it all quite amusing.

She turned back to Lady Norris and Lady Martin but the women were no longer beside her. The duo moved into the crowd, Lady Norris furiously waving her fan at another subject to gossip about.

Out of the corner of Alexandra's eye, the purple turban reappeared. Lady Dobson made straight for Alexandra, her face wrinkling up like a prune.

"Your uncle has requested your presence," Lady Dobson hissed. One claw-like hand caught Alexandra beneath her elbow. "Come. How fortunate you are that he cares enough to find you a suitor. He could have just put you out on the streets as soon as he sells the estate."

Alexandra didn't *feel* fortunate. She felt as if she would faint at any moment. She did not wish to marry and even if she did, it would not be to suit her uncle. Alexandra needed a moment to think.

"Lady Dobson, I wish to use the Ladies Necessary Room," Alexandra said in as modest a tone as she could muster.

The purple turban shook. "Down the hall," she said as she pointed a boney finger, "to the right, then a direct left. No wandering about. You are to return within a quarter hour. I shall inform Lord Burke."

Alexandra nodded politely, lowering her eyes so that Lady Dobson couldn't see the avid dislike in them. "Yes, my lady. I won't be but a moment. I fear several of the pins in my hair are coming loose."

Lady Dobson glanced at Alexandra's hair. "I'm not sure all the pins in the world would help *that*." The purple turban quivered and walked away.

Alexandra clenched her teeth, willing herself to walk calmly towards the doorway Lady Dobson indicated. She took a deep breath, trying to ignore the fact that she felt like a lamb being led to slaughter. She hated London and hated the overdressed collection of snobs that constituted the *ton*. Alexandra considered herself most firmly "on the shelf," and planned on staying there. The notion of her uncle marrying her off was ridiculous and laughable. No man had ever looked at her twice.

Lost in her own thoughts, she didn't immediately notice the quiet. The music from the ballroom sounded mute and distant. She had missed the turn for the Ladies Necessary Room and a dark hall, dimly lit with sconces, stretched before her. Alexandra turned, meaning to go back the way she had come when a small ping sounded on the marble beneath her feet. She sighed in frustration, knowing a pin restraining her hair had given out. An unruly curl, delighted with its freedom, spiraled down her back. Another ringlet sprang free, accompanied by another ping.

"Damnation!" She squinted in the dim light. One runaway pin twinkled on the floor and she grabbed it. Now where was the other? She looked up and spied a slice of light farther down the corridor with something glinting in it. She moved to collect her other pin and came to a dark paneled door, standing slightly ajar. The crackle of a warm fire greeted her ears. She rubbed her shoulders, chilled from the cooler air of the hallway. Alexandra looked down the hall. Surely no one would mind if she popped into the room and warmed up before returning to the ballroom. Curious, she snuck a peek into the room and gasped in pure pleasure. A library. A beautiful, lovely library!

She clasped her hands with joy, inhaling the musty smell of paper and ink mixed with leather. Books! Wonderful, wonderful books! Obviously, Lord Dobson had to be a great reader, for certainly it couldn't be Lady Dobson. That earnest lady lectured Alexandra on the evils of young ladies being too well read from the moment Alexandra first met Lady Dobson. Alexandra moved forward, the hairpins clutched in her hand as she spied the large walnut bookcases lining the room.

Wandering over to the far wall, she ran her finger over the spines of fine Moroccan leather. Titles jumped out at her, books on history, geology, and science. Her hand hovered over a large book on farming. Fingers shaking, she pulled her hand down.

Two weeks ago the thought of her uncle even remembering she existed, let alone deciding to marry her off, would have been absurd. As she lay dying, Aunt Eloise assured Alexandra that Helmsby Abbey would belong to her when she reached her twenty-fifth birthday. Oliver Burke would have no claim to the estate or Alexandra's small inheritance. Her birthday, two months away, would free her. She was positive Odious Oliver was oblivious to this fact. The family solicitor, Mr. Meechum, would assist her in getting away from her uncle. She sent a missive to Meechum & Sons just this morning urgently requesting the solicitor's help.

"Bloody hell!" Alexandra whispered to the quiet room. It felt good to use such foul language. The current circumstances warranted it. Her much unloved uncle needed money and the only things left to sell were Helmsby Abbey and Alexandra.

A chilling embrace wrapped around the smooth bare flesh of her arms. The possibility of what would happen to the people of Helmsby Abbey, should Oliver sell it, filled Alexandra with dread. Too elderly to find other positions, Mrs. Cowries, Jameson, and Cook would have nowhere to go should Oliver turn them out. They depended on Alexandra. Uncle Oliver dangled the fates of all she loved in this world over her head. She felt very much like a rabbit caught in a hunter's snare. How in the world would she escape without chewing a limb off?

Footsteps, firm and measured, sounded in the hallway. She heard the sound of a man's laughing baritone as a dark shape hovered outside the library door.

Alexandra frantically searched for a place to hide herself. Large damask curtains hung from the windows and she slid behind the dense folds. She shook the curtain, making sure her slippers were covered, and pressed herself against the wall. Alexandra held her breath, afraid to stir the curtain as the man moved into the room.

"Are you hiding from me, Lord Cambourne?" A woman's husky voice sounded in the hallway. "Making me give chase, you wicked, *wicked* man."

❧ 2 ❧

Alexandra stood very still behind the curtain. *Lord Cambourne? Satan Reynolds?*

She heard the click of the library door as it shut.

"Hello, darling! What a boring party! Lady Halston nearly put me to sleep with her gossip. She finds you quite depraved, by the way."

"Lady Halston should be more concerned about Lord Halston's wickedness than mine." The deep baritone vibrated down Alexandra's spine. An image of Lord Cambourne as he appeared in the ballroom leapt in front of her. His voice sounded as beautiful as he was.

The woman laughed lightly. "I adore your depravity. Besides, it certainly hasn't stopped every mama in London from pushing their simpering daughters at you."

"Mmmm. I'm not interested in virgins, simpering or not. I find them tiresome."

"Your grandmother does not. I'm told she interviews young girls by the dozen. Her specifications are quite exacting. She wants you married with an heir."

Alexandra peered through a small crack in the curtain and snuck a look at the couple. Lord Cambourne had his back to her. Her eyes traveled down to the spill of inky black hair over his shoulders. She looked lower. His trousers were indecently tight. She looked away. Ladies did not notice such things.

Lady Fellowes moved to stand in front of Lord Cambourne, pushing her breasts forward suggestively.

Lord Cambourne lifted a hand. His fingers drummed against the redhead's bodice. "Caro. You should go back to the ballroom instead of tempting me." The dark head pressed a kiss against the white flesh mounded over Lady Fellowes's bodice.

"*Do* I tempt you, Cam?" Lady Fellowes purred.

Alexandra nearly had a fit. She quivered in a mixture of excitement and embarrassment as she shrank back into the curtains. Could she sneak out while Lord Cambourne occupied himself with Lady Fellowes? What if they saw her as she tiptoed to the door? She could just imagine waving nonchalantly to Lord Cambourne, telling him to 'carry on' as she waltzed out.

A muted sigh of satisfaction reached Alexandra's ears. Lady Fellowes clearly relished whatever Lord Cambourne was doing to her. Alexandra tried to summon up disgust and revulsion, but instead her own traitorous breasts began to ache in response to the sounds she heard. She forced herself to stay still even as every nerve in her body tingled. *Think of something else, Alexandra! Like cleaning out the stables!*

The thump of a body landing on the couch, accompanied by a rustle of clothing piqued her curiosity. *I shall only peek.* She popped one eye around the edge of damask. *Good Lord!* Lady Fellowes had wrapped her legs around Satan Reynolds's torso and she was attempting to wrestle him to the couch. Lady Fellowes's bright green garters were in shocking contrast to her pale thighs and stark black gown. She tried to pull Lord Cambourne's hand inside her skirts.

"Come be naughty with me." Lady Fellowes pouted her red lips and swiveled her hips.

Lord Cambourne smiled indulgently. Long elegant fingers ran down Lady Fellowes's legs in appreciation. "I don't think this is an especially good time for this, Caro."

Lady Fellowes hugged him with her legs. She took one of Lord Cambourne's hands and placed it on her breast. The redhead sighed dramatically.

Alexandra stood frozen.

"Cam, Cam, I want you so badly."

The broad shoulders shifted as Lord Cambourne shrugged his dark hair back. A piece of green glinted amidst the inky strands, dangling and beckoning to Alexandra.

He has an earring? Pirates and all sorts of other disreputable characters wore earrings. Something dark swirled down Alexandra's stomach and between her thighs when she watched Lord Cambourne. As he had in the ballroom, he sufficiently squashed all thoughts of her dire circumstances with his presence. Alexandra sniffed the air. The library smelled of cinnamon.

Lady Fellowes thrust herself against Lord Cambourne and tried to pull him closer. The gloved hands ran through the long locks of his hair.

Alexandra stood transfixed, knowing she should look away, close her eyes, and possibly put her hands over her ears. She clasped one hand to her stomach. A flutter danced its way back and forth, twirling across her body. She wondered if the champagne she drank earlier caused her discomfort. Her drawers felt damp. One gloved hand wandered down to lay between her legs. Shocked at herself, Alexandra snatched her hand away.

Lord Cambourne kissed Lady Fellowes, pushing her

down into the sofa cushions. The redhead, pinned in place against the couch, moved suggestively under Lord Cambourne as he kissed her. Alexandra saw the flick of his tongue against the woman's lips before he broke away from her.

Lady Fellowes narrowed her eyes as she regarded the man in front of her.

"Oh, my."

Oh my indeed! Alexandra panted a bit. She told herself it was only the thickness of the curtain and the dust in the air. Aunt Eloise said kissing was disgusting, particularly if one kissed in the 'French' way. Alexandra looked at Lady Fellowes. The woman did not appear disgusted. Her face bore a silly, blissful expression. Alexandra thought perhaps her aunt's opinion of relations between a man and a woman had been colored by marriage to Odious Oliver.

Lord Cambourne gently disengaged Lady Fellowes's legs and took a step back from the couch. He watched the redhead with amusement. "Caro, go back to the ballroom. Even though this has been a vastly amusing *discussion*."

Lady Fellowes giggled. Her gloved fingers wiggled at him, curling and begging him to come closer. "Have you lost your sense of adventure, Lord Cambourne?" She plucked at his trousers.

"No, but I have better sense than to tumble you in my host's library during a ball. Besides, didn't you ask Danvers to escort you tonight?"

Lady Fellowes frowned a bit. She put her hand between Lord Cambourne's legs as if she were massaging something.

Oh, Good Lord! Intrigued, Alexandra continued to watch. Lady Fellowes was touching his... She covered her mouth as a small squeak emerged. She knew exactly what Lady Fellowes was touching.

Lord Cambourne pushed the grasping hand away from his

pants and chuckled softly. "Go back to the ball, Caro, before you are missed."

Lord Cambourne stepped away from Lady Fellowes's grasping fingers and faced the curtain. His beautiful features looked thoughtful and a bit melancholy.

Alexandra's heart gave a small, odd lurch. Something about his countenance made her want to comfort him. Ridiculous as that sounded.

"Darling?"

Lord Cambourne walked over to the fireplace and poured himself a glass of Lord Dobson's brandy. "You should not have followed me, Caro. An association with me would likely end any future match with Danvers."

Lady Fellowes smiled. "I don't give a fig for what Danvers thinks. He's *only* a baron. You are a Marquess. A gorgeous, lovely Marquess."

"Why how very mercenary of you, Caro. And you hardly out of mourning for your *dear* husband. No doubt you would mourn me just as fiercely. You do make a lovely widow. Black becomes you. I suppose you were hoping someone would see us?"

The sarcasm of his words sliced across the room into the empty air, hanging above Lady Fellowes like swords.

The redhead frowned. She flounced about the couch pretending to straighten her clothing with an aggrieved air. A calculating look came over her lovely face.

"Lord Danvers is quite taken with me."

"I'm sure he is. Don't let me keep you." Lord Cambourne waved his hand at the door.

Lady Fellowes did not care for his reply. The redhead postured, thrust out her chest, and gave him a petulant look.

Lord Cambourne ignored her.

She flipped her head and allowed a bright red curl to dangle down her shoulder in a fetching manner. "Fine. But should you come looking for me later, you shall have to fight Danvers for my attention."

"I stand duly informed, Lady Fellowes." Lord Cambourne downed the brandy.

Lady Fellowes glared fiercely and waited for Lord Cambourne to say more. At his silence, she stood in a huff and flounced to the door in a swirl of black silks. The library walls shook as she slammed the door.

Lord Cambourne shrugged and moved closer to the fireplace. His brow furrowed in contemplation as he reached into his pocket to produce a cheroot. A brief flare of light lit the beautiful planes of his face. He touched the flame to the end of the cheroot with a sensuous flick of his wrist and took several deep drags.

Alexandra scratched her nose, careful not to disturb the curtain. The dust really was deplorable. She watched Lord Cambourne with her left eye. His hair glimmered like a bolt of black silk, the strands curling just a bit on the ends. The man should consult another tailor, possibly one who knew how to fit a gentleman. She could see the muscles of his thighs outlined by his breeches.

The smell of tobacco reached her nostrils making them twitch. Terrified of sneezing, she scratched her nose and prayed he would leave. Lord Cambourne blew smoke rings into the air as if he had all the time in the world. How long had she been gone? Her uncle would bring the house down around her ears if he discovered her missing. *Damnation! Why doesn't the blasted man adjourn to the conservatory? I'm sure there's a tasty countess or two waiting for him there.*

The dark head swiveled in her direction as if hearing her thoughts.

Alexandra's heart hammered in her chest. Carefully, she stepped deeper into the folds of the heavy gold damask. Her nose twitched again. *Damn dusty curtains!* She heard him approach her hiding place, the steps leisurely, as if he were merely taking a stroll in the park. The smell of the cheroot mingled with the cinnamon hanging in the air. Her hands began to sweat inside her gloves. Dust tickled the back of her throat.

The footsteps stopped. What was he doing? She took a shallow breath, beginning to feel slightly claustrophobic behind the curtain. Could one suffocate in a curtain? She closed her eyes. A dust mote danced on her nose. If she gave a fig for Lady Dobson, she would tell her the deplorable state of her maid's housekeeping.

Suddenly a hand shot through the heavy fabric, reaching towards Alexandra and startling her so that the edge of her slipper caught on the bottom of the curtain. She tripped and grabbed at the material, inadvertently twisting it around herself as she tried to flee. The curtain pulled free from the rod as she tipped forward. Swaddled in the folds of the heavy curtains, she landed at Lord Cambourne's feet like a tiny gold damask-wrapped mummy.

Lord Cambourne cursed and dropped his cheroot.

Which is how the curtain caught on fire.

3

Good Lord! Sutton Reynolds watched as his cheroot burned a hole in the writhing curtain. A small feminine chin came to rest on the toe of his boots. As jaded as he was, even Sutton could appreciate the irony of yet another woman literally falling at his feet.

He bent to swat at the ember that rapidly burned through the curtain. The bundle at his feet made a muffled sound of protest. The bundle deserved his abuse. She *had* been spying on him. He hoped it wasn't Lady Halston's daughter, Eunice. The girl had been stalking him for weeks now. He had last seen Eunice leaping at him from a topiary at the Earl of Trent's a fortnight ago.

"Ow!"

Yes, he definitely swatted her too hard. The pleasingly plump bottom below his palm was likely stinging from his ministrations. Couldn't be Eunice, then. Eunice was much taller and so thin she looked as if she would snap. Lord Cambourne smacked the plump bottom again.

The bundle stiffened in indignation.

An eye peered at him through a gap in the fabric. The bundle twitched, struggling to roll over and free itself. After several minutes of twisting and turning like an earthworm, he heard a feminine sigh of frustration.

"Excuse me," the bundle addressed him, "I realize we have not been properly introduced, but would you mind unwrapping me?"

"How incredibly provocative that sounds." The bundle stiffened and gave a small snort of disgust.

Sutton grabbed the end of the curtain and gently unrolled. A profusion of chestnut curls spilled out, accompanied by an overabundance of bosom and snapping gray eyes. The girl struggled ungracefully into a sitting position. One dark curl fell over her brow. She pursed her lips and blew a puff of air to dislodge the curl. The spiral moved, and then snapped back over her eye.

He held out a hand and pulled her up to face him. Petite and curvy, she barely reached the middle of his chest. The oval of her face was pale, her skin a delicate porcelain, her features altogether ordinary. Except that they were surrounded by a magnificent, dark-brown mass of curling tendrils. She didn't look frightened in the least, just irritated, and apparently with him. He found her demeanor quite interesting.

"Eavesdropping is a dreadful occupation. Do you see where it gets you? Nearly roasted to death like a tiny partridge." His gaze ran over the ringlets threatening to escape what remained of her coiffure. He absolutely *adored* curls. One might even call it a fetish. Sutton toyed with running his fingers through the twisting mass when a better idea occurred to him. "I had a devil of a time making sure the fire was out. Perhaps I should just check again." He leaned to examine her posterior.

She jumped out of his reach, the tendrils of her hair

swaying across the ivory tops of her breasts. He tried not to stare. Her breasts were magnificent. Between the breasts and the hair, his interest was definitely piqued. The tightness in his breeches proved it.

"Are you all right?" he asked politely. She stared at him. Most women *did* when they first met him. Sutton knew of his effect on women. The female sex tended to look at him as if he were some sort of dessert. Although, this girl looked hostile. Perhaps she didn't have a sweet tooth.

Shooting him a look of reproach, she rubbed her abused bottom.

It was only her quickened breathing that gave away her distress. Each breath tightened the silk fabric of her bodice against the ivory globes of her breasts. He hoped she would inhale deeply enough so that one of those magnificent mountains would pop out. Or at least a nipple. His left hand twitched with the urge to cup one of those perfect breasts in his hand. The thought made it difficult to remember that he needed to chastise her soundly for spying on him.

"I wasn't," she sputtered. Her brow wrinkled in consternation. Another curl sprang free.

Sutton watched in fascination as the curl unwound, spiraling down her shoulder to lie in the valley between her breasts. "Wasn't what?" He forgot what they were discussing. Her lips were plump, like tiny pillows. Sutton forced his look from her lips back to her face and assumed a bland expression.

"I wasn't eavesdropping," she began to explain hastily. "I was looking for the Ladies Necessary Room. The pins....in my hair...you see they were falling out. My hair is quite unruly and the pins..." She spread her hands in front of her. "I got lost and then I saw the light and thought perhaps it was the Ladies Necessary Room. But it wasn't. I saw books and I...." Two spots of red appeared on her cheeks.

A flair of annoyance washed through him at her words. Why didn't she have the good sense to shut up? Women had been lying in wait for him since he was fifteen. The situation had only gotten worse since his return from Macao when his grandmother announced "open season" on his bachelorhood. Granted, wrapping oneself up in a curtain and being caught on fire was a bit drastic, but he knew many women who would do far more to snatch a title. Disappointment filled him. Just another dull virgin of the *ton*, out husband-hunting. Albeit one with magnificent hair and an overabundance of bosom.

"The books? Do you mean to tell me you traipsed in here purely to look at books? In Lord Dobson's library? During a ball?" A dark brow lifted. "What an interesting excuse."

The girl gulped in disbelief. Loudly. Small, gloved hands clenched tightly at her sides as if she were strangling something in her fists. The gunmetal gray eyes narrowed.

His already foul mood worsened. He wanted only a moment's peace from the muttering gossips that graced the ballroom. He detested these affairs. Then Caro appeared, begging to be seduced. He should have ended things with her weeks ago. Could this girl be in league with Caro? Caro did so want to be a Marchioness. Or possibly this girl wanted to be a Marchioness.

Her nostrils flared. The bodice stretched, but held.

"Are you here at Lady Fellowes's behest or are you a mercenary yourself? Perhaps you thought to jump out after she left?" He waved his hand, dismissing her. "Go back to the ball. You have been found out. I hate to dash whatever you hoped to achieve, but neither you nor Lady Fellowes are Marchioness material. Keep that in mind should you decide to call ruin. I would hate to kill an outraged father or brother for such ridiculous behavior."

A squeak of outrage popped out of her luscious mouth. He had an urge to nibble on that plump lower lip.

Another thought occurred to him. "Maybe I disturbed *your* assignation? Were you meeting a lover?" A bit of contempt bled into his words. He could not help it. The women of the *ton* tended to either be twittering virgins or bed-hopping matrons. "Please take a word of advice. You really need to work on your excuses. Bluestockings are a rarity at these gatherings. No one will ever listen to such nonsense as 'I was looking at the books.'" The girl's face reddened. She gritted her teeth and gave him a look full of daggers.

Sutton's breeches twitched. The proper thing to do would be to allow her to run back to the ball, having sustained only minor emotional distress during her encounter with Satan Reynolds. But her reaction to him was so atypical. For some odd reason he was enjoying himself. A rarity.

"Well? What do you have to say for yourself?" The baiting of virgins should become a sport or a gentleman's pursuit. Like fencing.

She muttered something; it sounded like 'bloody arrogant bastard,' and a small foot stamped in an effort to gain his attention. Gray eyes, gone the color of a winter storm, flashed at him. "I was *not* eavesdropping. I am not in league with your Lady Fellowes. I was not meeting a lover. I especially was not, *heaven forbid*, following *you* in a pathetic attempt to be ruined! You vainglorious, arrogant, depraved ...*peacock*! Until tonight I had no idea you even existed. In addition, you have the most ridiculous nickname I have ever heard! I think it likely you made it up to entice shallow females who would fall for your dubious charms." She pursed her lips and puffed away an errant curl.

Sutton's breeches twitched again. The little bit of fluff in front of him had called him a peacock! Held him in contempt! Women simply did not talk to him this way. Actually no one did. He wanted to kiss her senseless.

"I *pity* the shallow women of the ton if indeed they are lining up for your favors." The girl's small shoulders squared as if she were preparing for a boxing match. "Your enormous ego and inflated sense of self-importance would make you a poor choice for a husband, for you are already in love with yourself! There wouldn't be room in the marriage bed for both a wife and the large mirror in which you admire yourself.

Sutton opened his mouth to defend himself but thought it wiser not to interfere with the most fantastic set-down he ever received. And he found it enjoyable. His status as Satan Reynolds, evil despoiler of women, seemed to have no effect on this girl. The tiny tempest intrigued him.

"I am a guest of Lady Dobson's. Had I known the *sordid* display that I would be forced to witness I would have stayed at home! Strange as it may seem to you, *my lord*, I *was* actually looking at the books. My toad of an uncle doesn't have a library. I love books. In fact, I find I like them much more than people, especially the ones I have met so far! Books are not rude, they do not insult a person and accuse them," she nearly yelled at him, "nor do they seduce dull-witted women on couches during balls! You likely wouldn't know anything about books, *my lord*, since I am doubtful you have ever picked up anything to read except the racing papers or the betting sheets at White's."

Sutton actually read a great deal more than the racing papers, he was in fact finishing a book on philosophy, but he didn't wish to interrupt her. Another curl sprung free and hung unnoticed by her ear. He resisted the urge to tweak it.

She continued in a shaky voice. "I just wanted to be somewhere peaceful—just for a moment. Away from all of *you*." Her voice caught. "I just wanted to look at the books." Her magnificent bosom heaved back and forth and her face flushed a becoming shade of rose as she finished her tirade. She looked away, and one small, gloved hand flew to her mouth in embarrassment.

Sutton watched her for a moment, wanting to be sure the eruption was over. Her reddened face and the clutching of her hands assured him it was. The gray eyes were watching him warily. She was adorable. Fierce. He wanted to put her in his pocket.

"What a ferocious little thing you are. Like a tiny badger. A *bookish* little badger." He laughed softly. This was the most amusing thing that had happened to him since his return from Macao. Where had this girl been hiding?

She stomped her foot, indignant again. "You compare me to an ill-tempered rodent?" Her nose scrunched in the loveliest manner.

"Did you enjoy watching Caro and me?" How incredibly mean of him to continue to goad her, but he couldn't help himself. Especially now that he knew she had not been spying on him intentionally. "Why did you not make your presence known? Or scream in offended outrage?"

Emotions played across her face. Her fingers plucked at her gown. She turned her face slightly and looked away. His question managed to stop her cold.

She didn't raise her head. "I don't know what you mean. I didn't watch your sordid display. I covered my eyes. The shock of what I witnessed has put me in a state of shock. I am leaving now. I bid you a good evening, my lord."

"Liar. Pretty little liar."

"I find your accusations disgusting. I find *you* disgusting."

And she did. He could tell by the look on her face. But something else shone in her features as well. Something he intended to draw out.

"Too bad." He leaned in. "I find you utterly adorable. Not the least disgusting."

The Badger was discomfited at his words. She backed away from him, not looking at him directly, but at the toes of his polished black boots. This was much more fun, Sutton thought, than all the jaded flirtations of the women that filled Lady Dobson's ballroom. He took another step forward.

She retreated.

Damnation!

He heard her say it under her breath as she realized she was cornered against the library wall. Neatly trapped, the Badger stared at him in defiance. A tiny Amazon attempting to face down an ill-mannered giant. No doubt she expected him to ravish her. His reputation would suggest nothing less. He *was* sorely tempted. Lust for this temperamental girl struck him again, surprising him with the sharpness of it.

He winked and lifted his hands, palms up in supplication, before he clasped them behind his back.

Her eyes widened.

Sutton often thought that so much of seduction could be accomplished with only the mouth and tongue. Words, in particular, were incredibly seductive, although he had found few women who understood that. This girl in front of him had no idea how her tart tongue had incited him.

The gunmetal eyes followed his progress. She said nothing, but her face remained flushed. She didn't order him to step aside. She didn't scream. The tilt of her head told him she wanted him to kiss her. The white column of her neck turned, just so, inviting him to touch it. She may not be aware of her actions, but her body knew what it wanted. He heard her breathing, like a frightened animal.

I really am a vile man.

Her gaze fell to his chest, then, back to his face. Her breasts lifted towards him, her body making an unconscious appeal to his. He sensed deep passion in the prickly badger.

Sutton leaned forward and caught her scent. Green apples on a spring day. How appropriate. He loved tart, green apples.

A tiny nest of curls, dainty and fine, hung underneath her ear. He blew softly towards the curls, watching them move as if they were caught in a gentle breeze.

She shivered. Deliciously. Her hands pressed against the back of the door as if to brace herself for his attentions.

He considered just reaching around her to open the door and waving her out. But she tempted him. Lured him.

Carefully, he nuzzled the nape of her neck with the tip of his nose, pushing aside the small tendrils to touch the skin underneath. Her skin was warm and soft. Delicate like fine satin. He couldn't help himself. He nipped her.

"Oh!" Two hands flew up immediately, like trapped doves, to place themselves on his chest.

Heat jolted through his chest at her touch. He wanted nothing more than to wrap his arms around her, pressing her small form to his. But he didn't. Instead he inhaled deeply and pressed his lips to the spot he nipped, savoring the Badger as if she were fine wine. He flicked out the tip of his tongue and traced a line from the spot to just below her earlobe. He took her lobe in his mouth and gently sucked on it.

"What are you, oh!" she said again, before she sagged towards him.

The magnificent breasts pushed against him. He imagined her nipples, the color of dusky ripe cherries, pushing through the lawn of his shirt. The beat of her heart could clearly be seen beneath the column of her throat.

She rubbed against him, like a cat wishing to be stroked.

He nearly came undone then but forced his hands to stay still. What started as virgin-baiting turned into something else entirely. Sutton pressed a gentle kiss to the side of her mouth. His tongue flicked out to run against the inside of her upper lip. Her head moved back an inch, unaccustomed to the sensation.

"No." He whispered against the corner of her mouth. "Be still."

Her eyes closed in surrender. Her touch ran up his chest, fingers tensing as she made her way slowly up to his neck. His lips brushed over hers, sucking on her bottom lip, pulling away gently from her.

Sutton's heart hammered in his chest from their kiss, a rare and unnerving experience. What in God's name was he doing?

SATAN REYNOLDS KISSED HER. EROTICALLY. DECADENTLY. And he smelled of cinnamon. She wanted this moment to last forever. The most notorious rake in London looked at her with seduction. She should run as far from this man as possible. Something about him made her want to be wicked. Wanton.

A puzzled look crossed his angelic face as he watched her. His eyes were the most glorious color she had ever seen, green with flecks of gold. Only one other creature in her acquaintance also possessed eyes of that color, her calico tabby cat, Marmalade. Thinking of Marmalade, who was likely sitting by the fire in Helmsby Abbey's kitchen, brought Alexandra back to reality. She was just a girl from Hampshire, who had never been kissed, desperate to outsmart her uncle to save her home. Were she not so muddled by the man standing before her, Alexandra would have laughed out loud. Her situation sounded very much like a plot of a Lord Thurston novel. The knob of the door ground into her back. She reached for it.

"What is your name?" The dark rasp ran over her like molten chocolate.

Her hand froze on the knob. "Alexandra Dunforth." She looked into those catlike eyes, truly frightened for the first time. She wondered if this was what the gypsy cursed him with, a magical allure that women could not resist.

"I'll be seeing you again, *Alex*." He smiled wickedly at her.

Alexandra cautiously opened the door, never taking her eyes off Lord Cambourne. She nodded a polite goodbye to him, as if they merely met for tea. She tried to pivot gracefully but stumbled a bit in her haste to exit. She cursed her clumsiness and forced her shaky legs to take her back to the ballroom. The side of her mouth tingled from the imprint of his tongue on her lips.

❧

LORD CAMBOURNE, KNOWN TO HIS FRIENDS AS CAM AND amongst the gossips of the *ton* as Satan Reynolds, felt his heart thump loudly in his chest as the delectable Miss Dunforth attempted a regal exit. She tripped over her gown, caught herself, and stumbled in a most ungraceful manner away from him. He thought to assist her but feared touching her would unleash all sorts of behavior best left for another time. Besides, her awkwardness charmed him. And he *did* desire her. That was quite apparent from the hardened arousal in his breeches, meaning he couldn't follow her immediately. He lit another cheroot.

One of his mistresses in Macao had given Sutton a puzzle box as a gift. The box was intricately inlaid with two different types of wood in a delicate pattern made to look like fish in a sea. He couldn't open it. He spent weeks looking at it, trying to discern where the secret latch could be hidden, how to push the button just so to reveal the mysteries hidden within.

Sutton flicked his wrist and the remainder of the cheroot fell into the fireplace, sparking briefly. He adjusted his breeches as he walked out of the library. Patience was one of Sutton's strong suits. After nearly a year, he had finally opened the box to his immense satisfaction. He didn't think it would take quite that long with Miss Alexandra Dunforth.

4

Donata Reynolds, Dowager Marchioness of
Cambourne, grabbed the head of her cane and
watched with interest as a small, slight girl slid to a
halt next to the couch where the Dowager sat. The girl was
dressed plainly, although still fashionably, in a watered blue-
gray silk gown trimmed in dark lace. She took several deep
breaths and patted her hair. The girl was either running from
a lover or *to* a lover. Intrigued, Donata leaned forward.

The girl's hand flew to her coiffure, or rather what was left
of it. She took one curl and pinned it back up, only to have
another fall down and take its place. Donata heard an unladylike curse erupt from her lips.

Damnation!

The girl proceeded to stab another pin viciously at the
back of her head, as if attempting to kill something hidden
there. The Dowager coughed politely to announce her
presence.

Wide gray eyes locked with hers in horror. No, not gray.
The girl's eyes caught the shimmer of the candlelight,
reminding Donata of opals. Her face flushed red and her

mouth gaped open. Her brow wrinkled in concentration as she worked on a plausible excuse for her behavior. Donata nearly clapped in delight. Finally. Someone interesting to talk to.

Cocking an eyebrow, Donata said in her most severe tone, "running from an amorous suitor, are you?"

The girl sucked in her breath and flushed a deeper shade of red, which seemed to seep down the ivory skin of her most generous bosom. She was quite well endowed for such a small woman. The girl's hair was rather forcefully restrained but was a lovely chestnut color, and exceptionally curly. Altogether ordinary-looking. Attractive but certainly no competition for the beauties that crowded Lady Dobson's ballroom. Donata nonetheless sensed something *sparkling* about the girl in front of her.

"No, my lady." The girl had the sense to curtsy. "I beg your pardon. I didn't see you sitting there. Forgive my intrusion." Ready to run from Donata at the slightest censure, she bit her lip and looked up at the ceiling, unsure as how to proceed. She reminded the Dowager of a vexed kitten.

"Here now, miss." Donata nodded towards the bench. "Sit next to me and catch your breath. I am sure your mother will find you directly. I shan't tell, you know." The Dowager smiled at her. Who was this child? Positive she knew every dull virgin of age to marry in London, Donata pondered the question. *Perhaps that's why I don't know of her, for this girl does not strike me as dull.*

The girl sat carefully next to Donata. "I'm here with my uncle, Lord Burke."

Donata hid her distaste as the girl mentioned Lord Oliver Burke. She did not know the man personally, but she knew his reputation. The man was a dull-witted glutton, known for gambling away his late wife's substantial fortune. He was related distantly to Lady Dobson. She did not know Lord Burke had a niece.

"I see. How are you acquainted with Lady Dobson?"

Donata nearly laughed out loud at the expression on the girl's face at the mention of Agnes Dobson. The girl's mouth curled as if she sucked on a lemon.

"Lady Dobson is kind enough to chaperone me. I had my first Season so long ago, you see. My uncle wishes that I find a suitable husband." She didn't sound grateful, as most girls would be, at having someone so well-known help her navigate the *ton*.

"I was not aware Lord Burke even possessed a niece."

"I wish he did not possess one as well." The girl clapped her hand over her mouth and looked at Donata in horror. "My lady, I apologize. I-"

Donata patted her hand. "It's all right, my child." Donata peered at her. "You do not sound happy about the prospect of a husband. Or is it just Lady Dobson you object to?"

The girl took a deep breath which sighed out of her. Clearly, the child was distressed.

"What is your name, my dear?"

"Alexandra Dunforth, my lady."

"Well, Alexandra Dunforth, if I may ask, what has caused you to run into Lady Dobson's ballroom with your hair coming down?"

Miss Dunforth reached up anxiously to tuck in several stray curls. "Nothing you would be interested in, madam, except that my hair does not appreciate the confinement of pins." She looked up and her nose wrinkled. "Oh dear, there's my uncle and Lady Dobson." It sounded as if she were accusing the duo of murder.

An obese man plodded his way across the polished parquet floor towards Miss Dunforth, with Lady Dobson following in his wake. Donata struggled to hide her distaste for her hostess, composing her features into something that she hoped would be regarded as bland and polite. Donata did not care for Agnes Dobson, finding the woman to be a social-climbing harpy who ruined the reputations of those she deemed unworthy for sport. Lady Dobson was afraid of Donata.

She thought that the only bit of wisdom the woman ever displayed.

Turning her attention to Lord Burke, Donata had to stop the sneer that threatened to curl her lip. The cravat he wore was tied in a bumbling knot, his mustache much too waxed, and his waistcoat. Atrocious. Donata could see a food stain, something dark, spotting the left side.

Lord Burke stopped directly in front of Miss Dunforth. "Alexandra! Where have you been? Lady Dobson told me you disappeared. You are so dull you fade right into the woodwork. It's likely she just didn't notice you." The beady eyes bored down on Miss Dunforth as he gave a short bark of amusement.

Donata wanted to swat the man with her cane. What a rude and vulgar man! Lord Burke was a brilliant example of overbreeding in the *ton*.

Lady Dobson winced as she noticed Donata and nudged Lord Burke.

He nudged her back with an irritated look on his face.

Lady Dobson thrust her chin, so pointed it could likely cut glass, in the direction of Donata. "Lord Burke, may I present the Dowager Marchioness of Cambourne." Lady Dobson curtsied and tried to pull Lord Burke into a bow.

Lord Burke gave a perplexed look as the words took their time filtering through what Donata assumed was a brain the size of a pea-hen's. Remembering his manners at last, Burke bowed deeply to her, stretching his waistcoat to its limits. Donata thought for a moment his enormous girth would split the fabric, sending the brass buttons flying into her face. She sighed with relief when he straightened.

Lord Burke lurched forward to grab Miss Dunforth's arm and pull her from the couch.

Clearly, Miss Dunforth needed a friend and Donata was ever taking in strays.

"Lord Burke." Donata inclined her head in a regal manner and used her most coldly superior tone, "I was just telling the *delightful* Miss Dunforth that she must come for tea."

Miss Dunforth gave her a surprised look.

Lady Dobson cleared her throat as the blood left her face.

"My granddaughter is of the same age and I feel certain they have much in common. I also find Miss Dunforth exceedingly entertaining. She is a treasure."

Lord Burke gave Donata a look of confusion.

Lady Dobson elbowed him.

Apparently, Lord Burke did not find his niece charming. The dumbfounded look on his face reflected his surprise that anyone did. All the more reason for Donata to champion Miss Dunforth.

"She would be most happy to." Lady Dobson answered before Lord Burke opened his mouth. She grinned like an idiot at Donata.

Donata wanted to swat the turban off of Lady Dobson's head with her cane. She didn't think she could reach it though. Lord, but she hated getting old.

Without waiting for Lord Burke to agree, since if he didn't she would overrule him anyway, Donata said, "Wonderful. I will send my coach for her. Tomorrow perhaps?"

Lord Burke seemed about to say something but thought better of it.

Miss Dunforth murmured her goodbye, surprise clearly written on her face. The girl had no idea, thought Donata, of the powerful ally she had just made.

Lord Burke grabbed Miss Dunforth by the arm and dragged her across the ballroom. As Donata watched them, a man darted from an alcove and followed. He was slender and impeccably dressed, with hair the color of ripened wheat. Donata blinked, shocked by a face she hadn't seen in years. When she opened her eyes, the man had disappeared.

She must be mistaken, or possibly her eyes were playing tricks on her. A trickle of anxiety ran down her spine. There was no mistaking the hair. It was the same color as her daughter-in-law's.

☙❧

ODIOUS OLIVER PINCHED ALEXANDRA'S ARM AND GAVE HER a shake.

"Stop it, Uncle. You are hurting me." She tried to pull her arm out of his grasp.

"What did you say to the Dowager? Where have you been?" He accused as he took in her flushed features. Sweat dripped from her uncle's broad brow and down his puffed, reddened cheeks. Spittle sat in the corner of his mouth. A vision of a rabid dog she had seen once ran through Alexandra's mind.

"Nothing, Uncle. I lost a pin from my hair, then another fell out. I went to the Ladies Necessary Room to fix it, but I fear I didn't do a very good job."

Her uncle snorted. "That's an understatement. You look like you have a rat's nest on your head." He chuckled at his joke. "No matter. Your suitor has arrived. Finally. He wishes to meet you."

Lady Dobson and her purple turban swayed. She clucked her tongue and gave Alexandra a look of disapproval.

"Agnes, I thank you for your assistance tonight. As you can see, I am overburdened with the girl." Her uncle mopped his brow with his free hand then wiped it on his trousers.

"How she attracted the interest of the Dowager Marchioness I will never know. What could they possibly have to talk about?" Lady Dobson shook her head in disgust and wandered towards a group of women who were gesturing to her.

Uncle Oliver looked at Alexandra with skepticism. "How did you insinuate yourself with such a woman?"

Alexandra pulled her arm from his grasp. "She only introduced herself and bade me sit down. What do you think I said, 'my uncle is forcing me to marry'?"

Her uncle snorted and eyed her with avid dislike. "Don't get lippy with me, girl. I am merely doing my duty as your guardian. You should consider yourself lucky I don't throw you into the streets to beg for food. Besides, I doubt that wrinkled aristocrat could care less who you married."

Alexandra swallowed the panic that rose at the truth in his words. She lifted her chin.

"And you will marry. If you wish to show your love for that ancient group of retainers you so adore. If you want to save that pile of manure you call a farm in Hampshire."

Fear welled in her throat. Possibly this mysterious suitor would find her wanting and decide to call off the arrangement. Alexandra was halfway across the floor, towed by her uncle like a tiny boat being pulled along in a frigate's wake when the connection hit her and stopped her cold in her tracks. The Dowager Marchioness was the *grandmother* of Satan Reynolds. The man those women had been discussing.

"Come along, Alexandra! Don't dawdle. What's wrong with you? Have you been drinking?"

"No. I'm just a little tired." Her uncle had certainly been drinking though. The fat man smelled of wine and she saw a purple line just underneath his mustache.

They wove through Lady Dobson's guests who were chattering like magpies as they dissected dresses, gentlemen, and marriages. The ladies' gowns were bright spots of color, lovely yellows, subdued rosy pinks, dark blues, and greens. Alexandra looked down at her blue-gray gown. Her gown contrasted sharply with the hues floating through the room and she suddenly felt like the drab country mouse Lady Dobson had called her. Casually, she looked through the crowd hoping to catch a glimpse of Lord Cambourne but his dark visage was nowhere to be found.

Her uncle brought her alongside a slender, blond gentleman who stood against a far wall. Apart from the other groups dotting the ballroom, he lay partially hidden in the shadows of a far corner. His eyes, a pale blue, immediately ran over her form in appraisal.

The color rose in Alexandra's cheeks along with anger at being inspected in such a way. But her ire dissipated as the man gave her a warm, kind smile. His evening clothes, a formal black, fit him to perfection. His cravat was expertly tied and in such a complicated knot that Alexandra marveled at his valet's talent. Hair, which reminded her of ripened wheat, toppled over his forehead. One pale hand rested on a fashionable walking stick. A wolf's head, the eyes glittering rubies, graced the top. Good breeding emanated from him and Alexandra wondered how in the world he knew Oliver Burke.

"Mr. Runyon, my niece." Her uncle practically pushed her into Mr. Runyon's arms. "Miss Alexandra Dunforth."

Alexandra stumbled a bit as Mr. Runyon took her arm. Her uncle discarded her none too gently. Humiliation made her face burn.

Mr. Runyon wrinkled his perfect nose at her uncle's manner but said nothing. His touch was light and polite, the elegant fingers warm on her arm. He was not as tall as Lord Cambourne, but still much taller than Alexandra.

"Miss Dunforth." His voice was smooth and melodic. He took Alexandra's gloved hand and brushed it with his lips. The pale blue eyes looked at her with curiosity.

Odious Oliver pinched the back of her arm, reminding her to dip into a small curtsy. "Mr. Runyon," she tilted her head, "It is a pleasure to meet you."

Lord Burke rubbed his ham-like hands together. "Well? We can sign the papers this evening." The ballroom wasn't overly warm, but beads of sweat clustered on her uncle's forehead. One of his eyes twitched.

Alexandra now knew how horses felt as gentlemen haggled over them. How she hated her uncle.

Mr. Runyon gave her uncle a pinched, unpleasant look. The lips under the light blond mustache curled a bit.

Alexandra was given the distinct impression that Mr. Runyon didn't care for Oliver Burke.

"Miss Dunforth, it is a great pleasure to meet you." He gave Lord Burke an icy glance. "Your uncle did not do justice to your looks or charm."

Alexandra nodded to him wondering at the oddity of having two handsome men flirt with her in the same evening. And Mr. Runyon was handsome. She'd wrongly assumed that her uncle would try to marry her off to one of his gambling cronies, most of who looked like wrinkled trolls. Not someone so obviously wealthy and attractive.

"I'm sure you are full of questions, Miss Dunforth, as well I would be if our situations were reversed. I would like to answer them." He turned to her uncle. "Lord Burke, if you don't mind, I would like to take Miss Dunforth for a turn about the terrace. I'm sure she could do with a respite."

Her uncle looked as if he might object. His eye twitched again.

"Of course, I-"

"Will wait for Miss Dunforth in your carriage. You should escort her home, as it is quite late." Mr. Runyon's pale blue eyes bored into her uncle.

Odious Oliver nodded dumbly. He held up one pudgy finger meaning to admonish her with it, before Mr. Runyon cleared his throat.

"Good evening, Lord Burke. You may call on me tomorrow."

Mr. Runyon turned his back on her uncle, dismissing him. "Come, Miss Dunforth. We shall take a turn around the terrace and get to know one another. I am not a monster." His eyes twinkled at her. "I've no wish for you to think me one."

Alexandra flushed, charmed by Mr. Runyon's easy grace. Her mind raced with the possibility that perhaps he would help her.

He guided her deftly to a row of tall doors, thrown open to let in the air at the back of the ballroom. A blast of cooler air slid across her arms and she sighed in relief.

Mr. Runyon chuckled. "Dreadful in there isn't it? Too much hot air!"

Alexandra laughed in return, delighted with his joke. "You are not fond of these events, Mr. Runyon?"

"No, I fear I am more of a homebody, thus my unmarried state." He grinned ruefully at her. "I have spent many years living abroad and have only just returned." He brought her over to the edge of the terrace. Alexandra could see the outlines of the garden lit dimly with colored paper lanterns. The muffled whispers of other couples hidden along the terrace reached her ears. Kisses were being stolen. She touched the side of her mouth briefly.

"I met your uncle quite by chance while playing cards with a group of friends. He mentioned during the game that he had a niece who he wished to have marry." He gave her an apologetic look. "Lord Burke proceeded to list your long list of undesirable traits, education, love of books, how you expressed your opinions..."

"Did he?" Alexandra interjected defensively hating her uncle even more if that were possible.

Mr. Runyon squeezed her arm. "Pray do not take offense. I found all of your supposed flaws to be highly valued. At least to me." The wind ruffled his fair hair and she caught the light masculine scent of him. She thought of Lord Cambourne and the smell of cinnamon. "I am quite shy, Miss Dunforth and not at all good at courting. Which is why I agreed to our meeting." One slender hand reached up and stroked his beautifully tied cravat. "Your uncle wishes you to marry and I—well—I am in need of a wife. My elderly father and I are estranged. I was quite the social disaster in my youth and much too naïve. I acted foolishly and brought some shame to my father." He held his hand up. "Nothing nefarious, I assure you. I made a cow of myself over a woman. I became quite despondent. I was the laughingstock of the *ton*. I've been loath to pursue a woman since."

"I will not agree to marry a man I do not know," Alexandra stated firmly.

Mr. Runyon's nostrils flared, and a glint of anger flared in his ice-blue gaze before his face transformed into politeness. The smile he bestowed upon her radiated kindness. Alexandra thought she must have been mistaken.

"Your uncle *is* pressing me to sign a betrothal agreement, but I have been very clear with him that I would not force you. We should try to know one another better before making such a decision. I wish a joyful marriage, Miss Dunforth. I do not want an ill beginning." He stroked his cravat again.

Alexandra regarded him. Mr. Runyon appeared to be

nothing more than a kind, gentle man who seemed a bit shy. Having witnessed the way nearly everyone gossiped since her arrival in London she did not doubt the cruelty he'd received.

"Surely there are dozens of more appropriate women, Mr. Runyon. I have been raised far away from London and am not as sophisticated as many women. I had only one Season before returning to Hampshire. Also, I am considered to be long in the tooth and on the shelf."

His gaze shifted from her questioning look. Shyly, he looked back at her face.

"As I stated," he cleared his throat nervously, "because of my prior disgrace I fear that many of the *ton*'s families find me *inadequate* for their daughters. Something of a milksop. I was so young and stupid. Chasing a girl who strung me along. I am pleased that you are not familiar with my previous embarrassment." His eyes bored into hers as he clasped her hands. "Miss Dunforth I am certain we would get on. I find you have a most pleasing disposition."

"But my uncle-" A plan formed in her mind. One that filled her with remorse but one that could save Helmsby Abbey and those she held dear.

"Leave your uncle to me, Miss Dunforth. I will tell him we are getting to know each other better and will sign the betrothal contract when we are ready. *If* we are ready." He winked at her like a conspirator. "My attentions will at least keep your uncle from casting his net, will it not?"

Mr. Runyon gave her a very firm look, his eyes full of protective furor.

As long as her uncle assumed that she and Mr. Runyon were betrothed, Odious Oliver would not attempt to find another suitor. She was certain her uncle didn't know his control over her ended soon. If she could just *use* Mr. Runyon for a bit.

Mr. Runyon she was sure, would understand her need for deceit.

Alexandra gave Mr. Runyon what she hoped was a dazzling smile. "Mr. Runyon, I would be honored to accept your terms."

"Wonderful. Simply wonderful. I feel certain we shall form a strong friendship that will grow into much more."

Alexandra ignored the twinge of guilt at his words. She forced herself to push it aside. She would do what she must. Helmsby Abbey and those she loved must be saved.

Mr. Runyon stuck her hand into the crook of his arm. "Come, Miss Dunforth. I shall escort you to your waiting carriage. I desire to call on you later in the week, business permitting. Would that be all right?"

She nodded and smiled her assent as Mr. Runyon led her back through the ballroom to the carriage where her uncle waited.

5

"I don't suppose the devil takes tea, so I should have nothing to fear." Alexandra smoothed the pleated folds of her yellow-sprigged gown and tried not to think about the fact that she was about to be entertained by Lord Cambourne's sister and elderly grandmother. Alexandra wondered again at the odd coincidence. Certainly, God must have a sense of humor.

A note arrived that morning written in a spidery, elegant hand. The note instructed Alexandra of the Dowager's expectation that Alexandra join the elderly woman for tea today. She tossed the note at her uncle and flew up the stairs to find something suitable in her wardrobe. The thought of escaping her uncle's townhouse, if only for an afternoon, filled her with delight and an odd sense of expectation. But what if she saw *him*?

Alexandra's fingers fluttered nervously until the digits found a curl lying across her shoulder. Her bottom wiggled against the settee as she tried to control her agitation. She twisted the curl round and round her finger, while she imagined what she would do if Lord Cambourne appeared. He won't remember me, Alexandra told herself for the tenth time. I am fairly plain and he was toying with me. Besides, if she would regain her independence and save Helmsby Abbey, she didn't need her meeting with the biggest rake in London to become common knowledge.

Her face grew warm in the cool air of the Dowager's parlor. Last night she had dreamt of Lord Cambourne and the infamous dragon tattoo. He had kissed her while the dragon's tail unwound from his torso to wrap around her. Her hands wove through the dark strands of his hair. She awoke this morning with her nightgown around her waist and a painful throb between her thighs. She could still smell the scent of cinnamon coming off his skin, the sound of his voice whispering, "*Alex.*"

The clock struck the hour and she jumped, her gaze flying to the door. The dark paneled walnut remained shut. She had been waiting nearly thirty minutes—giving her far too much time to dwell on fantasy. Her aunt had warned her about men and marriage long ago, using the examples of Grandfather Dunforth and Lord Burke. Men were trouble Aunt Eloise instructed her, titled men more so because they felt they *deserved everything*. Alexandra plucked at her sleeve. Lord Cambourne was nothing more than an adventure, something for her to remember in the autumn of her life.

She leaned back into the couch and allowed her eyes to roam over the comfortable sitting room. The walls were a muted cranberry color with a motif of leaves drawn in a pattern around the edges of the ceiling. A large, plush Persian carpet in soft tones of brown and green covered the floor. The carpet's weave was so deep that her heels sunk into it. She had never seen any room so elegant. Certainly nothing in her uncle's garish townhouse compared to this. A light breeze blew through the open window and Alexandra could smell a combination of floral aromas from the gardens behind the house. The comfort of the room made her homesick for her study at Helmsby Abbey.

She had written out yet another note to Mr. Meechum, the family solicitor, the third in as many days. She wondered at his lack of reply thinking that he possibly was out of town. Not trusting Tilda, the lady's maid her uncle hired to wait on her, Alexandra asked one of the stable boys to take the note to Meechum and Sons. The young lad tugged his forelock and went running down the mews from her in what she hoped was the right direction. Upon her return to the house, Tilda, her bulldog-like countenance twisted into a snarl, asked her what she'd been up to. Alexandra ignored her. Tilda was more jailer than lady's maid. Alexandra did not owe the woman an explanation.

Where on earth *was* the Dowager? When she'd arrived, the butler apologized profusely as he directed Alexandra to the lovely sitting room. The Dowager was not quite ready to receive her, he said. Alexandra tapped her toe and struggled to keep her posture ramrod-straight. Aunt Eloise always insisted on perfect posture, especially for Alexandra. *"Sitting up straight will give you presence, my dear."*

"Hello." A stunning young woman walked into the room, her long inky curls bouncing jauntily against her waist. She entered with broad, unladylike steps, exuding confidence and a friendly air.

Alexandra liked her immediately. She stood and curtsied, assuming the girl in front of her to be the Dowager's granddaughter, and her hostess for tea.

The sparkling green eyes were so much like her brother's that Alexandra was taken aback. The young lady gave her a sly smile. "You are Miss Dunforth. Grandmother has told me *all* about you. You quite shocked her, you know."

"I did?" Alexandra wondered what shocked the Dowager more—her cursing or her unruly hair.

"Why yes. She never expects to meet any young woman who is not a complete dimwit. The Dowager gets positively *thrilled* when she finds a girl who seems to have a mind. According to Grandmother, young ladies who can think on their own are rather the exception. I'm Lady Miranda, by the way."

Alexandra began to curtsy, but Miranda caught her arm. "Please! Let us not stand on ceremony. I find that all tiresome." She winked at Alexandra and laughed, a light tinkling sound which made Alexandra think of bells. "You must call me Miranda. Only my mother insists upon proper address at all times. At least they don't call me *Satan* Reynolds—they reserve that for Sutton." She laughed again.

Alexandra wasn't sure what to say. She expected that Miranda said the last bit to shock her or possibly even test her in some way.

"Sutton is my brother, Lord Cambourne. You'll likely meet him. Most of his friends call him Cam—short for Cambourne, but his given name is Sutton. Satan Reynolds is just a play on his first name and last name. I'm really not sure where the nickname came from. I mean, my brother has always been a bit wicked even as a child, but I don't think that's it. It may be because he has a tattoo." Miranda's eyes blazed bright green.

Miranda is trying to scandalize me. "I believe I heard that." Alexandra nodded, wondering what sort of comment she could make. *Maybe I should shock Miranda and tell her that I met her brother in a dark library and he kissed me.* Alexandra sat with her hands on her lap, composing her face into what she hoped was polite interest as Miranda continued to chatter.

"I'm certain those horrid boys at Eton started it. He had a terrible time of it there. Or possibly the *ton* started calling him that when he returned from Macao, no—that can't be right because the Chinese also called him 'Satan' in Macao." She paused and looked thoughtful. "I don't know how you say 'Satan' in Chinese. Have you ever heard of Macao? I've read loads about it and I've asked Sutton to take me there, but he says it's much too wild and full of unsavory characters." Miranda gave a careless shrug. "I think Macao sounds positively decadent. My brother had a monkey named Jonas when he lived there. Jonas wore a little red knit cap and smoked opium. Can you imagine? Oh, there's the tea cart."

Alexandra's head was spinning. She wasn't even sure Miranda had taken a breath in the last ten minutes.

Miranda sat back in a profusion of lavender silk, making her look as if she were perched in a giant orchid. "Now what about you, Miss Dunforth? Grandmother said you were newly arrived in London and you are *unhappily* looking for a husband." She gave Alexandra another sly look.

Alexandra nearly laughed out loud. She could clearly see the Dowager's strategy, sending in Miranda just to make sure Alexandra was worthy of tea. She chose to be blunt and hoped the elderly woman was listening at the door.

"My uncle has engaged his distant cousin, Lady Agnes Dobson, to find a suitable match for me." There was no need to relay her true circumstances to Miranda. "I would prefer to simply return home and begin breeding my livestock." Alexandra decided she could be shocking as well. Young ladies did not discuss livestock or breeding, ever. And especially not in a parlor over tea. She waited for Miranda's reaction.

Miranda's eyes widened, before she burst into charmed laughter. "Oh, Grandmother was so *right* about you, Alexandra. I may call you Alexandra?" She reached out and patted Alexandra's knee. "I hope I haven't offended you."

"Not in the least." Alexandra's gaze flicked to a book on the side table. *Lord Thurston and the Wicked Countess.*

Miranda saw her look and burst into a fit of giggles. "Yes, it's mine. I do so love Lord Thurston. Have you read any of them?"

Alexandra gave a nod of assent. "All but the last two." The books were likely still sitting in the study at Helmsby Abbey. She had forgotten to pack them in her distress over Odious Oliver summoning her to London.

"Oh, but this is wonderful. The author of the Lord Thurston series quite intrigues me. The books are only known to be authored by the mysterious, 'J'. A friend of my father's, Lord Wently, is the owner of the publishing house that prints the Lord Thurston novels. I am quite sure he knows who the mysterious *J* is, but he refuses to tell. I keep asking Sutton to pressure Lord Wently but he refuses, and—"

"Enough, Miranda. I can hear you chattering down the hall. Miss Dunforth has not said a word, I merit. She is likely to slash open the sofa pillows and put the stuffing in her ears. Pray do quit talking." The Dowager Marchioness strolled in assisted by a young footman. Her silver hair was piled high atop her head. She looked tired and walked stiffly, but her eyes sparkled as she saw Alexandra.

Alexandra stood and curtsied. Apparently, she passed the Dowager's test.

"Oh, do sit down Miss Dunforth. I'm afraid the only one who demands all that pomp and circumstance at home is my daughter-in-law." She clasped Alexandra's hands in her own and squeezed them. "Miranda, will you please pour?"

The Dowager began asking questions. She wanted to know all about Alexandra's upbringing, what languages she spoke, what subjects she had studied, and what she knew about farming, of all things. She was rapt with attention as Alexandra explained how she'd managed Helmsby Abbey first for her aunt, then on her own. She spoke lovingly of Mrs. Cowries and Jameson. How Cook made the best scones in England. The Dowager laughed and clapped her hands as Miranda related the "livestock breeding" comment while Alexandra blushed in embarrassment. The older woman seemed inordinately pleased to hear that not only was Alexandra a bluestocking, but also a gentleman farmer, of a sort. When Alexandra told the Dowager she knew how to make an apple pie, the elderly woman insisted that Alexandra must make her one straightaway.

"Once you marry, will you be bringing Cook and her excellent scones to your new home? Or are you planning on living at this Helmsby Abbey? I can tell you miss it terribly." The Dowager's brow wrinkled at the question.

Alexandra twisted her hands and tried to choose her words carefully. "It is my sincerest hope."

The Dowager watched her with hooded eyes. "Indeed?" She peered at Alexandra waiting to see if she would say more.

Alexandra stubbornly stayed silent.

"I hope, Miss Dunforth, that you consider myself and Miranda to be—"

The Dowager was interrupted by the appearance of the butler.

"Madam, the Marchioness of Cambourne." The butler quietly opened the door to allow a stunning blonde, dressed in ice-blue silk, to enter. The blonde looked at the butler with disdain, waving him away with an elegant flutter of her hand. She sauntered over to the Dowager, leveling a look of muted distaste at Miranda.

"Well, well. Quite the little tea party you're having, Donata. I assume you just neglected to tell me we were having guests." She looked pointedly at Alexandra with a tiny sneer on her perfect pink lips.

Alexandra's first thought was that she was seeing a fairy

princess from a fable come to life. The woman's beauty was
what poets wrote odes to and men fought duels over. The
Marchioness's golden tresses, the color of ripened wheat,
curled into an ornate coiffure that pulled artfully back from
her temples. Arrogance and entitlement dripped from her
like the diamonds in her delicate ears. Alexandra couldn't tell
how old she was, for her face was as unlined as Alexandra's
own and her complexion reminded one of fresh cream. *Was no
one in this family plain?* Alexandra looked at Miranda and the
still lovely Dowager. *I am a duckling amongst swans.*

"Jeanette, *dearest*, why don't you join us for tea? I assumed
you were still abed. You danced so late into the night with our
dear Herbert." The Dowager's voice dripped with sarcasm.

Alexandra didn't understand the sudden tension in the air,
but the parlor was rife with it.

Lady Cambourne stiffened at the Dowager's tone. Her lip
curled into a sneering imitation of a smile.

The Dowager looked ready to hit her daughter-in-law
with her cane. She stared down Lady Cambourne.

The two women reminded Alexandra of cats disputing
territory.

Lady Cambourne's hands curled into themselves giving
her nails the appearance of talons. The perfect features tightened. "Herbert's a dear, isn't he?" Lady Cambourne's cultured
tones said politely. "Just imagine, if Robert hadn't married
that vicar's daughter in the *nick of time*," Lady Cambourne put
special emphasis on the words, "well...things would likely be
much different. How *fortunate*, don't you agree, Donata?"

The Dowager's lips tightened. "You forget yourself,
Jeanette."

"Well, that's all ancient history now, isn't it?" Lady
Cambourne sounded like a hissing teapot.

"We have a guest, Jeanette." The Dowager gave a nod in
Alexandra's direction. The warning in her voice was implicit.

Lady Cambourne gave a sniff of her perfect nose, ignoring the Dowager. "I have some errands to attend to. I shall be gone the rest of the afternoon. Friends to visit." She turned to Miranda. "Miranda, pray drink nothing but tea. No cakes or scones. I see in you a tendency towards stoutness. Now that your brother foolishly declined Percy Dobson's offer for your hand, I am assured of nothing but difficulty in finding you another suitor. If you grow stout, it will only complicate things. Had you married during your first Season I would not now be faced with rescuing you from spinsterhood." She shook her head. "You could have been a duchess."

Miranda reacted as if she had been slapped. Her lovely face reddened, and her whole form deflated like an overdone soufflé.

The Dowager banged her cane on the floor.

"*Dear* daughter-in-law, I fear I am out of patience this morning. Pray do not try *me*."

The air around the two prickled with animosity.

Miranda looked away and plucked at her skirts.

Alexandra wished to fade into the tapestry of the sofa. She lowered her gaze to her lap.

"As you wish, my lady." Lady Cambourne curtsied low to the Dowager smirking with disrespect. Her skirts rustled softly. The icy gaze pierced the Dowager with dislike.

She quirked a perfectly plucked eyebrow in Alexandra's direction, as if she suddenly remembered Alexandra was in the room. "Donata, you haven't introduced me. And you are?" Her tone spoke volumes. Lady Cambourne couldn't care less who Alexandra was.

Alexandra rose and curtsied. "Alexandra Dunforth, my lady."

The golden head didn't nod in acknowledgement. The pale blue shards of ice flickered with what Alexandra thought was recognition. Then the Marchioness turned her back on Alexandra.

"Well, I will leave you to your *scintillating* conversation." She turned her conversation back to the Dowager. "Please make sure that Miranda drinks only tea. Sutton is so tight with every farthing, I can ill afford to let out her gowns if she eats too much." The Marchioness flounced out of the room in a flurry of blue silk.

Alexandra exhaled slowly. She had been holding her breath. What a horrid woman. And she was a Marchioness.

The Dowager suddenly looked very old and tired, as if her previous liveliness were taken by the dark fairy who just sailed from the room.

"That's my mother. Lovely, isn't she? She thinks Sutton is the reason no one has offered for me. Ha!" Miranda gave a toss of her head.

"You've declined so many suitors that few now have the inclination to ask." The Dowager clutched her cane. "Perhaps you should lower your expectations."

A soft knock came at the door. Alexandra prayed it wasn't Lady Cambourne returning.

"Come," the Dowager uttered in her commanding tone.

The butler opened the door and bowed low. "Lord Cambourne is here, madam."

Alexandra's teacup shook. She struggled to set it down without spilling her tea.

The Dowager cast her an odd look.

The scent of cinnamon wafted into the room followed by Lord Cambourne. "Hello, *Rainha*. Hello, Miranda. I've come to chase away your demon. I believe she bolted to her carriage when she saw me coming." He smirked like a child caught in mischief as he walked through the door but stopped in surprise when he spied Alexandra. The green gaze ran over her figure on the couch, lingering on her bosom before lifting to her lips.

Damnation! He does remember me! She felt ridiculously happy that he did then chided herself for caring.

His features immediately composed into cold curiosity. "Forgive me, Grandmother, I didn't realize you had a guest." He drawled with what sounded to Alexandra like insolence.

Alexandra stiffened her spine. *Does he think I am here to scream ruination? Well, I don't give a bloody damn what he thinks. I wasn't snooping, and I certainly don't wish to acknowledge our previous meeting.*

"Sutton, this is Miss Alexandra Dunforth. Grandmother met her at Lady Dobson's ball the other night. Miss Dunforth, my brother, the Marquess of Cambourne." Miranda, no doubt still smarting from her mother's remarks, defiantly bit into a slice of raisin cake.

"Must you refer to me in a foreign tongue? Portuguese is only slightly better than Chinese. At least the Portuguese aren't heathens." The Dowager sniffed.

"But *Rainha* means queen. I thought you would appreciate the sentiment."

Alexandra made a dutiful curtsy all the while wishing she could run from the room. Lord Cambourne was more beautiful than she remembered, in spite of the slight frown he directed at her. The dark, silky locks of his hair were pulled back and tied neatly with a leather thong. The earring, dangling jauntily from one ear appeared to be a jade figure. The smell of cinnamon grew stronger as he moved into the room. He bent down to bestow a kiss on his grandmother's forehead before moving his tall form to the window where he leaned against the sill. The green eyes, so like his sister's and grandmother's, watched her appraisingly.

An awkward silence engulfed the room. Alexandra clasped and unclasped her hands. Lord Cambourne's presence caused her no end of nervousness. Did he think her appearance was to denounce his behavior at Lady Dobson's? She certainly wasn't here to curry favor with his family or force him into marriage. Marriage was the farthest thing from Alexandra's mind. In fact, she was actively avoiding it.

The dark head nodded curtly, "A pleasure, Miss Dunforth."

His long legs encased in leather riding breeches, stretched out in front of him as he leaned against the window. The leather outlined his muscular thighs, clung to them in fact, a bit *indecently*. A blush stole up her cheeks again. She realized she was admiring him as one does a prize stallion.

He caught her looking and raised an eyebrow.

Alexandra lowered her eyes. The man really *was* a conceited ass.

"Miss Dunforth was just telling us about her estate in Hampshire, Helmsby Abbey. She's quite the gentleman farmer, Sutton. You might learn a thing or two from Miss Dunforth."

Alexandra sincerely doubted that Lord Cambourne gave a fig for managing an estate and nearly said so to the room. He likely had dozens of minions to do that for him. She wished she could march right over to him and tell him to stop looking at her with his beautiful accusatory eyes. Thankfully, at least, he did not seem inclined to acknowledge their earlier meeting.

"Indeed? Are you familiar with animal husbandry as well, Miss Dunforth?" Lord Cambourne drawled the words. His gaze slid over her breasts as if he were contemplating a delicious roast at a banquet and deciding which prime cut to slice off.

He is a horrid, arrogant man.

A spurt of heat ran through her. Alexandra did not miss

the innuendo, although thankfully it looked like Miranda had. She wasn't sure about the Dowager.

"I am, my lord."

"I thought as much." Lord Cambourne smirked. "You have that look about you—as a *gentleman* farmer does."

Rude, insulting peacock. She knew she was plain, but she *certainly* didn't look like a *man*. His glance at her breasts should be enough to disprove that. She wished to leave before she marched over to him and gave him another setdown. A set down he most certainly deserved.

The parlor grew warmer.

"What else have you ladies been discussing today? Gowns, I suspect, and other fripperies?"

"Sutton, don't goad me." Miranda looked as if she would throw a piece of the raisin cake at him. "We are not like your Lady Fellowes. There's a woman with nothing but vacant space between her ears. Her personality is that of a potted plant. A fern or some other dull shrub."

"Miranda!" The Dowager flinched and sounded stern, but her eyes laughed.

Lord Cambourne shook his finger at his sister. "She is most *definitely* not *my* Lady Fellowes." He didn't appear chagrined with his sister in the least. Clearly, he and Miranda were very close.

The Dowager put one wrinkled hand to her forehead as if in pain. "I am thankful she is not. There are enough plants in this house."

❧

SUTTON SHOT HIS GRANDMOTHER AN AMUSED GLANCE. HE knew of her dislike for Lady Fellowes. The Dowager made no secret of it. He narrowed his eyes and flicked an imaginary piece of lint off his sleeve as he surveyed the sumptuous Miss

Dunforth. What in the world was she doing here? The lovely ivory skin of her face and neck flushed a delightful shade of red. The opal eyes flashed at him in disapproval along with an odd vulnerability. If his grandmother and sister hadn't been present, he would ravish Miss Dunforth on the settee.

Miss Dunforth popped up in the most unlikely places. Hiding behind curtains in libraries. His grandmother's parlor. Oddly enough, he'd visited his grandmother today to ask if she knew Miss Dunforth. And low and behold here was the Badger. He told himself again that he was merely bored, and Miss Dunforth only intrigued him. Perhaps that was it, he thought with disdain as he looked at her severe coiffure. The chestnut curls were sedately and unfortunately restrained. Not even a tendril was attempting to escape. Pity. The gown she wore was of good quality, but the colors were muted and dull. Miss Dunworth apparently wished to fade into the shadows of his grandmother's parlor. Her back was rigid as if a fireplace poker held her in place. How incredibly ladylike and prim was Miss Dunforth. He wanted to throw her skirts over her head and make her beg him to take her.

She looked away unconsciously biting her luscious lower lip. A rebellious, tiny curl, almost as if it had heard his earlier thoughts, sprung from her coiffure.

Sutton shifted slightly. His cock stood at full attention. The Badger's appearance today reminded him that leather breeches were unforgiving. He treated Miss Dunforth to a polite, interested smile.

"How long have you been in London, Miss Dunforth?"

The Badger choked as he addressed her directly. The opal eyes flashed at him in annoyance. He had the odd sensation she wished he would ignore her completely. Impossible.

"A fortnight only, my lord."

"Lady Dobson's was the first social event Miss Dunforth has attended. Lord Burke, Miss Dunforth's uncle, is a distant relation of Lady Dobson's. Miranda piped in helpfully, plopping another piece of raisin cake into her mouth.

Sutton watched Miss Dunforth's reaction to his sister's recitation. Her hands twisted in her lap and she studiously avoided his gaze.

So that was her cause of distress in Lord Dobson's library. Her uncle launched her into society and expected to find her a suitor. The look on her lovely face told Sutton she was none too happy about it. A smart girl, one with ambition, would be screaming that the Marquess of Cambourne compromised her honor at Lady Dobson's. Her uncle should be here demanding marriage. Curious.

"Sutton?" His grandmother banged her cane on the floor in a demand for his attention

"Sorry, woolgathering. I was just wondering if Lady Dobson was successful in making introductions for Miss Dunforth." An unwelcome spurt of jealousy welled in him as he waited for her answer.

Miranda regarded him with astonishment. The question was much too personal for a first meeting. His grandmother gave a calculated look of surprise that he would show such interest in their little guest. The question bordered on rudeness. Sutton didn't care. It was suddenly very important to him.

The Badger raised her chin defiantly. Annoyed. He could tell by the set of her jaw. Brave little Badger. She wanted to throw something at him. He could tell. Then she winced painfully and dramatically.

"Forgive me, my lady," Miss Dunforth moaned in false pain to the Dowager. "I suddenly feel quite unwell. My head feels as if it is splitting. I beg your forgiveness, but I must take my leave."

"Indeed?" His grandmother tried to sound shocked. Grandmother was not a stupid woman. She noted Sutton's interest in Miss Dunforth. "Your headache came on so suddenly."

He nearly laughed out loud. Badgers tended to be crafty little creatures.

Miss Dunforth tried to look ill. A hand fluttered to her temple. She grimaced again as if in horrible pain. She was a terrible liar and a worse actress.

"Miss Dunforth? Alexandra? Are you sure you must leave?" Miranda pouted. "I wanted to show you the library. We haven't even talked about the latest Lord Thurston novel."

"I am so very sorry, but I find that my head aches terribly. My constitution is delicate at times, or so I'm told."

"Indeed." The Dowager gave a small snort of disbelief. "And you a sturdy lass from Hampshire. Who ran a farm. Alone." His grandmother's knowing gaze flicked to him, then to Miss Dunforth.

"Miss Dunforth, I do hope it's not that sudden illness I've heard is making the rounds of the *ton*. Young ladies suddenly struck down as they drink their tea. You must get home immediately before you find yourself unable to do so." Sutton composed his face into one of bland concern knowing it would irritate the little Badger. He was not disappointed.

Miss Dunforth, *Alex,* looked as if she would argue with him, saw his grandmother watching her and changed her expression to one of illness. "Possibly, my lord. There are all kinds of *ill humors* and *vile things* to be found in London that I, growing up in Hampshire, am not accustomed to. I was likely *exposed* to something at Lady Dobson's which didn't agree with me."

Most women did not compare Sutton to an *ill humor* or *vile thing*. Her subtle insult made him want to laugh out loud. Or kiss her senseless. He strode over to the settee. "Please allow me to escort you out, Miss Dunforth."

"That's not necessary, Lord Cambourne." The Badger stood. "I am quite capable of finding the front door myself." She gave a false wobble and pretended as if she would faint at any moment. "Lady Cambourne, Lady Miranda, I bid you good day. My apologies again."

Sutton leaned over Miss Dunforth, *Alex*. "I insist." The look of horror on her face was so comical he bit his lip to stifle the laughter bubbling up inside of him.

She ignored his arm, prickly thing that she was, and proceeded to the door determined to see herself out. She stopped only when his grandmother spoke.

"I would take it much amiss, Miss Dunforth, if Sutton didn't see you out."

Alex's shoulders slumped as she paused for effect and whispered, "I don't wish to trouble Lord Cambourne, my lady." The pathetic tone in her voice had an edge to it. "Your footman is right down the hall."

"It's no trouble at all." Little coward. He held his arm out again, daring her to take it.

Alex's fingertips brushed the top of his arm lightly, as if he was a leper she was forced to touch.

"You cannot be too careful, my dear Miss Dunforth. A headache can make one so weak and dizzy. I would not have you fainting in the hallway. Sutton will put you in my carriage least you collapse on the steps." The Dowager commanded in a severe tone, but her eyes twinkled in delight. "It has been a *most* illuminating afternoon, Miss Dunforth. I cannot wait to further our acquaintance. We shall call on you soon, won't we, Miranda?"

Miranda nodded and took another bite of the raisin cake.

Sutton led the subdued Miss Dunforth out of his grandmother's parlor. She looked like she was being escorted to the gallows instead of being seen to the waiting carriage of a Marchioness. He heard the laughter of the Dowager behind him. No doubt his grandmother would be full of questions.

❧

ALEXANDRA FELT THE HEAT OF LORD CAMBOURNE through her fingertips. The sensations seeped down her arm, through her chest, and lodged between her legs. Her emotions vacillated between anger at his high-handed behavior, embarrassment at his acknowledgement, and a nervous, filmy excitement that rushed through her in waves.

As always, Alexandra tried to think logically. She decided that his goading of her was nothing more than dismay in finding her taking tea with his grandmother. Fine. She could understand his confusion. She would explain the situation to him. She would likely run into him again, if she were to further her acquaintance with the Dowager and Miranda so she would like to smooth over any misconceptions he may be under. She couldn't fault him in thinking that most women would try to use their previous meeting as leverage. Her irritation abated, though she still thought him a conceited ass. She snuck a look at his beautiful profile.

"My Lord." Alexandra turned, taking a deep breath. His eyes were so green and mesmerizing that it took her a moment to continue. "Please let me explain. I met your grandmother purely by chance at Lady Dobson's and she invited me to tea. My appearance is in no way related to our unfortunate meeting last night. My discretion is assured." Surely, he didn't wish for anyone to know that she'd witnessed his assignation with Lady Fellowes. Or, their previous meeting. She certainly did not.

His eyes widened a bit. The gold flecks in his emerald eyes twinkled in the light.

"Let us begin again," Alexandra said proudly, impressed

she could even think with the exotic allure of Lord Cambourne's surrounding her. She managed to sound as if his company caused her little distress. A feat of incredible magnitude, for the smell of him, like a warm cinnamon bun, played havoc with her senses.

The green gaze settled on her bosom then wandered down between the valleys of her breasts.

Why was he being so....so *improper* with her? It was unwarranted. He had intimated that she was plain and mannish in front of his grandmother. He could not possibly be attracted to her. Maybe he was trying to get her to apologize for losing her temper. She was beneath him socially and the setdown she gave him *was* incredibly incorrect. He didn't strike her as a stickler for those types of things, but maybe he was.

"I am also truly sorry for my unladylike display of temper." There, she thought. That should placate him.

"Yes. Your very unladylike display of temper." His brow wrinkled, and he frowned slightly, as if it truly disturbed him. The big body moved closer to her.

Alexandra felt overly warm, as she had in the parlor. Apparently, Cambourne House was not well ventilated. Surely, a maid or footman could open a window. Besides being warm, her irritation returned at his manner. He didn't need to sound so...*put out*. If she recalled correctly, he'd called her an educated, overgrown rat at their last meeting. That was *much* worse than being called a peacock.

"My lord," Alexandra said through clenched teeth. His closeness made it difficult to concentrate. She thought of the green dragon tattoo and imagined the tail moved and reached out for her. "If you will not accept my apology then I bid you good day." The words came out in a slight stutter, and she winced.

"Prickly, aren't you little Badger? I did not find our

meeting unfortunate. I found it precipitous." He stood so near she could clearly see the stubble on his chin. The green eyes danced under lashes longer than any man should have. His lips were full and sensuous. She tried to focus on the tiny jade figure in his ear. It looked like a baby.

"Do not call me that. It is not flattering to be likened to a foul-tempered rodent."

"No, it is not. Nor is it flattering to be likened to a strutting bird known for its beauty and stupidity." This time he grinned, showing even white teeth.

Alexandra's heart began a dull thud as she looked up into those green eyes. Her breath stopped. She stood frozen, mesmerized by Lord Cambourne. Were he a cobra about to strike she would cheerfully stand still and allow the bite. Alexandra realized with growing trepidation that she was out of her element with this man. As mistress of Helmsby Abbey, she gave orders to a group of ancient servants and farmhands. Her intelligence and authority were never questioned and no man, not a farmhand, a villager, or even the peddler that sometimes passed through ever dared flirt with her. The man before her was a dangerous, handsome Marquess with a scandalous reputation. His attraction to her was illogical and ridiculous. She was both frightened and thrilled by his apparent interest in her.

"Miss Dunforth, I would love to further a discussion of animal husbandry with you. Perhaps you can give me pointers. About my sheep." A mischievous grin broke across the beautiful face.

He's flirting with me. Teasing me. Her heart fluttered like a trapped butterfly. "I would be happy to. The next time your grandmother invites me to tea." The words came out sharply. She turned her back on him, anxious to escape to the safety of the carriage and the dubious company of Tilda. She took a step forward.

A warm finger slid along her neck and inserted itself in the back of her gown. The finger tugged her back, towards Lord Cambourne. She could not move forward without risking a tear in her gown.

"Stop blustering for a moment, Badger. Even though it makes you *quite* delectable."

The words fell over her in a caress. He'd called her delectable. Something dark and dangerous twisted through her. Her skin tingled. The hall grew even warmer. Surely this was only a game to him.

"You are unkind to toy with me in this fashion." She nearly wept the words. Every nerve in her body screamed. "Are you so jaded by life that you amuse yourself by torturing your grandmother's guests?"

The finger slid out of the back of her neck and was joined by his whole hand as it trailed down the length of her spine. Her back exploded at the warmth of his touch. A gasp escaped her mouth. She prayed he hadn't noticed.

"I would enjoy torturing you *endlessly*. In a most *kind* fashion."

The dragon's tail wrapped around her middle, sensuously winding around her.

"Alex." His breath, warm against the back of her neck, held a note of longing.

An odd ache filled her chest. "I did not give you leave to call me by that name." She tried to sound harsh, but instead her reprimand sounded seductive.

"I did not ask for it." The words floated around her as he planted a kiss below her ear, the skin sparking with flame at the touch of his lips.

Alexandra blinked, stunned that he would dare kiss her, here at Cambourne House, but did not turn around to face him. It was all she could do not to fall into a puddle of adoration at his feet. She was a bookish, plain spinster from Hampshire, more comfortable discussing the planting of crops than the whispering of seductive flirtations in the shadows. Notorious rakes did not desire her. Did they?

She pivoted round, determined to confront him with the logic of her thoughts, but he was gone, the elegant hallway of Cambourne House quiet. Lord Cambourne disappeared as if he had never been there at all.

❧ 6 ❧

"**M**y lord, you have a guest awaiting you in your study." McMannish wrinkled his enormous bushy black eyebrows and frowned as he saw the tear in Sutton's jacket and the scrape against Sutton's cheek. "My lord? Have you been teaching Viscount Lindley that Chinese fighting again? Looks like he got one off on you."

Sutton nodded to McMannish but didn't answer. The man who attempted to slit Sutton's throat as he left the solicitor's office decided to have his windpipe crushed rather than tell Sutton who employed him. Sutton was sure that even without the man's confession he knew who'd hired the would-be assassin. Three attempts on his life in such a short time span, one prior to his departure from Macao, the other just after his return to London, and the third today, left Sutton little doubt as to the identity. She was the only one with much to gain by his death and everything to lose if Sutton continued to live.

He shook his shoulders, trying to force the dampness of London from his body. He had been back from Macao for nearly two years, but still he couldn't get warm. Every fireplace in the townhouse was kept stoked day and night to banish the cold. Still Sutton shivered. McMannish complained of slowly being cooked to death and suggested his lordship wear wool undergarments.

"Can you be more specific as to the guest?"

The two giant, black caterpillars over McMannish's eyes attempted to climb into the man's hairline. A sure sign of trouble. McMannish was a large man of Scottish extraction and made quite an imposing butler. Sutton had found him drunk and surly in a tavern on the wharf one evening. The man bemoaned his fate. He came to London to escape the poverty of his Scottish village only to be unable to find work. His imposing size, stern countenance, and Scottish burr gave potential employers pause. Sutton, knowing how it felt to be an outcast, hired McMannish on the spot. The grateful Scotsman was both butler and bodyguard.

"Robbins tried to warn you. He sent 'round a note." McMannish lowered his tone.

"A lady, McMannish?" Damn Robbins. Sutton had found his erstwhile valet at a house party held by the Earl of Lantham. Robbins spilled out of an upstairs window after being discovered with the Earl's mistress. The man was a decent valet but could be distracted by a show of leg or a pretty smile. He was likely just now recalling he needed to get a note to Sutton.

McMannish sniffed. "I'm sure some would call her that. No lady I know would show up at a gentleman's home, unescorted in her widow's weeds."

Ah. It was Caro then, and not his stepmother. Thank God. He really wasn't up for sparring with Jeanette this afternoon, especially since she was trying to have him killed. The morning at the solicitor's had been quite illuminating. Jeanette spent the Cambourne fortune at a furious pace. Her dressmaker's bills alone boggled the mind. She ordered jewels and fripperies by the dozen. Employed a servant just to hold a parasol over her in the garden least the sun spoil her complexion. Her allowance, exceedingly generous, seemed to disappear amongst the pile of gambling debt she accumulated. Sutton instructed the solicitor that the Marchioness no longer had an open line of credit, anywhere. He alone controlled Jeanette's allowance. She was not going to bleed Cambourne any longer with her excess.

"Cam, darling? Is that you?" A feminine voice echoed down the hallway.

McMannish wiggled his brows in distaste. His lips pressed firmly into a grimace of disapproval. "It's *that* Lady Fellowes."

"I see." Sutton sighed in frustration. Caro refused his polite brush-off at Lady Dobson's. He did not wish things to become nasty, but Caro wasn't taking the hint.

He approached the study, swinging the door open.

"You should shut the door, darling. I wouldn't want to catch cold," Caro giggled.

Lady Caroline Fellowes was spread across his leather coach in nothing but a lacy chemise. The filmy garment hid nothing of her form beneath. Her flaming red hair trailed over the arm of the couch to pool on the floor below.

"Come warm me up." Her arms opened wide to greet him, a seductive smile on her lips.

Sutton quietly shut the door. He would have to instruct McMannish that Lady Fellowes was not to be let in the townhouse again. A headache began behind his eyes. His near murder and the excess of his stepmother exhausted him. Sutton wanted a drink, a warm fire, and to be left alone.

Her blue eyes widened as they took in the scratches on his cheek and the torn jacket. "What happened? Did you fall off your horse?"

Anxiety and worry suffused her lovely features. He admitted that Caro probably *did* care something for him. She *loved* the jealous looks from other women when he chanced to escort her out. *Loved* his wealth. *Adored* his title. So transparent, his dear Caro, but one had to admire her tenacity.

"I stumbled in the street. It's of no import."

Rain trickled down the study windows in rivulets, giving a wavering appearance to the street outside. Sutton shivered. Damn, he was cold. The flames in the fireplace roared into a crescendo of heat. Caro looked nice and warm, even in her chemise. No, it was England that chilled him. This cold, hard island of his birth. Did he even belong here?

At night he dreamt of a suffocating heat, a heat so wet with warmth a man had difficulty breathing. The kind of heat in which no cold could live. A man woke every day with sweat already clinging to his brow. The dense, green jungle, reeking of rotting vegetation mixed with the exotic, floral scents he much preferred over the rotting refuse to be found in the streets of London. Mornings in Macao, he awoke to the sound of monkeys chattering in the thick brush that surrounded his compound. Well, he mused, he still heard the chattering of monkeys, but here the monkeys were called the *ton*. Sutton chuckled.

"What's so funny?" Caro sat up. She lifted one ivory shoulder, allowing her chemise to dip low, nearly exposing one round breast.

Sutton ran his hand through his hair, determined not to bodily throw her out. "What are you doing here, Caro?" He didn't bother to hide the irritation in his voice.

Caro ignored his tone. "Well, the other night," she said, stretching like a cat, "you seemed quite put out with me and I think I know why." Her full lips pursed in apology as she tossed a coppery strand over her shoulder. The chemise rode up her thighs.

Sutton walked to the sideboard and poured himself a large glass of brandy. Clearly Caro was bent on seduction. It was much too early in the day for brandy, but Sutton didn't care.

The brandy was from his father's private store, and quite expensive. His father, he thought with a smile, enjoyed a good brandy. He sipped the smoky warmth and wished his father still alive. He missed him. Sutton thanked God that Donata had forced him home, even though the circumstances were not of Sutton's choosing. He had been with his father at the end.

Caro gave a puff of irritation. She hated to be ignored.

"You were saying?" He didn't even bother looking interested, because he wasn't, not in the least. He imagined the woman on his sofa to be smaller, but no less voluptuous.

Alex.

The hair a profusion of chestnut curls, not copper strands. The eyes, gray, not blue. The smell of tart, green apples filled his nose. An image of Alex, naked on his lap, reading to him, her mass of hair trailing over his arms, as he turned the pages of a book, flashed before him. He took another sip of the brandy.

"Darling, I sense you are cross with me. Have I made you jealous?" Caro batted her eyes at him and tried to sound despondent. "Viscount Lindley did steal a kiss, but it meant nothing. I should *not* have taken a turn around the terrace with him. You aren't going to *challenge* him, are you?" Her face fairly beamed in delight at the thought of two Wickeds fighting over her. How Caro would enjoy the uproar.

Sutton snorted. Nick, Viscount Lindley, could care less about Lady Caroline Fellowes. Nick thought Caro a witless, vapid creature with only a nice pair of tits to recommend her. Caro's machinations did not impress Sutton's best friend. Nor did they impress Sutton. His patience with Caro and her maneuvering in and out of his bed were over.

"You ignored me at the opera, Cam. I'll admit when Viscount Lindley asked me to take the air with him, I thought to make you jealous. I had no idea," she paused dramatically, "that he would try to take liberties." Caro slid across the couch, perching herself on the edge in a display of half-naked flesh.

Sutton swirled the brandy in his mouth. Caro had flounced over to Nick begging him to take her out for a breath of fresh air, lest she faint.

"You know I'm not interested in Viscount Lindley. His eyes...." Caro shuddered delicately, "Well they terrify me. Besides, it's you I adore. I love everything about you. There is no other man for me," she declared, allowing her breasts to spill out of the chemise.

Sutton pretended to mull over her declaration. "Hmmm. What is my younger sister's name?"

Caro froze, looking like a startled deer. She bit her lip, at a loss.

"Well, I'm not sure you ever mentioned her to me."

"Her? I have two sisters. I'm positive I've mentioned both. You've met Miranda several times, I believe. Elizabeth, the younger, is away at boarding school in Scotland. I'm quite sure you know my grandmother, don't you?"

Caro frowned, offended. Everyone in London knew the powerful Dowager Marchioness.

He wagged a finger at her, enjoying her discomfort. "Here's an easy one then. How many properties do I have?"

She smiled brilliantly, sure of herself. "Five. Cambourne House, this townhouse where you currently live." She waved her arms about the room. "A bachelor's house with ill-mannered servants, which we will sell, once we're married. I can't imagine why you prefer this place to Cambourne House."

Sutton raised a brow but didn't stop her. Apparently, Caro didn't care for McMannish.

She held up a hand, counting off the Cambourne assets.

"Blackburn Heath, the family's seat, Gray Covington, and Baylor Manor in Scotland."

"Well, at least you know I have a home in Scotland." Sutton clapped his hands at her recital. Greedy, greedy Caro. She made the Prussian mercenaries look like schoolchildren. "I'm sure you know my income from each of my estates as well, do you not?"

She smiled and proceeded to tell him. She stood and strode over to him, her hips swaying and a lascivious look in her eye. The chemise floated about her hips. Her nipples, small and dusky, pointed through the thin silk. Smooth white arms wrapped around Sutton's neck as she kissed him on the cheek. "See. I do know everything about you." She shook her head as if he were a naughty child.

Sutton mused that Caro was no better or no worse than any other woman of her station. Groomed from childhood to be the ornamental wife of a wealthy, titled man, Caro simply did as she was trained to do. When Sutton was no more than a child, Jeanette, his stepmother, reminded him on a daily basis that Sutton's only value in this world, his only meaning to others, was as heir to Cambourne. Oh, he was beautiful, Jeanette would admit, women would adore him, want him and he would have no lack of lovers. No Marquess had a lack of lovers. Cambourne was everything, and without the estate and title, Sutton was *nothing*. Jeanette would remind him that Cambourne didn't actually belong to Sutton. Not really. She knew the truth. As soon as she produced a son, well, Sutton would be sent off to the army in India or some other place. Robert would want his *real* heir, an heir Jeanette would produce, to inherit Cambourne. Robert, his father, regarded Sutton as a duty, an obligation, and would expect Sutton to do the right thing.

Sutton took another long, draught of the brandy, praying for the dark liquid to do its work and numb him to the past.

Jeanette was a greedy, ambitious, depraved bitch. He witnessed the depth of her depravity with his own eyes. She convinced him, ice blue eyes spilling with tears, to not tell his father.

I am with child. A son. I'm sure of it. Your father's heir.

Jeanette pleaded with Sutton. Think what the scandal would do to the Cambourne family. What about Miranda, Sutton's adored younger sister? She would be spat upon. *Shunned.* Jeanette was the only mother Sutton had ever known. If he had an ounce of love for her, he would leave England, never confessing Jeanette's accidental misstep to Robert.

Sutton loved her then. He *believed* her. Stupidly, he did as Jeanette asked and left for Macao. What a fool he had been. He deserted Miranda and left his newborn sister, Elizabeth, all because of that harpy. Jeanette hadn't even been with child.

Sutton gently set the brandy glass down on the table. The brandy failed to warm the chill in his heart.

Caro waited, her face turned up to his, waiting for his declaration of...love? Caro reminded him so much of Jeanette at that moment he found it difficult to look at her.

He pulled Caro's arms from around his neck, pushed her body away from him. "You need to leave, Caro. Do you require assistance?" He pointed to her gown, crumpled and lying on the floor. "Or can you manage? I can call one of the maids if you wish." Jeanette's wounds on his soul reopened, freshly bleeding. Bitterness and resentment soured the taste of brandy on his tongue.

Caro's mouth gaped open, fishlike, then closed abruptly. She trembled, but her eyes remained hard on him.

Sutton knew Caro told nearly everyone in the *ton* that he was about to offer for her. She took out credit, telling merchants all over London she would be the future

Marchioness of Cambourne. She had done it all with poor Lord Danvers on her arm. Sutton felt no pity for her.

Caro's perfect porcelain complexion flushed until it turned mottled and red. She stood tall. Staring down her patrician nose she gave him a haughty look and lifted her chin.

"Are you casting me off? Dismissing me?" Her voice remained cool. "Don't be a fool. Danvers will offer for me in an instant. He wants me terribly. Do you want him to have this?" She pulled down the chemise, baring her large breasts, the nipples erect. "We have an understanding, Sutton. Everyone knows that." Her blue eyes watered in the most fetching manner.

"Do we?" He looked her straight in the eye, trying desperately to keep the disgust he felt for her out of his words. "I believe you have misunderstood." He picked up the brandy glass, intending to refill it. "Good day, Lady Fellowes."

Caro reeled back against the couch as if he slapped her. "Oh, come now, Cam," she cajoled, "surely, you can overlook a minor transgression with Viscount Lindley. It was a kiss. He took advantage."

"This has nothing to do with Viscount Lindley. Although I do admire you for attempting to become a duchess as well as a marchioness."

Caro's face contorted into a mask of ugliness. Her lip curled into a sneer. "*Bastard.*" She said the word slowly, emphasizing the syllables.

Sutton halted, the glass held mid-air. Brandy sloshed out. He could feel the heat rise in his cheeks. He nearly killed a man recently for inferring the same thing about his parentage. How dare she?

Caro gave a short nasty bark. "Oh yes, all the *ton* knows. Did daddy really marry your lowly born mother before you were born or after? What side of the blanket did Sutton come into the world on?" Caro's voice was brittle. "A *vicar's* daughter, a nobody. Some tart who was your father's mistress! Little better than a whore. Who marries their mistress?"

A horrible rage built inside Sutton at Caro's words. He knew about the scandal that surrounded his birth, mostly he ignored it, and sometimes he made an example of the person stupid enough to challenge him with it. There was no proof of his birth prior to his parents marrying. None. He *was* the Marquess of Cambourne. He doubted anyone alive knew the real truth except the Dowager. The gossip would have died but for Jeanette. She planted the seeds of the rumor when Sutton was a child. Nourished the scandal when she carried his sisters, hoping she would give birth to a son and Sutton would be pushed aside. He should have sent his stepmother to exile the moment he returned to England. But he hadn't. Instead he tolerated the whispers, tolerated his nickname. But he would *not* hear a word against his mother. Not Madeline. Lord Robert Cambourne grieved Madeline's loss every day of his life. His father kept a miniature of Madeline in his pocket with him always. His father's last breath on this earth had been *her* name. Madeline may have only been a vicar's daughter, not wealthy, or titled, but she had been deeply loved. Something the pampered, spoiled bitch in front of him would never understand. Madeline deserved respect. The woman who stood smugly before him wasn't good enough to *speak* his mother's name. Whatever brief affection or kindness he felt for Caro died.

"Tread carefully, Caro."

Caro backed away from the threat in Sutton's voice.

"Oh my God. I... You... I was just angry. I'm sorry. I didn't mean..."

"Yes, you did. I'll be sure and remember you to my grandmother." Sutton knew that was petty of him, to threaten her social standing. His grandmother could ruin Caro with a flick of her cane.

Caro paled.

"McMannish will escort you out." Sutton pulled the bell cord and the butler immediately opened the door. The damned Scot was probably listening at the door.

"Sir?" McMannish kept his eyes focused on Sutton's face, choosing to ignore the scantily clad, red-faced Caro.

"Please have Lady Fellowes's carriage brought around. She is leaving. Immediately."

McMannish raised a bushy brow at the evident disrespect in Sutton's tone, but merely nodded and left the room.

Caro jerked her gown over her head. He'd long suspected Caro would be a complete bitch if thwarted, but never did he think her stupid enough to disparage his mother, Madeline, to his face.

McMannish stepped back into the study.

"Ah, my lady, your cloak." He held it out to her, careful to keep his eyes averted from her state of undress.

Caro ripped the cloak from the butler's hands, wrapping the wool around her half-dressed form.

"You will regret this, Cam. I am not some common whore."

"No, you are not," he scoffed, "a common whore has better manners." Sutton filled the brandy glass from the sideboard and walked from the room just as Caro began to scream.

7

"**M**y dear, Miss Dunforth, how absolutely charming you look this evening." Mr. Runyon greeted Alexandra, bending over to brush a kiss upon her knuckles.

Alexandra smiled back. "The peonies you sent yesterday were lovely and so thoughtful."

"Did you enjoy the book on Roman history?"

Alexandra nodded with enthusiasm. "Of course." She enjoyed everything Mr. Runyon chose for her. Over the last two weeks, some small token from Mr. Runyon arrived at her uncle's nearly every day. Flowers, books, even a charming print of an etching of the Parthenon, found their way into her hands. Mr. Runyon appeared just as often, coming for tea and once escorting her to a play at the Royal Theater. While she did not desire marriage to him, her false courtship by Mr. Runyon certainly bore benefits. Helmsby Abbey was safe, at least temporarily, and her uncle brought her no other suitors. "The book was fascinating. I fear I read it in one evening!"

"Your mind is as inquisitive as my own. Perhaps we are

destined to be together." His hand cupped her elbow as he guided her down the hall.

Alexandra ignored the sudden stab of guilt.

"How kind of you to invite my uncle and me for dinner." Alexandra quickly changed the subject. She used this gentle, intelligent man for her own ends and it did not sit well with her. Alexandra focused her attention on the beautifully decorated entryway.

Art niches were set in the walls at various intervals and each seemed to contain a tiny statue or urn of some sort. A vase of white roses, extremely rare this time of year, sat on an expensive looking table to her right.

Alexandra turned her head and a curl spilled free. Her coiffure needed attention before they dined or it would likely fall down during the soup course.

"Mr. Runyon? Is there an area where I can see to my hair?" Her hand ran up to a group of curls threatening to break free of the carefully placed pins.

His gaze flickered over her hair in appreciation. "I would adore your hair down, Miss Dunforth. But I suppose you must repair it." He said the last regretfully and squeezed her elbow. "Down the hall is a small sitting room, possessed of a large mirror with which you can make your adjustments."

What a thoughtful man! Alexandra made her way down the hall to the room Mr. Runyon indicated. She could hear her uncle muttering to Mr. Runyon about requiring drink before dinner. Her uncle cared nothing for the nuances of conversation, his only concern seemed to be gluttony. She shook her head and opened a door to her right.

This was no sitting room. Heavy, dark walnut furniture dominated the room. Paintings, the colors dark and muted, hung from the paneled walls. Her sense of direction, always questionable, led her to the wrong room. Curious, Alexandra stepped closer. Mr. Runyon's taste, based on what she saw in the entryway, was exquisite. She thought perhaps she ventured into his private collection.

Her eyes attempted to adjust to the dim light as she stepped up to the first painting, a large landscape framed in gilt. Upon closer inspection, she could make forms and shapes. A satyr and several nymphs lay on a field of red poppies. Naked bodies writhed together making it difficult to actually decipher what belonged to whom. Alexandra blinked. The scene before her was erotic, but also obscene. The satyr held a whip in one hand. Her gaze ran to the other paintings in the room. All were filled with even darker depictions of the sex act. She should not be here. She spun around to leave, fear pricking her spine.

"There you are, Miss Dunforth. You seem to have no sense of direction. This room was not the one I intended you to find but find it you did. Is the art to your taste?" The silken tones greeted her exit. Mr. Runyon stood directly in front of her. He stared at her bodice in an assessing manner.

Startled, Alexandra took a step back. "I fear I chose the wrong door."

Mr. Runyon hovered over her like a vulture.

Unease rippled through her. Did he intentionally send her to this room?

Fingers touched her lightly on her arm.

Alexandra jumped.

"Miss Dunforth? I see the paintings in this room have left you a bit unsettled. Your hair can wait. Let us have a sherry in the parlor." His voice had taken on a soothing quality and the shy, polite man she'd come to like returned. Tucking her hand securely in the crook of his arm he urged her forward. "Come, Miss Dunforth."

Alexandra felt a bit foolish. Mr. Runyon's art had only surprised her. There was nothing sinister about him, he was simply an art collector. Yes, the paintings were a bit obscene, but Alexandra's knowledge of the arts was rather limited. She did not wish to seem naïve.

Observing Mr. Runyon from beneath her lashes she surmised that her own guilt was giving her misgivings where there should be none. The man next to her had been nothing but kind. Polite. Courteous. Mr. Runyon did not deserve such quick, harsh judgment.

"Miss Dunforth?" Mr. Runyon watched her anxiously, his brow wrinkled with concern. "I feel I must apologize. When I lived in Italy, I studied art, in all its many forms. I fear that the Italians have much more sophisticated tastes than we English. The paintings you saw are considered questionable here in London, but in Italy you see the like in nearly every drawing room. I should not have brought them back with me but as an art lover, I could not bring myself to simply put them in storage. I sincerely hope I have not offended you. I'll have them removed before you visit again." He stated the last bit firmly with a shake of his blond head.

"Oh please. It is I who may have offended you, Mr. Runyon." Never had Alexandra felt more like a backward country girl. "I fear that my lack of exposure to the arts may have made me a bit judgmental."

A smug look crossed Mr. Runyon's face, then just as quickly disappeared.

Alexandra paused, deciding she definitely needed a sherry. "Tell me about the paintings. I assume by your comments you purchased them in Italy."

Mr. Runyon maneuvered to the parlor, leaving her to sit on a lovely green velvet chair. Odious Oliver, already seated, was working his way through a large glass of wine. He tipped the glass back, downing the red liquid in one swallow. He snorted, pig-like. "What do you know, girl, about art? Or Italy, for that matter?" Her uncle shook his empty glass at Mr. Runyon's butler.

The butler, a tall, lean man of uncertain age, shuffled slowly to her uncle's side. The butler's eyes remained flat as he served Oliver Burke. He bowed only slightly, as if it offended him to wait on her uncle.

"More wine, my lord?" The butler's tone, though polite, held a note of mockery.

Uncle Oliver's face, hardened. He turned to Mr. Runyon, a complaint on his fat lips, but just as quickly lowered his eyes. He held out his hand for the wine.

Alexandra watched the exchange with curiosity. Mr. Runyon looked at her uncle, as one does a rodent accidentally found on the doorstep. Her host caught her curious glance and quickly smoothed out his features. He gave a conspiratorial wink and leaned over to Alexandra.

"My dear," he said close to her ear, "forgive me. I do not approve of your uncle's disposition or the way he regards you or your opinions. I am so sorry for being unkind. He is your uncle after all."

I am a horrible person. Mr. Runyon protected her from her uncle, brought her lovely gifts, and treated her with every kindness. Meanwhile she used and exploited this sweet man for her own ends. Her guilt caused her to assassinate his character at every turn. "You, sir, are forgiven for your prejudice."

Mr. Runyon deserved her gratitude, not her speculation. His courtship of her gave her a reprieve from her uncle's plans. Now that her uncle assumed her betrothal to Mr. Runyon to be well under way, Odious Oliver left her in peace. He no longer threatened the servants of Helmsby Abbey with expulsion. In fact, he'd stopped mentioning the estate to her completely. Now, if she could only reach Mr. Meechum, her aunt's solicitor.

The note she sent Mr. Meechum the morning after Agnes Dobson's ball remained unanswered, as well the note she sent yesterday. She could not travel to Meechum & Sons without arousing her uncle's suspicion and he would certainly not allow her to make the trip. Her gaze fell to Mr. Runyon. She would have to ask his assistance. He was a kind, decent man. Honorable. Unlike Lord Cambourne.

Alexandra exhaled slowly, closing her eyes. She could hear the whisper of Lord Cambourne's voice as he said her name. *Alex*. Alexandra had not seen him since that day. She played their two meetings over and over. She relived the erotic kiss of his lips, the smell of cinnamon that swirled about him, and the green of his eyes.

"Miss Dunforth? I fear my conversation is dull, for it appears I am putting you to sleep."

Alexandra's eyelids flew open. For a moment, she had been back in that hallway, a warm hand running down her spine while a dragon's tail wrapped itself around her.

"No, Mr. Runyon," she sputtered, embarrassed to be caught daydreaming. Especially about Lord Cambourne. "That delicious aroma I smell put me in a trance. I must confess I am looking forward to whatever your chef is serving." She sniffed the air. The smell *was* delicious. Her stomach grumbled in hunger. Odious Oliver ate most of his meals at his club and the cook he employed at his townhouse could barely prepare anything that might be mistaken for a meal. Alexandra thought perhaps her uncle attempted to starve her into submission.

Mr. Runyon clapped his hands in delight. "You will be more than pleased, Miss Dunforth. I promise." Mr. Runyon dipped his wheat-colored head. His hair looked recently trimmed. A single lock of gold fell across his forehead, artfully curled and put in place. The dark blue jacket and lighter blue waistcoat was expensively tailored and set off his coloring to perfection. Mr. Runyon appeared to have stepped out of a painting himself. Perfect. Surreal.

Too perfect.

Unease filled her before she firmly shooed it away. So what if Mr. Runyon was a bit of a dandy? A cultured man, like Mr. Runyon, paid attention to his appearance. He did not have the unearthly male beauty, or the sense of exotic danger that clung to Lord Cambourne, but that did not detract from his masculinity. Alexandra gave Mr. Runyon's styled hair another glance and sighed. She really must quit thinking of Lord Cambourne and comparing the two men. She had Helmsby Abbey to save. The attractions of a rake were something she could ill afford.

"As you can probably tell, or smell in this case, my chef has prepared an outstanding dinner for you this evening." He held out his glass for the butler to refill. "I found Henri quite by accident, cooking in the villa of an impoverished noble-man's family in Tuscany. He was about to return to France, since the family could no longer afford to keep a chef of Henri's talent. Apparently, their daughter," Mr. Runyon frowned, "was promised to a wealthy suitor. But the girl preferred to run away with the estate's groom, much to her family's horror. The family was counting on the marriage to rescue them from dire straits."

"How sad. Did they ever see their daughter again?" Alexandra asked.

"Alas, no. The daughter was found dead of a broken neck shortly after she fled her family. The groom disappeared. The authorities assume he murdered her." Mr. Runyon shook his head sadly. "I did what I could to help the old man. In fact, several of the statues you admired were from his private collection. I purchased them from him. Paid way too much, I'm afraid." His smooth brow wrinkled in consternation. "I wish I could have helped them more. But I did manage to rescue Henri and his marvelous way with Cornish game hens." He waved a hand at the tall butler. "Hobson, please ask

Henri if dinner is ready. I cannot have Miss Dunforth wasting away!"

What a nice man! Alexandra felt the flash of guilt again. She would make it up to him. She would assist him in his search for a bride once her uncle's guardianship ended and Helmsby Abbey safely in her hands.

Hobson emerged from the shadows by the open parlor door and nodded respectfully to her host. He turned, staring at Alexandra. A smirk pulled at the corner of his mouth.

"That will be all, Hobson, until you call us for dinner." Mr. Runyon said softly, though his voice held a hint of steel.

The butler twitched. He lowered his eyes to the floor and shuffled from the room.

"Hobson is a decent-enough butler," Mr. Runyon explained, "but I keep him mostly out of pity. He's quite simple, you see." Mr. Runyon tapped his temple with a finger. "I need to constantly remind him of his manners. He is one of life's unfortunates."

"Your care of others is apparent in all you do, Mr. Runyon." Alexandra took a sip of sherry, letting the cherry taste slide down her throat. "It speaks well of you to offer such charity to others."

Uncle Oliver chuckled from his position by the fireplace.

Mr. Runyon shot him an ill-concealed look of dislike.

Uncle Oliver grinned into the fireplace. Obnoxiously merry this evening, she expected that he was simply anticipating shoveling a five-course dinner into his mouth. Alexandra envisioned him choking on the game hen. That would certainly solve her problems quickly.

Odious Oliver grunted, rubbing his stomach in anticipation.

Mr. Runyon threw a look of disgust in her uncle's direction.

She knew exactly how he felt.

"I try to be of a service to others when I can, Miss Dunforth, especially those less fortunate than myself."

Alexandra nodded and took another sip of sherry as she surveyed the room. The art, paintings, and knickknacks on display were all lovely and expensive. She and Mr. Runyon sat on finely made Chippendale furniture, easy to recognize by its exquisite lines and elegant upholstery. A book on India lay on the table before her. Dark green curtains, velvet and quite expensive, hung from the windows. A fire warmed the room, crackling merrily in the hearth. The room, as comfortable and cheerful though it was, bothered Alexandra. The fire, the way the furniture was situated, even the tassels of the curtains, gave the impression of being all *too* perfect. Staged. Nothing in the room showed the least bit of wear. The room, immaculately clean, did not feel used or lived in. It struck her that she saw nothing personal in the room. No portraits of Runyon ancestors. In fact, Mr. Runyon barely made mention of his family, only speaking in a vague way of his father and a cousin. The feeling of unease returned. Something was odd here, but she couldn't quite put her finger on it, and wasn't sure she wished to. Mr. Runyon may well be the only person who could help her.

Watching her host from beneath lowered lashes, Alexandra wondered once more why Mr. Runyon wished to marry her. It didn't really matter of course, since she had no intention of actually becoming his wife. It was a pity, since Mr. Runyon would likely make an excellent husband for any woman. He was kind, possessed a quick mind and wit, and was thoughtful and intellectual. Exactly what Alexandra, had she any desire to marry, would wish for in a husband. She glanced again at the too-perfect room.

I am being foolish.

Alexandra reached to the table before her and casually picked up the book on India she noticed earlier. Flipping open the front cover, she noted that the binding of the book was stiff, as if it had never been opened. The sherry made her bold. "Are you enjoying this book on India, Mr. Runyon? I've read several on the Far East. The area is of particular interest to me. I've heard all sorts of tales of Macao—what a wicked place it is. Have you –"

"Alexandra!" Her uncle sputtered. His moonlike face took on a horrified look.

Mr. Runyon's pale eyes held an icy chill. A light purplish flush crept up from the top of his cravat, ruining the perfection of his skin.

What had she said? Both men regarded her as if she committed murder.

"I beg your pardon, Runyon." Odious Oliver apologized. "My niece speaks before thinking. This is what comes from overeducating women. Letting them read and have opinions."

Mr. Runyon took a deep breath and pinched the bridge of his nose. His eyes fluttered closed for a moment as if composing himself before addressing Alexandra.

"Mr. Runyon?" She leaned forward in concern. She put down her sherry.

"I'm sorry, my dear." His eyes opened, and an apologetic look came over his face. "My stomach can be contrary at times and I fear that the sherry," he swished the dark liquid in his glass, "does not agree with me on an empty stomach. Shall we?" He stood and offered his arm to Alexandra. "A bite of food and some of the excellent Madeira I've chosen for dinner will no doubt put me to rights." He patted her hand and leaned closer. "And I find your opinions on everything quite to my taste."

Alexandra stood and bit back the retort she was about to fling at her uncle, but she didn't wish to upset Mr. Runyon. Soon. Soon she would reach Mr. Meechum. Mr. Runyon would assist her. Then she would be rid of Odious Oliver and return to her beloved Helmsby Abbey. She lowered her eyes, afraid her thoughts would show, as she allowed Mr. Runyon to lead her to the dining room, in as docile a manner as she could muster.

ॐ

WHAT A LOVELY DINNER! ALEXANDRA SWAYED SLIGHTLY with the movement of her uncle's carriage as they pulled away from Mr. Runyon's elegant home. The conversation over dinner ran the gamut of politics, art, and history. Alexandra delighted in showing off her knowledge of history, enjoying her uncle's discomfort. Oliver had little to contribute. Her uncle was ill suited to any type of conversation that didn't involve food or drink. She knew he detested educated women. She quoted Plato just to annoy him. Odious Oliver sat in terror all evening, fearful that her display of intelligence would put off Mr. Runyon. It had been delightful to see the fat man fidget about in his seat.

The carriage hit a bump and she flopped back against the squabs, head spinning a bit as she giggled to herself. Mr. Runyon kept her glass full of Madeira all through dinner while regaling her with tales of his travels. The name of the wine escaped her just now, something Spanish, but it tasted delicious, like ripe blackberries. Wine was never served with dinner at Helmsby Abbey. Her aunt thought it a luxury. A pity. Wine gave one such a different view of the world, a wonderful feeling of lightness, and whimsy. She decided that when she returned to Helmsby Abbey, wine with dinner would be a necessity.

An excellent host, Mr. Runyon seemed truly interested in her opinions on a variety of topics. Alexandra was surprised to find that she enjoyed his company immensely. Perhaps she *should* marry Mr. Runyon. True, he might be considered a bit bland, but bland was safe. Comfortable. He was nothing like Lord Cambourne, the dark Marquess, who made her want to throw off her clothes, and act wanton. And Mr. Runyon hadn't compared her to an ill-tempered rodent all evening. She thought that a huge point in his favor.

"You got on quite well with Runyon, Alexandra. He will make you an excellent husband. You'll be well taken care of."

Her uncle's words surprised her. First, because she was sure he cared nothing for her happiness, and second because she assumed he had fallen asleep as soon as the carriage left Mr. Runyon's elegantly furnished townhouse.

A self-satisfied smile stretched across his face. "Well?"

Apparently, the fat man wished her to converse with him. She decided to have a bit of fun. "Yes, he's quite amiable." Alexandra frowned a bit and tapped her temple with a finger, pretending to contemplate something. "Although, Uncle, he did tell me that when he agreed to the match, he did not realize exactly *how* educated I was. He claims you failed to mention I was a bit of a bluestocking." Alexandra frowned slightly. "I hope it does not put him off."

Her uncle sat up so quickly she thought his backside was on fire.

"What do you mean, girl? Put him off? You got on well at dinner." Spittle formed at the sides of her uncle's mouth.

Alexandra widened her eyes in an innocent manner, enjoying her uncle's dismay. "Oh, just that he said I was a bit more opinionated than you led him to believe. He said I didn't appear to be, now what was the word he used? Pliable. Yes. Pliable. He actually needs a more *pliable* wife, although he certainly enjoys my company. I took that to mean he thought me a bit too bookish for his taste." Kind Mr. Runyon said no such thing to her. Her uncle, so consumed with eating everything on his plate, missed most of the dinner conversation.

She could hear her uncle's labored breathing, as if he'd run down the street. The wine emboldened her. "I'm sure he meant nothing by it, Uncle. After all, Mr. Runyon does not strike *me* as the type of man to go back on his word." She smiled sweetly. This was by far the best evening she'd had since arriving in London.

⚜

OLIVER BURKE WATCHED HIS DRUNKEN NIECE TEETER UP the steps of his townhouse. If he pushed her down the steps, her neck would snap, and he could end this ridiculous charade. The fingers of his hand curled into a fist. He should have gotten rid of her instead of trying to marry her off. But that damn solicitor of Eloise's checked on the girl at regular intervals. Oliver had convinced Meechum that Alexandra wished to marry so the solicitor would advance funds for Alexandra's debut. If she suddenly disappeared, suspicion would fall on Oliver. Besides, now he needed her.

Had she put Runyon off? Oliver didn't think so. He'd tried to pay attention to their conversation this evening, but honestly, talk of history and what Parliament voted on bored him to tears.

Sweat broke out on Burke's forehead as he contemplated the exorbitant amount of money he'd lost to Runyon playing faro. Runyon held Oliver's fate in his hands. But Runyon was desperate, too. Estranged from his father, Runyon needed a bride of unimpeachable virtue to present to his elderly father. Oliver did some checking on Runyon. None of the families of the *ton* would give him their daughters, and Oliver knew why. Runyon found Alexandra, his worthless niece, attractive enough to take her in payment of the debt. She was perfect, Runyon said, for his particular needs.

Oliver watched Alexandra ascend the stairs and wave

goodnight to him. He prayed for her to trip. She looked so smug. Assured.

Little bitch.

She wouldn't be so confident once she was married to Runyon. He waddled down the hall to his study. An evening of his niece's company and his acting her concerned guardian called for a drink. Perhaps he could induce Tilda to join him. He had known Tilda for near twenty years, when she had been a gin whore near the docks. She was never too busy to spend some time with Oliver.

He walked into his study and ignored the chipped furniture and the worn Persian rug. *Eloise.* This was all her fault. What remained of the Dunforth money and even Helmsby Abbey, should be his. Eloise's only use to him had been her money. Why else would he have married some squire's daughter in Hampshire?

Oliver smoothed back the few strands of gray hair that sprang across his eyes. How he hated Eloise. Two years ago, Oliver snuck back to Helmsby Abbey to see his wife as she lay dying. He spent his monthly allowance almost as soon as he received it. He was tired of the duns beating a path to his door. Tired of begging Eloise for money. Her father, crafty old bastard, hadn't trusted Oliver completely. Eloise held the purse strings. As he stood over Eloise pale and stinking of death, Oliver decided he'd had enough. He would never have to ask her for money again. Eloise laughed at him. "Not *everything.*"

Oliver took out a handkerchief and mopped the sweat from the top of his lip, pausing to run a finger through his mustache and twist the ends into points. The action helped calm him. Oliver detested being laughed at. Before he realized it, he had a pillow over his dying wife's face. He just wanted to shut her up. He didn't mean to *actually* kill her, but he was vastly relieved she was dead. Oliver slipped out before

Alexandra and the ancient servants even noticed his presence.

The notice of his wife's death the next afternoon prompted an immediate visit to Meechum & Sons for the remainder of the Dunforth fortune. Oliver was informed that while he would certainly receive a vast sum, Helmsby Abbey and the remainder of the Dunforth money was Alexandra's upon reaching her majority. Oliver heard nothing after Meechum said *vast sum*. He directed the solicitor to send the money to Oliver's bank account. Burke cared nothing for his niece and even less for Helmsby Abbey, and thus pushed them both out of his mind. He walked out of Meechum & Sons without a second thought, already deciding how to spend the Dunforth money.

After paying his creditors, Oliver focused the remainder of his attention on spending the money he'd long waited for. He celebrated the death of Eloise by taking a mistress and gambling. Unfortunately, he was a terrible gambler. The plump whore on his lap urged him to play faro with Runyon. An unwise decision. Runyon let him win several hands and Oliver, drunk and filled with overblown confidence, bet *everything*. The whole of the Dunforth money went to Runyon on the turn of a card. Oliver was ruined. Then he remembered his niece and that pile of rubble in Hampshire. But time was running out.

Oliver waddled into his study and over to the massive oak desk. Opening the drawer, his sweating hands closed over a small blue bottle. How fortunate that Runyon, who was as rich as Croesus, needed a wife. Runyon would forgive the debt. Oliver could keep Helmsby Abbey and Alexandra's money. But Alexandra *must* marry Runyon. Now Oliver was about to lose everything because that little twit possibly offended Runyon at dinner. She was always trouble. Even as a child. Always mouthing off. He suspected she thought to outsmart him. He knew perfectly well her birthday was still two months hence. After all, his entire life depended on knowing the terms of his guardianship. Silly, stupid, little girl. Her marriage to Runyon would take place well before her birthday.

Alexandra would awake tomorrow with a headache from the enormous amount of wine she drank tonight. Oliver, as a concerned uncle, would send for a doctor who would prescribe medicine. The doctor would explain to her that her headache was the result of nerves from the move to London and her still unresolved grief over Eloise. He would prescribe medicine for Alexandra.

Alexandra *would* be biddable. She *would* marry Runyon. Oliver would keep the rest of the Dunforth money and sell Helmsby Abbey. His only regret was that Eloise was no longer alive to witness it.

8

"Miss Dunforth?" James opened the parlor door. "Mr. Runyon is here to see you."

Alexandra put down the last of her tea and smoothed down the sprigged green muslin of her gown. The special tea the doctor prescribed gave her a lazy feeling, but the headache abated. The headaches started soon after her dinner with Mr. Runyon, but the tea managed to keep the worst of the pain at bay. The doctor her uncle summoned, a stern, older man who spoke with an upper crust accent, told her she had anxiety due to exhaustion. The sudden excitement of London, after spending so many years in the country as well as the lingering grief over her aunt's death had overtaxed her mind.

Alexandra normally scoffed at such diagnoses of women's ills. She rarely even contracted a cold. But the tea did make the headache go away. And when the headache returned, the tea helped again. The tea *did* tend to make her forgetful. She nearly forgot about Mr. Runyon taking her to Thrumbadge's today.

Mr. Runyon's visits become a daily ritual after dinner at

his home. She looked forward to seeing him. Today, he was taking her to Thrumbadge's, London's premier lending library and bookseller. Her uncle's library left much to be desired. It was full of ancient tomes dedicated to medieval armor. She thought the books likely left by the previous owner, since the only thing she ever saw her uncle read were reports of horse races. The thought of coming back to her uncle's dismal townhouse with a carriage full of books filled her with delight. And anything purchased today she could take with her to Helmsby Abbey upon her return. She couldn't wait to leave London, though she would miss Miranda Reynolds and the Dowager, with whom she had twice had tea, and even attended a musicale. She considered herself lucky that Lord Cambourne and she did not cross paths again, although she did spy him from across the room at the musicale.

Lord Cambourne escorted a beautiful tall brunette that evening, who clung to his arm as if their skins were fused together. Thankfully, he didn't see her, or at the very least he ignored her presence. The brief flirtation they shared was apparently over. She told herself how grateful she was he no longer toyed with her.

Alexandra stood and greeted Mr. Runyon with a bit of nervousness. Today she must ask him to do something of the utmost importance for her. She took a chance, she knew. Mr. Runyon might easily go directly to her uncle, but no other alternative existed. Alexandra had sent several messages to Mr. Meechum but received no reply. At least now she knew why.

Yesterday, she wandered by her uncle's study, curious at the sheaf of paper on his desk. The writing paper closely resembled her own stationery. Knowing that her uncle had left hours ago for his club, and Tilda was occupied in the kitchen brewing Alexandra's tea, she decided to investigate.

Alexandra leafed through the papers on her uncle's desk

finding every one of the notes she'd written to Mr. Meechum. Her uncle had intercepted them all. The last note, given to the stable boy, sat on top of the stack. Nervously she felt for the note placed in her reticule this morning. Mr. Runyon might be her only hope. The crackle of paper assured her that the note still lay safely inside.

"Miss Dunforth. Are you ready for our excursion?"

Alexandra swung her thoughts from the treachery of her uncle to the appearance of her friend. Mr. Runyon, impeccably dressed as usual, wore a dark blue coat with dark brown breeches. He jauntily swung his walking stick as he strode towards her.

Mr. Runyon smiled down at her. "I've sent for Tilda to await us in my carriage." He frowned. "I am sorry, my dear, that we need to bring Tilda, but I did promise your uncle to observe every propriety."

"I am excited beyond words to be able to go to Thurmbadge's. You cannot imagine how appreciative I am. My uncle's library is ...a bit lacking."

"Your uncle does not strike me as an avid reader, just an avid eater." He laughed, then covered his mouth with a gloved hand as if he had spoken out of turn. "My apologies."

Alexandra laughed merrily. "No apologies necessary, Mr. Runyon. You and I are of a like mind and I am grateful for it." She stood and reached into her reticule. "There is something I need to discuss with you." She hesitated, unsure if she should proceed.

He watched her politely, the blond brows raised in question.

Alexandra stood abruptly and shut the parlor door. She knew now that Odious Oliver kept her from Mr. Meechum, but her uncle didn't know she knew. He likely had the servants spying on her. She kept her voice low.

"Mr. Runyon. I am so sorry to impose upon you, but I

have nowhere else to turn." She took out the note and handed it to him, pausing to clasp his hand in hers. "I hope that you will not mind assisting me."

Mr. Runyon turned the note over. He frowned when he saw the name written in Alexandra's neat script across the front. His pale blue eyes narrowed.

"It's not what you think!" Alexandra said urgently. "Please let me explain."

Mr. Runyon looked displeased. Very displeased. Then the look vanished, replaced by one of polite confusion.

Alexandra swallowed, relieved that he would listen to her. "Mr. Meechum is my aunt's solicitor." Alexandra wasn't certain how much she should tell Mr. Runyon. After all, he would likely not want to help her if it meant their betrothal would be annulled. She decided to be discreet. "This is about Helmsby Abbey. The estate is to go to me on my marriage," she lied, "but I think my uncle means to sell it sooner and keep the profits himself."

"You mentioned that you grew up there."

"He is threatening to throw out my servants, many of whom are elderly. These people are my family, the only family I have left. My aunt, on her deathbed, made me promise never to sell Helmsby Abbey and to always look after the loyal retainers who are part of the Dunforth family. I cannot allow him to sell my home."

"Are you suggesting that Lord Burke doesn't truly own this Helmsby Abbey? That he is attempting fraud? To repay your servants' loyalty to your family with homelessness?" The cultured voice sounded shocked.

Alexandra sighed in relief that he seemed to be on her side. "I do not think my family solicitor is aware of the situation. I must consult him so that he may delay the sale. My uncle cannot sell it."

"Please do not distress yourself." The blonde head nodded

to her. "Miss Dunforth, words cannot express how deeply I am honored that you entrust such a task to me. After our excursion today, I will personally deliver your note to Mr. Meechum and wait on his reply. If it is positive," he took her hand gently, "I will escort you there immediately. However, if it is not, will you promise to accept Mr. Meechum's response and look towards your future? Perhaps with me?" He reddened slightly, seemingly embarrassed by the expression of his emotions.

Alexandra looked at the kind man before her. She should tell him everything and rely on his discretion. His honor. But his honor might just as likely force him to tell her uncle of the plans Alexandra was making. She detested lying to Mr. Runyon, but once Helmsby Abbey was firmly in her hands, she would explain everything and pray he understood.

She nodded her assent. "Yes. Thank you so much for helping me."

He patted her hand. "Then let us be off!"

Mr. Runyon escorted her to his smart black carriage and took the seat across from her. Tilda, ever vigilant, sat on Alexandra's left. Mr. Runyon kept the conversation light until the carriage halted in front of an enormous gray stone building with large glass windows facing the street. A large sign hung above the entrance from a burnished copper pole. "Thrumbadge's," then underneath, "Booksellers and Lending Library."

Alexandra jumped up as soon as the carriage doors opened. Excitement ran through her at the thought of all those luscious books waiting for her discovery.

Mr. Runyon gave her an indulgent smile, taking her hand to assist her from the carriage. He squeezed her fingers.

Tilda heaved her herself up from the squabs, grunting in displeasure. A visit to the booksellers did not sit as well with the maid as it did with Alexandra. The scowl on her features gave credence to her lack of interest.

"Thank you, Tilda. Your presence is not required in Thrumbadge's. Miss Dunforth shall be very safe with me."

Tilda nodded mutely, sitting back down in relief.

Mr. Runyon gave Alexandra a wink and extended his arm.

She squeaked in delight as they entered the booksellers. Alexandra simply couldn't help it. The size and breadth of the establishment left her in awe. Through the windows facing the street, Alexandra could clearly see the hundreds of volumes stacked neatly within. It looked as if the shelves stretched on forever.

"Thank you for bringing me, Mr. Runyon." She dropped his arm and ran to the entrance, urging him with a wave of one gloved hand to hurry.

He laughed at her urgency to enter. "Miss Dunforth, your pleasure is all the thanks I need. You look like a child at Christmas!"

Alexandra giggled, waiting impatiently for him to catch up. He caught her hand, tucked it securely in the crook of his arm and nodded to the doorman. Blue eyes twinkling at her, he opened the door with a flourish and waved her inside. "Welcome to Thrumbadge's, Miss Dunforth."

"Oh my." It was all she could say. Alexandra valued knowledge above all else, and books represented knowledge. She looked at the hundreds of leather-bound tomes, the stacks of periodicals, and the small army of male clerks who bustled amongst the customers and sighed in exquisite delight. Thrumbadge's fit very neatly into what Alexandra's version of what heaven must be like.

"May I?" She looked at Mr. Runyon eagerly. She trod over to a large brass plate affixed to the end of one aisle. The plate read, "History and Geography."

"Of course! I shall seat myself just there. I haven't yet read the *Times* today." He pointed to an area with several large wing-backed chairs. "Peruse to your heart's content." He bowed slightly.

Alexandra didn't know where to begin. Choices abounded. She decided to explore, starting with the aisle before her. Perhaps a book on the Far East. Or Macao. She had a driving curiosity about Macao.

❧❧❧

LORD CAMBOURNE LISTENED TO HIS SISTER, MIRANDA, chatter non-stop, as they walked through Thrumbadge's. His days had been filled with inquiries into the latest attacks on him, poring over dozens of account books for his various estates and weeding through the stack of bills his stepmother sent round to him on a daily basis. The amount of money she planned to spend on her birthday celebration at Gray Covington was costing a bloody fortune. He ran a hand through his hair. The irony of paying for Jeanette's birthday ball when she'd attempted to have him killed was not lost on Sutton. He needed to be sure that she was the culprit before he took action. Very sure.

Sutton eyed the rows of books. Books calmed him. He wondered if Miss Dunforth, who he imagined shared his love of the written word, shopped at Thrumbadge's. He should ask her, if he saw her again. He knew Miss Dunforth to be fast friends with Miranda. The two women attended a musicale together, and he'd spied Miss Dunforth rapidly retreating into a hallway to avoid speaking to him.

The Badger, or rather his attraction to her, gave Sutton a muddled feeling, as if he had drunk too much brandy. Until his desire for her was under control, or until the Badger cast aside caution and allowed herself to be in his presence, he thought it best to keep his distance. He entertained himself with some of the most beautiful women in London, namely Countess Rutherford, but even that woman could not push aside the image of Miss Dunforth.

Alex.

The Dowager dropped Miss Dunforth's name repeatedly within Sutton's hearing, waiting for him to ask after her. Cagey old bird, Donata. He needed to be careful around his grandmother.

Sutton walked down a long row of books on geography and wondered why one small, bookish Badger held him in thrall. He barely knew her. Her prickly manner and her sharp tongue would flay a man alive.

"Sutton, I am going just over there." Miranda pointed to the other side of Thrumbadge's where he suspected the Lord Thurston novels were shelved. "Look, there are some dreadfully dull books on botany, filled with ruminations on the structure of various fern plants in the Indies. I'm sure you'll be enthralled for hours," Miranda said saucily before sauntering down the aisle. Impishly she looked over her shoulder. "Perhaps we should get mother a book for her birthday." Miranda opened her eyes innocently and burst into giggles. It was doubtful Jeanette Reynolds ever read a book in her life, except for possibly Debrett's Peerage.

Sutton pretended sternness. "Begone, you minx." How Miranda sprang from Jeanette Reynolds mystified Sutton. Miranda and his younger sister, Elizabeth, bore little resemblance to their mother, for which Sutton gave eternal thanks. "No plants today. Instead I will be here amongst the Pharaohs," he called after her. "I have a desire to read about mummies."

Miranda turned, and a shadow crossed her beautiful face. "Mummies? I used to adore mummies."

"I have you to thank for starting my obsession with that book you gave me on embalming practices." He said to her departing back. He couldn't fathom that his sister was ever interested in Egypt but the scores of books in the library told him different. He thought Lord Thurston was really more her taste.

The sound of humming came from the next aisle. Heels clicked across the wood floor, so the hummer must be female. An elderly spinster. Few attractive women were interested in the contents of the aisles on either side: Plato and travel essays.

Curiosity got the better of him. He peered through a stack and was rewarded by the view of a green bonnet perched upon a mass of chestnut curls. The heavy mass of hair, already escaping the bonnet, sat atop an ivory column of neck and was situated on a delectable female form with an overabundance of bosom.

Miss Alexandra Dunforth.

As if in thinking of the Badger he'd conjured her up from thin air. His appreciation grew for her ability to appear in the most unexpected places. The tiny, bonneted head disappeared as she rounded the aisle.

The click of her heels sounded from behind him. The heels stopped. A gasp sounded in the aisle.

Sutton turned and caught Miss Dunforth trying desperately to flee before being seen. The tiny form skittered down another row and around a giant stack of periodicals from the Historical Society and out of his view.

Sutton stopped moving. When he'd lived in Macao, he went on a tiger hunt with a group of Portuguese dignitaries. The men, all hunters confident in their abilities, stomped through the jungle in an attempt to flush out the beast. But not Sutton. He'd climbed the highest tree within reach. While the rest of the hunting party continued to track the beast through the jungle, Sutton waited on a branch, feet dangling and gun ready. The tiger eventually appeared behind the hunting party. Sutton bagged it. He was a patient man. Besides, Badgers weren't nearly as subtle as tigers.

He heard a tiny sniff, like the sound of a mouse choking on a piece of cheese. Whirling to his left, he looked through the stack of periodicals. Wide gray eyes, the color of a stormy sky popped up, then vanished, as Alexandra attempted to escape in another direction.

He caught a flash of her green gown as she hurried down the aisle. Sutton turned abruptly and calmly walked the way he had come. He simply stood still and let her run into him.

"Oomph!" It sounded most unladylike.

Her head hit him squarely in the chest. An unexpected shock of desire ran through him as her small form made contact with his larger one. Every nerve in his body came to life in an instant. Blood rushed to his groin and he stifled a groan. The books she carried dropped with several loud thuds across his black Hessian boots. He heard her tortured sigh of disbelief and frustration that she hadn't eluded him.

The tiny figure straightened like a spike as she geared for a confrontation with him. Several curls escaped the bonnet. A small foot stamped in dismay.

God, how he wanted the tiny tempest before him.

He took in her small, gloved hands. The way her nose crinkled in anger. The stormy gray eyes, and the heaving, generous bosom. The tops of her breasts pushed her bodice back and forth, straining the fabric as she struggled to maintain her composure.

Sutton tamped down the sudden urge to push her against the stacks and lift her skirts, wrap her legs around him and thrust into her. He felt like an untried lad of fifteen instead of the jaded roué he was.

"You." Her face flushed. "You nearly scared me out of my wits."

"Doubtful, Miss Dunforth. I sense you don't scare easily. Besides, *you* ran into me."

Her cheeks puffed out. Clearly, she was not pleased to see him. Unlike most women, she did not care to be attracted to him or have him desire her. The Badger was most difficult.

She put her hands on her hips, glaring as if she could scare him away. It was all Sutton could do not to burst into laughter. She resembled an angry chickadee. Wrenching heat ran down his body making him stiff with arousal. He wanted her. Badly.

"What are you doing here? Stalking innocent women?" Her voice shook slightly.

Ah, Sutton thought. Not angry. *Nervous.*

"How can I stalk something I cannot even see? Perhaps little Badger, you should wear a bell like a cat to announce your presence. Good Lord, I nearly stepped on you!" He teased her, hoping to annoy her into erupting. He much preferred her anger. He didn't want Miss Dunforth, *Alex,* to be skittish around him.

Miss Dunforth's mouth opened as if she would scream. He could see she wanted to. She truly took offense at being compared to a badger. He must call her that at every opportunity.

Instead of screaming, she took a deep breath. Her voice sounded calm and polite though he could see she struggled for composure.

"If you will excuse me, I will get my books and go least you feel the need to tell me I remind you of a speckled toad or a diseased rat. My apologies Lord Cambourne, for my clumsiness." She bent at his feet, eager to pick up the scattered tomes.

Sutton knelt down to assist her, noting with pleasure the angry snort of surprise that erupted from her. His hand fell on a particularly large book about the Far East. Next to that tome lay a memoir of a sea captain who had traded spices in Java. Not exactly required reading for a young woman. Nothing on fashion or etiquette. He held out one of the books to her and raised an eyebrow in question.

Angrily, she grabbed the book from him, shooting him a look of annoyance. She pulled back so fiercely on *Tales of a Seadog*, she lost her balance and fell back on her bottom. Green muslin puffed around her as she slid back on her elbows. Her legs fell open to reveal a glimpse of slim thighs encased in sheer stockings.

Sutton took a deep breath. Her skin would be creamy and feel like satin underneath the stockings. He wanted nothing more than to run his hand down her calves and thighs and take one lacy garter between his teeth. The rock-hard arousal in his breeches was becoming uncomfortable. *Painful*. He reached for her hand to offer assistance.

She ignored it.

Miss Dunforth sat up and attempted to smooth her skirts. "Oh, just go away." She sounded miserable as if being near him caused her undue pain. His Badger was rapidly losing her bravado.

"Alex. Let me help you."

"No. And don't call me that." She pulled back from him.

"Why ever not?" He moved towards her.

"It doesn't matter why. Go away." She made a futile effort to push against him. Her cheeks pinked, and her eyes lowered. Grabbing one of the larger books she held it against her chest as if it were a shield.

"Are you interested in the Orient, Miss Dunforth? Or travel to faraway places?" He gestured to the large book she clasped to her chest. "I read many such tales in my youth and decided not to trust the opinions of those who wrote the books. I wanted to travel myself. I lived in Macao until a few years ago. It's a fascinating place."

"So I am given to understand. The *ton* speaks of nothing else," she said tartly. The Badger watched him from underneath her lashes and cocked her head.

Sutton winced. She *had* heard the gossip surrounding him. "I'm not sure anyone in the *ton* knows where Macao is," he said under his breath, ashamed for just a moment of his reputation in front of this blazing, fierce girl.

Alex let out a small laugh, catching him off guard. "I've *heard* that Macao is full of unsavory characters. Heathen Chinese. Pirates. Have you ever met a pirate, Lord Cambourne? Or been one?" Boldly, she looked up meeting his eyes.

Sutton didn't speak for a moment, enthralled with the way her mouth moved as she said "unsavory." All he could think of was touching his tongue to her lips again as he had in the library. "Macao is indeed full of unsavory people. I should know. I was one of them."

Alex gave him a forthright look. "Your sister claims you kept a monkey who smoked opium. What was it like? The jungles? Do you speak Portuguese? I've read about the Chinese and their customs. It all sounds so interesting and I think I should like to go there someday." She looked at him, waiting for him to dissuade her or tell her she shouldn't wish such things. The lovely gray opals shimmered with curiosity. A chestnut curl sprung out across her forehead.

What would she do if he touched her?

Sutton was at a loss. The seduction of women came easily to him. He adored the female of the species but didn't necessarily respect them, outside of his grandmother and sisters. And while he certainly enjoyed the company of the fairer sex, especially in bed, he didn't actually have intelligent conversations with them. Nor did he give much thought to *liking* a woman. Until Miss Dunforth.

Alex.

A spurt of warmth hit Sutton right in the middle of his chest. The feeling so intense, he restrained himself from rubbing his breastbone. The Badger *knew* Portuguese was spoken in Macao. She actually *knew* where Macao was. Miss Dunforth, while she didn't know it, was the most exotic, seductive creature Sutton had ever met.

"I do speak Portuguese and Chinese. Jonas was my monkey and he smoked opium like a fiend. I could not bring him to England with me. When one is being shanghaied, one does not have time to pack."

"Shanghaied?"

"Kidnapped."

"Oh, yes. It took ten men, *ten men*, to bring you back."

Sutton laughed. She imitated the tone of Lady Agnes Dobson to perfection.

"Why? Why did your grandmother have to kidnap you? Didn't you wish to come back and be a Marquess?" Her honest question gave Sutton a thoughtful pause. He didn't know how to answer it. The title and the money, even his looks, he considered of little import to who he really was. He'd lived by his wits in Macao. Penniless upon his arrival, he'd built a successful trading post. He'd explored vast areas of jungle and studied the flora of the peninsula. He traded with the Chinese, smoked opium, and generally did as he chose. A Marquess had no such luxury.

"There is more to life than a title, Alex." He didn't shirk from her gaze. It was heresy for someone of his standing to say such a thing, but he didn't care. Something told him Alexandra didn't either.

Her gray stare shifted and ran along his torso. He could see her mind working. She imagined the tattoo. Every woman in London knew about his tattoo so it was no surprise Miss Dunforth, *Alex*, did. Women found the tattoo erotic. It added to the allure of bedding Satan Reynolds.

The Badger shot him a curious, appraising look.

"It is indeed a green dragon. The eyes are red."

Alex shook her head, mortified that he'd guessed her thoughts. "I didn't mean——"

His hand stayed her. "It's all right. I don't mind telling you. The dragon covers the whole of my back and the tails wraps around the lower part of my waist." He waited for her to blush and run from him, as most young ladies of proper breeding would do if body parts were discussed. But Alex never looked away.

"Why did you have it drawn on you?"

"I don't have it by choice. The tattoo was painted on me as a type of punishment, to mark me. I was put in charge of some property for a friend, a Chinese warlord, while he saw to his business elsewhere. He did not appreciate the way I handled his property and decided I needed to be punished for my indiscretions. One of his concubines told him that the English called me Satan Reynolds. The warlord thought it a great joke that my own people likened me to the devil. He decided to mark me so that all who saw it would know I was cursed." Sutton had, in fact, nearly seduced the man's young, fourth wife. If he had succeeded, he no doubt would be dead now. The punishment was for the girl to tattoo Sutton with the face of the devil, but she had no idea what the devil looked like. She chose a dragon instead.

"Did it hurt?"

He nodded. "Like the bloody dickens. I stayed drunk for nearly a week, the pain was so bad."

Her hand lifted, as if she would touch him but she quickly put it down. She smiled shyly. "Did the warlord's 'property' object to your punishment?" She met his gaze and looked into his soul without judgment, only concern and tempered amusement. He felt the pull towards her. Stronger. Insistent.

"No." Slowly he reached a hand towards her waiting to see

if she would run like a frightened animal. "She was the one who drew it on me." His hand cupped the side of her face.

Her eyes widened in surprise at his touch, then fluttered closed. She gave a small sigh of satisfaction and tilted her head into his hand. Sheer need punched Sutton in the gut. Primal. Fierce.

Sutton reached swiftly with both hands and grabbed her shoulders. He stood up, drawing her small form against him.

Alexandra's eyes popped open. Her mouth rounded in an "o" of surprise.

A shock of heat coursed between them as their bodies melded together. His hand ran down her spine, clutching her around the waist. One hand held her tightly as the other roamed down her tiny form to grab underneath her bottom, cupping her buttocks. Deliberately, he pushed her against the hardness nearly bursting through his breeches.

She struggled half-heartedly. The action rubbed her breasts against him in an agonizing rhythm. A gloved hand swatted ineffectually against his chest. The hand stayed against his shoulder, the fingers caressing him, seemingly of their own accord.

"Put me down, Lord Cambourne." It was the same tone she used with him in Lord Dobson's library. Two spots of color stood out on Alexandra's cheeks. Her body softened against him. She stopped struggling.

"You are depraved to think I wish to be accosted by the biggest rake in London, in a *bookshop* of all places, next to a shelf of ...of..." She peered over his shoulder and squinted. "*Etiquette for Young Ladies!*" I know what you are about. I have no desire to become yet another conquest of the great Satan Reynolds. As a plain girl, far beneath you socially, you might imagine I would welcome your amorous attentions, but I assure you I do not."

Plain? Alexandra thought she was plain? Sutton thought

she sparkled like a tiny snowflake that had by mere chance, landed on his tongue. Unique and beautiful. He pushed her harder against him, which earned his shoulder another ineffectual swat of her hand.

Alex's chin lifted in a determined manner. She thought this a game to him. Sutton couldn't blame her. He had a rather black reputation, especially with women. Their mutual attraction to each other confused her. He saw the fear of rejection in her eyes even as he moved her against the fiercest arousal he'd ever had in his life.

"Shut up, Alex." He wound his arms around her, kissing her deeply and possessively. He nudged her mouth open, touching her tongue to his. Gently he sucked her tongue into his mouth. Her body shivered in his embrace. He kissed her harder, all the need he felt for her spilling into the kiss.

Alexandra wiggled her hips, which happened to be pushed against Sutton's breeches. He pushed her against the hardness in his breeches and she wiggled back. He lifted his lips from hers.

"You misunderstand, little Badger." His breathing ragged as he struggled to control himself. "I cannot believe that a woman with your intelligence fails to notice all the signs of a man who desires her." He kissed her hard. "And I find you most beautiful." He wrapped his arms completely around her. She fit against him perfectly. "*Most* beautiful."

He heard her gasp at his words. His mouth brushed lightly against her neck, nipping at the tender flesh. His lips traced a trail back to the corner of her mouth and she let out a small moan as he ran his tongue over her bottom lip. Virgin she might be, but Alexandra's body held a wealth of sensuality. Sutton could think of nothing but encouraging that sensuality. He imagined the things he would teach her. Of whole days spent in bed. He wanted to pleasure her endlessly. She tentatively opened her mouth, and her tongue darted out shyly, seeking his.

Sutton groaned and pulled her closer. A book fell from the shelf and the title glared up at him. Dear *God*, he *was* seducing her against a stack of etiquette books.

His fingers massaged her buttocks, caressing them through her gown, feeling for the crevice that split them apart. He grunted and pushed her slight form against his arousal more firmly. He had been hard since he'd spied her through the book stacks. If he reached under her skirts to the slit in her drawers, he knew she would be wet and ready for him.

Alex pulled her face away from his. Her eyes were heavy-lidded, erotic. One small hand reached up to caress his cheek, then moved to his ear to touch the piece of jade. She brushed her lips against his. Her fingers tickled his scalp.

Sutton shuddered. A thought came to him, something he had never offered to any woman. "Alex. I would not misuse you. I will buy you a lovely apartment anywhere you wish. We can travel, even to Macao if you like. I shall buy you more books than you could read in a lifetime. I——"

She stiffened in his arms like a board. Her face full of shocked hurt, she gave him a look of distaste. "How dare you." The words were rough with emotion. Her mouth was set in a grim line.

"Sutton? Where are you?" Miranda's voice floated from one aisle over.

"Put me down!" Alexandra hissed. She pushed at him, twisting from his embrace. Her face turned from his, but not before he noticed the sheen of tears in her eyes.

He put her down reluctant to end their contact. Alexandra stood and straightened her skirt, her hands jerking quickly over her wrinkled gown. Hostility emanated from her. And hurt. The Badger apparently did not find his asking her to be his mistress quite the boon that Sutton thought it to be. His wanting of her consumed him, and the words had popped out of his mouth, unbidden. Sutton spent years in control of his emotions, particularly around women. But not this *one* woman. The thought confused and unnerved him.

Alex's small form trembled. She struggled to the floor, kneeling to pick up her books. She refused to look at him. He could hear her gulping in air. The thought that he'd injured her enough to make her nearly sob out loud gave him a physical ache.

"Alex," he said contritely, "I'm sorry I—" He reached for her. If she would just let him explain. Let him hold her.

She shied from him like a dog afraid to be kicked.

"I don't need your help, Lord Cambourne. You might dirty your fancy breeches."

He flinched from the sarcasm in her tone.

Miranda rounded the corner. "Oh, there you are! I'm in shock! You won't believe who is here, calmly reading the newspaper as if—" She stopped, spying Alexandra on the floor.

"Miss Dunforth? Alexandra? Whatever are you doing here? What happened? Let me help you." Miranda shot a pointed look at him as she went to Alex.

Sutton watched Alex while she picked up her books. Her shaky shoulders and stilted movements told him how his words had hurt her. Alexandra was a decent woman who deserved marriage. *Expected* marriage. No matter her nonchalant attitude towards the institution. He wished fervently he could take back his words.

9

Alexandra thought she would burst into tears right in the middle of Thrumbadge's. She rarely cried. Lord Cambourne, that conceited titled ass, had made her chest ache and tears well in her eyes. He didn't deserve to see her cry. Rake. Despoiler of women. Dear God, she'd practically allowed him to ruin her. How could she have allowed him such liberties? His mistress. Did he know how incredibly insulting that was?

I deserve some respect. I realize I am only a spinster from Hampshire, with no great connections to recommend me, but does he really think so little of me?

That's what hurt the most. He'd almost convinced her that he desired her. Liked her, even. Aunt Eloise had warned her about men like Lord Cambourne.

"Miss Dunforth? It's time we left."

Oh no.

Alexandra, still trying to stack her books, heard Mr. Runyon approach. His footsteps stopped abruptly. He cleared his throat.

She looked up in time to see Mr. Runyon pale as his

features hardened into a mask of cold dislike. The cordial gentleman who escorted her to Thrumbadge's earlier disappeared. A vein in his temple pulsed, bulging a dark blue. His lips curled into a murderous sneer.

"Hello, Archie. What a surprise to see *you* here. In London. I thought you had exiled yourself to the Continent," Lord Cambourne drawled in a voice thick with distaste.

A chill ran down Alexandra's arms. Lord Cambourne sounded so foreign.

Mr. Runyon's fingers grasped her upper arm.

"I missed being in the bosom of my family, Cam." Mr. Runyon looked down at Alexandra. "I wondered where you had gotten off to, my *dear*." He emphasized the last word, making it sound intimate.

"I see you know the delightful Miss Dunforth."

Lord Cambourne raised a dark brow at her. "How interesting." His body tensed like a deadly jungle cat about to pounce on its prey.

Miranda's mouth hung open. Her gaze never left Mr. Runyon. She clutched her brother's forearm tightly.

"Yes, Miss Dunforth and I are birds of a *feather*." Mr. Runyon smiled at Lord Cambourne, a smile that did not reach his eyes.

Two pairs of emerald-green eyes flicked over Alexandra. Miranda's held surprise, Lord Cambourne's, a look of disgust.

Mr. Runyon implied something with his words. She supposed he meant she shared a love of books.

Lord Cambourne's mouth formed into a grim line. A muscle ticked in his cheek. The air around the two men was thick and black with tension, the heaviness suffocating Alexandra. A dull ache started at the back of her head. She wanted her tea. Urgently.

"I dropped my books." She swallowed, desperate to diffuse the hostility emanating from both men. "And-"

"I found Miss Dunforth lying in a heap!" Miranda lied smoothly. "Thank goodness I saw you, Miss Dunforth. You could have injured yourself." She walked confidently to Alexandra and knelt to assist her.

Alexandra noticed Miranda gave Mr. Runyon a wide berth, walking as far from him as she could, not even allowing the silk of her skirts near him.

"Mother didn't tell us you were in town." Miranda spoke to Mr. Runyon in a frigidly polite tone Alexandra didn't recognize. "Forgive our surprise."

"Yes, Archie." Lord Cambourne snapped. "Perhaps you'll come for tea. My grandmother will no doubt be *delighted* to see you." He smiled grimly at Mr. Runyon. "Alas, you'll miss Elizabeth. She's away at boarding school." His tone was ominous and deadly.

Alexandra sensed something hidden behind his words.

Mr. Runyon jerked immediately, almost pulling Alexandra over as she attempted to stand. She gave him a questioning look. *He is afraid of Lord Cambourne.*

"Miranda, we need to return home and leave Miss Dunforth and Archie to their...pursuits." Lord Cambourne looked directly at Mr. Runyon.

Miranda stood, backing smoothly away from Alexandra. "I shall see you soon, Miss Dunforth."

"Possibly you will see her." Mr. Runyon snarled. "Miss Dunforth and I are quite busy. She is newly arrived in London and I am showing her the sights. What free time I have is devoted to my business pursuits. I am stretched to make time for my dear cousin's birthday celebration." Mr. Runyon's pale slim hand gripped the wolf's head atop his walking stick so tightly Alexandra imagined the ruby-red eyes of the beast bulging and popping out.

Lord Cambourne smiled wryly. "Pity. I should *so* adore discussing old times with you. My father, before he passed away, regaled me with tales of your adventures in London while I was in Macao."

Mr. Runyon blanched, becoming even paler as Lord Cambourne spoke. Alexandra could see a fine mist of sweat collecting just above his perfectly groomed mustache. She could smell his fear.

"Miranda?" Lord Cambourne gently steered his sister away from Alexandra and Mr. Runyon. His face held a contemptuous look. "I shall look forward to seeing you at Jeanette's party." The dark head nodded to her. "Miss Dunforth. You should be careful where you step in the future." He turned and strode away. Miranda hurried next to him, struggling to keep up with his long strides.

Mr. Runyon watched them depart. He sighed deeply, his body visibly relaxing as Lord Cambourne departed. He turned to regard Alexandra, and a sad smile came over his features. "Come along, my dear." Mr. Runyon took the books from her, tucking them under his arm, and steered her to a waiting clerk.

The scene Alexandra just witnessed replayed in her mind. Mr. Runyon and Lord Cambourne obviously knew each other. Hated each other. She wondered what had occurred between the two men to create such animosity. She thought of the look Lord Cambourne gave her before he walked away. His green eyes had been filled with utter contempt. His attitude angered her. His treatment of her was unwarranted no matter his issue with Mr. Runyon. And how exactly did the two men know and despise each other? "Mr. Runyon? What is the nature of your association with Lord Cambourne, if I may ask?"

Mr. Runyon hiccupped. He cleared his throat as his shoulders sagged in defeated despair.

Alexandra touched his sleeve. She didn't wish to upset

him further, but she needed to know. "Forgive me for asking, but—"

He stopped walking. He reached into his pocket and pulled out a handkerchief, blotting his eyes. "I am sorry, Miss Dunforth. I am so sorry for that dreadful scene you witnessed and my ungentlemanly behavior. Pray forgive my loss of composure."

"It's none of my affair." She gave his arm a squeeze. The poor man looked wrung out like a damp napkin. "Let's just go back to my uncle's. A cup of tea will restore your composure." She waited as Mr. Runyon paid the clerk for the books. The clerk took his time wrapping their purchase and Alexandra took a moment to scan the bookstore for any sign of Lord Cambourne and Miranda. Why did she feel the need to clarify her association with Mr. Runyon to Lord Cambourne? Her mind whispered back. *Because you care what Lord Cambourne thinks of you.*

"Shall we?" Mr. Runyon thanked the clerk and moved Alexandra towards the entrance.

"You have a right to know." Mr. Runyon stopped just outside the door.

Alexandra looked up at him. He looked sincere and very, very sad.

"Cam, or Lord Cambourne as you know him," he said, "is the stepson of my beloved cousin, Jeanette."

Alexandra swallowed hard. The Marchioness, that horrid woman who interrupted her tea with the Dowager at Cambourne House, was Mr. Runyon's cousin? The resemblance, once she looked for it, was strikingly clear. Mr. Runyon and the Marchioness shared the same pale blue eyes and identical heads of wheat-colored hair.

"So, Cam and I are cousins of a sort," Mr. Runyon continued. "I have not seen Lord Cambourne for many years, not since before he left for Macao. I fear that Cam and his family do not think too highly of me. I had a misunderstanding with Robert, that's Lord Cambourne's father." Mr. Runyon's eyes began to fill with tears again. "Robert was a horrible man." He winced. "I'm so sorry to speak ill of the dead, Miss Dunforth, but he always blamed others for his own failings. At any rate, I had only returned to my father's good graces when Robert felt the need to give my father details of what he considered my character flaws. Very embarrassing. Humiliating. Robert harbored an insane jealousy of my relationship with Jeanette." He shrugged. "He loved my cousin madly. I fear it unhinged him. He treated her terribly. Cam treated her even worse. She tried to be a real mother to him. He threw all of her efforts back in her face. She cried on my shoulder many an afternoon. She so wanted to be a true mother to Cam.

Alexandra thought of the cold, hard woman she met at Cambourne House. Mr. Runyon seemed to be speaking of someone else entirely.

He patted her hand and gave another sad smile. "I do not wish to say much, for I am trying to put the past behind me. I tried to protect Cam, you know. We are only a few years apart in age, but worlds apart in every other way. While I studied, he seduced women and fought duels bringing dishonor to his family. Cam is a devil with women. His looks, you know." He shot Alexandra a speculative look. "You can imagine the pain his escapades brought my cousin. She caught him in an indelicate situation." Mr. Runyon looked away. "I tried to help him. He fled to Macao soon after. Robert blamed me for that, I'm afraid. He waited for years to make me pay. The next time he and I butted heads it was quite a row. I decided to tour the Continent soon after."

Alexandra's stomach twisted in knots. Mr. Runyon's assessment of Lord Cambourne's character did not ring false. Unfortunately, all the pieces fit. If Lord Cambourne truly wished her company, he would seek her out. Instead, he attempted to seduce her when he chanced upon her. Likely, his treatment of her after the appearance of Mr. Runyon was nothing more than irritation at having his seduction interrupted. She clutched at her stomach. The ache in her head spread to envelope her entire body. Silly spinster from Hampshire. Lord Cambourne almost had her believe he held her in some esteem. If you thought that being offered the position of mistress meant you were well thought of.

She had misjudged Lord Cambourne's character and perhaps she'd also judged Lady Cambourne too harshly. Mr. Runyon clearly adored his cousin and had no reason to lie. If what Mr. Runyon told her was true, Alexandra could forgive Lady Cambourne her coldness.

Mr. Runyon looked at her in expectation.

"I am so sorry, Mr. Runyon, for what you have suffered." Alexandra offered comfort, chiding herself for allowing Lord Cambourne to take her mind off of her objective, the safety of Helmsby Abbey. She truly felt sorry for Mr. Runyon, but she must not allow herself to involve herself too deeply out of pity. She pressed fingertips to her temples. She felt a bit dizzy.

"I can see my tale has distressed you." Mr. Runyon took her arm and instructed the clerk to deliver the books to Lord Burke's address. He walked her to the carriage, concern etched in his features. "I shall never forgive myself if you become ill over these events." Gently, he placed her in the carriage.

Tilda snored in the corner, barely stirring as Mr. Runyon followed Alexandra in.

"Mr. Runyon." Alexandra spoke across the seat from him, "please do not distress yourself, you are not the culprit. It is just a headache. I have them sometimes." She reached over and gently took his hand. "I admire your fortitude in trying to put the past behind you."

Mr. Runyon gave her a half-hearted smile as if a heavy weight lifted from his shoulders. "You are a treasure, Miss Dunforth. I am blessed to have a companion such as you. I am hopeful that once you and I are married, my father and I can mend our breach. I feel certain you are the instrument of my redemption." He gave her hand a squeeze. "Perhaps even Cam and I can be in the same room together, if not friends. Nothing would make my cousin happier."

Alexandra stole a look out the window. She felt doubly terrible now that she used him for her own convenience. He would be devastated. But she must push on. For Helmsby Abbey.

⚜

THAT HAD BEEN NEARLY TOO EASY. ARCHIBALD RUNYON sat back in his carriage after escorting Alexandra inside Burke's townhouse and congratulated himself. What a boon to have Cam and his worthless sister confront him at Thrumbadge's today. He couldn't have planned it better himself. Alexandra barely needed a push to accept that Cam and his father, were the reasons Archie was reviled. His little pigeon was so trusting! Adorable! Cam's reputation as the great Satan Reynolds, which Archie wisely cultivated had paid huge dividends. He clapped his gloved hands in delight.

Reaching into his vest pocket he pulled out Alexandra's note to Mr. Meechum. Calmly he ripped it into tiny pieces and tossed them to flutter over his head. The creamy paper landed in a muddy puddle and disappeared from view. Listening to Alexandra rattle on about beloved servants and such today was tiring and a trifle boring. But it had given him an idea.

His beautiful little Hampshire rose. That buffoon, Lord Burke, claimed Alexandra to be plain and devoid of any feminine attributes. Burke was an idiot. True, she was no conventional beauty, but he found conventional beauty to be tiresome. She certainly could never hold a candle to his beloved Jeanette. Few women could. And there was the bonus of Alexandra's innocence. She was pure. Untouched. Innocence in women was to be relished. He loved to be the person to shake the gentle perceptions of a young woman, defile and degrade her. Introduce her to perversions she didn't know she desired.

His delicious thoughts of Alexandra faded away as he thought of Cam. How he hated the man. Cam's baiting made it clear that Lord Robert Cambourne, before dying, confessed everything to his son. Damn Robert. Jeanette convinced herself that Robert would become malleable if only she bore a son. Well, Archie sniffed, she didn't. Just daughters. Leaving only one heir to Cambourne.

Archie stretched his slender fingers inside the fine leather of his gloves. He bet that Alexandra did not spill her books by chance. Miranda, that chattering simpleton, did not just happen upon Miss Dunforth in need. Archie stroked the wolf's head absently. He saw the way Cam looked at Miss Dunforth. The thought of Cam's pain when Archie married Miss Dunforth was simply delicious. Imagine! The great Satan Reynolds enamored of a virgin, a bluestocking from Hampshire no less. Incredible. Wait until he told Jeanette.

He leaned back into the leather squabs of his carriage and contemplated the delicate bones of Alexandra's hands. Her hands were so small, her wrists so slender he would need to have special cuffs made for her. He couldn't risk Alexandra slipping out of them at an inopportune moment.

Archie thought of the beautiful leather crop he had fashioned in Italy. Long narrow strands sprung from the top of the crop, each ending in a small glass bead. The handle of the crop was made to fit his hand perfectly, so as not to lose the grip when the crop was being used. Just today he tried it out on the downstairs maid, a drab little girl who dutifully submitted to him. He imagined it was Alexandra beneath him the entire time. His elderly father would adore Alexandra. Archie would finally appease the old toad and return to his rightful position in the family.

And Archie would be appeased as well. The idea of buying a woman and making her a slave to his needs held much appeal. Alexandra's intelligence challenged him, which would make the breaking of her spirit that much more exquisite. He planned all types of activities after their marriage. Once she broke, his friends could use her. Archie would watch. He would beat her, pulling back the dark curls of Alexandra's hair so hard, a scream would come out of her luscious mouth. He needed to be careful. He didn't want her too bruised. He imagined Alexandra's firm plump bottom, pushed towards him. Archie felt himself grow hard just thinking about it. He rapped on the top of the carriage.

"Take me to Madame LeFleur's." His coachman acknowledged the command with an abrupt turn, heading toward the direction of the most notorious brothel in London. Madame LeFleur would have forgiven him by now for that unfortunate incident. It had been years ago when Archie had less control of his emotions. The girl, no more than fourteen, had balked at all his suggestions for play. It wasn't Archie's fault her neck snapped. He hoped Madame LeFleur hired sturdier whores now.

❧ 10 ❧

Alexandra sat down on the drawing room couch, a tray of tea before her. She pressed her fingertips to her temples and took a deep breath. Lord, how her head ached. Dinner had been a long and drawn-out affair. The meal exhausted her. Her appetite usually so robust, deserted her. A few sips of consommé were all she could stomach. Odious Oliver cheerfully stuffed his face full of food, ignoring the fact that the duck was dry, the fish over-cooked and the vegetables mushy at best. Mr. Runyon noticed. He ate mostly bread, downed with a glass of red wine. Alexandra cared little only wishing for the meal to end. Mr. Runyon had visited with Mr. Meechum and she desperately needed to know of Mr. Meechum's response to her note.

The door to the drawing room opened and Mr. Runyon entered with Lord Burke trailing behind him.

"May I have a word alone with your niece, Lord Burke?" It was phrased as a question, but the words from Mr. Runyon sounded more like a command.

Her atrocious uncle gave one of his pig-like snorts. He

disgusted her. She thought him larger, getting fatter like a goose before Christmas.

"Of course. I'll just have a glass of port in my study. Leave you two lovebirds alone." Odious Oliver blinked one bleary eye at Mr. Runyon.

Alexandra watched her uncle with apathy.

"Try to stay awake to entertain Mr. Runyon, Alexandra. It amazes me he's interested in anything you have to say. I certainly am not." Her uncle gave a huge wheezing chuckle and headed towards the door.

"You will not speak to Alexandra in such a way again, Lord Burke. Do I make myself clear?" Mr. Runyon glared at her uncle, his knuckles white as he clenched his fists.

What a lovely man to defend her. Mr. Runyon stood firmly in Alexandra's corner. He didn't take advantage or try to seduce her on books. Not like Lord Cambourne.

Alexandra's eyelids fluttered down as she thought of Lord Cambourne. He toyed with her. But she ached for him all the same. She dreamt of the dragon tattoo and the earring nearly every night. Felt the dark sable hair beneath her fingers. Oh, she knew how foolish her feelings for the notorious Lord Cambourne were. Ridiculous actually. His torturing of her was merely a game for him, ruining women a hobby. Oh, but to be ruined by a man such as that. A wistful puff of air escaped her lips as she imagined such a thing.

"Um, yes, Runyon. I meant nothing by it. Alexandra doesn't take offense, why should you?" Her uncle shuffled his feet as his fat fingers nervously tapped against a thigh.

"I will join you later, Lord Burke." Mr. Runyon gave a chilly dismissal.

Odious Oliver nodded with a warning glance at Alexandra. He needn't have bothered. She would never say anything to hurt kind Mr. Runyon.

Mr. Runyon sat down gingerly next to her on the couch.

His golden hair gleamed in the candlelight. She found him attractive. He did not have Lord Cambourne's angelic beauty, but he was a rather good-looking in his own way. He took one of her hands, rubbing it gently in his larger one. His hand circled her wrist, squeezing for a moment, then, letting go. The pale blue gaze settled on her, the pupils dark as he squeezed her fingers.

"Miss Dunforth," Mr. Runyon sighed. "I spoke at length with Mr. Meechum." His voice trembled slightly.

Dread settled over Alexandra like a dark mist. The consommé threatened to leave her stomach.

She took another sip of the tea. Her head began to throb. "Yes?" How pathetic and hopeful her voice sounded, even to her own ears.

"I am sorry, Miss Dunforth. I regret to inform you that apparently your aunt may have misled you." He glanced away and refused to meet her eyes. "Unintentionally, I'm sure."

She put the tea down, sloshing a bit on to the saucer. She tried to pull her free hand from Mr. Runyon, but he resisted. "Misled me? How?"

Mr. Runyon coughed. He gave her a wan smile, his blue eyes troubled. "The terms of the will, I'm afraid. There is no expiration on your uncle's guardianship and Helmsby Abbey most assuredly belongs to him. Not you."

Her vision narrowed to pinpoints.

"What do you mean?" *Aunt Eloise lied?*

"I'm afraid that your uncle is your guardian until you are married. Helmsby Abbey and everything that goes with it," he paused, "belong to your uncle. It is *you* that has no claim on the estate."

Alexandra sat back against the cushions of the couch pulling her hands free from Mr. Runyon. A giant whoosh of air forced through her lungs and out. She told herself to breathe. Her hands clutched at the arms of the couch.

"Please, Mr. Runyon. Please do not say this to me." My God. What would she do? Odious Oliver would sell the estate. She had failed Helmsby Abbey and all who depended on her.

"Miss Dunforth. I am deeply sorry to bring you this news." He moved closer to her on the settee, his voice low and empathetic. "I suspect your aunt misled you to keep you from leaving her. She never encouraged you to marry, did she? Perhaps she didn't wish to be alone or perhaps she was incapable of running the estate without your assistance."

Alexandra's stomach clenched. A deep wracking pain centered there. Could it be true? Her mind, sluggish and tired as it was, searched for a rationale.

"Dearest?"

Alexandra looked up at Mr. Runyon, startled out of her despair by the endearment on his lips. An odd thought occurred to her, of watching cows run about the pen as the herders manipulated the animals to drive them down the chute. The cows fought the men's guidance, but in the end allowed themselves to be led down the chute, where the butcher awaited them.

"Forgive me for having to be the one to destroy your hopes." He reached for her hands again, this time clutching her fingers tightly. "To tell you of your aunt's betrayal."

Alexandra's throat was very dry. A feeling of hopelessness, of having her choices all taken from her, like the cows, hit her.

"You have nothing to apologize for, Mr. Runyon. You are unfailingly kind and a true friend to me." Panic made her voice shaky. "Thank you for speaking to Mr. Meechum."

"Miss Dunforth, I wish to be so much more than a friend." He peered at her with fervor. "I desire to be your true companion. I wish to be your husband. Pray forgive me for the timing of my proposal coming, as it does, on the heels of you finding yourself without recourse." He squeezed her hands. "But you are *not* without recourse. I wish to be your knight in shining armor. I spoke to your uncle before dinner. I have told him that I wish to purchase Helmsby Abbey from him." His eyes gleamed in excitement. "Your uncle drove a hard bargain, but in the end I triumphed. Paid him more than he asked to assure your future happiness. We shall live there always, if you wish it. Your family, your beloved servants, shall be safe. I will grow to love them as you do, my dearest!"

"You would do this for me?" Her voice sounded far away. "Ensure that all whom I love there would always be welcome? Helmsby Abbey, my home, would forever belong to me?"

"Oh, my foolish little dove. Of course. Just say yes and all shall be returned to you."

Alexandra closed her eyes. The chute gaped wide. All of the exits, blocked. The butcher waited. What choice did she have? An image of Helmsby Abbey at sunset, floated through her mind. She could smell Mrs. Cowrie's scones. The housekeeper sent a letter just yesterday, asking Alexandra when she would return. All of her extended family had no idea how precarious their situation actually was.

"We would live at Helmsby Abbey? Truly?" She sounded like a beggar in the street. Shame washed over her. The choice remained simple. Marry Mr. Runyon and keep Helmsby Abbey safe. There really was no other choice.

"Miss Alexandra Dunforth, would you do me the honor of becoming my wife?"

The smile on Mr. Runyon's lips did not match the look in his eyes but she ignored the wave of dread that filled her. He had promised to restore her home. He would make a decent husband. Most marriages started with less.

Mr. Runyon's nostrils flared as he waited. A lopsided grin crossed his face, giving him the look of an earnest puppy.

"Please say yes, dearest. I know I am not perhaps the man of your dreams, but I shall strive to be."

Her heart, the heart that yearned for the smell of cinnamon and dragon tattoos, screamed her refusal. It was her mind, ever logical, that answered. "Yes, Mr. Runyon. I'll marry you."

☮

Archie watched in pleasure as his little Hampshire rose agreed to the match. She must adore that pile of manure in Hampshire. She practically salivated as he mentioned returning the estate to her. The very thought of her dusty group of ancient retainers at the estate becoming homeless nearly made his pigeon faint. He would have to watch her future attachments to servants. He simply did not approve.

Archie had practiced his proposal all day in front of the large mirror that hung in his chambers to ensure he conveyed the correct amount of emotion. He toyed earlier with the idea of getting down on one knee, but honestly, the thought of kneeling before Alexandra was so preposterous, he was afraid of bursting into a fit of laughter. Playing the besotted suitor had been a rather laughable annoyance and he would be glad to discard the façade. On their wedding night, he would explain in great detail how he'd fooled her. That he tore up the note to Mr. Meechum. That Helmsby Abbey was gone and her retainers sent from the estate without a farthing. Lord Burke informed Archie of the sale of the estate two days ago. His dove would be devastated.

He pressed a kiss to Alexandra's cold cheek. "Wonderful. This is just wonderful news. You make me the happiest man in the world. I shall inform your uncle right away." And he *was* happy. The thought of having Alexandra completely in his control made him lightheaded. The special cuffs he'd ordered from France would arrive by the end of the week.

Alexandra closed her eyes. Her small hands shook as she pressed against her temples with the tips of her fingers.

Archie wasn't pleased. This was not quite the reaction he hoped for. She had acted odd, at dinner, but he put that down to nervousness over his supposed meeting with her solicitor.

"Alexandra, dearest?"

Sweat beaded on her forehead. "I'm so sorry. I fear I'm a little tired. I have not been sleeping well. Would you mind ringing Tilda to bring another pot of my special tea?"

"Special tea? Are you ill?" If Burke sold him a sickly bag of goods, the fat man would pay dearly. Did Alexandra have consumption or some other distasteful disease? She seemed well enough on their recent outing to Thrumbadge's. He noted the paleness of her skin. The way her hands shook.

"It's nothing, Mr. Runyon. The doctor told me I am prone to nervousness and stress."

Archie found that statement absurd. He rang for Tilda.

When the maid brought the tea, Archie poured Alexandra a cup. The dark steaming liquid gave off an acridly sweet smell. She'd barely eaten tonight. Her pupils were slightly dilated. The headaches.

Alexandra took a deep swallow of tea and relaxed into the cushions of the settee.

Damn Lord Burke! Damn him! Did Burke think Archie stupid? "I will be back, my dove." He patted her hand. Burke had overstepped his bounds and risked damaging something that belonged to Archie. He'd killed men for less. "If it suits you, we will make a formal announcement of our betrothal at my cousin's birthday fete."

She nodded slowly. "Of course. Whatever you wish." The words filtered out but her lips barely moved.

Archie stood and strode out of the parlor, pausing only

to grab his wolf's-head cane where it sat in the foyer. His angry footsteps echoed on the bare wooden floor as he beat a path to Burke's study. *Really!* He was so incensed he considered killing Burke tonight instead of waiting until after the wedding. He flung open the paneled door. Burke sat behind an enormous desk, his eyes closed, his large, ham-like hands clasped across the bloated rise of his stomach.

Burke grunted in surprise as Archie entered. His hands flew down below the desk even as he wiggled to pull up his trousers.

Tilda crawled out from under the desk. Wiping her lips with the back of her hand she gave Archie a sly grin.

If only he had a pistol handy to shoot the shameless old whore. And Burke.

"Get out. Now." He pointed the wolf's head at Tilda.

Casting a baleful look at Archie, Tilda scurried from the room in a cloud of brandy laced with the aroma of body fluids.

Disgusting!

Burke faced him red-faced and blustering. "You should learn to knock Runyon. A man deserves some privacy in his own home." Burke pushed away from the desk, still adjusting his trousers. His eyes were bleary with drink.

"Sit down you fat, disgusting toad." Archie hurled the words at Burke.

Burke complied immediately with a wounded look. He mopped his brow with a hastily produced handkerchief as his eyes widened in terror, like a child who has been caught doing something vile by a parent.

Archie expected Burke *was* terrified. The fat man should be. Archie's blood boiled with rage. He felt this same insane rage when he'd killed Lucia and her groom in Tuscany. No one defied him. Undermined him.

"Alexandra agreed to marry me." He spat the words out, his voice choked with anger.

Burke sat back and resumed mopping his forehead with the handkerchief. "Well there was no need to barge in on me with the news. Isn't that what you wanted? You didn't want her forced. You told me she must come to you of her own free will. My congratulations." Burke lurched one arm across the desk and poured himself another brandy.

Archie swung the cane over his head towards Burke.

Burke put his hands over his head in a defensive gesture, spilling the brandy. He sobbed in fear. The wolf's head slammed down on the center of the desk sending pieces of wood into the air.

Burke jumped up, his chins wiggling.

"You've *drugged* her." Archie was livid. "Laudanum. Do you think me so *stupid* I wouldn't notice? No wonder she barely spoke at dinner. How long have you been drugging her?" He wished to tear the fat man limb from limb. This wasn't how the game was played. Burke ruined it for him. *Ruined it.* Archie wanted to sob in frustration. He had such *plans* for Alexandra. The cuffs!

"I didn't know what else to do." Burke blubbered. "The night we dined at your home she told me you didn't want her as a wife. She said her opinions put you off and you wanted a woman more biddable. I just made her biddable."

"She was toying with you. She hates you." He swung the cane again enjoying the pounding sound it made as it hit the wood of Burke's desk.

Burke swatted away the bits of wood flying at his face as he tried to squeeze his corpulent form underneath the desk.

"You've made her an addict. She barely knows what is going on around her." He clutched the cane in his hand. He wanted to beat Burke until the man's head split open like a pumpkin.

"Wait." Burke held up a fat hand. "Please. Don't you see I've done you a favor? Alexandra is the most tiresome twit. She won't break easy. She's stubborn. But now," Burke sputtered, "you have leverage. You can threaten to take away her tea. Use it to control her. Won't you like that?" Burke's brows lifted up to his greasy pate in an expression of hope.

Archie stopped swinging his cane. The suggestion had merit. Her addiction could prove useful.

"Think what she'll do for her tea. Think how Alexandra pleading for the tea will entertain you. She'll let you do anything. The laudanum will always give you control, especially once she finds out I've sold Helmsby Abbey."

Runyon stroked his chin. A vision flashed through his mind of a naked Alexandra handing him the cuffs, allowing him to do anything if she could have her tea. *Anything*. He pursed his lips, tapping one finger against them. A begging Alexandra *would* amuse him.

He would give the fat man a reprieve. Pointing the cane at Burke he warned, "Tilda is not to increase the dose, do you understand? If Alexandra's given any more, she's likely to become a blithering idiot and she'll be of no use to me. I want her to still have the presence of mind to fight me. Or beg."

Burke nodded effusively. "I swear, Runyon. No more than she already takes. I don't wish to be the man to spoil your fun."

"No, I don't expect you do." Runyon looked at Burke, wishing he could just gut the man like a fish. He couldn't *wait* to rid the world of Burke.

"Tell Miss Dunforth the Dowager Marchioness of Cambourne and Lady Miranda Reynolds have arrived to call on her." Donata commanded the snide butler at Oliver Burke's townhouse. How dare he refuse her entry. The man smelled of onions and his clothing disheveled. *Atrocious*. Donata did not care for his insolence one bit. She rapped her cane against the door.

"Madam, Lord Burke is not home. He left specific instructions for Miss Dunforth to rest with no visitors." The butler put his hands in desperation against the door, attempting to politely shut it.

"I am not just *any* visitor. I am the Dowager Marchioness of Cambourne. If you wish to find gainful employment after Lord Burke falls into poverty, which is likely at any moment given the state of your uniform, you will step aside this instant. Or I shall have you removed." Donata's silvery head gestured to the large Cambourne footman hovering protectively over her. "Do I make myself clear?" Her tone brooked no disobedience.

The butler eyed the muscular young footman and moved aside, muttering to himself he'd be sacked for sure.

Donata was neither impressed nor surprised. Few people *ever* defied her.

"Grandmother, are you sure? Perhaps Alexandra is ill or—"

"Absolutely! Harry," Donata smiled at the footman. "Please stay here." The Dowager gestured to a space just under the stoop of the door. She turned to Miranda. "If she is ill, all the more reason to see her. And Harry, should you hear me raise my voice, I am in need of your assistance." Donata stared down Lord Burke's butler as she walked through the door.

"Yes, my lady. I shall come running." Harry nodded, his eyes never leaving the butler.

Donata thought Harry a good boy and a very capable footman. He adored Donata.

Burke's butler nodded to Donata, leading her and Miranda down a dark entryway. "This way, milady."

"This visit is most overdue. *Most overdue*. Several invitations have been sent to Miss Dunforth inviting her to join us for tea, *and* an outing to Thrumbadge's, *and* a drive in Hyde Park. She refused them all. Strange behavior from a woman with Miss Dunforth's lively and curious mind. I refuse to believe she means to keep herself sequestered in this... house." Donata choked on the word as she took in the state of the hallway the butler led them down. She stared in horror at the garish decorations of Burke's home. It was enough to make her run screaming back to her carriage.

"Good Lord! What a hideous display of poor taste," she said out loud to the butler's back as he shuffled ahead of them.

Miranda's eyes widened, taking in the dim corners of the

hall. One gloved finger touched a side table. She gasped as it came back black with dust.

"And filthy to boot," Donata muttered, seeing Miranda's ruined glove. "Does Lord Burke not employ a housekeeper?"

The butler ignored her question. He opened the door to a small salon. He studiously avoided Donata's question, only nodding as he stepped aside.

Donata's eyes widened at the state of the salon. The entryway and hallway, while horridly decorated, were in relatively good repair. This room, however, spoke of neglect and desperation. She could not help but notice the chipped paint around the doorway, or the way the corners of the wallpaper peeled away from the window edges. She could clearly see the oval and square shapes left behind on the walls that bespoke of pictures sold long ago. The rug underneath Donata's feet was worn and threadbare. The design of the rug was so faded it was impossible to guess the original design. *So, Lord Burke is on his way to the poorhouse.* The pompous ass was no doubt busy selling everything within his reach, including Miss Dunforth. Alexandra's association with that depraved cur, Archie Runyon, started to make sense.

Donata shivered, not from the room's dampness but at the thought of Archie Runyon once again on the loose in London. She prayed fervently that he would never return, but Miranda's near-hysterical arrival from Thrumbadge's two weeks ago crushed Donata's fragile hope that he was gone from their lives.

"Grandmother, he's back!" Miranda sobbed that day. She collapsed against her grandmother hugging Donata tightly.

Confused, Donata stroked Miranda's dark hair, wondering whom Miranda could possibly be talking about. "Who, Miranda?"

"Archie! We saw him. Spoke to him. He was at Thrumbadge's with Miss Dunforth. How could he possibly know Alexandra?"

A chill settled over Donata at the mention of Archie Runyon. She recalled the man she saw across the room at Lady Dobson's ball. Archie *had* been there. Hiding in the shadows.

"Sutton didn't speak a word on the carriage ride home. Not a word. I know Archie did something awful, truly terrible to make Father and Sutton hate him so."

Donata stayed silent. Miranda had every right to know, but Donata did not have the strength at that moment to tell her granddaughter such a vile story.

"I think Sutton means to kill him." Miranda's green eyes were wide.

"Well, I wish someone would," Donata said as she comforted Miranda. She did indeed know what Archie had done, or had almost done, and to *whom*. The thought solidified her hatred of her daughter-in-law, Jeanette. Donata dried Miranda's tears that day and sent her granddaughter up for a nap before dinner. She needed to think. Her grandson had not come into Cambourne House after dropping off Miranda. Sutton's coach pulled away before Donata could have Harry fetch him.

Archie was a fool. He had come back to London at his own peril. Donata did not doubt Sutton would kill the man. But what of Miss Dunforth? Donata could not allow a young woman, *any* young woman, to be taken in by that monster. Especially as she suspected Miss Dunforth's affections lay in another direction. Later that same day after several unsuccessful attempts to find her grandson, Donata sent her favorite footman, the same Harry who now guarded the door, on an errand.

Lord Burke's offensive butler cleared his throat bringing

Donata back to the dismal parlor. At least a fire lit the hearth, although the flames needed stoking and another log should be added. The curtains of one window were open a bit to let in the weak morning light. Donata thought she spied a form perched in the corner.

"Lady Cambourne?" Alexandra's voice sounded from the dim room.

"Open these curtains immediately!" Donata thumped her cane. "Send someone in to tend to the fire!"

The butler rushed to open the curtains, scattering dust throughout the room.

Miranda sneezed.

Miss Dunforth sat on a faded, overstuffed chair with a book, unopened, in her lap. She had been peering through the crack in the curtains at the garden outside. Or what passed as a garden, thought Donata, a kind word for the weed-infested expanse she glimpsed through the window.

"My child!" Donata hobbled over to Alexandra. She lowered herself onto an ugly couch, wincing at the pain in her hip. How she detested old age! "Are you ill? Why are you sitting here in the dark?"

"Forgive me, my lady. I've had headaches that leave me quite exhausted. The dim light seems to help."

"Headaches? Really, Miss Dunforth, that is not a valid excuse for ignoring the Dowager Marchioness of Cambourne. I've issued you invitations for delightful outings. Invited you for tea. You have ignored me. I had to venture out into this dreadful weather to search for you," Donata raised a brow. "Me. The Dowager Marchioness. Forced to call upon *you,* Miss Dunforth. Why, it simply isn't done."

Alexandra didn't flinch at her tone. She gave Donata an apologetic smile. "I'm so sorry to have disappointed you."

Donata cheered silently at the note of sarcasm in Alexandra's words.

"Such a *tone,* Miss Dunforth. Remember to whom you are speaking." She squeezed Alexandra's hand, which was cold and slightly clammy. "Miranda is here as well. Poor Miranda cannot enjoy tea when her mother is around, you know."

Miranda agreed cheerfully. "It's true, Alexandra. I'm not even permitted a tea-cake. No scones or sandwiches nor even a cube of sugar with my tea. Mother says I'll become stout and pop my stays." Miranda swept her hands down her trim figure. "Going somewhere else for tea is the only chance I have." Miranda sneezed again.

Alexandra raised her arm to grab at the bell-pull just behind her.

The girl's arm shook slightly, though she did not seem especially sickly, only tired. Weak. Miss Dunforth showed neither of those tendencies earlier. She did not strike Donata as nervous and given to physical ailment. Donata's sixth sense, ever useful in these situations, told her something else was wrong with Miss Dunforth.

The parlor door flew open, the knob thrusting into the opposing wall with a bang. A bulldog in female form gave a snarl and fixed beady eyes on Miss Dunforth. "You rang?" The woman stopped at the sight of Donata and Miranda. The bulldog cleared her throat. "You ain't supposed to have company, Miss Dunforth. Lord Burke says you're to rest. You have headaches and you must get better." The woman's gaze shifted to the ceiling as her tone sweetened.

Donata found the servant appalling. *Appalling*. What an ugly woman. So *seedy*.

"Balderdash. *I* am not company. *I* am the Dowager Marchioness of Cambourne, and this is Lady Miranda. She nodded to her granddaughter. "You." She pointed her cane at what she considered another worthless servant of Lord Burke. "Bring us tea and sandwiches. Now."

The woman's features contorted into a mask of blank

pleasantness. "As you wish. I will let Lord Burke know you are here, Lady Cambourne."

Donata snorted. "Lovely. I look forward to renewing my acquaintance with your master, although I was under the impression he was not at home." She raised her chin, queen-like. "Don't dawdle. Go get us some tea."

The woman didn't move. She snuck a look at Alexandra.

Donata pounded her cane on the floor. "Harry!"

The young footman appeared magically at the door of the parlor. He gave the servant an evil look. "Yes, my lady?"

"This is...?" Donata pointed to the servant who seemed to shrink a bit under Harry's regard.

"Tilda." Alexandra interrupted from the couch. "My maid." Alexandra put her hand to her mouth to stifle a giggle, as if she knew how ludicrous it was that Tilda was a maid. "My uncle is a bit short-staffed it seems, and Tilda must do double duty."

Donata was suitably horrified. "That woman is not a ladies' maid," She shook her head. This was far worse than she thought. "Tilda is bringing in tea, Harry. Once she does, you are to stand by the parlor door in case I need you. We shan't like to be disturbed."

Tilda bit her lip.

"Well?" Donata pointed at Tilda with her cane. "I am the Dowager Marchioness of Cambourne and I do not like to be kept waiting!" Tilda dropped an awkward curtsy and scurried out of the parlor.

"I fear you have frightened Tilda. No easy task is that." Alexandra brushed a curl off her head. "Her bark is much worse than her bite. I'm not sure where my uncle found her."

"Hurrumph." Donata snorted in disapproval. *Probably in the sewers along the Thames.*

Miranda flitted around the room like a hummingbird.

Every so often, her eyes met Donata's over Alexandra's head. She regaled Alexandra with the latest brace of suitors to cross the steps of Cambourne House, making Alexandra laugh softly.

Tilda reappeared, her bullish looking face red and determined. Two teapots sat on a tray along with an odd assortment of tiny cakes and some bruised fruit.

"Interesting." Donata wondered at the two teapots. "Is there a reason there are *two* pots of tea?"

"Well, Miss Dunforth likes a special kind of tea. I make it just for her. The doctor says it helps with her headaches. You and Lady Miranda would not enjoy it so much." The beady gaze shifted to the right, away from Donata.

"Thank you." She waved at the maid, dismissing her. "You may go."

The woman remained rooted to the spot, unwilling to leave the tea. A nervous tic appeared in her cheek.

The woman was really terrifyingly ugly. "Well? You may go. I shall pour." Donata commanded.

Harry's head appeared around the doorway. "My lady, is all well?"

Nervously, Tilda looked at Harry, then back to Donata. She bobbed once and left the room sparing a glance at the tea as she exited.

"Yes, Harry. Pray do shut the door."

Donata waited until the door shut, relieved Harry stood guard. They would not be disturbed again. Not even by Lord Burke if he appeared. Donata poured three steaming cups of tea from the second pot ignoring Alexandra's "special" tea. She handed a plain cup of tea to Alexandra.

"Lady Cambourne, I should drink my tea." Alexandra pointed to the first pot. "The doctor prescribed it for my headaches."

Donata pretended deafness. She pushed aside the first pot.

While Miranda chattered lightly to Alexandra, distracting her, Donata lifted the first teapot's lid. She sniffed. A sickly, sweet smell wafted up into her nostrils. She knew that smell. Memories of her husband, the elder Marquess, flooded through her. Her husband reeked of that particular odor the entire last year of his life. He had died slowly and painfully, but the laudanum helped to ease his passage into the next world. Many doctors favored prescribing laudanum for headaches. Particularly for wives who perhaps were considered unruly, opinionated, or full of female complaints. Her gaze flew to Alexandra. The girl left early during her first visit to Cambourne House due to headache. Donata assumed that headache to actually be her grandson. The spark between the two was so bright one would be blind not to see it. But perhaps she was incorrect? Donata cocked her head, taking stock of Miss Dunforth. Alexandra wasn't ill, exactly, but she did not sparkle quite as brightly. Donata was sure the diagnosis of Alexandra's headaches was false.

The Dowager's mind raced. She had plans for Miss Dunforth. Plans which did not involve headaches or special tea, but which did involve her grandson, Sutton. Lord Burke was no match for Donata Reynolds. Nor Archie Runyon. Miranda, her chattering, but highly intelligent granddaughter, would no doubt be delighted to help.

Donata pasted a smile on her face. "Miss Dunforth? How would you like to go to the Royal Exhibition today? An outing is just the thing to clear the cobwebs out of one's head! I'm told Lord Bishop is lecturing on his travels to the Far East."

Miranda clasped her hands. "Yes. You must come."

Alexandra's face lit up. "Oh, that would be lovely. But I'm not sure my uncle—"

"Oh pish! Lord Burke is likely at his club and will never know you've gone, my dear. I would so hate for you to miss a lecture by Lord Bishop. He's famous, you know." Donata detested dry, dull lectures. But she was correct in assuming that Alexandra did not. Nor did her grandson. He adored them.

"**A**lexandra?" Miranda sounded as if she were speaking from far away.

Alexandra dozed. She snuggled deeper into the leather squabs. The green hills of Helmsby Abbey dotted with bluebells, lay before her. She walked through the rolling green grass. Birds sang and swooped overhead. She twirled and spun amongst the grass and flowers until she fell to the ground. The sweetness of the meadow filled her nostrils. She rolled over and Lord Cambourne, his glorious green eyes watching her with warmth, lay next to her. Bluebells caught in his dark hair and fell down his chest. He rolled on top of her, smothering her with kisses, pressing against her. Then he sat back, slowly unbuttoning his shirt and pushed the fine lawn off his shoulders. The dragon's tail was as green as his eyes and the meadow that surrounded them. Her fingertips touched the tattoo and the tail wound its way around her fingers, pulling her closer to Lord Cambourne.

"Alexandra?" Fingers bit into her knee as Miranda shook her. "You must wake up. We are nearly at the Royal Exhibition. I let you doze off." Her brow wrinkled in concern. "You seemed tired earlier."

The dream faded. She wanted to cry out as the dragon's tail slipped from her fingers and floated back to Lord Cambourne.

"No."

"No? No, you don't wish to wake up?" Miranda giggled. "You must wake up. This is an adventure. I don't believe I've ever kidnapped anyone, although of course my grandmother is quite good at it."

The last hour came back to Alexandra. The Dowager and Miranda unexpectedly appeared for tea. The two kidnapped her from her uncle's home for an excursion to the Royal Exhibition. Well, not truly a kidnapping. Alexandra went willingly. Oliver Burke would likely have a fit, but Alexandra didn't care. She felt good. Not wonderful, but good. The nap restored her.

"I like 'shanghaied' much better. It gives the impression I am dangerous and exciting." Alexandra grinned back at Miranda. The green gaze, so like her brother's, gave Alexandra pause. All of her dreams of late featured Lord Cambourne and the dragon tattoo. She looked out the window, so Miranda wouldn't see the moisture in her eyes. In spite of everything, Lord Cambourne held a wicked fascination for her. She imagined him seducing various widows and torturing other virgins with his handsome face and teasing demeanor. Cutting a swath with a bevy of beautiful women. Lord Cambourne only thought her good enough to be his mistress. She must remember he was a cad. A rake. But still she craved him desperately.

"I find you terribly exciting, even though you breed livestock and speak Latin. I've never managed to master that particular language myself. Or anything other than English.

French, I'm passable in. Grandmother says a proper lady must speak French."

Alexandra smiled. Miranda was the first real friend Alexandra ever had. Except for Mrs. Cowries, the housekeeper at Helmsby Abbey. But Mrs. Cowries was at least sixty and more mother than friend.

"You will enjoy Lord Bishop's presentation very much," Miranda enthused. "He's traveled all over the world and brought dozens of exotic animals back with him. My brother knows Lord Bishop quite well. Though I'm not surprised that my grandmother deserted us. She detests lectures but knows how Sutton and I love them."

Alexandra's heart leapt at the mention of Lord Cambourne. She folded her hands sedately in her lap and pretended to be engrossed in a fight outside the carriage between an orange girl and a customer.

"I told Sutton to be late. Lord Tasterly is expected to be in attendance. He is absolutely terrified of my brother." Miranda smoothed her skirts.

Lord Cambourne is attending the lecture? Not usually a fainter, Alexandra wished she could faint now and avoid seeing Lord Cambourne. Her glance flew to her friend's reticule and wondered if there were smelling salts hidden in its depths. She may need them.

"I was unaware that your brother would be attending."

Miranda cocked her head and gave a silly laugh. Her eyes, like bits of emerald glass, bored into Alexandra.

"Sutton will likely see us home as well. I do so hope he doesn't scare away Lord Tasterly. I must confess to a fondness for Lord Tasterly, though Sutton finds him a bore."

Alexandra's stomach fluttered uncomfortably. The feeling was like being at the edge of a precipice and wanting to jump. But afraid to take the plunge.

"May I ask you something, Alexandra?"

The fear of seeing Lord Cambourne warred with a light giddiness at the thought of seeing him. She couldn't breathe. "Yes." The word snapped at Miranda like a whip.

Miranda sat back and raised one perfectly shaped dark brow. "I hope that you don't mind me asking, but I am curious about your association with Mr. Runyon. Did he explain his relationship to my family?"

"Yes." Cautiously, she took a breath, waiting for Miranda to continue. Alexandra hoped she and Miranda could enjoy the outing without the subject of Mr. Runyon popping up, but she saw that was not to be the case. Her hand trembled in her lap. How to explain the situation in such a way that Miranda would understand? Her stomach contracted and not with excitement. The slow hum of a headache made its way through her temples. Would Miranda understand the need Alexandra had to keep Helmsby Abbey safe? Her betrothal could not be kept a secret forever. Mr. Runyon intended to announce their future marriage to everyone at the Marchioness's birthday ball at Gray Covington, the Cambourne estate, next week.

Miranda was beautiful, titled, and loved. She had a family and possessed several homes. The desperation Alexandra felt would be foreign to her friend. She stifled the bit of jealousy rearing its ugly head as she looked at Miranda. Lord Cambourne's sister was a vision in light yellow, with tiny peridots dangling from her ears. Did Miranda ever want for anything?

Alexandra cleared her throat and said softy, "Mr. Runyon is courting me."

Miranda sat back in a whoosh against the squabs. Abruptly, she turned her head to gaze out the coach's window. Gloved hands twisted the reticule in her lap as if she were trying to strangle it.

"Miranda," Alexandra spoke haltingly, "he has been unfailingly kind to me. My uncle supports the match. I know that there is a...a difference of opinion between him and your family. I truly hope—"

"While I do not know the exact nature of my brother's dislike, my father shared the feeling. Grandmother forbids Mr. Runyon's presence at Cambourne House. Over Mother's objections."

"Your father and he disagreed, that much I know. I'm sure if Mr. Runyon and your brother sat down—"

Miranda held up her hand, effectively silencing Alexandra. "I wish to hear no more." Her friend's expression became thoughtful. "My mother and Archie were raised together, as siblings, even though they are cousins. Ten years separates them. They are much alike. Two peas in a pod." Miranda stared at Alexandra. "Ask yourself, Alexandra, how you can dislike my mother and not see her in Archie?"

Alexandra murmured a half-hearted protest.

Miranda shook her head. "Something happened to make my brother hate him. There are rumors about Archie. Where there is smoke, there is often fire."

"What are you saying? He has been nothing but kind to me. A friend where others have not been. What would you have me do?" Alexandra almost revealed that he would return Helmsby Abbey to her.

Miranda, as sharp as the Dowager said, "What has he promised you?"

Alexandra looked away. Miranda's guess at the truth made her squirm. "Nothing. He is a decent man." Alexandra looked down into her lap. "I am very sorry you do not approve my choice, Miranda. Perhaps you haven't noticed, but I am not exactly inundated with offers for my hand. You wouldn't understand. You who have been given everything." Alexandra wished the words back the moment they left her lips.

Miranda reacted as if she'd been slapped. Her face became

carefully composed, a look no doubt cultivated by the nobility for just such an occasion as this.

"Not everything," she said quietly. "There is much you do not know about me, Alexandra. But you are right. I do not understand. I would ask you to consider one thing. Understand this is no reflection on you or your social standing. But please ask yourself, Alexandra, why the cousin of *the Marchioness of Cambourne* cannot find a woman of his class to marry him. *He* should be inundated with girls eager for a match. Yet, he is not."

Alexandra's hackles rose up. Lord Cambourne and his sordid proposition filtered through her mind. The headache rose to a crescendo at the back of her neck, the tentacles of it covering her scalp and piercing her temples.

"It is not your concern, Lady Miranda, whom I wish to befriend, or whom I allow to court me."

"As you will, Alexandra." Miranda smiled grimly. "I meant no insult. But you are an intelligent woman. Please start acting like one." She glanced out the window. "We're here."

The carriage rolled to a stop in front of the Royal Exhibition. Alexandra had never been here, but she'd read about it. Her aunt Eloise received some of the London papers and Alexandra read about the adventurers who had lectured here as well as the exotic beasts that were kept as part of the zoo, and the amazing exhibits put together by the Royal Academy of Sciences. The Royal Geographical society gave lectures here on a regular basis and sponsored several expeditions to the jungles of Africa, India, and the Far East. Alexandra wished she were visiting these hallowed halls under better circumstances. The adventure of the day dimmed with Miranda's condemnation of Alexandra's association with Mr. Runyon. Alexandra determined she should enjoy herself, no matter the circumstances. There was a treasure trove of knowledge waiting for her inside these walls.

If only she could have some tea for her headache.

The Cambourne footman climbed down from atop the coach and guided the ladies out. As Miranda and Alexandra made their way towards the tall, wooden doors they passed several groups of gentlemen milling around the front of the building. A young boy ran among the men passing out flyers and receiving a coin here and there for his troubles. Miranda gave the boy two coins. She handed a flyer to Alexandra, keeping one for herself.

Miranda took Alexandra's arm. Her face was perfectly composed, the false sense of gaiety evident in her tone. "Come. You will enjoy this greatly, I promise."

Alexandra followed her in, a sinking feeling infusing her entire being. It struck her that this may likely be her only visit to the Royal Exhibition with Miranda. Perhaps Mr. Runyon would bring her in the future. The thought of never seeing Miranda after today saddened her. The conversation inside the coach left no room for debate. The Marquess of Cambourne and his family did not tolerate their cousin. That lack of tolerance would extend to Alexandra once she married Mr. Runyon.

The crowd inside the hall was thick where they entered. Alexandra saw several other ladies in attendance, but women were definitely in the minority. A lecture did not take precedence over shopping on Bond Street, it seemed, or making calls. Miranda pulled her along as they moved through a large atrium that comprised the main foyer. Four hallways veered off in separate directions and Miranda led her towards an entrance on the left. The lecture hall. The marble floor vibrated with the footsteps of dozens of people. Titled gentlemen mixed with scholars and well-heeled businessmen swung their walking sticks and chatted with members of the government. Lord Bishop was well known in London and revered for his scientific explorations.

Alexandra paused to push a curl off her cheek. Her neck prickled. Someone was watching her. Scanning the crowd, her eyes lit on a tall dark form. Lord Cambourne. His arms were clasped across his chest and his face carefully devoid of any emotion. But he watched her. His green gaze lingered on her, following her progress with Miranda.

Nervously, she looked away, pretending she didn't notice him even though her entire body flamed to life. Focusing on a fresco that covered one wall she suspected Miranda saw her brother, but she made no move to greet him. When Alexandra dared look again, Lord Cambourne was gone. Her heart fluttered, and she pressed her free hand to her chest, hoping to ease the sensation.

Miranda drew her into the lecture hall, pointing out a podium situated atop a large wooden stage.

"That is where Lord Bishop will speak, Alexandra." The lecture hall was of medium size. Rows of chairs lined the interior of the room. Watercolor paintings of exotic birds, some so realistic they seemed to leap off the canvas sat on easels against the walls. Alexandra looked at the paintings in wonder. She could not wait to examine each one in detail.

"Aren't they beautiful?" Miranda looked at the paintings, mesmerized by the colors and depictions of birds as well. "Lord Bishop is having engravings made for a book. I've already ordered a copy from Thrumbadge's."

Alexandra nodded in agreement and pointed to a sign that read, 'Zoological Exhibition of Lord Bishop.' "Is that where the animals are?"

"Yes, although I'm not sure what is contained within. Sutton did say there were monkeys."

Alexandra consulted the small pamphlet purchased outside. Lord Bishop's collection was extensive according to the pamphlet and contained not only monkeys but birds and tropical plants. She rubbed her temple. Her headache throbbed dully, and the closeness of the crowd made her a trifle dizzy. She shook her head to clear it.

Miranda lifted an eyebrow in question then took her arm again, making an effort to match her longer strides to Alexandra's shorter ones.

"There are my friends, Lord Atkins and his sister, Lady Atkins." Miranda waved in the direction of an attractive young girl with glasses and a man about Alexandra's age. "Oh my, *and* Lord Tasterly." Miranda blushed furiously, which only served to make her more attractive.

Alexandra watched in amazement as Miranda transformed under Lord Tasterly's regard. Miranda's dark lashes slid over her green eyes in a coy manner. She gave the young man a shy smile, so unlike her usual confident grin. Alexandra found her unrecognizable as the chattering bluestocking she adored. Clearly, Lord Tasterly piqued Miranda's interest.

"Lord Tasterly," the name escaped Miranda's lips in a whisper, "is quite handsome, don't you think, Alexandra?"

Alexandra did indeed find Lord Tasterly attractive. His hair, a dark brown, curled pleasingly around his ears. His gaze, rife with adoration for Miranda, worshipped her from where he stood. He plucked at his neatly trimmed mustache and smiled broadly at Miranda's approach.

Lady Atkins, dressed in pale yellow and resembling a studious canary, waved furiously to Miranda, motioning her to come forward. "Lady Miranda, I wondered when you would get here. Lady Atkins's brown eyes shone behind her glasses. "I hoped I would see you before the lecture started. We can all sit together." Her eyes widened as if in secret code to Miranda. No doubt it had to do with Lord Tasterly.

"Lady Atkins, Lord Atkins, Lord Tasterly." Miranda greeted the three with a slight nod of her head. Both men bowed to Miranda and Lady Atkins dipped in a small curtsy. Miranda, as the sister of a Marquess, outranked them all.

Lord Tasterly grasped Miranda's gloved hand and brushed it with his lips. He was clearly delighted to see Miranda. "Lady Miranda. I hoped we would run into each other here. How many times have you told me the story of your brother's monkey?" His hazel gaze ran down her form in appreciation. "You are as pretty as a rose."

Miranda blushed again and gave him a coy look. "A rose? Such a common flower. I was hoping I resembled something a bit more exotic."

Lord Tasterly's eyes lit up at Miranda's flirtatious reply.

Lord Cambourne was such a flirt, Alexandra mused. The image of his tall form leaning against the wall in the atrium flashed through her mind. Stubbornly she pushed him away. She must not think of him. She was to be married to a lovely man. Her gut clenched painfully. A simply lovely man.

"May I present my friend, Miss Dunforth." Miranda introduced her.

Lady Atkins and Lord Tasterly greeted her politely. Lord Atkins held her hand a moment longer than necessary. He winked at her, squeezing her fingers tight.

Shocked at his forward behavior, she looked to see if Miranda or Lady Atkins noticed. No one was watching. The two ladies listened to Lord Tasterly with rapt attention as he led them to a row of chairs.

"May I, Miss Dunforth?" Lord Atkins made a sweeping gesture, allowing her to follow the trio ahead of him.

Alexandra walked carefully up the aisle. Lord Atkins's stare bored into her back. Something about the man filled her with trepidation.

"Ladies," Lord Tasterly said from up ahead, "let us sit." He directed Miranda and Lady Atkins into a row of seats.

Lord Atkins moved swiftly from behind Alexandra and put himself next to Lord Tasterly, seating Alexandra next to the aisle and furthest away from the other two women. He waited until she was seated and said, "Dunforth, I'm certain I've heard the name bandied about."

Alexandra gave Lord Atkins a confused look. She was certain they had never met. He didn't look the least familiar. If his sister was a friend of Miranda's, possibly Alexandra had been introduced to him.

"Lord Atkins, I am at a disadvantage. Have we met?" Alexandra's mouth was dry as cotton and it gave her voice a raspy quality. She was terribly thirsty. She could do with a cup of tea. Lord Atkins made her very uncomfortable.

Lord Atkins leered at her. He assessed her bodice with shocking frankness. "But I know you, Miss Dunforth." He whispered into her ear. "I've met your uncle at the gaming tables. What a terrible faro player he is, but you likely knew that. I'm a business associate of Mr. Runyon. His eyes roved over her body, resettling on her bosom. "You don't look the type, truth be told." He smacked his lips.

Alexandra pursed her lips. "And what type is that, Lord Atkins?" Her temples throbbed. She waited for his answer even though she wanted to sprint as fast as she could from this disturbing conversation.

"The type that Mr. Runyon likes." He winked again. "You've the look of an innocent about you. I must say, I find it quite desirable as well. That bodes well for any future acquaintance, don't you think?"

Alexandra sat, stunned into silence. What did he refer to? The words and tone spoke of depravity, as did the way he continued to look at the tops of her breasts. The urge to flee became stronger. "I'm sure I don't know what you mean, Lord Atkins. I find your tone overfamiliar."

"No need to be distressed, Miss Dunforth." His fingertips grazed her knee.

Alexandra jumped. She shrank back from Lord Atkins.

"I meant no offense." His voice was smooth and reassuring. "Mr. Runyon and I have similar tastes. There's no need to pretend shyness around me. You should look on me as a friend. I would certainly never betray Mr. Runyon's confidence." Lord Atkins's stare, his eyes like black pebbles, hardened on her.

What was he insinuating? Her hands trembled. "If you don't mind, Lord Bishop is walking towards the podium and I would like to listen to his lecture."

Lord Atkins chuckled softly. "As you will, Miss Dunforth. It wouldn't do for the others to get wind of anything would it?" He threw a look at Miranda. "Especially Lady Miranda, the daughter of Mr. Runyon's *dear* cousin." He turned and faced the podium.

The dread mixed with the smothering feeling of despair reared up again, this time nearly suffocating her. Alexandra's hand twitched in her lap. She stood, her knees nearly buckling underneath her.

Lord Atkins didn't spare her a glance. She saw the hint of a smile on his lips. Her distress amused him.

Miranda's head peeked around Lord Tasterly. "Miss Dunforth? Are you going somewhere? Lord Bishop is about to begin."

"I simply need refreshment. My throat is quite dry. I believe I saw a lemon ice vendor in the atrium. I shall return promptly." Her voice stammered out of her, sounding guttural as she choked on her words. Fear and despair mixed until it formed a large stone sitting in her chest. If she stayed, she would not be able to breathe. Lord Atkins's comments made her ill. Doomed. Trapped like some wild animal. Perhaps she could catch a hackney outside. Home. Tea. She wanted nothing more.

Miranda rose to accompany her.

Alexandra put up a hand to stay her. "I'll just be a moment, Lady Miranda. Please don't fret." Alexandra flicked a glance at Lord Tasterly, who was watching Lord Bishop mount the podium. "Besides, you'll miss the lecture."

Miranda sat back down. "I don't know where Sutton is. If you see him, tell my brother I've saved him a seat." She patted a chair to her left.

Lord Tasterly turned his attention from Lord Bishop. His pleasant expression disappeared and his face paled. "Lord Cambourne is joining us?"

"Yes of course. You didn't expect us to be without escort, did you?" Miranda gave a shy chuckle, turning from Alexandra.

It was all the distraction Alexandra needed. She stood and fled down the aisle. Sliding through the walnut doors at the end of the room, she found herself back in the foyer. Sun shone through the skylight above her. Devoid of the crowd, the foyer was quiet, even peaceful. Now, she need only avoid Lord Cambourne.

Alexandra turned towards the main entrance. Lord Cambourne might be lurking just outside. Her gaze flicked to the right. A sign for the Ladies Necessary Room sat prominently displayed, so she turned. Miranda would search for her there if Alexandra did not return to the lecture hall. The corridor to the left had a sign posted before it. 'Exhibition of the Flora and Fauna Discovered by Lord Bishop.' She spun on her heel and made for the exhibition. A back entrance could be found there. She would make her escape and hail a hackney.

Her temples ached. She needed her tea. Lord Atkins's words rang in her head. Miranda's pained expression in the carriage flashed before her eyes. Her thoughts jumbled. She could not make a connection between the two incidents.

Turning the corner, the familiar musky smell of animals and hay assailed her nostrils. The aroma comforted her. Calmed her. If she closed her eyes, she could imagine herself in the barn at Helmsby Abbey. Tears welled in her eyes. She wanted to go home. After her marriage, Alexandra intended to take the first coach to Hampshire. Mr. Runyon *promised*.

Alexandra marveled at the transformation of this section of the Exhibition Hall. Plants abounded from various corners, their pots cleverly hidden to give the appearance of walking into a jungle. Rich, earthy aromas filled the air. The hall was deserted. According to the pamphlet, Lord Bishop would lead a guided tour into this part of the exhibition after his lecture. Alexandra moved forward, taking a deep breath. The urge to flee lessened.

A loud screech made her jump. Clasping hands to her heart, she laughed at her own foolishness. The screech came from the cage before her. Cautiously, so as not to startle the inhabitant of the cage, she tiptoed closer.

A mass of palm fronds wiggled back and forth, quivering as if someone or something hid behind them. The fronds jiggled wildly, batted by an unseen hand.

Entranced, Alexandra moved until her nose nearly touched the cage bars. Then she stood still.

Curious black button eyes peered at her from behind a frond.

Alexandra smiled.

The eyes disappeared. Two tiny brown hands clutched the frond. The frond shook.

"Hello, little man." Alexandra whispered.

A small face emerged. Covered with dark fur, the eyes outlined in black, the expression on the face was one of interest.

Alexandra forgot about leaving in her desire to examine the monkey. She unrolled the pamphlet she still clutched in her hand slowly, not wanting to frighten the animal. The pamphlet contained illustrations of various animals Lord

Bishop had collected for the exhibition. She flipped several pages until she found the engraving she sought.

"There you are." Alexandra gave her friend a tiny triumphant smile. "You are a capuchin monkey."

One small hand, the fingers tiny and black, rose up and reached towards Alexandra.

Alexandra held her breath.

The animal chattered. The hand retreated.

She thought back to the story of Jonas, Lord Cambourne's monkey who smoked opium and wore a hat. That seemed a lifetime ago. Pain lanced through her breast. The panic returned, along with fear and loneliness. She sucked in a breath. Alexandra rarely cried, but in the last few weeks the urge to do so was with her daily. If she burst into tears, only her new friend, the monkey, would witness her lack of composure.

"I am so sorry you are in a cage."

The monkey's head bobbed in agreement.

"If I could, I would set you free. But then, you would be alone in London, with no one to help you." She wiggled a gloved finger at the animal. "I know what that feels like. I would not wish that for you, my friend." She put a hand to her mouth, trying to stem the anguish erupting from her lips "I miss my home as well." Her voice broke.

The monkey blinked at her. A chirp of sympathy came out of the animal's mouth. Suddenly the monkey screeched loudly and disappeared into the foliage of the cage.

Disappointed, Alexandra watched the monkey's retreat, her heart aching. She was so immersed in her own sadness she didn't hear the footsteps behind her.

"Alex."

13

S utton resolved to stay away from Miss Dunforth. Her
association with Archie Runyon filled him with disbelief and an angry possessiveness. Jealousy. An emotion
Sutton had never felt for any woman before, and he shied
from it. But then he saw her, walking smartly into the atrium
of the Royal Exhibition in the company of his sister. Again,
the Badger surprised him with her appearance in the most
unlikely place. Miranda neglected to inform him she was
bringing Miss Dunforth today.

He waited before entering the lecture hall, intending to
sneak in after Bishop began speaking. He would stand during
the lecture and avoid Miss Dunforth. Then Alexandra burst
through the heavy doors of the lecture hall, scurrying away
like a frightened mouse chased by a housecat. He'd followed
her. He told himself it was only to ensure her safety. Not to
accost her. Not to demand an explanation of her relationship
with Runyon, though God help him, he needed one.

He watched as she spoke to the monkey. The Badger's
voice, so lost and forlorn, undid Sutton. The very sight of her

trim form with the overabundance of bosom, and the curling mass of hair, made every muscle in his body come alive. He longed for her. There simply wasn't another way to describe this deep, intense yearning for the small, prickly woman before him.

Alex didn't move or turn as he said her name. She looked straight ahead, as if frozen in place before the cage. Her voice quivered.

"Stalking innocent women again, Lord Cambourne?"

"Perhaps. Or badgers. I am partial to badgers."

"Are we back to seeing me as an irritable rat again, Lord Cambourne?" Still, Alex refused to face him. The pale blue gown she wore made her chestnut curls shine and the pale skin of her neck gleam like a slice of moonlight. Her outlandish hair struggled mightily to escape its confines. One shiny hairpin busily worked its way loose as he watched. His gaze fell to her waist, running up her back to the long string of satin covered buttons. Sutton had an unnatural fascination for her back. He longed to see the naked flesh hidden behind the satin.

His fingers wandered to the line of buttons. He rotated each one, wiggling the button just so as he imagined undressing her.

"Please leave me be, Lord Cambourne. I beg you. I have not the strength of will to fight you." Sad and despondent, her voice shook as she spoke.

He resolved to comfort her only. "Turn and look at me. Tell me what is wrong that has you weeping on the shoulder of a capuchin monkey."

Her head shook in denial. The hairpin fell to the floor. A curl flowed down her back and fell on his fingers where they touched the buttons.

Sutton's finger shook. He determined to just hold her. To offer assistance.

She shivered under his touch, arching as he twisted the buttons. "Why?" Her shoulders moved. The satin rippled underneath his hand. "Why do you care?"

Sutton pondered that difficult question. How to explain to Alex that he wanted her. But it was more than wanting. He desired the whole of her for an inexplicable reason. She called to something deep inside of him. The Badger belonged to him. Just thinking about Alex with Runyon filled him with blinding rage. No amount of brandy, nor the charms of every beautiful woman in London, not even the thought of returning to Macao, drove thoughts of Alex from his mind. Seeing Runyon put his hands on the Badger, his *Alex*, made Sutton nearly insane. Sutton had many reasons for wanting Archie dead, but he had found another. Alex.

Afternoon sun peeked through the skylight above their heads, casting shadows across the path through the exhibit hall. The silence was so complete he heard each breath she took. His fingers lingered over the buttons.

"I wish you to call me Sutton." The words hovered in the quiet.

Why didn't she say something? Move away?

Sutton blew a puff of air on her neck, unable to resist the tiny curls at the base. The curls swayed as if buffeted in a breeze. He tugged the long curl that fell over his hand.

The Badger moaned softly. She arched her back, lowering her head slightly to give him access to her neck.

Sutton's heart thudded. He pressed his lips to her skin and nibbled, teasing a path with his tongue. He wanted to devour her.

Her hands grabbed the bars of the cage in front of her, as if she would fall without support. She gasped.

Sutton thought of throwing her skirts up and taking her here, in the exhibition hall while she grabbed the cage. A growl escaped his throat.

"Please." Alex gave a smoky whisper.

"Please what, Alex? Please take you here? Please kiss you? Fuck you until you are senseless?"

He heard her intake of breath at the crudity of his words, but she didn't flinch. He was nearly blind with the lust he felt for this woman. Sutton wanted nothing in his life as much as he wanted Alex. His bookish badger from Hampshire.

Alex made a small cry like a trapped bird. She turned slightly as if to flee him.

"No." His lips whispered against her neck. His arm wrapped around her waist. "I want you."

"Lord Cambourne." She panted. "Sutton," she implored. "Please let me go. We cannot. I *cannot.*"

"Don't be afraid of me. Badgers are fearless, are they not? Certainly not afraid of peacocks." Sutton swiftly turned her to face him.

Gray eyes, full of trepidation and want looked up at him.

His eyes fell to her breasts, her magnificent breasts, and he imagined he could see the nipples tighten beneath his gaze.

"Come with me, little one." His arousal was uncomfortably hard in his breeches. He pulled her against him and brushed a kiss against her lips. "Please, Alex."

A gloved finger reached up and ran down his face. Like the kiss of a butterfly. Fear warred with desire. He could see it in her face.

She gave a hesitant nod.

Sutton's mind chided him for taking undue advantage of the Badger in her distress. He didn't care. His hand closed around her wrist tightly, giving her no opportunity to flee. Sutton pulled her down the exhibit hall to a small door he noticed earlier. A maid's closet. Grabbing her by the waist, he nudged her into the small space ahead of him. He pulled the door shut, plunging the closet into darkness. The room smelled of lye and beeswax. Sutton kicked a pail aside with his foot and hauled Alex up against him.

❧

I HAVE LOST MY MIND. ALEXANDRA WONDERED AT HER actions. A bit of light filtered underneath the door, enough so that she could see Sutton's outline, if not his features. She could smell lye. He'd pulled her into a cleaning closet. She should open the door and run as fast and as far from this man as she could. But she hadn't the strength or the will. She wanted him. Just for a moment. Before she faced reality. Mr. Runyon. Betrothal. Marriage.

Strong hands moved down her arms from her shoulders. Heat shot out from his fingers as he caressed and molded her flesh.

A shaky breath escaped her lips. She must tell him. Tell him the thing that now hung around her neck like some ill-gotten albatross. "I shouldn't be here with you, Lord Cambourne."

"Sutton."

"Sutton," she pleaded. "I will be missed."

"You won't be missed for a time."

"There are circumstances that you may not be—" The rest of her sentence was cut off by the warmth of his mouth. His lips pressed against hers, insisting and demanding a response. Tenderly, he forced her mouth open. The tip of his tongue touched her own. Her lips responded as her tongue twined around his.

Sutton groaned in satisfaction. He enveloped her in his arms.

Cinnamon. He smells of cinnamon. She clutched at him

tighter. Her hands worked up the muscled chest and around his back to lie against his shoulder blades. She imagined the dragon on his back sensuously moving against her palms.

One large hand moved from the small of her back to cup her breast.

An unladylike moan came from her lips.

Fingers slowly circled the nipple. He flicked the hardened peak.

A spurt of warmth rushed down between the apex of her thighs. The sensitive peak of her nipple throbbed deliciously.

He pulled his mouth from hers. The tip of his tongue blazed a trail up her neck to her ear, lightly skimming the lobe and laving the inside with tiny, darting strokes.

Alexandra felt taut, wild, and trapped in too many layers of chemise and petticoats. Her entire body ached with need, a need she didn't understand.

Sutton pushed against her, gentle but demanding, forcing her to bend to him. He twisted sensuously, so she could feel the hardness of his arousal. Cool air ran across her breasts, the skin puckering as the buttons popped on her bodice. She jumped in shock as the warmth of Sutton's mouth closed over her nipple.

He suckled, nipping at the peak with his teeth.

Alexandra thrust her breasts up to Sutton. She behaved as a wanton. Her fingers wrapped themselves in his hair, urging him to suckle harder. All rational thought flew from her mind. A low moaning sounded in the closet and she realized with astonishment the noise came from her. Boldly, Alexandra nipped Sutton on the neck, tasting the cinnamon of his skin.

Sutton made a primal noise. His mouth moved from her breast.

"No," she begged.

"Shush." Sutton's large hands cradled her head. He leaned forward.

The pad of his thumb ran over her swollen lips.

Alexandra panted lightly. She didn't want him to stop.

"Alex." Sutton carefully put his nose against hers, rubbing them together gently. The gesture was so intimate, so loving, she came undone.

"Sutton, please, I must tell you..."

"Shush. Not now. Not here. Later."

He brought his large body down in one fluid motion, his hands around her waist. One hand strayed from her side, reaching beneath the layers of silk and petticoats to run up her leg. Her calves tensed, the cool air of the closet a tickle against her hose. Something brushed against her thigh—his mouth.

"I want to bury myself in you. Wrap your hair around my wrist and bind you to me." The words, possessive and sexual, flew from his lips in a harsh whisper.

The pressure between her thighs mounted. The ache intensified at his words. In the darkness it was easy to imagine the dragon's tail winding around her and Sutton, binding them together.

Warm fingers traveled to the middle of her thigh, stopping at her garter. The other hand let go of her waist. Taking a grasp of her skirts, he twisted them and threw the folds of fabric over his shoulder.

"One day soon I will have you spread before me," the dark, husky voice intoned, "with your hair spilling around you, clad in nothing but your stockings and garters. Your very essence open to me."

Aroused at the image his words brought to mind, Alexandra almost fainted.

His fingers glided over the thin cotton of her drawers,

seeking the opening. Fingers, warm and sensual, plucked at the fabric.

Her mound thrust against his questing hand. The warm mist of his breath scorched her drawers. He pulled the string of her drawers gently with his teeth until they fell away. Intimately exposed, she shied in embarrassment.

"Mmm. No." His thumb prodded at her slit, parting the folds of flesh to massage the hidden nub. Sensations shot through her. The thumb ran back and forth over the tender peak.

"Oh, God," she gasped.

One large finger slid inside her folds, inside her, while his thumb continued to put pressure on the nub. The pleasure was intense, excruciating, *forbidden*.

"Does that feel good, little Badger?"

"Having seduced many women," she panted, "I would assume you know it feels good. Arrogant p-pea-peacock." The pressure inside her built.

Sutton sucked in his breath. "Yes, but none I wanted to pleasure as much as you, my Badger. Put your hands on my shoulders." His voice was rough. Demanding.

She complied, grasping the fabric at his shoulders. The dragon nipped at her fingers.

Alexandra was immediately rewarded for her compliance as another digit joined the first. Her inner core expanded, stretched wickedly to wrap around his fingers.

"Oh, my."

The thumb suddenly stopped its ministrations.

Alexandra wanted to scream in frustration. Was he stopping? Like an animal she moved her hips towards his hand seeking, wanting.

The two fingers inside her, wiggled.

"Oh God, *please* Sutton."

"Please what, sweetheart?"

Her heart flipped at hearing the endearment from his lips. Her nipples hard and sensitive begged for his ministrations. Alexandra would burst if he didn't touch her again.

She sobbed. "I don't know what I want. I don't know what to ask for."

"Tell me you want me. I want to hear you say it."

His tongue flicked lightly against the sensitive nub. His fingers, still buried deep within her, moved in time with his tongue.

She thrust herself against his mouth.

Sutton held her firmly. The tongue flicked and retreated. The ache built inside her, needy, demanding.

Alexandra's muscles clenched around his fingers, "Please." She wanted his mouth on her again.

"Say it." His tongue rasped against her flesh. "Say it or I'll stop." The sensation traveled all the way down her body. She heard herself moan.

"I want you. Only you." She said it as if she were begging for food. As if she were burning in flames, and only he could rescue her.

His mouth settled back over her as he thrust a third finger deep into her. Alexandra cried out. The intensity of his fingers and the stroke of his tongue gave way to a fine, intense pinpoint of pleasure. Her body tensed. The pressure of his mouth increased, his fingers thrust into her.

A white-hot bolt of intense ecstasy shot through her. Wave upon wave of pleasure so powerful, so forceful, that she cried out. Nothing she'd ever read, nor any cautionary tale heard from her Aunt Eloise, had prepared Alexandra for the wealth of pleasure she experienced at Sutton's touch.

"Sutton, Sutton." She sobbed his name, her heart and body filled with this man. Only this man.

He clasped her tightly. His tongue continued to stroke her until her body stopped its wild movements.

The sensations faded. The jerking of her body stopped. She felt bloodless, boneless, limp and weak. If he hadn't held her, she would likely have collapsed into a heap on the floor.

His hands left her body. A kiss pressed against her womanhood. Then the kisses moved down her leg, as he carefully retied her drawers and lowered her skirt. He murmured something against her thigh in a soothing tone. His lips touched her thigh in reverence. Breathing heavily, his fingers trailed down her leg to her ankle.

Sutton grabbed her hand and pressed it against the arousal in his trousers.

Alexandra didn't flinch. Instead she traced the hard, uncompromising shape with her fingers.

He groaned, the sound loud and male. He brushed his mouth against hers.

She could taste herself on his lips.

Standing, he held her in his arms. One hand stroked the side of her neck. He whispered dark, erotic words of the pleasure he wished them to find together.

She nestled closer to his chest, wishing for this to never end. Ashamed and broken with the knowledge of what she needed to tell him, she pulled from his arms. She was betrothed to a man Sutton hated. He would never forgive her.

"Alex? What is it, Badger?" He grasped her shoulders in the darkness, the fingers gently fitting the buttons of her bodice. "Did I hurt you?"

Alexandra made a small cry of distress. "Sutton." She cleared her throat and pushed his hands away. She couldn't make him out in the darkness, but she sensed he was frowning at her, perplexed by her attitude. "I must tell you. Please try to understand—"

Sutton backed away from her so violently his large body collided with the shelves behind him. Cleaning supplies fell to the floor and the smell of lye filled the small space.

"Alex. What have you done?" he rasped.

"You need to understand. People depend on me. People—"

"Runyon. You have *betrothed* yourself to Runyon."

Alexandra made tiny sobbing noises, her heart breaking apart like a glass vase someone had dashed against a stone floor. "Please let me explain. I deserve your disgust. Truly." Tears ran down her face. "But Helmsby Abbey. My home. I had no choice, don't you see? There is no one else. He promised...." She babbled, sounding like a lunatic in Bedlam.

"You are marrying him for a *farm*?" He shoved her against the wall, hurting her. "You scoffed at my offer, made me feel as if I was the very epitome of depravity, for even suggesting that the innocent Alexandra Dunforth be my mistress."

"I thought you toyed with me. I know now that's—"

He continued as if she hadn't spoken. "What a pity I didn't know your price to become a whore was an acre of dirt in Hampshire. The highly principled Miss Dunforth. In the end, you are exactly like every other woman I know. You are just much *cheaper*."

"Please, Sutton. Listen to me."

"You would rather be Runyon's whore? Then so be it." Sutton snarled. "To think I actually considered—" His words ended abruptly.

Alexandra shook her head. Her blood drummed in her ears. "It's not like that. I need to make you see—"

"Shut up." He grabbed her chin roughly, turning her head so that he could whisper in her ear, his tone full of disgust. "No better than a *whore*." He dropped her chin as if the feel of her flesh tarnished him. "Is that what you were doing that day at my grandmother's? Did you think to tell her I seduced you, so you could negotiate for your farm? No wonder you were so surprised when I appeared. I scuttled your plans, didn't I?"

Pain and hurt roared through Alexandra, making her stomach twist into knots. *I will not survive this. I cannot listen to any more*. A horrible retching sound came from her mouth. She opened the closet door and picked up her skirts. Her eyes filled with tears, blinding her, as she stumbled out into the hallway. She ran full tilt into someone who held her by the shoulders. Miranda.

"Alexandra. What's happened?" Miranda's brow furrowed in surprise as she looked at Alexandra. She quickly leaned over, adjusting Alexandra's bodice. "Oh, Alexandra."

Alexandra shook her head. "Oh God, what have I done?"

"Look at me, Alexandra," Miranda said in a low tone, "others are watching."

Lord Tasterly, from behind Miranda, cleared his throat. "Lady Miranda, your brother is here."

"Miranda," Alexandra whispered, "I need to leave. Please, away from everyone. Especially your brother." She was dying inside. Her heart would stop beating. Her noble sacrifice on behalf of Helmsby Abbey brought her little comfort. She destroyed her heart's desire. How could she marry Mr. Runyon? How could she not?

Miranda straightened, shielding Alexandra's much smaller body with her own. "It's all right," she said to the small group that rounded the corner of the exhibition. "A snake in the exhibition startled Miss Dunforth. I believe she's turned her ankle."

Someone in the crowd gave a gasp of fright. Alexandra thought it sounded like Lady Atkins.

"Come Miss Dunforth, Lord Tasterly will see you to my carriage." Miranda waved at Lord Tasterly. "My lord, would you assist us?"

"Of course!" he choked out, sparing a glance at Lord Cambourne to see if the Marquess would disagree.

Alexandra wanted to cry out that Sutton would not

object, in fact, she was quite certain Sutton could care less whether she expired on the spot or not. Grief wracked Alexandra's body. She shook uncontrollably.

Gingerly, Miranda led Alexandra away to the main hall, assisted by Lord Tasterly. Alexandra heard Lord Tasterly murmur a "my lord" as they passed Lord Cambourne. She did not look up.

Sutton did not attempt to stop them.

Miranda made soothing sounds as she led Alexandra towards the main entrance. "I will have the Cambourne coach take you home."

Every step took Alexandra farther from Sutton. She'd misjudged him. Loss, dark and gaping, smothered her taking her breath away. She stumbled.

Miranda caught her and gently placed Alexandra inside the Cambourne coach. "Please see Miss Dunforth home," she instructed the groom. "You may return for Lord Cambourne and myself, later." Miranda squeezed Alexandra's hand. She looked over her shoulder at her brother, who watched them with hooded eyes from the entrance. "Alexandra?" She lowered her voice, so the groom would not hear. "What happened to leave you in such a state?"

Alexandra blinked back tears. She would brave this out. Her chin lifted. "I simply informed Lord Cambourne of my betrothal to Mr. Runyon."

Miranda said nothing. She swallowed hard. "Oh no, Alexandra." Miranda's lovely face crumpled. She shook her head and disengaged Alexandra's hands from her own. The groom shut the carriage door. Alexandra could stand it no longer. She began to weep.

Damn her! His mind refused to accept the truth of Alex's words. Refused to acknowledge the anguish her words caused to his heart. He convinced himself it was only that he was thwarted in his lust. There were many women in the world. He did not need to suffer the loss of a temperamental spinster from Hampshire. Alexandra was like every other woman. Runyon simply made her a better offer. Sutton merely made a mistake. Alexandra was *not* different. Providence allowed him to find out before he made an ass of himself. Sutton made the incorrect assumption that Alexandra wanted *him*. Not the Marquess of Cambourne. Not Satan Reynolds. *Him*. Pity he didn't know earlier her price was a farm. No matter. He intended on either killing Archie or sending him to the continent.

An unexpected wave of longing washed through him. *Alex*.

Did she care for Runyon? Share his proclivities? The thought made Sutton ill. No. Her response to Sutton had been innocent and untried. Alexandra had not been with another man. He did not believe the awful words he flung in anger at her. He refused to believe she married Runyon because she wanted to.

A distant memory came to him, from his time at Eton. Three boys, all despised by the other youths, and tormented daily by the headmaster for their perceived flaws. Colin smuggled in a bottle of whiskey, good Irish whiskey, from his father's study. The three ran and hid on the edge of the woods, drinking until the bottle emptied. Nick said a man in the village told him that an old gypsy woman lived by the river. She told fortunes.

Drunk, but in agreement to have their futures told, the three made their way to the river and spied the Gypsy wagon. An old nag, barely able to stand, was tethered to the wagon. The old woman didn't flinch as the trio approached. Laughing, the three sat as the crone cackled in delight at their appearance.

Colin shouted they wanted their fortunes told. Our fates should make the other boys respect us. Make us sound dangerous he said, so that the other boys will learn to stay away.

'I've been waiting for you, my Wickeds,' the crone laughed. 'All cursed, aren't you?' Her gaze fell on Nick. *'We share an ancestor.'*

Nick shrank back in horror.

The crone reached out and grabbed Sutton. She held his chin, turning his head back and forth, as if examining him for flaws. One claw-like hand stroked his cheek. *'A terrible beauty you are. They say the devil was once an angel as well.'* His looks were a curse, she said, for no one would ever look past his face to see the soul encased therein.

The crone terrified Sutton. He tried to pull away from her grasp.

She laughed, coughing up brown spittle. The spittle hung from her withered lips. Grabbing his left hand, she traced the lines of his palm with a yellow cracked nail. Her eyes, nearly concealed by sagging folds of flesh, sparkled with a supernatural intelligence. *'Women will desire you. You have only to look at them to seduce them. No woman will be able to resist you.'* Colin and Nick burst into gales of laughter, their fear momentarily forgotten. Nick made several lewd comments. *'But your life will be controlled by the jealous envy of others. You will be marked for it.'* Sutton shrank back, his eyes never leaving the crone's face. *'And love? You will love only once, the same as your father.'*

Nick dropped the whiskey bottle. Colin coughed nervously.

Sutton pulled his hand away from the crone. How could she know? How could she *possibly* know about his parents?

The crone chuckled at his discomfort. *'The woman you desire above all others will belong to one whom you wish to destroy.*

You will never possess her. You will yearn for her all the days of your life.'

The memory dimmed. He was once again at the Royal Exhibition. Sutton clenched his fists tightly. He didn't believe in prophecy.

14

Nicholas Tremaine, Viscount Lindley, strolled into White's, watching with amusement as liveried toadies ran to take his cloak. He shrugged the wet wool off his massive shoulders and threw the cloak at one of the scurrying men. The other toadies looked at Nick in thinly veiled disapproval, but their mouths remained firmly shut. Nick was barely admitted at White's and he was sure the admittance committee brought up his disbarment from the establishment on an annual basis. It was of no import. If one was the heir to a wealthy dukedom, no matter the infamy of that dukedom, one was admitted to White's. Besides, he wasn't here to bask in the aura of the indolent gentlemen that filled the rooms. He was here for Satan Reynolds.

Nick called earlier for Cam at his friend's home only to be told by the butler, some arrogant Scot that Cam employed, that his lordship had left that afternoon to hear Lord Bishop speak. No one adored a boring, tedious lecture more than Cam, but it was past the dinner hour and his friend had not returned home. Given that Cam seemed to attract persons who wished to murder him since his return from Macao, Nick thought it appropriate to locate his best friend.

Nick next visited Cambourne House, praying as he rarely did, that he would not have to make polite niceties with Cam's stepmother, the Marchioness. Lady Cambourne annoyed Nick so fiercely that when he saw her his hands itched to snap her neck. He well remembered her treatment of Cam during his entire childhood, and how she'd forced his departure to Macao. Nick hated the woman.

He had started to ask for the Dowager at the door but was stopped by the appearance of Miranda. Cam's sister was not a woman given to hysterics. She looked quite lovely in her distress, but Nick ignored the attraction as such a thing could cost him a valued friendship. Miranda was firmly off limits.

Instead, he sat down with Cam's sister and gently asked her what in bloody hell had happened? Between sobs, Miranda related that Archie Runyon was back in London and betrothed to someone named Alexandra. Before Nick could ask why any of that mattered, Miranda flew up the stairs in a fit of tears.

Nick pushed aside Miranda's behavior earlier and returned his attention to the great room of White's. *Ah! There he was.* Satan Reynolds! Nick adored calling Cam by that hideous nickname since he knew how his friend detested it. Ridiculous though the name was it suited Cam. Cam was entirely a devil when it came to women. He avoided innocents and those women who seemed to be in love with their husbands, although those females were few and far between in the *ton*. Nick thought that sporting of Cam, not to take undue advantage. Because Cam could, if he wished. Women flocked to him like bees to honey, throwing themselves at him like lemmings going over a cliff. Cam said he only seduced the women that *deserved* to be seduced by Satan Reynolds.

Nick lifted one dark brow at the sight of Cam holding a

glass of whiskey with one unsteady hand. How the *ton* would be shocked to know that the terribly foxed man sitting before Nick spoke five languages, wrote travel essays under a pen name, and would have done well as a professor or scholar.

Cam sat in a dank, dark corner of White's with a large, expensive bottle of whiskey his only companion. He grunted in greeting at Nick and proceeded to wave an unsteady hand towards a chair to his right.

Nick assumed that an invitation of sorts. Eyeing the narrow leather chair, he grimaced. Did White's have nothing bigger in this blasted place? For God's sake, what did he pay a fortune in dues for? White's should provide proper furniture for all its members. He twisted, trying to mold his large, muscular frame into the fragile chair. The chair protested his weight, squeaking and wobbling a bit, but held. Nick sighed in frustration.

"Dear God, Nick." Cam slurred. "Pray, do not destroy yet another piece of furniture. The Dowager is still distressed about the couch in her music room."

"Hmm. Well that was shoddy workmanship, although I didn't wish to risk her offense by saying so."

Cam grinned. "Cobbs!"

A man standing discreetly in the shadows stepped forward.

"A glass for Viscount Lindley."

"Yes, my lord." The unflappable Cobbs scurried off.

"So, this is what has become of the great and dangerous Satan Reynolds. Sitting alone with nothing but an overeager servant and an expensive bottle of whiskey." Nick peered at the bottle. "Looks Scottish. Likely quite peaty." As he sat back the chair groaned in protest. "You're horribly foxed, Cam. What calamity has occurred to put you in such a state? Did Bishop's lecture not sufficiently bore you to tears? Did your latest volume of the history of the pyramids not arrive on time?"

Cam scowled at him.

"Oh, I know. A woman was immune to your charms." He winked at Cam, grinning evilly. Nick was afraid of nothing in this world, certainly not Cam in a foul temper. Now the *next* world, if one believed in such things, was open for discussion. Nick wasn't concerned. Being one of the damned, and already destined for hell, meant one didn't worry about such things.

He stretched out his long legs deciding how to broach the subject of Runyon, without Cam going completely mad. Nick suspected the unknown Alexandra played a part in Cam's drunken revelry. *Curious*. Cam did not drink himself into a stupor over women. Time to go fishing and see what he caught.

"Who is she?" He took a sip of the whiskey savoring the warmth that flowed down to his stomach. *Delicious*. A bit peaty, with a smoky finish, as he'd assumed.

Cam huffed and looked away.

Nick swirled the whiskey around the inside of his mouth. The stuff really was quite good. He held his glass out to Cobbs, who promptly refilled it. "Give over, Cam."

"Alexandra Dunforth." Cam muttered. One of his eyes nearly shut, then snapped back open. He spilled a bit of the whiskey on his breeches.

Nick tried to keep the shock from his face. It took an enormous amount of liquor to make Cam unsteady. In fact, the last time Nick heard Cam slur in such a fashion had been at Eton. Whiskey was the culprit that time as well. Cam's tolerance for alcohol added luster to his nickname at Eton, since he drank like the devil, with few ill effects. Unlike poor Colin, who could be found stumbling after two glasses of Madeira.

"Alexandra Dunforth? I don't believe I've made her

acquaintance. I rather thought someone died with the long face you're wearing and your sister sobbing away on my shoulder."

Cam sputtered.

"Oh, don't *frown* so, I didn't touch Miranda. She cried *properly* on my shoulder." Nick popped his knuckles and took another sip of the whiskey. He waited.

Cam remained stubbornly silent.

Nick shrugged. He had no other entertainments scheduled for tonight and his curiosity was piqued. Cam's face had grown dark and he resembled an angry, avenging angel. St. Michael or another enraged cherub, perhaps. A multitude of women would swoon over Cam should they see him so upset. Females found Cam most attractive when he brooded.

"I'm not sure what the problem is," he chuckled. "One woman is much like another. You lift their skirts over their heads, and it's difficult to tell them apart. I find throwing the skirts up cuts down on female chattiness. The silk tends to muffle the noise."

Cam shot him a look of distaste.

My, this is serious indeed. He assumed a stern demeanor, determined to get to the bottom of things. "Really Cam, what is this Alexandra Dunforth to you? You've shown no pointed interest in any woman since your return. I've *never* seen you give a fig for any of the fairer sex, excepting your sisters and the Dowager. Did she injure you in some way?" Nick's opinion of females tended to be low in general, although he did have a deep affection for his own sister and a healthy fear of Cam's grandmother, which he supposed could be construed as a type of affection. "Is she trying to have you murdered? London is suddenly populated with assassins and you their prey."

Cobbs coughed delicately from the shadows.

Cam's head lolled sideways. It took more than a moment for him to respond.

"No! She is a tiny, foul-tempered, opinionated little Badger! With curling hair. Lots of it." Wistfully he sighed, sloshing whiskey over the fine leather chair.

Cobbs pursed his lips and immediately wiped up the spill.

"You know how I love curls." Cam struggled to focus. "Love them."

Nick would soon need an interpreter if the evening went on much longer. Cam was *very* drunk. "Yes, you've mentioned that to me before. Every curly-haired whore in London propositioned you after you voiced your preference at Covent Garden. Ladies of the *ton* swarmed Bond Street purchasing every curling iron available after you spoke of your obsession at Lord Meriam's fete. So, this Alexandra is curly-haired. That is not an excuse for your present state. Did she refuse your attentions? Is she insane? Crazed? Does she not know you are a great seducer of women?"

"Yes. I mean, *no*. Well, I don't know. I don't think she's mad." Cam struggled to sit up. "Nick, she is *betrothed*."

Nick had never seen Cam so unhappy. Especially not over a woman. He must tread carefully. "Perhaps you can have Alexandra after the wedding? I'm not sure a husband in the picture presents much problem if a woman is willing. I still remember Lord Ranson shooting off his toe." A deep belly laugh erupted from Nick.

Across the room, a group of gentlemen sat discussing politics or something equally dull. The men turned towards Nick in unison all bearing frowns of disapproval. One man, over-dressed in a hideous dark plum jacket, put his pudgy fingers to his lips and made a *shushing* noise. The man turned back to his friends, nodding as if to say he'd taken care of the issue.

Nicholas bared his teeth and growled.

A portly man sitting next to Mr. Hideous Plum Coat

mouthed the words *"Devil of Dunbar"* and attempted to point discreetly at Nick.

Mr. Hideous Plum Coat looked chagrined and much less smug. He swallowed, and Nick saw the folds of fat around the man's chin shake. After a moment, the men scattered like a flock of frightened geese.

"You see, Cam, I can clear a room in no time." Sometimes, Nick mused, it was *hard* to be one of the damned.

His friend took a deep breath, his forehead creasing with consternation. Worry stamped every line of his handsome features. "Archie is back, Nick. He is *here*, in *London*. That bitch my father had the bad sense to marry neglected to inform the family. The news sent Grandmother to bed for two days."

"A terrible pity that bastard didn't die abroad. It would have saved you the eventual trouble of killing him. Shame your father spared his life. What is he up to, do you suppose? Does Elizabeth—?"

"No. She remembers nothing, thank God." Cam's brow furrowed again. "At least, we don't think she does."

"I would be happy to dispose of him, should you wish it. Consider it a favor." Deadly serious, he sipped at his whiskey. Nick was quite good at killing men. A useful skill if one was already destined for hell for there were no repercussions to be concerned with.

"No. I will do...do...do it myself. When the time comes," Cam stuttered.

Nick thought the time likely near. The hourglass measuring Archie's life had started to run out the moment he foolishly returned to London. It was no coincidence that Archie returned just as the attempts on Cam's life multiplied. "What does Archie have to do with your Miss Dunforth?"

"She's...she's...inclined to wed him." Cam's entire form

deflated as if he would fall into a pool of despondency at any moment.

Nick wasn't quite sure how to address *that* comment. "What would you *want* with a woman that is inclined to marry Runyon?" He pretended to pick a spot of lint off his coat. Archie Runyon was well known among the *ton* for his depravities, some acts so repulsive that even Nick was shocked by them. A rarity.

"She is a *badger*. Badgers are not like other women. She is only marrying him because of the Abbess."

"She is marrying him because some papist nun is forcing her?" Good Lord he could barely make out Cam's words.

"No. Jush lishen to me." Cam's head rolled around. "Abbey. I meant Abbey. Helmsby Abbey. It's a place where all badgers wish to be."

That didn't make a bit of sense to Nick. The only thing that *did* make sense was Cam's obvious infatuation with this Alexandra. Unless Archie Runyon had changed drastically after receiving a beating from Sutton's father, which Nick found doubtful, a woman who would wish to marry Archie would have to share the man's *tastes*.

"Are you sure, Cam, there is no possibility that this Alexandra just *prefers* Runyon to you? He promised her an estate she covets, and possibly they share common...*interests*." There were some women who enjoyed the types of sex play that Archie and his cohorts engaged in.

"Women are shallow, vapid creatures, as well you know. I personally have dozens throwing themselves at me regardless of my faults." Nick waved a large hand across his frame. "The Dunbar fortune and the possibility of being a Duchess is enough to entice any woman of the *ton* to spread her legs. Even if she is afraid of me. Perhaps Alexandra is no different, though possibly you wish her to be."

Cam's face contorted in rage.

"I shall beat you to a bloody pulp for that remark. She is a *badger*!" Cam turned and swallowed the entire contents of his glass, gesturing to the attentive Cobbs for more.

Nick wondered what Alexandra had in common with a large rodent. Certainly, the lady in question could not find it flattering.

A growl sounded from Cam. "I want her."

Nick was certain, especially after this conversation, that what Cam felt for this Alexandra was a bit more than lust. He attempted to twist himself into a more comfortable position. Impossible. The chair was simply too small. *Damn*. Wasn't it enough to be cursed with his freakish eyes? Must he also look as if he'd descended from giants?

A curious sense of déjà vu floated over Nick as he threw one leg over the arm of the chair. In his mind's eye he saw three young men, misfits of the *ton*, tormented relentlessly by the other youths at Eton. The gypsy. She'd made a prophecy for each of them. A sense of unease filled Nicholas as he remembered what the old woman foretold for Cam. It was a coincidence, nothing more.

He pushed aside the prediction the hag had made for him.

"You want her, so have her. Cuckolding Runyon certainly could not cause you to lose sleep, besides you're likely to make her a widow soon at any rate if I'm not mistaken."

"But she is innocent. She is a *badger*." Cam spilled whiskey onto the dark leather of his chair once more.

Cobbs rushed forward like an industrious mouse to mop it up.

"But yet, your paragon is willing to marry Runyon?"

Cam gave a despondent nod. A great sigh came from him.

Nicholas wondered how long Cam had sat at White's nursing his whiskey along with his anger.

"Cobbs?" Nick said to the servant. "How long and how many?"

Cobbs held up one finger. "He finished the first bottle completely before you arrived. He's been here since before tea."

Good Lord. This was most serious indeed.

Nick stood and pulled at the cuffs of his jacket to straighten them over his wrists. The chair creaked in relief as his form left it. Nicholas shot the offending piece of furniture an exasperated look.

The drunken idiot sitting across from Nick muttered something incomprehensible, before closing his eyes.

"Cam," Nick peered down at his friend. "You realize you are in love with her?"

A drunken snore was the only answer he received.

Nick waved an arm at the helpful Cobbs. "Help me get him to his carriage. I'll see him home.

❧ 15 ❧

Jeanette Runyon Reynolds, the current and forever Marchioness of Cambourne, if she had her way, surveyed the ballroom of Gray Covington with a militant eye. She adored Gray Covington, the Cambourne estate just outside London. Not because she liked the country, of course. Country life was dull and drab. No, it was because the building and grounds bore a vague resemblance to the gardens of Versailles, the grand palace built for the French kings. There was simply no finer setting for Jeanette's beauty nor a better place to remind the *ton* of the wealth and affluence of the Cambournes. Particularly Jeanette.

Mentally she checked off the myriad of decorations ordered earlier, making sure all was *just so*. The staff of Gray Covington complained that what Lady Cambourne wished was *impossible*. They could not complete the Herculean tasks given them to her satisfaction. Jeanette replied that it had better be done to her exact specifications or she would find a staff capable of handling her instructions. Did they all wish to sleep on the streets of London tonight? The entire staff ran around her skirts like rats after her casual question, anxious to serve her. She shrugged her silk-clad shoulders. Threats were necessary when dealing with underlings.

Jeanette's gaze lingered over the beauty of the ballroom. The walls and ceiling of *her* ballroom were hung with yards upon yards of gleaming blue silk, dyed so dark it gave the appearance of a midnight sky. Brilliants sewn into the silk represented the stars and the constellations. The designs took a staff of six seamstresses nearly two months to complete. Orion hung just above her head and to her right, Andromeda. She didn't remember the names of the rest. She found astronomy to be a dull subject that was best suited to unattractive old men.

The candlelight flickering in the crystal chandeliers shone against the brilliants, making them wink and sparkle. She adored brilliants. The dazzling stones set off her hair and complexion perfectly. Even a giant silver moon hung in the corner. She had been born at midnight. She wished all of her guests to experience the magnificence of the sky at the time of her birth.

She sniffed the air, enjoying the perfume of her special roses. Midnight Rose was a rare and difficult variety of rose to cultivate. How many gardeners had she fired before finding the one man who could breed the rose? Her cousin Archie loved them as well.

Pale white roses glowed against the dark wall hangings of the ballroom. Large vases filled with the roses were placed in every corner of Gray Covington. Unfortunately, the gardens of Gray Covington had produced only enough blooms for the ballroom. More were needed for her celebration and she was forced to use her florist in London. The ungrateful vendor balked at the large order. She demanded to know why. After all, the florist only grew the roses for Jeanette when she was in London, *didn't he?* Was he selling Midnight Roses, her signature flower to another patron? The florist assured her, bowing and scraping as he did so, that never would he sell the Midnight Rose to anyone else.

The roses had arrived by the cart-load just this morning.

She smiled and allowed the delicate scent to invade her nostrils again. Her birthday ball was *the* event of the Season. The *ton* would talk of nothing else for months. Possibly, even years. Everyone clamored for an invitation. The cost of her birthday celebration was staggering.

Jeanette didn't care a bit about the extravagance. Her dear stepson, Sutton, was paying for it.

Just the thought of Sutton caused a surge of hatred so clear and precise one could cut veal with it. But her face did not betray her thoughts. She'd spent years perfecting a smooth, cultured look that never gave anything away. A frown or a wrinkled brow never crossed her countenance. The ivory porcelain of her skin remained unmarred by the passage of time. Thoughts of that *bastard*, that *usurper* to the Cambourne title, could not be permitted to damage her looks. The women of the *ton* routinely commented on her youthful appearance, in spite of the fact she was mother to a son of Sutton's age. Jeanette gritted her teeth. *Stepson*, she would remind the mindless twits who said such things to her. How could anyone possibly assume she gave birth to him? The thought made her feel soiled.

She had been so *hopeful* he would do the correct thing and die while he was traipsing around the Far East. How that man survived pirates, filthy disease, Chinese warlords, a slight opium addiction, and the assassins Jeanette had dispatched, was anyone's guess.

"You there!" Jeanette's scalding voice touched on a manservant carrying a tray of wine filled goblets.

The manservant quivered like a frightened rabbit as he met Jeanette's gaze.

"Bring the tray."

The manservant lowered his eyes and carefully approached.

Jeanette surveyed the frightened man before her. He displayed the appropriate amount of servitude. She waved him away without taking any wine. She could ill afford to dull her wits for the evening ahead.

The return of Sutton.

She blamed Archie. If only her cousin hadn't been so greedy. The business with Elizabeth had caused Jeanette to lash out at her cousin in anger. Oh, not for Elizabeth's sake, another dull daughter when what Jeanette needed was a son. No, her anger at Archie was for his sheer *stupidity* in putting Jeanette in a most delicate position. Robert, her deceased husband disliked her, but after Elizabeth he actively despised and distrusted her. Robert had beaten her beloved Archie so severely, Jeanette had to spirit Archie away to the Continent. Archie's father soon learned of his son's behavior, courtesy of Robert, and disowned his son. Jeanette cajoled Archie's father as sweetly as she could, but the pair remained estranged. Although it was some comfort that the entire incident caused Robert to collapse in a fit of apoplexy.

Her daughters whined endlessly for their father and prayed daily for his recovery. Jeanette sat dutifully by his bedside, hoping each time he wheezed it would be his last. He clutched that ridiculous miniature of Madeline in his hand, speaking to the dead woman as if she sat holding his hand and not Jeanette. Not that she cared a whit. As soon as Robert died, Jeanette meant to cajole Herbert Reynolds, Robert's cousin, to marry her. Herbert, the poor simple-minded dear was the only other heir to Cambourne besides Sutton. She planned to be the merriest of widows. Then Donata, that meddling battle-ax, intervened.

"Lady Cambourne, felicitations on your birthday." Lady

Thomlinson, her round face wearing a beggar's smile, curtsied low to Jeanette.

Lady Thomlinson's voice forced Jeanette back into the present, away from Robert's sickroom and the mother-in-law she detested. She focused on how much her dear, unlamented husband would detest the fortune spent on her birthday. Jeanette looked down her nose at Lady Thomlinson and nodded, accepting the woman's fealty.

A couple stood to Jeanette's left, politely awaiting notice.

Jeanette turned, flashing a regal smile to hide her dislike. Lord Witherstone and his featherbrained wife. Jeanette found Lady Witherstone particularly tiresome. The woman bore a striking resemblance to a horse. And her voice. High-pitched with a slight lisp like a child, Lady Witherstone's speaking annoyed everyone within hearing. Jeanette wondered how her husband could tolerate the sound. She'd heard rumors he was a bit of a drunkard. That may explain things.

"How lovely the ballroom is Lady Cambourne. I don't believe I have ever beheld such a glorious display!"

Jeanette tried not to cringe outwardly at the sound of that lisp. The woman would be better off not speaking at all.

"Your taste rivals Lady Halston's." Lady Witherstone continued, trying desperately to curry Jeanette's favor. The patronage of the Marchioness of Cambourne was necessary for Lady Witherstone's charity. Something about war orphans. *As if I care. Children are tedious, especially orphans.*

"The roses are simply *divine!*" Lady Witherstone fawned.

Lord Witherstone bowed deeply. His polite gaze rested a bit longer than necessary on the swell of Jeanette's bosom. The aroma of gin clung to him.

Jeanette sent them both an icy grin. She noted with distaste that she could see down Lady Witherstone's bodice.

Lady Witherstone, it appeared, padded herself quite aptly. No wonder her husband searched out greener pastures.

Lady Witherstone raised her head, struggling to stand after the mewling curtsy she bestowed upon Jeanette. Suddenly her nostrils flared like the startled mare she resembled, and her eyes bulged in a most unbecoming fashion. A quiver went through her frame part fear and part anticipation. The way patrons at the zoo looked at tigers. Lady Witherstone's gaze was fixed on something just beyond Jeanette's shoulder.

Jeanette's lips tightened. She had seen the look many times. Bracing herself for the inevitable, she turned.

"Mother, *dear*, there you are." Sutton's deep baritone resounded like a thunderclap.

The absolute hatred she felt for her stepson bubbled up inside her. How *dare* he call her mother! She despised the words from her own children's mouths. Jeanette wondered if it would be bad form to poison Sutton during her birthday celebration.

Sutton Reynolds, Marquess of Cambourne, bore down on her. More handsome than any bastard should be, he bowed low, kissing her hand.

Jeanette felt her lip curl at his false show of solicitude towards her and it took all her strength not to pull her hand back in revulsion. The resemblance to his father, Robert, was so striking it momentarily startled her. Robert, the handsome, rich Marquess who courted her during her first Season. Jeanette had been envied by every unmarried woman in London. He was perfect in every way. At parties she would stare entranced, her arm in his, as they walked by mirrors. She looked simply *divine* on Robert's arm. He had been the perfect setting for the *jewel* of her beauty. Pity he had turned into such a bore.

"Sutton, there you are." The words spilled from her lips

smoothly, without a hint of the dislike. She turned to Lord and Lady Witherstone. "May I present the Marquess of Cambourne."

Lady Witherstone gave a girlish giggle but shied from Sutton, as if he would fall on her like a mad dog. Lord Witherstone clutched her arm in a possessive manner, obviously afraid the depraved Satan Reynolds might abscond with his wife. The couple nodded politely and hastily walked away. Lady Witherstone peered discreetly over her shoulder at Sutton as her husband led her off.

Jeanette stifled a laugh. She hated Sutton but the thought of him pouncing on the horse-faced Lady Witherstone was truly laughable.

"I see you are as charming as ever, aren't you darling?" She threw him an icy glance. "Why, poor Lady Witherstone nearly burst a Bible from her reticule to ward off the *evil* Satan Reynolds."

The large body of her stepson tensed.

Jeanette smoothed her gown and pretended innocence. The nickname started as a tool to humiliate Sutton. Archie thought that cultivating a distasteful reputation for her stepson could prove wise. It was a dreadful miscalculation. The nickname gave Sutton's persona a dark patina but did not destroy him but seemed to make him more attractive.

Sutton lifted one black brow, the green eyes, so like Robert's, filled with dislike. "How you love calling me that, Jeanette. One would think you coined the nickname yourself."

Jeanette smoothed her hair. Her beloved Archie spewed out a continuous stream of venom against Sutton while her stepson had resided at Eton. Jeanette whispered about Sutton's scandalous birth in London, stirring up doubt about his legitimacy. Her plan, naïve in retrospect, was to use the scandal surrounding Sutton's birth as leverage with Robert when Jeanette bore a son. The entire plan had worked to perfection. Sutton unknowingly assisted Jeanette when he seduced the wife of the headmaster at Eton. Unfortunately, Sutton returned unexpectedly to London, to face his father's wrath and witnessed she and Archie 'playing'.

Jeanette had fallen on her knees to plead with her step-son, convincing Sutton that she was pregnant, this time with a son. If anything happened to the child she carried, Robert would be devastated. Between Sutton's behavior at Eton and the questions of his legitimacy, shouldn't he do his father a favor and leave London? Do this one honorable thing for Robert after the disgrace Sutton caused?

Convincing Sutton to leave had been almost too easy. He'd been so malleable as a youth and so uncertain of his legitimacy.

"Ah, what a delight to see the mind of the black widow working through her next scheme. And on her birthday! Well, it goes to show," Sutton whispered low, "that wickedness does not take a holiday."

Jeanette grimaced. Her plan worked, for a time. Sutton disappeared into the jungles of Macao. Unfortunately, he used that ridiculous nickname to his advantage. It became her stepson's calling card. Now men feared and respected Satan Reynolds. Women threw themselves at him in a more appalling manner than before. The whole of it sometimes made her weep in frustration. The worst, however, was his return to London.

"You are the authority on wickedness. I'm afraid I don't have time for your silly accusations," she hissed. "Guests are arriving, and I am the belle of the ball."

"So the bills I continue to receive from your dressmaker, the florist, and a variety of tradesmen I can't even name tell me. I wonder how you shall afford such extravagance in the future."

Jeanette ignored his blatant threat. Eventually, she would hire an assassin that could actually kill her troublesome stepson. Sutton's survival skills, honed during his time away from London, were greater than she'd originally suspected. Thank goodness Archie was back to assist her. "Where is that halfwit sister of yours? I finally resorted to having her maid take her books away, so Miranda would ready herself for this evening. It's bad enough Elizabeth is missing my birthday celebration."

"If I have my way, you will never see Elizabeth again." Sutton smiled, conscious that the room was filled with guests who watched their conversation. His eyes, like green shards of glass, sliced into her flickering with rage.

Jeanette's face froze. Her mind whispered that the man before her was no longer the motherless child she had once abused. Ignoring the trickle of alarm that ran down her spine, she lifted her chin.

"It will be no great disservice to me if I don't see the little twit again, you can be sure. Elizabeth is even duller than Miranda, which is difficult to fathom. Your father made such a fuss. It was only a misunderstanding."

Sutton sucked in his breath.

Her stepson could be *so* predictable. He wished to strangle her. She simply adored ripping out his emotions and waving them in front of his face like a matador's cape with an angry bull. If Sutton had *proof* of Archie's abuse of Elizabeth, her cousin would be dead. Nor could he possibly suspect she was behind the attempts to have him killed. However angry he was. Sutton likely still worshipped her as he had when he was a small boy. How could he not?

She smoothed down his cravat pretending motherly concern "I don't think I shall ever forgive you for refusing Percy Dobson's suit for Miranda. Your sister is a bluestocking and only passably attractive. She chatters incessantly. I once had great hopes for her but now?" Jeanette gave an elegant shrug of her shoulders. "What other man will offer for her? She's practically on the shelf."

Sutton relaxed. He didn't pull away from her touch. Instead, his mouth curved into a smile that did not reach the green glass of his eyes.

Jeanette much preferred his anger. This simply would not do. "She is a—"

"Shut up." He said it quietly. His face shone with manufactured affection.

Jeanette frowned before she could stop herself, then she smiled indulgently. Her guests would remark on what a *loving* relationship she and Sutton shared.

Intolerable.

"Mother, *dear*. Don't frown so. You don't want to wrinkle the perfection of your skin do you? Besides, at your age, *Mother*, you can ill afford wrinkles." His lips still held an affectionate bent, but his words bit through her. "You ceded all responsibility for your daughters. *All*. You are dependent on my charity. You will learn to behave, *Mother*, or I will have you banished to the Continent. Never to return. Perhaps I shall do so anyway."

Sutton lied. The boy who longed for her love was still in the man before her. She knew it. She could still manipulate him. Smiling warmly, she murmured, "Tsk, Sutton, you would never send me away. I am the only mother you have ever known." She placed her hand on his sleeve in a show of affection.

"Then you had better find a more skilled assassin."

Jeanette blinked, and her hand froze.

Bastard. He knew.

She changed tactics to something more proven. "Did I ever tell you that I saw your mother once? The exalted Madeline?" It wasn't true of course but Sutton didn't know that.

A muscle in his cheek twitched.

"Sweet, sweet Madeline. We all know how...*pious* she was. Not her fault she became a rich man's mistress. A vicar's daughter spends all her time on her knees...praying. Right?" She leaned into Sutton's tall form, smelling the musky exotic cinnamon scent that clung to him, wishing for a knife to plunge into his chest.

His nostrils flared, but he said nothing. He merely raised a brow and walked away into the crowd.

Jeanette turned, her lips twisted into a half-smile, to greet Lady Worth. Sutton wouldn't be able to keep his temper in check for long. Archie had imparted the most *delicious* secret to Jeanette.

❧ 16 ❧

There she was. His little pigeon.

Archie Runyon stood just inside the entryway watching in anticipation, as Alexandra and her uncle entered his beloved Jeanette's ballroom. Lord Burke he dismissed with distaste. But Alexandra. Pale and fragile as one of his cousin's beloved roses, she glided towards him. Her dark curls gleamed like a bolt of sable silk in the candlelight. Her manner demure and unassuming. The dark gray silk of her gown clung tightly to her generous breasts while the overskirt of silver floated around her hips. The effect was of Alexandra gliding through a cloud of mysterious mist. Lovely. His gaze ran to the press of her breasts against the bodice of the gown and his mouth watered. Soon.

"Miss Dunforth, my dove, at last you have arrived." He walked forward, clasping her hands in his own.

He noted with distaste that he could feel the iciness of her hands even through the beautiful handmade gloves he'd gifted her with.

Alexandra watched him with detachment. The pupils of

her gray eyes were enlarged. This would *never* do. How much laudanum had she been fed? He glared at Burke.

"Lord Burke. It is only two hours ride from London to Gray Covington. I have been awaiting my fiancée. Impatiently."

Burke flushed at the censorious tone. "Business, Runyon. My apologies."

Archie turned back to Alexandra. "My dove, do you approve of your room? I requested that particular room as it is down the hall from my own. I hoped you would enjoy the view of the gardens. And it is in the family wing. After all, tonight you become my family."

Alexandra murmured a polite reply. Her hands slid from his and hung limply at her side. Good Lord! She looked about to slump to the floor in a stupor. Damn Burke.

"Come." He took her hand, tucking it into the crook of his arm. Archie made a determined effort to control his anger. He had warned Burke about giving Alexandra too much laudanum. Apparently, Burke had ignored Archie's instructions. He would make sure the fat man paid later for his blatant disobedience. "I must introduce you and your uncle to my beloved cousin." He cast a look at Burke. "I'm sure she'll be *delighted* to meet you."

Burke tried to hide his fear and failed.

Archie was sure that Burke would much rather run all the way back to London than face Jeanette Reynolds. The man looked like a fattened pig, about to meet its fate with the butcher.

Lord Burke's steps faltered. He nodded grimly to Archie. "Yes. Of course."

Archie gave Burke a satisfied smile and turned towards his cousin, not waiting to see if Burke would follow. Burke would. Archie owned Burke and his debts.

Archie led Alexandra through the gathered crowd,

ignoring the stares of the curious, and the rudely raised eyebrows as they passed. *Cretins!* Once his estrangement from his father was ended, he and Jeanette would make every gossiping twit in this ballroom pay for the manner in which he was regarded. He made mental notes of who pointed at him from behind fans and whispered behind gloved hands. Once his father welcomed Archie back, and the old codger would once he saw Alexandra, Archie's social standing would be reinstated.

Archie beamed in appreciation as he spied his cousin.

Jeanette's glorious wheat-colored hair sparkled in the candles. Brilliants twinkled at her temples. The tiny crystals were also sewn into her midnight-blue gown, the color of which matched the hangings in the room to perfection. She looked like a fairy princess come to life and walking among the lesser folk. No, Archie thought, a human star, a goddess sparkling amongst the dull women of the *ton*. His heart lurched. He and Jeanette would have done well as man and wife. But Jeanette deserved far better than to be the wife of a third son. He only wished she had found a duke to marry. Or a prince. Not Robert the Rotten.

"My dear Marchioness." Heads turned to watch him and Jeanette.

"Dearest?" Jeanette swung around at the sound of his voice, completely dismissing Countess Rutherford. The glacial gaze fixated on Alexandra for a brief moment, then a stunning smile crossed her face, making her shine as if she were the sun. A light floral scent floated to his nostrils as she moved to take his hands.

Archie disengaged Alexandra's hand from his arm to press a kiss against his cousin's cheek. He bowed and made a sweeping gesture towards Alexandra.

"Lady Cambourne, may I present Miss Alexandra Dunforth."

Alexandra lowered her eyes. She dipped into a perfect curtsy.

Archie was beside himself. Exquisite. He thought of having her half-naked as he forced her to curtsey to him in the evenings. The breaking of Alexandra filled him with anticipation.

"Greetings, Miss Dunforth. It is so lovely to see you again." Jeanette's words held just a note of distaste.

Alexandra paled, the first sign of emotion since she walked through the doors of Gray Covington. She shot Archie a nervous look from beneath her lashes.

Archie smoothed down the ends of his mustache, enjoying her obvious discomfort. Silly pigeon. He knew everything she said or did. He knew she went to tea with the Dowager and to the Royal Exhibition with Miranda. He cataloged her every move.

"Felicitations on your birthday, my lady." Alexandra's voice was low and polite. Respectful. "It is a great honor to attend this occasion."

Jeanette raised an eyebrow while her gaze ran over Alexandra in an attempt to find some insolence or incorrectness in Alexandra's tone.

Archie's chest burst with pride. His dove was perfect.

"A pretty speech, Miss Dunforth." Jeanette turned to Archie, her face relaxing into affection. "How are you this evening, my beloved cousin? I am so thrilled that you are here with me on this important occasion. I could not imagine celebrating without you." She kissed him on both cheeks, making sure everyone saw.

Everyone.

SUTTON WATCHED THE SCENE BEFORE HIM. ARCHIE AND Jeanette fawning over each other made him slightly ill. The memory of that long-ago day, of what he'd witnessed, had dimmed with time, but it was clear enough. His gaze ran to Alexandra. She looked pale and delicate in a diaphanous gray gown. Demure. *Quiet*. Sutton frowned. Quite unlike his Badger. Though she wasn't his at all, it seemed. He considered killing Archie immediately. The man certainly deserved it.

"Your gaze will drill holes through her." The Dowager stomped her cane, as she leaned in next to him.

"Jeanette? I wouldn't do that to her guests. Evil would spill out of her as if she were a sieve, crashing down in a flood infecting her guests."

"Tsk. Obtuse as always. I was speaking of Miss Dunforth." The Dowager pointed with the end of her cane as Alexandra dipped low to pay homage to Jeanette.

"Why would I stare at Archie's betrothed? I've no interest in the girl other than that she is a friend of Miranda's and should know better than to marry Archie Runyon."

"Pish! You are deliberately trying to irritate me, Sutton. Your interest in her is marked and remarked upon," the Dowager stated mysteriously.

"Really? Miss Dunforth is a spinster from Hampshire and a bit long in the tooth. She is engaged to a man I consider the vilest human being in the world. Why would I give a fig for her?"

"I should hit you with my cane. It may knock some sense into you. I have paraded every eligible virgin of the *ton* before you. I have looked the other way at your scandalous behavior with the multitude of women who seem to be enamored of your looks." The Dowager pointed her cane at Jeanette Reynolds. "I have tolerated your lack of ability to dispose of her out of some misbegotten sense of responsibility and duty to your sisters and the reputation of Cambourne. Or perhaps you still seek her love."

Sutton shot his grandmother a disgusted look. "That boy is dead."

"I miss him. He was sweet and scholarly. I failed him." Her gray head dipped.

Exasperated, Sutton touched her hand. "*Rainha*, please." He gave her an imploring look. "Get to the point."

"The point? You want Miss Dunforth."

Sutton sucked in his breath. "She is betrothed to Archie. Nothing short of ruination will break a betrothal. Whether I want Miss Dunforth or not is inconsequential."

The Dowager peered at him in a calculating manner. "Just so."

What was his grandmother up to?

"I will see you in a bit, *Rainha*. I need something stronger if I am to tolerate this evening." He kissed her cheek and headed into the depths of Gray Covington in search of some good French brandy or some of his father's whiskey. Anything to ease the sight of the Badger on Archie's arm.

MR. RUNYON ERUPTED INTO SHRILL GALES OF LAUGHTER AS Lady Cambourne whispered into his ear. Two identical stares of icy blue pierced Alexandra and she had the distinct impression the laughter was at her expense. She didn't care. She wanted nothing more than to drink a cup of Tilda's tea and get away from this teeming mass of people. Alexandra longed to sit somewhere dark and quiet where no one would bother her. Odious Oliver disappeared immediately after greeting Lady Cambourne, no doubt en route to the gaming tables. Alexandra wondered if her uncle would return without his cufflinks, for she doubted any of the Dunforth money still existed.

"Sit here, dear one. I am going to play cards." Mr. Runyon's silken words interrupted her thoughts. He firmly deposited her on a divan situated in a dim alcove.

Two giant potted ferns flanked the divan, no doubt her only companions for this evening. That suited her perfectly. Would anyone mind if she lay down? The divan was surprisingly soft.

"Alexandra?" Mr. Runyon snapped his fingers before her nose.

Why didn't he just go away? She had performed to his expectations. He'd paraded her about the room. She'd curtsied to his beloved cousin. Now all she wanted was to be left alone, to nurse her wounds and perhaps get a glance of Sutton.

"Yes. I shall sit just here." Alexandra nodded as the crowd swirled about her.

He frowned, putting deep creases in his forehead. Did her obedience delight or irritate him? She thought it the latter. She didn't care.

"Hmm." He stroked the ends of his mustache. Alexandra noted that his hair curled a bit farther on the right side. Why had she never noticed the bald spot?

"See that you *do*. Sit here. I shall return in time for our announcement. After we enjoy everyone's good wishes, you and I will be the first into the midnight buffet, directly behind Lady Cambourne. We are to be seated next to her. I hope you appreciate the honor my cousin bestows upon us."

Yes, the great honor being given to poor, spinsterish Alexandra Dunforth. Mutiny flared briefly but faded just as quickly. What did it matter?

"Yes, of course," she murmured.

Appeased, he squeezed her hands and strode in the direction of the gaming tables. She folded her hands into her lap and decided to spend the entire evening watching the colorfully clad ladies of the *ton* and their doting escorts. Now that she had been properly introduced, not one person expressed any inclination to speak to her. She stared into the crowd. The incessant chatter and music now that she was no longer in the midst of it, soothed her nerves.

"Alexandra?"

She jolted upright. Had she dozed?

Miranda appeared before her, looking like a fairy princess in a light green silk gown that matched her eyes. Miranda was so beautiful, just like her brother. Alexandra's heart hurt. Now that having him was out of the question, she missed Lord Cambourne. Dreadfully.

"Alexandra? What is wrong with you?" Dark curls dangled at Miranda's temple as she tilted her head to peer at Alexandra. She waved her fingers in front of Alexandra's face. "Are you foxed?"

"No. I'm fine. My head aches a bit from the excitement. I just need some of my special tea." She had in fact, drunk an entire flask of tea before the ball to steady her nerves. But she wanted more. "I am nervous about the announcement of my betrothal. It's to be tonight." Silently Alexandra wished Sutton to appear. She smiled to herself, imagining the earring swinging jauntily from his ear. He would lean in and-.

"Alexandra?" Miranda moved her face inches from Alexandra's nose.

"Miranda, whatever are you doing?" Alexandra giggled. "Are you going to kiss me?"

Miranda sat back. Her lovely face bore an odd look. "The betrothal is to be announced tonight? Here? Damn."

Alexandra giggled again. "Miranda, such unladylike language. This is not a Lord Thurston novel."

Miranda stood and clasped Alexandra's hand. "I have to

go speak to my grandmother, but will return to collect you promptly. Do not move from this spot."

Alexandra nodded dully. "Everyone wishes me to stay *just here*." She patted the cushions of the divan.

❦

MIRANDA PUSHED THROUGH THE CROWD OF TOADYING sycophants that filled the ballroom of Gray Covington. All here to pay glory to the Marchioness of Cambourne. Her mother. Her lying, deceitful mother. It almost felt as if Gray Covington was being tarnished with the presence of her mother and Cousin Archie. Miranda's father would most certainly not approve.

While she didn't know the exact details of Archie Runyon's banishment to the Continent, Miranda knew it involved her younger sister, Elizabeth. Archie had been at Cambourne House that night with her mother. Miranda had gone to bed but could hear her parents raised voices. She'd come down the stairs and watched in horror as her father hit Jeanette across the face. Mother's head had snapped back before she collapsed sobbing against the wall. Then Father raced out the door, calling for his coach.

Miranda scanned the crowd for either her grandmother or Sutton. The pure fright of that horrible evening washed over her. She remembered seeing the blood on her father's hands upon his return to Cambourne House. He'd beaten Archie Runyon nearly to death. She recalled that her father sent out several letters that night and locked Mother in her chambers. Miranda could still see Father, pale and shaking as he buttered his toast at breakfast while not meeting her eyes. He collapsed before the footman poured his tea. But most of what Miranda remembered was her mother's smug, self-satisfied smile while Father lay dying. A smile that disappeared once Sutton returned to London only days before Father's death.

"Lady Miranda! How lovely you look, why—"

Miranda brushed by Lord Jacobi without a second glance.

She wished with all her heart that her father was still alive. How was it that he died, yet the viper known to the *ton* as Jeanette Reynolds still lived? And now Archie was back. And he was betrothed to Miss Dunforth. The Dowager confided her suspicions to Miranda and warned her to watch Alexandra closely. She had searched the ballroom relentlessly for Alexandra, only to find her dozing on a divan in a dark corner. Alexandra's movements were slow, her speech stilted. Laudanum. Grandmother, as usual, was correct.

Miranda saw Zander, the head butler of Gray Covington, bustling about in the shadows. She must find her grandmother. Miranda realized as she looked over her shoulder to see Alexandra wilting against the couch, that the scheme Grandmother concocted should be implemented immediately. Miranda waved a gloved hand at Zander to get his attention and marched forward. He would know where to find her grandmother.

❦ 17 ❦

Bored, Alexandra dozed against the cushions of the divan. How long since the visit from Miranda? It felt like ages. Likely her friend had forgotten all about her and even now wove across the dance floor with a handsome beau.

She stood, feeling the pinpricks in her legs as they woke up. Smoothing down the gray silk ball gown, she admired the beauty of the garment. For once she didn't look like the poor country mouse she was. If Sutton saw her, would he find her beautiful?

A dull pain radiated from her stomach. Thinking about Sutton caused the most dreadful agony. Not even the tea could mask it. As she relaxed on the divan, she searched the crowd endlessly for his dark visage and finally gave up. It was terrible disappointment. She just wanted to look at him. Just a glance. He need never know. Alexandra wanted just a bit of him to remember, especially tonight. The most horrible night of her life. The betrothal already signed by her uncle made her marriage to Mr. Runyon a foregone conclusion. Tonight's announcement a mere public formality.

Alexandra put a gloved hand to her stomach. Truthfully, she felt a bit ill. The air in the ballroom was heavy with the smell of roses and too many bodies. A brief respite would refresh her. Unsteadily, she made her way to a short, impeccably uniformed man introduced to her earlier as Zander, the head butler.

Zander was a slightly built man, but one of imposing presence. In one hand he clutched a sheaf of papers dense with notes that he seemed to study over and over as he directed the team of servants at his disposal. Seeing Alexandra approach, he executed a perfect bow.

"Miss Dunforth. Is there something I may assist you with?" Zander smiled helpfully.

Alexandra pursed her lips to stifle the words her mind screamed her lips to utter. *Yes. You can assist me by packing me back off to Hampshire immediately. Tell Mr. Runyon I have expired of nerves.*

"Miss?"

"Yes, Zander. I feel the need for some air. Can you direct me to the easiest path to the terrace?"

"Oh, Miss, you cannot go around the terrace and gardens just now. The lamps are just being lit and you could hurt yourself. The gardens are quite dark at night. Shall I find Mr. Runyon?" Zander's tone, coolly polite, held a note of dislike at the mention of her fiancée.

"No. No, that won't be necessary. I simply wish to sit in the quiet for a moment. I find the celebration overwhelms me."

Zander shot her a look of concern. "Just so. Miss Miranda told me you are from Hampshire."

"Yes." *And I want desperately to return.*

The butler smiled kindly. "I know a place where you can collect yourself, safe from prying eyes. Let me direct you to the orangery."

"The orangery?" She really needed some air. Pain twisted between her eyes.

"Gray Covington's is one of the finest. I had the privilege of assisting Lord Cambourne in the building and installation. His lordship adored oranges. The orangery is quite safe. No one will bother you. Besides, the smell of the orange blossoms is quite soothing for nerves, I'm told."

"Thank you, Zander. You are so thoughtful."

Zander led her down the hall to a small alcove one would never find unless looking for it. Stone steps lead to a paved walkway that ended in a small, gated door. He turned the large brass handle carved in the shape of a tree and swung open the door. "Just through there, Miss. Stay on the path. When you have recovered, come back up the steps and turn left to return to the ballroom. His gaze looked back up to the entrance of the alcove, skewering a serving boy who was leaning against the wall. The butler made a short bow to Alexandra and marched back up the stone step barking orders at the boy.

Alexandra walked through the doorway, sighing as the smell of oranges filled her nostrils. Zander was right. The smell of oranges was incredibly soothing. She tilted her head back. The ceiling of the orangery was glass. Horribly expensive. Hundreds of stars, *real stars*, unlike what could be found in the ballroom, twinkled merrily. The moon, pale and full, hung heavy in the sky, seeming so close Alexandra wondered if she could touch it. A sigh of relief left her lips as she enjoyed her brief escape from the excess and false gaiety of the ballroom.

The smell of orange blossoms and damp earth lured her deeper into the greenhouse. Alexandra had read about orange trees but had never actually seen one. Oranges did not often grace the table of Helmsby Abbey. The ache in her head and heart eased a bit. The outline of a bench was before her and Alexandra walked towards it, marveling at the sky above her.

"Bitch!"

Alexandra froze at the sound. The toe of her slipper connected with the hard wood of the bench and she winced.

"Shall I show you who is really master? You spread your legs willingly enough earlier. Now it's time to play some more."

Alexandra held her breath as her heart raced with fear. What had she happened upon?

"Ow! M'lord your 'urtin me." The female voice etched with pain and sexual excitement lingered in the quiet air of the orangery. "Not so rough."

Two bodies scuffled in the dark. Alexandra moved back from the bench, sliding herself along the wall. Her foot nudged a clay pot. She froze for a moment, but the pair didn't seem to notice they weren't alone. Shaking, she lifted her foot over the clay pot.

The sound of a riding crop cracked through the air.

Alexandra halted. A riding crop?

"Please, sir. I'll be a good girl. Ye don't have to hit me so hard. I'll do whatever ye wish," the female voice pleaded.

The bushes directly in front of Alexandra shook, parting to allow her a glimpse of two bodies moving in unison. The figures of a man and woman shone with the light of the moon. The woman's gown sagged down around her waist, exposing her breasts. The man behind her had one hand on the woman's back and her skirts clutched in his hands. The woman's buttocks appeared ghostly against the dark of the orangery.

Alexandra heard a whistle then a snap of leather against flesh.

The woman jerked, whimpering in pain.

Alexandra pushed her fist against her mouth to keep from

screaming. The man thrust his body forward in an urgent manner. "Who is your master?" the man commanded the woman, his voice laced with lust. But even lust could not disguise that voice.

Bile rose in Alexandra's throat.

"Who?" The crop came down.

The woman moaned and jerked.

Alexandra flinched as the crop made contact again. Her body collided with a clay pot and the pot tipped over, shattering on the stone floor.

The woman lifted her head. Her eyes, dull and heavy-lidded stared at Alexandra through a hole in the bushes.

Mr. Runyon followed the woman's stare. He stopped thrusting.

His breathing came out in gasps. He leered at Alexandra, white teeth reflecting the light of the moon. His eyes never left Alexandra's face as he moved his hips into the woman, grunting softly.

"Care to join us, my sweet? Archie can please more than one, can't I?" He pushed into the woman and brought the crop back down on her buttocks.

Alexandra ran.

18

She fled as if the very devil himself were chasing her. The image of what Mr. Runyon did to that woman burned into her mind. Her skirt caught in the doorway and she jerked it free, not caring as the fabric tore.

Wildly, she looked around. Was this the way she had come? Where was Zander? Frightened, she turned, hearing a man's steps on the walkway leading out of the orangery. *He is coming after me.*

She ran down the hallway, desperately searching for a servant, another lost guest, or even the door to the terrace. Bile rose again in her throat, halting her progress. She slowed and pressed herself against the wall, panting and wheezing, unable to catch her breath. A wave of dizziness stuck her, and the hallway swam before her eyes.

"Alexandra?" The silken tones echoed along the corridor. "Where are you hiding, my pet? My perfect pigeon? Shall we play hide and seek? I adore hide and seek. If I find you though," his voice roughened, "you will pay a forfeit."

Alexandra looked back the way she had come. Nothing

moved. Ripples of fear coursed through her. Mr. Runyon hunted her.

A heel squeaked across the floor. "Silly girl. Are you jealous? There's no reason to be envious, darling. She is just a servant, while you," his words belied an evil intent, "are to be my wife. My...*property*."

Alexandra's heart raced. The hallway tilted again. Sconces dotted the paneling of the walls but gave off little light. The strains of music from the orchestra could be heard but were muted. The last time she had gotten lost during a ball she met Sutton Reynolds. Hysterical laughter bubbled out of Alexandra's mouth. The outcome tonight would be very different indeed.

"This is becoming tiresome, Alexandra. Your jealous fit bores me. Stop hiding. I am a man after all, and I have my needs. Needs I am longing for *you* to fulfill."

The sound of the riding crop slapping against his leg jolted Alexandra out of her immobility. Her gaze swung down the dark hallway, trying to discern a door, a window, anything. Her ears perked up. She could swear she heard the creak of a chair in the silence. Someone was down this hall. Maybe someone who would help her.

"Alexandra, *sweet!*" The crop snapped from behind her. "Do not make me drag you back into the ballroom. Or maybe I should. Do you like being forced, Alexandra?" Mr. Runyon's brittle laughter rang in Alexandra's ears. "Do we need to take a turn around the orangery so that you may regain your... balance? You are most un-balanced, Alexandra. *Pigeon.* Sometimes, you even rave nonsense at me. Everyone knows your nerves are...delicate. I've made sure."

He was insane. *Oh God, I have to get away from him.* Grabbing her skirts, she dashed across the marble floor, her slippers not making a sound. Her head ached terribly, the dizziness came at her in waves. Her right foot caught on the torn part of her skirt, and she faltered as one foot skidded across the polished marble. With a thud, her knee slammed into the floor. She sprawled across the tiles. Cold marble pressed into her cheek. She tried to keep still, hoping he would think she fainted.

A shadow loomed over her prostrate form. "Really, my pet, do you think I would let you get away? You are bought and paid for. Like the breeding stock you no doubt loved while you played farmer at Hermsbut Alley." He deliberately mangled her beloved home's name.

"Helmsby Abbey." A gasping sob escaped her throat. She sounded like a wounded animal. The hallway tilted again.

"Oh, yes. That was the name. A dreadful hovel peopled with ancient servants who should have been sent out to pasture long ago. Come, let me help you up." His words dripped with false solicitousness. "How you long for your home. Hopefully, you will see it again. Hopefully, your servants won't starve. There are no guarantees, of course."

"You-" Alexandra choked out, tears of shock running down her cheeks. "You said you would buy it for me. You said-"

"That's right, pigeon. I did promise it as a gift, a *wedding* gift."

A scorching pain seared through Alexandra's chest. "You cannot possibly believe I would still agree to marry you. You are depraved," she whispered as tears puddled on the marble floor beneath her face. She wished to be dead.

"Yes, you will. We've been betrothed for weeks now and money has exchanged hands. Lots and lots of money. Your uncle is a terrible faro player. It's simple really."

Alexandra clawed at the marble in desperate attempt to move herself away from him.

Mr. Runyon slid one foot onto the train of her dress, pinning her to the floor.

"Lord! You look like an inchworm, my dear Alexandra. As I was saying, your uncle owes me quite a bit of money. I promised to forgive his debt in return for *you*."

At her horrified gasp he continued. "I thought you worth far more than what he owed, pigeon. Your uncle simply doesn't value you."

Dawning comprehension settled over her. She had never been free. Odious Oliver had sold her like a prize mare to pay off his debts. Her plan to wait him out had been in vain. Her betrothal had been decided before she ever arrived in London.

Odious Oliver *gambled* her *away*.

"I told your uncle I would purchase Helmsby Abbey from him as a gift to my betrothed. But if you don't *marry* me, your uncle will not only be homeless, which I realize you could care less about, but your retainers at that estate as well. I shall throw them out into the streets and make beggars of them all. I shall burn that pile of manure to the ground while you watch."

Her vision dimmed as if she were looking down a tunnel. Tiny pinpricks of light flashed before her. "Why would you do this to me?"

"Because I can. I've paid for the privilege." Hands, gloved in the finest leather, wrapped around her wrists. He pulled her upright so hard her arms were nearly wrenched from their sockets. Ice blue shards of glass watched her dispassionately. His handsome face contorted into a menacing mask. The monster before her in no way resembled the gentle man who once paid her court. The pressure on her wrists intensified. "My dear, sweet, clumsy little *whore*."

Alexandra flinched. She thrashed, causing her head to ache as she sought to free herself.

Mr. Runyon sighed in disgust. "Just stop it." He shook her until her head snapped back on her neck. "You are behaving like a child. You will learn to enjoy the things we do together, the things you will do with my friends. Lord Atkins is looking forward to furthering his acquaintance with you."

"No. Never. You are sick. Disgusting. What you did to that woman-"

"Was only what she wished. I'll admit Mary isn't as fond of the crop as I would like her to be."

"Please," she begged.

He gave her a rueful smile. "You and I are going to have such *fun* together." Grabbing both her wrists in one hand, he reached out with the other. The gloved hand lingered over the mounds of her breasts, squeezing them as if he tested their ripeness. "Lovely and tender like an unblemished peach." His thumb rubbed against her left nipple, slowly.

Horrified, Alexandra felt her nipple harden into a point under the gentle urging.

Mr. Runyon chuckled, a nasty, rasping sound. "See? Whore." Abruptly he pinched the nipple.

Alexandra shuddered in pain.

Lord Runyon licked his lips. "Oh, yes. Such *fun* we will have, for year and years."

Ashamed and more frightened than she had ever been in her life, Alexandra began to weep in earnest. She continued to struggle ineffectually against him, nausea and dizziness nearly overwhelming her.

Mr. Runyon swung her around like a child. "Alexandra, I fear all this defiance on your part has done nothing but whet my appetite. I think we must find a quiet parlor before returning to the ballroom."

"No. I'll scream!" Alexandra stuttered between sobs.

"Then I shall gag you." He shook her. "You need to learn proper respect for me, your master."

"Hello, Archie. Am I interrupting something?"

Lord Cambourne, his tall form barely more than a shadow, stood in the hallway before them.

Sutton. Alexandra's heart beat wildly.

Mr. Runyon stopped swinging her. He thrust her behind him, still holding her wrists in a bruising hold.

"Bugger off, Cam," he sneered to Sutton. "My future wife and I are having a private discussion that is no concern of yours."

Sutton took in Alexandra's wrists, bound by Mr. Runyon's hands. His gaze lingered on her face, before turning to Mr. Runyon. "Private discussion or not, betrothed or not, no woman is to be abused under my roof. Let her go."

"You have no say, Cam. She's my property. My betrothed."

"Mary is missing. Have you seen Mary? Plump lass who takes care of things in the family's wing?"

Mr. Runyon's grip on Alexandra tightened. One slender hand reached around and caressed Alexandra's face, the fingers tapping along her cheek. He viciously grabbed her chin, forcing her to look at Sutton. "A maid's disappearance? Why should I care about the disappearance of some lowly servant when I hold my perfect Hampshire rose? Lovely, isn't she, Cam?"

Alexandra closed her eyes against Sutton's penetrating stare and her own shame. What must he think of her? Deep, wrenching humiliation flooded through her. Her stupidity had cost her the affection of the man before her. She disgusted him.

"Miss Dunforth." Sutton addressed her but did not look at her. "Your dress appears to have a slight tear in it. Down the hall there is a small parlor where my sister is attending my grandmother. I will escort you there and call for a maid to repair your gown."

"I don't think so, Cam. I will escort my betrothed to a room where she can be waited on by her maid, Tilda. I can't bear for Alexandra to leave my side. We are announcing our betrothal tonight." Archie sneered at him.

A slight tic appeared in Sutton's cheek. He cocked an indulgent smile. "I don't think so, Archie. Miss Dunforth will sit in the parlor with my sister and the Dowager."

Mr. Runyon sputtered. The dark vein in his temple bulged as his gaze settled on Sutton maliciously. "You want her. Don't deny it. I've seen the way you look at her."

Sutton regarded him with an unwavering stare. "Your betrothed is of no import to me, other than that she is a woman, perhaps in need of assistance. A woman under my roof is in my care. Do I make myself clear?"

Alexandra swallowed. It was true then. He had no affection for her. He would leave her to her fate.

Mr. Runyon's nostrils flared in irritation. He pulled at Alexandra.

"Don't." Sutton stepped forward. "If you persist, you will force me to explain your demise at my hands to the crowd assembled in the ballroom. And the reasons for it."

The hall became deathly quiet.

Mr. Runyon's voice was soft. "You wouldn't."

"Wouldn't I?"

Archie flung Alexandra away from him, his face full of loathing, his breathing choppy from fear.

She fell to her knees against the paneled wall.

"You have no proof, Cam. None. The ravings of a dead man." Archie lifted his chin. "The scandal would destroy any hope either of your sisters has for a decent marriage. Think of the shame the Dowager would endure."

"Do you think I care a fig for scandal? I'd much rather you were dead," Sutton drawled.

Mr. Runyon backed away from Sutton, his hands clenched into fists. The comparison between the two men was laughable, a pampered housecat attempting to challenge a panther.

Alexandra pushed her head against the wall. Nausea rolled through her.

"Miss Dunforth?" Sutton said softly. "Can you stand?"

She nodded. "Yes."

"Please go down the hall. The door is closed, but Harry stands outside. Will you recognize Harry?"

She nodded again, not daring to look at Mr. Runyon.

Sutton's hand rested gently on her arm as he helped her up. "Allow me."

Alexandra could hear Mr. Runyon panting in frustration. "Don't you dare, Alexandra. I shall throw them all out. What will poor Mrs. Cowries do? A widow on her own."

Alexandra gasped. He knew her housekeeper's name.

"Oh yes." He'd noted her distress. "I've seen them all. I will throw them out. Make them beggars. Your slow-witted groom, Michael? Who will employ him and see that his ill mother is fed? And Mrs. Cowries? I suppose begging in the streets will suit her," Mr. Runyon snarled. "I shall destroy Helmsby Abbey brick by brick."

"No." Alexandra sobbed. She shook off Sutton's hand. "I have to-"

Sutton stared down at her. "Badger? Is this what you want?"

"Of course, it's what she wants. The contracts are signed, Cam. Not even you, the great Marquess of Cambourne can undo that legal document." Spittle formed at the corner of Mr. Runyon's mouth.

Sutton inhaled deeply. "Miss Dunforth?"

Alexandra looked at the two men. Terrified and in a panic, she simply could not think. Her head ached.

"Mr. Runyon, my head aches. I wish a small respite."

"Fine. You had better appear in a quarter of an hour or I shall come looking for you, Alexandra. And I will not be pleased. Your defiance tonight has cost you one retainer. I shall tell you later which one it is to be."

Alexandra put a hand to her mouth too horrified to reply.

"Archie, if you do not walk away now, I will kill you where you stand."

"Please, Mr. Runyon. I beg you."

"Remember, Alexandra. I hold Helmsby Abbey." Mr. Runyon jerked a thumb at Sutton. "He cannot help you. Only I can. Fifteen minutes." Mr. Runyon strode down the hall to the ballroom and disappeared.

"Badger?"

"Please, Sutton." She clutched at his arm. "I cannot speak about this now. I need to sit. My head. I need my tea."

Sutton shot her a curious look but said nothing.

Alexandra inhaled deeply of the cinnamon scent that swirled around him. She felt some of the tension ease from her body at his closeness. How she wished to wrap her arms around his body, to bury herself and her misery within him. Did he feel anything for her except a sense of duty?

Not daring to break the spell his presence wove around her, she desperately tried to ignore the rising panic within her breast. Fifteen minutes with Sutton was all she would ever have.

❈ 19 ❈

A quarter of an hour. That was all the time given Alexandra before she must put herself back in that monster's hands. She looked down at the floor, contemplating her fate, wishing the ache in her head did not match the one in her heart. The gray silk of her skirts brushed against Sutton's long legs as he walked her down the hall. Warmth from the large body next to her seemed to waft underneath the gown, comforting her. Calming her. She was safe for the moment. Mr. Runyon's words shouted inside her head. The vile words, threatening all she held dear if she did not return to him. Thinking of what Mr. Runyon would do to her, she stumbled.

Sutton caught her arm in a firm grip. Still, he said nothing.

A lump caught in her throat. Sutton rescued her, but not out of affection. He saw her as a responsibility, where once he desired her. Alexandra glanced from underneath her lashes to look at his profile. The dark locks of his hair fell forward across his cheekbones, the ends curling around the edges of his collar. The smell of cinnamon, exotic and sensual, buffeted around her. The need Alexandra felt for

this man, this intense yearning, was beyond her comprehension.

And I will never have him.

She looked back down at the floor, desolate. Sutton was
lost to her. Her association with Mr. Runyon sufficiently
snuffed out any feeling Sutton may have once had. She
belonged to Mr. Runyon now.

The hand clutching Sutton's sleeve shook with emotion.

Harry stood guard outside a paneled door. The young
footman greeted Sutton with a bow before glancing curiously
at Alexandra. He discreetly turned his eyes from her
disheveled state and tapped at the door with his knuckles
before giving Sutton entry.

Sutton pushed her forward with a gentle hand.

Had Alexandra been in a different frame of mind she
would have marveled over the lovely little parlor. The walls,
painted a light cream, were stenciled with flowers, bees, drag-
onflies, and other woodland creatures. Soothing and tranquil,
the parlor's atmosphere was a balm to her jarred nerves. She
desperately wished for a pot of her special tea.

Miranda and the Dowager sat on a green velvet couch
embroidered with butterflies. Their heads were bent
together. Surprised by her appearance and on Sutton's arm,
they looked askance.

Miranda shot her a guilty look before turning her attention to Sutton.

Alexandra's mind played tricks on her, for what did
Miranda have to feel guilty about?

"Alexandra? Whatever are you doing here?" Miranda's eyes
widened as she took in Alexandra's agitated state and the torn
gown.

The Dowager, her surprise now under control, merely
lifted a brow.

"I tore my gown." Alexandra muttered stupidly. "I

tripped. Lord Cambourne happened upon me and offered to escort me here in the hopes a maid could be found to repair the damage. I beg your pardon for disturbing you both." The words came out in a rush. Alexandra felt her cheeks flame as the lie rolled off her tongue.

The Dowager turned her gaze on Sutton.

"Yes, my grandson seems to ever be *happening* upon you, Miss Dunforth." Her tone was crisp. "I find it fascinating." She cleared her throat. "Why has your betrothed allowed you to roam without escort? Perhaps Miss Dunforth, you have had a change of heart?"

The Dowager stared her down until Alexandra wisely looked away.

"I could not remember where the room set aside for the female guests was located so-"

The Dowager lifted a gloved hand, effectively halting Alexandra's pathetic explanation and gave a small snort. Her emerald-green gaze pierced Alexandra.

"I can see you need a refreshment. Tearing one's gown, accidentally, can be very traumatic, especially since your betrothal shall be announced shortly. I see the thought of becoming betrothed, and your gown in such a state, has caused you to weep." The Dowager gestured to Alexandra's tear-stained cheeks. She patted a spot on the couch next to her. "The madeira is excellent."

Trembling and trying to maintain what composure she had left, Alexandra gingerly perched on the edge of the sofa.

The Dowager handed Alexandra a glass filled with a dark, ruby-colored liquid. "Drink up. It will restore you." The elderly woman watched as Alexandra took several sips of the wine.

Alexandra closed her eyes in pleasure as the warmth of the wine spilled through her veins. She did not wish to imagine what awaited her after she left the safety of the

Dowager's parlor. Responsibility warred with self-preservation, causing her mind to reel with panic. Her hand shook as she pressed the wine to her lips again. *What am I to do?*

"Sutton, have you congratulated Miss Dunforth on her impending nuptials?"

Alexandra choked. The wine sloshed in her glass. The Dowager seemed determined to work Alexandra's fate into every sentence.

Sutton gave his grandmother an appraising look and spoke quietly. "What are you about, *Rainha?*"

"I'll not tolerate such tone from you, Sutton." The Dowager pursed her lips in disapproval. "I am still your elder and deserving of your respect. Miranda."

Miranda, her eyes wide and unsure, watched the exchange between her brother and her grandmother in growing alarm. "Yes, Grandmother?"

"Please escort me to my room. I fear I am near collapse from exhaustion. You will send a maid to Miss Dunforth immediately, then return to escort her to the ballroom once repair is made to her gown. Understood?" She turned to Sutton. "Act the gentleman for once. I insist you stay with Miss Dunforth until the maid arrives, and Miranda returns. Miss Dunforth's safety is *your* responsibility."

Sutton opened his mouth to interrupt.

"Silence! I will not argue with you this evening. Disrespectful scamp." The Dowager stomped her cane at Miranda. "Come take my arm."

Miranda, still wearing a look of confusion at her grandmother's antics, steered the elderly woman to the door.

"Harry!"

"Yes, my lady." The young footman's head popped from around the door.

"Lord Cambourne will await the arrival of a maid to repair

Miss Dunforth's gown. The door should stay open, with you just outside, to ensure no impropriety occurs."

Alexandra drained her glass of Madeira. A feeling of euphoria washed over her. She would be with Sutton until the maid arrived! The wine gave her a light, fluffy feeling.

"Grandmother, I really think–" Miranda tried to interject.

"Be quiet, Miranda. After you send the maid, be a dear and let Archie know where he can find his *betrothed.*"

Alexandra thought she had at least ten more minutes before she had to face the nightmare of her impending marriage. She poured herself more madeira.

⚜

SUTTON STOOD IN STUNNED SILENCE AS HIS GRANDMOTHER made a most dramatic exit. She left him alone with Alexandra. The Dowager was no fool. She'd plied Alexandra with wine, calming the Badger until the anxious look her features bore had disappeared. Then, pretending to be affronted and outraged by Sutton's actions, she'd stormed out like an offended queen and instructed a footman to guard Miss Dunforth's virtue. Ridiculous. The centerpiece, of course, was the Dowager's instruction to make sure Archie knew where to find his betrothed. His grandmother had ensured Alexandra's ruination at the hands of Satan Reynolds. The scandal would be enormous. However, Alexandra's betrothal would be broken. The Badger would belong to him.

❦ 20 ❦

"**W**hy didn't you tell me?" Sutton advanced on the Badger who steadfastly ignored him. He settled himself next to her small form on the sofa.

Alexandra's gaze remained fixed on the wine swirling in her glass.

"Badger." He took her chin in his hands, forcing her to meet his gaze. She exhaled at his touch and a light, sweet smell filtered to him. The scent, familiar, but out of place. Not the aroma of the madeira. The smell reminded Sutton of his time in Macao.

Sutton peered into her eyes. Alexandra's pupils, large and unfocused, gave her the appearance of a curious owl. Two glasses of wine had not caused such an effect. Sutton's pulse quickened. Opium wasn't readily available in London, but laudanum was prescribed for every woman with a mild complaint.

The headaches. She mentioned headaches.

Sutton grimaced. That bastard not only threatened the

Badger but drugged her as well. Sutton added this to the ever-increasing list of reasons to kill Archie Runyon.

Alexandra bit her lip and a small sob escaped her. "I thank you for your assistance tonight, Lord Cambourne, but I can see that I disgust you."

"Shush. Stop, my Badger. You do not disgust me."

Her eyes, glazed with laudanum and wine, filled with tears. "You mustn't call me that." A shaky hand set down the glass of wine.

"Why ever not?" Sutton rubbed his thumb over her swollen lower lip. Just touching her made every nerve in his body tingle. His want of Alexandra blunted nearly everything else in his life.

Her hands fluttered in her lap. She tried to turn her head and avoid his stare, but he didn't allow her to move away. Lightly, he brushed his lips over hers.

The Badger moaned softly. Her body leaned towards him.

Sutton shot a glance at the door, just in time to see it swing shut. No doubt Harry followed the Dowager's instructions.

Sutton pressed soft kisses over Alexandra's temple and down to her ear, pausing to nibble at the lobe.

She placed her palms against his thighs. "Sutton," she whispered against his mouth.

Gently, he pressed his lips to hers. His heart beat erratically, as if this were the first girl he'd kissed. The kiss became urgent, possessive. He should stop. Guiltily, he knew Alexandra would take exception to being manipulated, even if she was willing. Even if it saved her from marrying Runyon.

Her hands kneaded his thighs. Alexandra's body became fluid as she molded herself to him.

He pressed her back into the couch until she lay underneath him. He half straddled her, one leg on the floor, the other pinning her small body down. The wispy lace of her skirt tore further as he moved his knee.

"Oh, no!" Her eyelids fluttered open. "This is the finest gown I have ever owned. I wanted you to see me in it. To see me for once as not a dull country girl."

"I find you beautiful in it and you are the furthest thing from dull." He answered the question he saw in her face. "My Badger."

Her arms wound around his neck. She smiled. Her hips moved underneath the layers of silk and petticoats.

Sutton's hand roamed over her bodice. He circled the tiny nub of nipple through the silk, massaging it until it hardened into a peak. Softly, he pinched the peak.

Alexandra flinched. Her eyes flew open.

Thinking he'd hurt her, Sutton moved his hand away.

"No." She took his hand. "He...I'm," Alexandra's face reddened, "bruised." She gave him an apologetic half smile.

Sutton swore under his breath. "He will never touch you again."

"You can't promise that." She closed her eyes with a small sob.

It occurred to Sutton at that moment that Alexandra truly had no idea she was about to be publicly ruined at his hands.

Voices sounded outside the door. Sutton heard Harry denying someone entry.

His lips lingered against the milky flesh of Alexandra's breasts.

"Try to remember how much I want you, as I've no doubt you will want to kill me after this," he whispered into her ear. "Forgive me. There was no other way." He pressed his face into the nape of her neck, inhaling the smell of tart, green apples. He pulled her bodice down farther.

The door burst open. Sutton looked up, covering

Alexandra with his arm. He hoped he appeared to be surprised.

The Dowager wore a smug, satisfied smile.

Lady Cambourne stared at their prone bodies with horror.

Archie Runyon howled with impotent rage.

⚜

ALEXANDRA WAS JERKED BEHIND SUTTON'S LARGER FORM AS the room erupted around her. Guests milled about the hallway outside the door in curiosity, each trying to catch a glimpse of the disgraced Alexandra Dunforth. Mr. Runyon would never marry her now. She nearly fainted the relief was so intense. Then fear enveloped her. Helmsby Abbey. My God, what had she done?

"You!" Mr. Runyon rushed at Sutton. "I should call you out for this insult. How dare you." Mr. Runyon's angry words sounded in a whine.

"Then why don't you?" Sutton answered. "Come on, Archie. I'm sure Jeanette would stand as your second."

A collective gasp came from the crowd outside.

Jeanette, her porcelain skin blotchy with anger, screamed commands to Harry and Zander, who ran to the door. "Direct my guests back to the ballroom. Immediately." She stabbed a terrified Harry with her index finger. "You will never work for any family again. Pack your bags. No references."

The Dowager pushed her cane between Jeanette and Harry. "I don't think so. Harry is under my protection and that of the Marquess of Cambourne." She smiled at the footman. "Run along to the kitchens, Harry, and get yourself something to eat."

Jeanette bared her teeth at the Dowager. "*You* did this. I

should have known. It has all the hallmarks of an addled, elderly-"

"Stop there, *Mother*."

Jeanette closed her mouth at the tone of utter command in her stepson's voice. Her chest heaved in fury.

Alexandra peered around Sutton's chest.

Mr. Runyon's face, a bright shade of red, gave him the appearance of an enraged tomato. His slender form vibrated with rage. The pale blue eyes were filled with the promise of retribution as he glared at Alexandra.

"No." Odious Oliver stood to one side of the door, clutching his chest.

Alexandra wondered idly if her uncle would have a fit of apoplexy.

Jeanette watched Sutton with a look of utter hatred on her face before she turned to the Dowager. "You planned this," she hissed with certainty.

The Dowager stood calmly amid the chaos, one silver brow raised in question. She barely glanced at Alexandra. "Really, Jeanette, you can't think I would ever sanction such *debauchery*." Looking towards Sutton, she composed her face into a mask of offense. "This is quite uncalled for, Lord Cambourne. Especially during Lady Cambourne's birthday celebration. Well, there's no help for it. You'll have to do the honorable thing."

Jeanette paled. She marched to the doors of the parlor and slammed them shut.

Mr. Runyon snapped at Alexandra from across the room. "I suppose Jameson will walk the streets tonight. How will he support his ill wife?"

"No!" Alexandra whispered from behind Sutton.

Sutton turned to look down at her. "I will not allow that to happen. Please trust me."

Alexandra put her hands over her face, terrified at the chaos erupting around her.

Jeanette bore down on she and Sutton like a crazed harpy. "Over my dead body will I allow this...this...*harlot*, who betrayed my cousin's good faith and honor, to become a member of my family."

Sutton laughed at her. "Honor? Oh, that's rich."

Jeanette's face mottled and her eyes bugged.

Sutton stepped away from Alexandra ready to do battle with his stepmother and Archie.

Alexandra slid from his side to sit on the couch hugging herself. *What have I done? I've betrayed those who depended on me.* Her head was throbbing unbearably as if it would split open at any moment.

A low growl sounded behind her. A beefy hand caught underneath her arm and attempted to pull her over the couch. Odious Oliver, his eyes bulging with hatred, gave Alexandra's hair a brutal wrench.

Pins fell to the floor as her uncle gripped the mass of curls and shook Alexandra as a dog would a rabbit.

"You whore." Spittle formed at the corner of his mouth. "Just like your mother, aren't you? You are going to fix this. You *will* marry Runyon. Beg for his forgiveness."

Miranda cried in alarm from across the room.

Every eye in the room turned to Alexandra's position on the couch.

Sutton spun about, returning to the couch so quickly Alexandra barely saw him move. The grip on Alexandra's hair was suddenly released as Odious Oliver flew through the air, landing with a thud. Several knickknacks unaccustomed to being rattled from their perch, fell to the floor and shattered.

Miranda came over to wrap Alexandra safely within her arms. She whispered into Alexandra's hair. "I'm so sorry. We didn't think it would be quite so...dramatic. My poor, dear friend."

Alexandra, still in shock from her uncle's attack, reeled with the implications of Miranda's words. Miranda and the Dowager...*planned* to have her ruined. Alexandra stiffened as Miranda hugged her. Was she nothing but a pawn in everyone's plans? To be used at their will?

Sutton sauntered over to Odious Oliver who lay mewling like an injured animal. Blood poured from his broken nose. Sutton nudged him with his foot. "Get out of my house. Now."

"I won't agree to this marriage! I am her guardian! She's to marry Runyon. She has to marry Runyon." Her uncle whined and shook his head erratically. Drops of blood rained across the Dowager's perfect parlor.

"Marry? Why, I wouldn't take this little tramp out to tea now that he's had her," Mr. Runyon sneered. He walked jerkily over to her uncle's prostrate form on the floor. "The deal is off. The betrothal is broken. The entire *ton* will be afire with the gossip of this scandal by tomorrow." Mr. Runyon's words sounded like shards of ice dropping on marble. "My solicitor will call upon you tomorrow, Lord Burke, to discuss the payment of the debt owed to me."

Her uncle wailed as if he'd been stabbed.

Mr. Runyon turned to her, and Alexandra immediately hid her face in Miranda's shoulder, desperate to avoid his glacial stare.

Sutton's large form blocked his path.

Mr. Runyon chuckled, holding up his hands, all signs of his earlier anger, gone. "Don't worry, Cam, I'm leaving."

"See that you do. There is an inn not too far away that you can stay at tonight, as you will not spend another night under my roof. Tomorrow, you can escort my stepmother back to London."

Jeanette gasped. "But my party! My guests!"

"Your guests are no doubt running to their carriages in a race to see who will make it to London first. They have gossip to spread. You wished for your party to be talked about for months. Now I'm sure it will be."

Jeanette's fragile grip on her emotions shattered. She ran at Sutton, her hands up, prepared to claw his face with her nails. "I hate you! How dare you do this to me. Why couldn't you have died in Macao?"

Mr. Runyon grabbed her around the waist. He smoothed her hair and whispered into her ear. "Come, cousin, do not waste your time on him."

Sutton regarded his stepmother as if she were no more than an insect in his path. A muscle ticked in his jaw, the only sign that her words affected him. "Good evening, Jeanette."

Jeanette gave a dramatic wail and leaned against Mr. Runyon as she allowed him to lead her out the door. "I will never forgive you, Sutton. Never. You will pay for this."

Mr. Runyon stopped abruptly. He swiveled his head to look directly at Alexandra. "I'll see you *soon*, Alexandra." A malicious smile graced the thin lips. Then he was gone.

Sutton turned to Zander. "Please dispose of this." Sutton jerked a thumb towards her uncle who lay sobbing and bleeding over the carpet. "Make sure that his valet and Miss Dunforth's maid are packed off as well. Immediately."

"Yes, my Lord." Zander snapped his fingers and two large footmen appeared. "Please escort Lord Burke to his rooms and stay with him until he is packed. See that his valet and Miss Dunforth's maid go with him."

The two footmen reached for Odious Oliver as he swatted ineffectually against their hands.

"No! She has to marry Runyon! She must!" He put his head in his hands. "I shall punish you for this Alexandra. You tedious little twit."

Sutton brushed aside the two footmen and wrenched her uncle up. "Have a care for the way you address the future Marchioness of Cambourne," he snarled. With one push he shoved her uncle towards the footmen. "Get him off my property."

Odious Oliver clawed at the footmen who restrained him. He sobbed and wailed. Alexandra watched in relief as the two footmen escorted her uncle from her sight. Sutton's words sank in. The future Marchioness of Cambourne? She disengaged Miranda's arms from around her waist. She remembered Miranda's guilty look.

"Thank goodness that is *over*," the Dowager intoned. "Sutton, the vicar of Covington owes me a favor. I'm sure he will be able to provide you with a special license."

"Stop it!"

The Dowager looked from Sutton to Alexandra.

"Does no one care what I wish for? What I want my future to hold?" Alexandra's head ached. Her heart hurt. Manipulated, first by her uncle and Runyon, now by the Dowager and Miranda. And Sutton? Had he been manipulated as well? Did he even truly want her?

The Dowager reached out and took Alexandra's hand. She squeezed gently.

Alexandra tried to pull away, but the Dowager's grip was surprisingly strong. "Sutton, why don't you and Miranda begin the arduous process of dismissing our guests? Ensure the viper is gone from Gray Covington. Miss Dunforth and I have things we need to discuss."

Sutton's gaze slid over Alexandra, his eyes unreadable. What was he thinking?

He nodded to his grandmother. "As you wish, *Rainha*."

"Alexandra," Miranda gave her an apologetic look, "I am sorry for the circumstances but not the outcome."

Miranda and Sutton walked out of the room, shutting the door quietly behind them.

"My lady," Alexandra stammered. "The preceding events have left me much distressed. If I could just lie down for a moment and catch my breath. Surely this conversation can wait until later. After I've had some tea."

"And allow you time to flee the premises with some ridiculous notion that you can find employment?"

Alexandra felt the guilty flush in her cheeks.

"I think not. Besides, you have an addiction to laudanum in case you have not noticed. You will need to be weaned." At Alexandra's look of surprised indignation, she said, "The tea, Alexandra. Have you not noticed the way it makes you feel? For such an intelligent girl you allowed yourself to be manipulated quite readily."

The Dowager hobbled over to the couch, frowning as she saw the tiny blood splatters left by Odious Oliver. "I shall have to have this couch re-covered. I doubt I can replace the pattern." She swung her cane, pointing at Alexandra. "Sit. I promise you will not be forced to marry if you truly do not wish it. I feel it my duty, however, to apprise you of your current situation."

Alexandra looked into the calculating green eyes of the Dowager Marchioness of Cambourne and sat.

S tubborn. Alexandra's penchant to be mulish rivaled Donata's own tendencies. An admirable trait, except when directed at Donata. In addition, Alexandra possessed a formidable backbone. The girl did not cry or sob, as most women would, after finding out they had been drugged with laudanum, sold to a depraved man for a gambling debt and ruined publicly by a notorious rake. *Most* women would collapse into a fit of hysterics. Alexandra did not.

"So, you don't wish to marry? Interesting. I assume you realize that you have not only been ruined, but *publicly* ruined. Even now your name and tonight's events are rapidly becoming *the* scandal of the Season. Everyone in London will know what occurred at Gray Covington by tomorrow morning. Not a door will be open to you. Women will cross the street to avoid making contact with you. Unless you marry Sutton, you will be a pariah. The only employment you will find will be on your back."

Alexandra sat back as if she'd been slapped.

"Oh, my dear, I do apologize for my candor. My age and

position give me license to speak my mind. I feel certain you would wish to know the truth of your circumstances."

"I will...return to Hampshire and possibly–"

Donata gave a sharp laugh. Stubborn! So very stubborn!

"You accepted your fate in marrying Archie willingly enough, but yet marriage to Sutton does not appeal to you? My grandson is wealthy and titled. I can name a handful of women who would cheerfully trade places with you in an instant."

"Then perhaps we should find one of those," Alexandra replied with a bit of her former spirit. "I have other concerns. Pressing concerns. Besides, Lord Cambourne did no more than kiss me."

Donata gave a wry smile. "Oh, my girl. No one cares. A kiss is akin to ruination, especially when it is given by a man whose reputation with women is somewhat infamous."

Alexandra looked away. "He does not wish to marry me. I would not have him marry me out of duty or honor. I am not a noble cause he must champion. He wished to rescue me from Mr. Runyon, and I am grateful, but he does not have to shackle himself to me."

Ah! So, that was Alexandra's concern. She stupidly believed Sutton didn't want her. She didn't yet realize that Sutton had willingly participated in her ruination. Just so. Donata would not tell her.

Tears formed in Alexandra's eyes and Donata's heart went out to her. But this was not the time to coddle the girl.

"Don't be ridiculous. He is not marrying you out of duty. Even I, Donata Reynolds, Dowager Marchioness of Cambourne, cannot make that scamp do anything he does not truly wish. He wants you."

Color seeped into Alexandra's cheeks. "I do not think he can forgive my association and stupidity where Mr. Runyon is concerned. I cannot even forgive myself." Alexandra bit her lip and looked directly at the Dowager.

"He wants you. You want him. I am only surprised he didn't finish the job before we entered the room."

The shade of Alexandra's cheeks deepened. "My lady, I do not think this conversation is appropriate. I am distinctly uncomfortable and my head aches. I would like to return to my room."

"Oh bother, Alexandra! Do not disappoint me and act like a dimwit! I despise martyrdom. Would you rather be marrying Archie Runyon?"

Alexandra shook her head. "No, my lady." She shivered. "No."

Donata did not press the point. She knew now how Lord Burke and Archie had manipulated Alexandra. If Alexandra would not admit to wanting Sutton, Donata must tip the scales. She had grown to care deeply for the girl and wished her only happiness.

"I see you will continue to deny the obvious. You are in love with my grandson."

Alexandra looked away. Her hands twisted in her lap, bunching the fine lace of her overskirt.

"A moment, Alexandra." Donata stood carefully, listening to the faint creak her bones made as she stood. Old age was a detestable circumstance. She made her way to the door and whispered to the footman who stood outside to bring Harry to her. Donata slowly made her way back to the sofa.

The girl continued to focus on her lap. She said nothing, but her breathing was shaky and uneven.

Harry arrived, bowing low to Donata. He handed her a folded document from his coat pocket.

He was such a dear boy. "Thank you, Harry. I will have need of you early tomorrow. Best you get some rest."

Harry bowed low. "Yes, my lady." He quietly trod out of the room and shut the door.

She turned to Alexandra, who still refused to look directly at her. "If your reputation or the state of your heart is not enough inducement to marry Sutton, I shall have to play my final card." Donata gave a deep sigh. "Archie enjoys toying with others. He receives pleasure from it. Had I known...well I don't suppose it matters now."

Alexandra looked up, a confused look on her face.

Donata held up the document. "Call it my wedding gift, if you wish. The papers are in your name only. I will have your promise to marry Sutton within the month." Donata handed the document to Alexandra. "Put your fears for those you love aside, Alexandra."

Tears ran down Alexandra's face as she agreed with a nod to Donata's terms. Her hands quivered as her fingertips took hold of the deed to Helmsby Abbey.

22

"May I come in?"

Sutton glanced up, surprised to see Alex and not the maid coming to clean the study. Alex was the last person he expected to see. He refused to marry her without her consent, no matter the scandal. Her words the night of her ruination pained him. Alex had the right to chose her own destiny, even if that destiny did not include Sutton.

The Badger hid well within the walls of Gray Covington. Since the disastrous night of his stepmother's birthday ball, he'd seen little of her. The Dowager, taking charge as few generals could, oversaw Alexandra's weaning from laudanum assisted by her handpicked physician, whose discretion was assured by the power and wealth of the Cambourne family.

His stepmother's return to London had been achieved with little fanfare. Jeanette said nothing as she left Gray Covington, but her icy glance spoke volumes. Her resistance to his marriage to Alexandra was evident in the toss of her head as she climbed into the Cambourne carriage. Correspondence from London assured Sutton that the scandal of

Alexandra's ruination had not died down. No great scandal had erupted to replace it. Thinly veiled references to Satan Reynolds and the spinster he ruined graced the London papers. Why, the rumors demanded, had no marriage yet taken place? Why was the Dowager Marchioness and Lady Miranda still in residence? The betting book at White's was full of odds on whether Sutton *would* actually marry Miss Dunforth.

"Hello, Badger." Sutton pushed back from the stack of papers that littered the gnarled walnut desk, laying down the letter he had been reading. The letter, from Lord Bishop, relayed the details of an expedition being mounted to explore a region of the Asian peninsula near Macao. Lord Bishop wished Sutton to lead the expedition. His answer would depend on the Badger.

"You cannot think of another way to address me? Must I always be a small and smelly creature?"

Sutton's mouth quirked, happiness filling him at the tartness of her tone.

"We must talk." She marched to the desk, demanding his attention in her prickly way.

He forced his features into a polite mask of curiosity, not willing to let her see how pleased he was to see her. Joyful was a better word to describe the sudden beating of his heart.

He *was not* pleased to see that she continued to twist her gorgeous mass of hair into a hideous bun that would make an elderly matron jealous. Not a curl so much as ventured from the tightly wound ball at her neck. Her gown, plain blue and bereft of adornment would be much more fitting for a governess. He preferred her in dark, vibrant colors and made a mental note to order her a new wardrobe no matter what she decided. A gray shawl hung about her shoulders, shielding the Badger's overabundance of bosom from his eager gaze. He wondered if Alexandra deliberately tried to make herself appear unattractive as a means to antagonize him. Perhaps he should tell her that the prim, dull appearance she adored cultivating did not deter him, and in fact, made him want her more. Sutton grinned.

The Badger backed up, not caring for his grin. She cleared her throat and placed her hands on her stomach, as if he irritated her so much she might become ill.

He quirked a brow and waited for her to speak. Had she come to tell him she would not marry him? That she would rather be a pariah? Sutton should take her on the desk right now, several times, until she became big with child. Badgers cannot flee when they are large and pregnant. The idea appealed to him.

Alexandra backed up another step and gave him an uncertain look. Then she lifted her chin, her eyes meeting his.

"Please sit, Miss Dunforth. You seem... *unsettled*."

She glared at him. Annoyance flashed in her eyes. "No, thank you."

Good. He much preferred her annoyed than the awful wraith she had been the night of the ball.

"I need to know. Why?"

"Why what?" He knew what she asked.

She turned her head away. "Did you do it only to save me from Runyon? If so, then I refuse to hold you to this absurd assumption that we must marry."

"Already your ruination at my hands is the talk of London."

"I will not return to London. I hate London."

"You cannot return to Helmsby Abbey. It's been sold."

Alexandra gave him an awkward look but said nothing. Her hands nested together. She took a shaky breath and looked directly at him. "I don't wish you to marry me out of duty."

"Then what *do* you wish to be married for?" he asked softly as he stood and moved until he stood before her.

The Badger bit her bottom lip. Her delicious plump bottom lip. She looked down at the floor, as if suddenly enthralled by the swirling pattern of thistles that edged the rug.

His fingertips grazed her chin, forcing it up. Her skin felt like silk. A tremor ran through her body as he touched her.

"For myself." She shot him a defiant look.

"Then we have that in common." He brushed his lips against hers.

Her gray eyes, flickering like opals, gave him a guarded look. "Tell me you did not do it just to save me."

"I am not that honorable. I would not marry a woman I didn't want, *especially* if I haven't had the pleasure of ruining her."

Alexandra sucked in her breath. Her hands moved nervously at her sides.

"Put your arms around my waist," he commanded her.

"You do not need to be so...so..."

"Domineering? Arrogant? Full of myself?"

She struggled not to smile. "I was going to say overbearing."

Gently, he took her hands and placed them on his waist. His whole being radiated with some emotion he wasn't prepared to name at her touch. He pulled her against his chest.

"I want you." He enunciated each word into her hair.

Alexandra swayed against him. Her hands ran over his back. She snuggled against him before pulling away.

"Why? Why me?"

"I don't know." How to explain to her that he'd desired her from the moment he'd seen her? No other woman had entered his thoughts since the second he touched her? That he dreamt of making love to her nearly every night?

Alexandra said nothing for a moment. "I see." Gray eyes flashed. The tiny chin lifted at a mulish tilt. A curl popped from its confines. "I suppose that will have to do."

Sutton grabbed the back of her head and took her lips in a possessive kiss that left no room for his intentions to be misconstrued. Her mouth opened under his, tongues twining about each other.

Alexandra sighed. The shawl fell to the floor, exposing the tops of her breasts. Another curl sprang free.

He pulled his mouth from hers and gave her a hard look. "This wedding can not happen soon enough. Consider yourself betrothed. Again."

23

The wedding ceremony took place at Gray Covington. Sutton did not wish to marry in London, surrounded by the curious glare of society and Jeanette's malicious tongue. Especially given the circumstances. It was no shock to him that Alex readily agreed.

The Dowager produced the minister who was witness to the marriage of Sutton's parents. He'd been visiting the Vicar of Covington, Madeline's father and Sutton's grandfather, at the time of the wedding.

Reverend Winkle was old and shriveled, like an overripe apple. His coat smelled of mothballs, and he had to be assisted into Gray Covington by a brace of footmen, each instructed not to allow the Reverend Winkle to fall. Even so, he took the time to seek out Sutton and assure him that while Sutton's mother was very close to giving birth, Robert and Madeline had most assuredly been married before Sutton came into the world.

Shortly after Alexandra's own vows, Donata had taken her aside and whispered, "I did not wish to dignify the rumors of my grandson's illegitimacy by speaking out about it, but now

I see that was a mistake. I feel certain that Reverend Winkle has put any doubts Sutton may have had to rest. Nor would I have you worry for your children's place in the world."

Alexandra hugged the Dowager tightly. "Does Sutton know how lucky he is to have you?"

The Dowager's only answer was to wipe a tear from her eye. "Dearest girl," she whispered as she squeezed Alexandra's hand. "Now go and enjoy the wedding feast."

She tried to enjoy the food, but her stomach was in knots at the thought of her wedding night. How did any bride get through the dinner?

"My lady?" A footman appeared at Alexandra's elbow intending to serve her a slice of roasted pheasant. She nodded in approval. Nervous, but trying desperately not to show it, she pretended to examine the pheasant. The food smelled delicious, but Alexandra had no appetite.

Her husband watched her down the long, beautifully set table while Miranda chattered enthusiastically to the partially deaf Reverend Winkle.

"How is your pheasant, my dear?" inquired the Dowager.

"The pheasant is exceedingly delicious," Alexandra murmured. She put her wineglass to her lips. Her mind kept wandering. What awaited her after this extravagant dinner? She felt the heat rise in her cheeks.

"I was not aware of my bride's love for pheasant." Sutton's voice came at her from across the table. "I was under the impression she favored peacock."

Alexandra sputtered and choked on the wine.

Amused at her discomfort, a smile hovered on her husband's lips.

She gave him an evil glare. Vile man. *Beautiful man.*

The Dowager looked at them both askance. "May we continue with dinner or must I endure more of what I assume passes for flirtation?"

"Flirtation? Grandmother we are speaking of fowl. Birds." Sutton lifted his brows in confusion.

"Hmmph." The Dowager stabbed at her pheasant with her fork. Alexandra could see she was trying not to laugh.

The rest of the dinner passed in a blur. By the time the dessert was served, an elaborate cherry confection that the cook had shaped into a heart, Alexandra found herself nearly bursting from her seat with fear and anticipation.

"Lady Cambourne?" Sutton's voice spilled over her in a caress. Without her knowing, he'd left his seat and now stood at her side. "I believe it's time we retired." He took Alexandra's arm. "Grandmother, Miranda, we bid you a good night."

Sutton guided her to the bottom of the stairs where Alexandra's newly assigned maid, Sadie, stood waiting.

"I'll be up shortly, Alex." Sutton pressed a brief kiss on her lips before heading down one of the darkened corridors of Gray Covington. "I've promised the Reverend a nightcap before he retires."

A sigh came from Alexandra's maid. Sadie was watching Alexandra's husband with a rapturous look in her eyes. Alexandra shrugged and started up the steps. Half the maids at Gray Covington sighed over him in such a manner she'd noticed, and Sutton seemed oblivious. The situation would likely not be any better in London.

"Ahem." Alexandra cleared her throat from her position on the steps to encourage the maid to follow her.

The maid startled, giving Alexandra a guilty look. Sadie was a sweet girl with bright red hair and a dense collection of freckles about her nose. She also possessed a mischievous disposition and the ability to tame the wildness of Alexandra's hair when not mooning over Sutton.

Alexandra tried to look stern but ended up smiling. The Dowager had instructed her to not be quite so familiar with the staff, although the Dowager's rules did not seem to apply to her own relationship with the young footman, Harry.

"I'm sorry, my lady. It's just that Lord Cambourne is very handsome. He quite takes your breath away." The maid reddened. "Begging your pardon, my lady, for saying so."

"Yes, he rather does." She smiled at the maid. "Lead the way, Sadie."

Sadie nodded and took a lamp off a nearby table. She led Alexandra up the sweeping grand staircase of Gray Covington towards the family wing. The room Alexandra occupied for the last few weeks as she went through the laudanum withdrawal was on the other side of the staircase. Her brow wrinkled. Those were dark days for Alexandra. Sweating, sleepless nights where she imagined that she had married Runyon after all.

"Here we are." Sadie stood between two doors and opened the one on the right.

Alexandra regarded the second door. She knew that must be her husband's bedroom, but she refused to contemplate it. Thinking of Sutton's dragon tattoo winding about his body made Alexandra blush to her toes.

Several lamps flickered in the darkness, giving the room a haloed glow. A fire crackled in the hearth. Light shone on walls hung with green damask, embroidered with the woodland animals and insects Alexandra remembered from the Dowager's parlor. This had likely once been the Dowager's suite of rooms. Thankfully, Jeanette hadn't used this chamber in years, preferring a suite of rooms especially constructed for her at the end of this wing.

Sadie had just begun to assist her in getting out of her gown when a knock sounded.

Both women looked up as a connecting door opened to reveal Sutton. He no longer wore a coat and even in the dim light, the outline of the dragon tattoo could be clearly seen beneath the fine lawn of his shirt. He sauntered towards them, his eyes never leaving Alexandra's face. The look he gave her made her feel...*naked*. She blushed.

Sadie stood agog next to Alexandra.

Sutton ignored the maid.

"Hello, Badger." He snapped a finger at Sadie. "Bring up a hot bath in two hours. To my room."

Sadie jumped at his command, nodded mutely, and scurried out the door.

"You've frightened Sadie," Alexandra said stupidly as her husband maneuvered her to the connecting door leading to his suite of rooms. "Shouldn't we," she stammered, "stay here?"

"No." Sutton shrugged. "After you." When Alexandra faltered, Sutton gave her a not so gentle push.

She turned to glare over her shoulder at him.

He was grinning at her. His fingertips ran along her arm. "Come, Alex. Come into the dragon's den. I promise I don't bite. Much."

Horrid man. Teasing her at this most *inopportune* moment. Torn between a sharp retort or simply pressing kisses all over his face, she did neither. The conflict was most disconcerting.

The room before her left no doubt it belonged to the master of Gray Covington. Dark burgundy drapes hung from the windows, matching the coverlet on what was the largest bed Alexandra had ever seen. She would be lost between the covers in a thrice and Sutton would never find her. An expedition would be launched to locate her whereabouts in the giant bed. She giggled.

"I see you find our wedding night amusing. Not quite the reaction I sought but..."

Alexandra gave his stomach a soft punch, surprising him.

He grabbed her hand and kissed the tip of her fingers, sucking her forefinger into his mouth.

Alexandra pulled her hand back, feeling the touch of lips and tongue down the whole of her body. *How was that possible?* "I was thinking, that I shall become lost in the depths of that giant bed. It will swallow me whole. Not even your Lord Bishop would be able to find me."

"But I would. I am an expert at hunting Badgers."

Sutton's playful words warmed her and some of the tension left her. Alexandra's gaze left her husband to run over the rest of the room. Maps covered one far wall along with a large stack of periodicals and books. Sheaves of paper and several inkwells were scattered across a desk that looked as if the legs had been gnawed on by beavers. The room was at odds with the image of Satan Reynolds. This room declared who her husband actually was, not the cultivated image the *ton* saw.

Two portraits sat on the large wooden mantel above the fireplace. She wandered over, conscious of Sutton watching her. She stood on tiptoe to get a closer look. Alexandra knew who they were immediately, Lord Robert Cambourne and his first wife and Sutton's mother, Madeline. Sutton's face stared at her from one miniature. No, she thought, not his face exactly but the resemblance to his father was markedly strong.

A young, pretty girl stared out from the other miniature, a winsome smile gracing her wide mouth. She appeared to be laughing at some private joke or she was looking at something that amused her. Another portrait of Madeline, clutching a plump child to her, hung in the music conservatory. Alexandra had studied that painting of Madeline and Sutton for hours. The love Madeline clearly had for her child had been captured by the artist. The Dowager told Alexandra that Jeanette had tried mightily to have the portrait taken down, but Sutton's father forbade it. Many nights, the Dowager said, she would find her son sitting quietly in front of Madeline's portrait, speaking to her as if she were there.

"My parents. Robert and Madeline." Alexandra could hear the slight ache in his voice from across the room. "My mother died when I was barely two, in childbirth. I have vague memories of a soft voice and the feeling of being loved, but that is all. I wish I had known her."

"I never knew my mother either." She gave him a regretful smile. "I remember her sending me to my Aunt Eloise when I was very young. She put me on a coach with a note pinned to my cloak." Alexandra turned back to the picture of Madeline. "I didn't see her again after that. She never even checked to make sure I made it to Helmsby Abbey. Nor ever visited. My father died before my birth. Aunt Eloise was his sister. She never spoke of my parents."

"I'm so sorry, Badger." Sutton came up behind her and put his hands on her shoulders.

Alexandra inhaled the cinnamon smell of her husband, reveling in his nearness and the comfort she drew from him. "Aunt Eloise raised me and was a most wonderful mother."

"Enough. I would not have us dwell on sadness tonight. Let us have some wine." A dark flame burned in the depths of his green eyes.

Sutton strolled to the table and poured two glasses of wine. He took one glass and carried it to a large chair that sat before the fire. He took a sip of the wine and casually swirled the red liquid around in the glass as he watched Alexandra who stood unmoving in the middle of the room.

The nervousness returned. Alexandra tilted her neck back and pretended to study the ceiling. What was she supposed to do now?

"Come here, Alex." Sutton's long fingers beckoned her from across the room. His eyes glowed like green coals. He threw one long leg over the side of the chair and sipped his wine.

Suddenly afraid, she lifted her head, trying to think of something witty to say.

Sutton laughed. "Don't be contrary. Well, you may be, but just now I wish you to do as I ask. Don't worry, I won't make a habit of it."

Alexandra perched on the edge of the chair across from him. The dragon's tail moved, clearly visible through the shirt, as he took a deep breath. She wanted to run her fingers over it.

"Tell me what you want, Alex." His voice, deep and melodic, caressed her. The wine glass dangled carelessly from his hand. His gaze fixed on her.

It was rather like being hypnotized by a cobra, Alexandra thought. She could feel the blood pulsing through her veins as she looked at Sutton. Finally, her curiosity got the best of her. "I – I want to see the dragon tattoo. I'm quite interested in how it was drawn. I've read about tattoos and the different inks used as well as the techniques."

"Liar. You are a terrible, horrible liar. Can you not ask me for what you want? I cannot guess at everything, as your mind is most complicated. What do you really want?" The green eyes took on a slightly lecherous glint.

Alexandra twirled a strand of her hair nervously. Right then she hated Sutton. "There are times, my lord, when I think of you as a horrid man."

Sutton gave a wry smile. "Indeed. I am vile. I torture virginal badgers."

She cleared her throat. "I should like you to take off your shirt so that I may examine your tattoo."

"Because you are intrigued by the technique used?" The huskiness of his voice slid seductively over her in a caress.

Alexandra's skin prickled pleasurably at his words. Boldly,

she replied, "No, because it arouses me." There. She'd said it. Damn him. He was deliberately baiting her.

A deep rumbling, erotic sound erupted from Sutton's chest. "Was that so difficult, Badger?" He set the glass on a side table and stood in one fluid moment. His features caught the firelight, shadowing and giving mystery to his face. Dark ribbons of hair, like black satin, swung about his shoulders. The tiny jade figure glinted from his ear. Sutton looked for all the world like a pirate. He just needed a knife between his teeth. An ache started between her thighs.

"I fear my fingers are clumsy from having so much wine. Come help me, Alex."

She wrinkled her brow in consternation. He had not even had a full glass of wine. Peacock! He was going to make her undress him.

❧ 24 ❧

lexandra approached the man in front of her cautiously. Her hand hovered over the first button on his shirt, grasping it between her fingers. Slowly, she undid the button, enjoying the feel of the fine lawn and the warmth of the skin underneath. The exotic scent of cinnamon that clung to Sutton moved around her. She thought she would faint from sheer delight. She looked up at him.

Sutton's mouth curled at the corners in amusement, though his eyes spoke of darker things.

"What is so funny?" she demanded. Horrid, *adorable*, man.

"Not a thing, Badger. Will you not help me out of my shirt, or will you just undo the one button? Should I call for my valet to instruct you? You've bred livestock, I assumed undressing your husband would not pose a problem." He gave a put-upon sigh. "I see I was misled."

She smacked his chest lightly with her fist. *Beast.* Her hands made quick work of the remainder of the buttons. Once undone, she took both edges of the fine lawn in her hands and pulled the shirt apart, as if she opened an expensive gift.

My goodness! Alexandra sucked in her breath, as she stared in wonder at the sight of the dragon's tail. The tail, dark green in color, came from the side of his torso and wound around his navel, seeming to weave in and out through the light dusting of hair on his abdomen. Without thinking, she ran her hand over the end of the tail, pressing her palm against his navel and the smooth planes of his stomach.

The dragon's tail jumped. Sutton's eyes, dark and unreadable, never left her face.

Emboldened, she stepped behind him. Her hands ran over his back and shoulders.

Sutton shifted, allowing one side of his shirt to dip down.

Alexandra's fingers traveled to the edge of the shirt. She pulled the cloth down the length of his back and tried not to gasp in wonder as the dragon slowly revealed itself. The enormity and beauty of the tattoo stunned her. "Good Lord, Sutton."

The dragon tattoo, exquisite and intricate, rivaled anything in Alexandra's experience. The exceptional skill of the artist was evident in every brush stroke. The dragon's almond-shaped red eyes, framed by dark sweeping lashes, looked down towards Sutton's waist. The head of the beast tilted regally over Sutton's left shoulder. The body wound down the spine of her husband's back, each scale drawn in detail, and outlined in ink that shimmered like gold. The dragon's smaller forearms stretched out, one arm reached for the right side of Sutton's back, the other clutched his left shoulder blade, giving the appearance that the dragon had crawled up Sutton to nest in his neck. The hind legs disappeared under the animal's body, only one clawed foot stuck out. The elongated tail wove around the right side of his torso, getting smaller and thinner as it wrapped around his right side and approached his navel. Sutton stretched and the muscles in his back undulated, making it seem as if the dragon came to life. The tattoo was a masterpiece.

"It's so real looking. I half expect it to pounce upon me."

"The dragon is not who you need to worry about," Sutton said lightly.

When he didn't move, or turn his head, Alexandra took that as a sign she could explore. Just touching Sutton, just letting her fingertips rest against his flesh, filled her with taut expectation. Tracing the dragon and feeling Sutton's muscles bunch beneath her touch pulled her into a sensual trance.

"It's beautiful, Sutton. Truly a work of art." She paused in her exploration. The pain he'd endured while this was etched on his skin must have been excruciating. She remembered the comments she'd overheard so long ago at Lady Dobson's. Sutton must feel like an oddity to have a tattoo, and especially one of this magnitude drawn on his body. A rush of tenderness filled her. The Dowager had been correct. Alexandra was madly, deeply, and forever in love. Not with Satan Reynolds, the man who stalked the ballrooms of the ton, but the man who dwelled within this room strewn with books and papers. The man who still mourned the mother he didn't remember.

Alexandra's fingers flowed around his midsection as she walked around to face him. Her hands ran up to his face, palms open against his cheeks. She loved this beautiful, complicated man with all her heart.

He pressed an open-mouthed kiss on her palm. The tip of his tongue darted out against her skin. "Turn around." His voice was husky. "I feel that since you have examined my back, the least I can do is return the favor."

Obedient and awkward, she turned, afraid he would find her wanting in some way. "I suppose I shouldn't ask if you need direction. I'm quite sure you're an expert." She cringed, immediately regretting the note of jealously she heard in her voice. Admitting her love for him, if only to herself, made her feel vulnerable. The intensity of the feeling frightened her.

"Shush, Badger. I have wanted no woman as I've wanted you."

Warm fingers ran down Alexandra's spine. The dress fell apart as his fingers did their work. Cool air sliced down her back. Slowly. Each time a new portion of her back became exposed, Sutton's mouth warmed it. Her legs shook. Her breasts felt heavy, almost painful.

Her wedding dress, a lovely confection of pale blue silk, fell to her hips. The silk hung suspended for a moment before cascading down her legs to form a puddle at her feet.

"Turn around."

Alexandra stepped out of the pool of blue silk and turned to Sutton. Her nipples puckered as she faced him. She knew he could see her breasts through the sheer fabric of her chemise. She covered her breasts with her hands, suddenly embarrassed to be nearly naked before him.

"Don't."

"Would it be possible, my lord-"

"Sutton."

Alexandra gave him a look under her lashes. Determination was stamped over his handsome face, as if he were a knight about to siege a castle. She supposed that was one way of looking at things.

"Sutton, would it be possible to perhaps turn down the lamps? I-"

"No. That is a distinct *impossibility*."

She forced her hands to her sides and tried not to tremble under his regard.

Sutton reached forward and pulled the ribbon that held the top of her chemise together. He pulled the ribbon slowly, purposefully, until the chemise parted. His dark hair fell across his face, his head bent to the task. The chemise loosened, the ends barely clinging to her shoulders.

He reached forward abruptly and wrenched the fabric down with both hands.

Alexandra's nipples hardened into points as the cooler air of the room caressed her exposed flesh. She turned her head, unwilling to look at him.

"God, you're beautiful, Alex." His breath drew in sharply.

Her hands clenched at her sides. She wasn't sure what was expected of her. The nipples of her breasts hardened into painful points, begging for his mouth. His tongue.

A low primal sound came from deep in his chest. The chemise ripped off her body, fluttering into a wispy heap on the floor.

"Pray be careful, my lord. I only have–"

"I'll buy you another. Dozens, if that's what you wish."

Alexandra was certain her drawers were next. She was not disappointed. One long finger grabbed the tapes of her underclothes. A harsh tug and the sound of fabric tearing met her ears. Naked now, except for her garters and hose, she stood before him. Feeling wicked and wanton, she met his stare as bravely as she could.

The green eyes smoldered as he took in her stance. His breathing quickened.

"Take down your hair." It was a command.

She stretched her arms up, conscious how the action lifted her breasts.

Sutton watched in rapt silence. His gaze flicked from her face to her breasts.

Alexandra pulled out the pins holding back her mass of hair. Chestnut spirals struck her shoulders and skimmed down her naked body to dance against her waist.

Sutton's arm shot out. He wound her hair around his wrist and gently but forcibly pulled her to him. His teeth nipped at her ear lobe. His mouth fell upon hers in a fierce kiss, demanding she give herself to him.

Alexandra responded by wrapping her arms around him. Her breasts rubbed against the hair on his chest. She groaned, tortured by the sensation of their bare skin. His arousal, thick and hard pushed against her.

"Wanton." He whispered. "Wanton for me."

Alexandra didn't argue. She nodded eagerly.

Sutton twirled her small form towards the giant bed. He picked her up as if she were no more than a housecat and tossed her on the mattress. Her hair fanned out across the burgundy coverlet and her legs fell open erotically.

"One day I will have you spread before me in nothing but your garters and hose, your very essence open to me." Alexandra blinked as the words came back to her. She sat up on her elbows to see Sutton watching her.

"You should not doubt me." He remembered as well.

The sound of boots and breeches hitting the floor met her ears. He would be on the bed in a moment. Her heart raced.

"Sutton?"

"Mmm?" The bed sank down on one end.

"The lamps. Seduction should take place in dim light, don't you agree?"

On his hands and knees, as naked as she, he approached her. She could clearly see between his legs.

"No, I do not. I wish to see you. Every lovely inch."

Alexandra stared at the canopy over the bed. She had been raised on a working farm. All male animals were possessed of the same basic equipment. Well, at least pigs and cows.

"Alex."

Sutton sat back on his haunches, a patient smile hovering on his lips.

Alexandra looked lower. A thick swatch of dark hair nested around his manhood.

Alexandra assessed the situation. She had felt his arousal through his breeches but underestimated its actual *size*. She bit her lip. It was so large. It was *much* larger than she'd anticipated.

Sutton leered at her. "Don't lose your bravado now, Badger."

The inky strands of his hair fell, framing his angelic features. The dragon peeked over Sutton's shoulder, watching her with the same intensity Sutton did. He got down on all fours and moved towards her. An exotic and beautiful tiger, stalking its prey. He hovered over her, his hair falling around her shoulders. His arousal brushed sensuously against her thigh.

Her eyes never leaving his face, she moved back against the pillows.

Fingers flicked one nipple.

Alexandra gasped, but she didn't move.

He rubbed the nipple, rolling it between his finger and thumb. The green of his eyes seemed deeper, richer, the flecks of gold lit by fire. Leaning forward, he took the nipple into the wet warmth of his mouth. He grazed the peak with his teeth.

"Oh, dear." Alexandra pressed her head back into the pillows. A spurt of moisture spread between her legs. The wicked feeling returned.

A finger ran through the soft fur of her womanhood. He gave a gentle tug before slipping his finger into her folds. "Wet already, Alex?"

Alexandra arched against his hand. "Sutton." His name stammered from her lips.

"Shush, sweetheart. I'll take care of you." He pressed feather-light kisses from her breasts to her stomach, nipping the tender flesh as she writhed beneath him. His fingers found the nub of flesh. Stroking it, he softly inserted a finger.

Alexandra moaned.

Another finger was inserted, stretching her carefully. More moisture seeped from between the folds of her sex. She ached for him to bring her to that precipice, as he had the day at the Royal Exhibition. He was preparing her to accept....

"Sutton." She panted, as he continued his ministrations. Her nerves flamed sensation across her body. "You must stop. We must discuss-" She mewled as his finger flicked her nub. "No matter how well you prepare me, I fear that...*that*...will not fit!"

Sutton laughed, the sound deep and erotic.

"You mean my *cock?*" His fingers wiggled inside her. He pushed in a third finger and she groaned.

"Yes." Alexandra was being slowly tortured. And she enjoyed it. "I realize that this is probably not the best time to tell you that it is too large, but I am sure-"

"Alex, don't be frightened." She felt the touch of his tongue on the sensitive nub and she nearly jolted off the mattress. "It will only hurt once, a pinch, sweetheart. It cannot be avoided. But your body will take mine in. I promise." He moved his mouth again.

Alexandra twisted, seeking to push herself more fully into his mouth. *Dear God! She would die from this.* She stiffened suddenly, as he slowly sucked the nub into his mouth. Alexandra cried out. The intensity of her response shook through her. She grabbed at the bedclothes and moaned his name.

As tremors shook her body, Sutton moved over her. His chest rubbed against the nipples of her breasts, the tiny hairs lacing her body with tendrils of sensation. He positioned himself above her, the tip of his manhood positioned at her entrance.

Irrational fear lanced through her. She tried to push him away. Her legs clamped shut.

"It's all right. Be still." He leaned over her, one hand cupped her face, the other, she felt slide to grasp her bottom firmly, forcing her to part for him. His eyes searched her face, looked into her soul.

She calmed. There was a strange glint in the green gaze, one she didn't recognize, but it calmed her. His eyelashes fluttered down. He rubbed his nose against hers. She relaxed.

"Alex." He thrust forward, imbedding himself in her.

Alexandra bucked, shocked at the pain of their joining. A pinch! She felt the wetness of tears in the corner of her eyes.

Sutton's eyes stayed shut. He didn't move. He barely took a breath. The muscles in his arms were tight and strained as he held himself back.

Her body stretched bit by bit to accept him. The pain still lingered, but a feeling of fullness slowly replaced it.

"I—I told you it wouldn't fit. Arrogant, vain, peacock," she whispered.

His eyes fluttered open and he gave her a pained smile. Then he shifted. Pulled back, and thrust again, sliding deeper.

Alexandra stroked his face and her fingers ran over his lips. "Sutton." The ache between her legs returned. She lifted her body to try to match his movements.

Sutton moved, circling his hips, putting pressure on her mound and the tiny nub that gave her so much pleasure. Every time he thrust their bodies caught at that sensitive spot until Alexandra could feel the pleasure inside her mount again to an unbearable pitch

Her breath came in short bursts. She arched against him.

Sutton thrust harder. He nipped her neck. Licked at the

nipples of her breasts. He whispered dark, seductive words against her neck as he rocked his hips against her.

"Wrap your legs around me."

Alexandra complied and felt Sutton's flesh sink deeper into her own. Her entire body was on fire, every nerve standing at attention, begging for release.

"Lift your hips, Badger." He pressed against the most sensitive spot. "I want to feel you come while I'm inside you." Sutton's voice was rough, his breath ragged.

An agonizing ache built within her. She felt herself stretch, like the taut string of a violin just before it breaks. The dragon moved beneath the palms of her hands, breathing fire on her fingers, as Sutton coaxed her into a rhythm to match his own. She grasped, hanging onto his shoulders as if she were going over a precipice, clinging to him as her body broke into a million pleasurable pieces. His name escaped her lips in a seductive moan as her body clutched tightly around his.

Sutton thrust once more, his breath stopping. He groaned as his body shook with the force of his own orgasm. His lips pressed a kiss to her neck. "Alex."

Alexandra lay still as the tremors left her body, her fingers threading through the ebony locks of Sutton's hair. Never would she have guessed it to be so...*amazing*. Why did women refer to this act as a duty? It was certainly no hardship. Maybe she didn't see it as such because she was in love with her husband.

The dragon's tail wrapped around her, holding her tightly to him. Binding her to him.

Sutton rolled to the side and lay next to her, careful to keep their bodies joined. "I told you it *would* fit." An angelic smile crossed his face. The green gaze, intense. "It fits *perfectly*."

THE TINY BUNDLE NEXT TO HIM STIRRED. MASSES OF DARK chestnut curls rioted over their bodies like vines spilling down a wall. He adored her hair. He absently twirled a dark strand around his fingers as he watched Alex doze. Impulsively, he hugged her to him tightly, against his heart.

Alex grunted and fussed. Prickly little thing. Even in sleep, she was determined to argue with him. Sutton sank into the pillows, enveloped in the warmth of the bed. For the first time since leaving Macao for England, he was blissfully and comfortably warm. All the way to his toes. He glanced sleepily to the fire, then the mantle above. His parents stared back at him, seemingly in approval. He felt certain Madeline would have liked Alex.

Alex shook her head, trying to dislodge a curl that tickled her nose. She tried to move and let out a cry when the curls of her hair remained trapped beneath his arm.

"Be still, Badger, let me untangle you." He laughed lightly. "Medusa."

Alexandra frowned and opened her eyes. Her nose scrunched in pretended offense. "Now I am compared to a woman with snakes in her hair? I think I prefer the small, irritable rodent."

He kissed the tip of her nose and carefully freed the trapped curls.

She placed her hand on his chest tentatively and traced the tail of the dragon.

Sutton hardened immediately. He wanted her again, but he needed to restrain himself. Alex would be lucky if she could sit a horse at any point during the next week. He squeezed her fingers.

"I'll ring for another bath." He nodded towards the brass tub. Sutton dimly remembered a knock earlier at the door and he'd growled them away. "You should soak." He looked at her with meaning. "It will help."

Alex shot him a confused glance. Her brow wrinkled as if she were working out a mathematical problem. Her eyes widened. "Oh!" Understanding spread over her lovely face. "Yes, a good soak will be most welcome."

Sutton turned his head quickly before he laughed outright.

"Please, Sutton. I know you are laughing at me. You must realize that Aunt Eloise's education was woefully lacking. She told me to lie still in the marriage bed and to think of books until it was over."

"And what book were you thinking of earlier, Alex?" He turned back to her, not bothering to hide the smirk on his lips. Alex perched in the middle of the enormous bed with her riot of curls covering her naked body. She gave him a mischievous look.

"Animal husbandry." Her lips twitched, determined not to spoil the solemnness of her answer.

Sutton's heart thudded in his chest. The opinionated, argumentative little tempest before him filled his heart and his mind, as nothing ever had. He saw nothing but Alex. Other women became nameless and faceless. Unimportant. His eyes ran to the miniature of his mother. Madeline smiled at him.

He padded over to the bell-pull. "The water will be here in a moment." He walked around the bed, releasing the curtains to create a cocoon for him and Alex before joining her on the bed.

She snuggled against him in the dark. He could hear her breathing, deep and contented, as she waited. A discreet knock came at the door.

Sutton poked his head out of the bed curtains. "Come."

A parade of maids entered, each lugging a pail of steaming

water. The tub was soon filled to the brim and a pleasant lavender smell invaded the room. As soon as the maids left, Sutton held out his hand to Alex. "Come, Badger." Sutton pulled back the curtain and stood.

"Turn your back," she said from the depths of the bed.

Alex's show of modesty, considering the time they had just spent in bed, was oddly amusing. The words tugged at his heart.

"Turn, please." Prim like a governess.

He turned his back, grinning to himself.

She came out the other side, pulling bedclothes with her as she approached the tub.

"Do not turn around." He heard the sound of her hand swish through the water, testing the heat. This was followed by curious grunting noises.

"Bloody hell."

Sutton wasn't the least bit shocked. The tub belonged to him and as such, the sides were taller than average. The maids neglected to bring a stool. Alex couldn't get her much shorter legs over the side.

"Is there a problem, Badger?"

"You know there is."

He turned to her. She had pulled his discarded shirt on in an attempt to cover her nakedness. The sheer lawn of his shirt clung to the curves of her breasts, billowing around her hips. The sight of her in his clothes, her nipples shadowed and pointed under the shirt, aroused him more than mere nakedness.

"Will you help me into the tub?" She clutched the shirt. "I'll take it off once I get in."

"You're being ridiculous. I've seen—"

Alex turned bright red. "I realize that. But I am still not completely comfortable with..." She waved her arms towards the lower half of his body. "...all of this just yet."

Sutton traced a finger down her cheek. "As you wish." He picked her up and laid her gently in the tub.

She immediately sank down and gave a groan of satisfaction. Her eyes closed as the water came up to her chin. She slipped her head under the water with a sigh of satisfaction, sputtering out the warm water as she came back up. A cake of soap made its way into her hands. Lather foamed between her fingers as she rubbed the soap.

"The shirt." The sight of her lathering the bar of soap was giving Sutton all kinds of ideas.

Reluctantly she pulled the shirt off, struggling to use one arm to keep her breasts covered. Every time she moved, a bit of flesh popped out. The entire display made him mad with lust.

Sutton took the shirt and flung it at the wall, where it made a loud, wet plop. His finger twirled through the water in the tub, inching ever closer to her breasts. The water of the tub rose and fell over the mounds of flesh. Fascinated he watched as her nipples played hide and seek. He flicked the tip of one pert nipple with his nail.

"Mmmm." Alexandra looked as if she dozed, but he suspected she watched the progress of his fingers through the soapy water. "I have a question," she murmured. "Please do not laugh. You must consider my inexperience. I have no one else to ask and you appear to be highly educated in these matters."

"Indeed." He pressed her nipple between thumb and forefinger.

"Is it possible for," she stammered, and a reddish tint rose from her breasts to her face, "for me to," she bit her lip, "do what you did with your mouth to you?"

It took a moment for Sutton to understand exactly what she referred to, as her breasts held his immediate attention. Alex never failed to surprise him. Or, to arouse him.

She gestured to his manhood, which swelled rapidly under her studious intent. Sutton coughed. "Yes." He stepped into the tub. He was afraid he would explode if she touched him, let alone if she-

Inquiring fingers, slick with soap and water, ran down the length of his manhood. Testing, touching. She placed her hand around the base and gave a tentative squeeze.

Sutton moaned.

"Am I hurting you?" The small hand fled away into the depths of the tub.

"No," his voice rasped. "No, it just feels...good." He tried to keep his voice even.

She touched him again. "This is not at all the way I thought it would feel. I was given the impression from Aunt Eloise-"

"We must establish Alex, that your aunt gave you the worst possible information in regards to relations between a man and woman. Can we agree to discard her advice?"

Alex moved her wet, lathered hand up and down his length and nodded. "Agreed. I doubt she would have approved of this." Her finger ran back and forth over the tip, circling round and round.

Dear God, was she trying to torture him? Her nail rasped the sensitive underside of his hardened flesh. Sutton panted and gripped the edge of the tub.

Alex moved until she positioned herself beneath his legs. His arousal was mere inches from her willing mouth. Her free hand ran up his thigh, swirling against the hair of his leg towards the sac that hung beneath.

"Is this right?" She squeezed.

Sutton held his breath. His arousal twitched, as if desperately trying to get between Alex's lips.

Suddenly, she let go.

Sutton shuddered with disappointment then shock, as he

felt her tongue flick against him. Alex mimicked Sutton's actions earlier, sucking and running her tongue and lips along the tip of his length.

Sutton wound her hair around his wrist. He pushed her head closer. He was going to spill his seed here in the tub, or rather in Alex's virginal mouth, if she didn't stop.

"Alex-"

Her mouth stopped torturing him. "Am I not doing it right?" Disappointment etched her features.

"No. I mean yes. If you do it any more correctly, I will stand here and spill myself into your mouth." He pulled her up against him. Water ran from the curling mass of her hair and down her back in rivulets. He picked her up and carried her to the bed. She smelled of lavender.

He laid her face down on the bed. His hand ran over the globes of her buttocks. "Sutton?" She twisted her head to look at him.

He ran a finger down her spine, watching as she trembled at his touch. He pushed her left leg up and knelt behind her. He pushed two fingers inside the warm cavern of her sex. His fingers slid in easily. She was already wet, ready for him. He thrust his fingers in again.

Alex made a mewling sound. Her body twisted on the bed. "Oh God," she said into the coverlet.

"God has nothing to do with this." He nipped her on the smooth skin of her bottom.

Alex wiggled and moaned.

He was so engorged, so hard, he feared he would come the minute his flesh entered hers. Sutton took a deep breath. He wanted to hear and feel her pleasure first. He caressed the sensitive nub, massaging it while his fingers moved in and out.

Alex bucked, her hips pushing up in the air.

He pressed kisses down her back, nibbling the pale flesh as he made his way to her plump derriere.

She pushed herself against his hand, rubbing herself frantically. Her muscles tightened around his embedded fingers. She would climax any second. He pushed her down, effectively ending the movement giving her so much pleasure. Sutton removed his fingers.

She pounded her fist into the pillow. "Beast." He heard her whimper. "Peacock."

Sutton leaned over and kissed her neck. "Not yet, love. Patience is a virtue. So I've been told."

She groaned in frustration. "Patience is not a virtue for me."

He pulled her back against him. His hands cupped her breasts, pulling at her nipples.

"What are you doing to me?" she murmured. "Please. I can't take anymore."

He pressed his arousal, hard and firm against her. One hand traveled leisurely down her body, fingers dancing through the down of her womanhood. He moved his hand over every part of her but did not directly touch the delicate flesh begging for his attention.

Alex tried to grind her body against his hand. She thrust ineffectually, pleading for him to touch her.

He pulled her face against his mouth, kissing her hard, and pushed her down on the mattress. Grabbing several pillows, he positioned them under her writhing hips.

Placing himself behind her, he thrust into her, burying himself deep within the slick folds.

Alex cried out and clawed at the coverlet.

He moved in and out with slow, deep strokes, careful not to hurt her. He reached down and worked his fingers against her nub.

She pushed back with her hips. "Harder. Please."

"God, Alex, what are you doing to *me?*" He pulled back and gripped her firmly about her hips. He should go slow, but he couldn't. He pounded into her.

Alex moaned his name. She exploded into an intense orgasm, the contractions of her body gripping him so tightly that they brought him to his own fierce climax. Her body milked him, wringing him dry. Panting, careful not to crush her with his weight, Sutton kissed the back of her neck. He pulled out, gasping as her body clung to his.

Alex flipped over, her breathing as heavy as his own.

"Is it always like this?" Her innocent question sparked some deep emotion in Sutton, causing it to flame to life. He pulled her to him, kissing her ear, then her lips.

"No. But it will always be for us." He hugged her close to his chest and wondered exactly when it was that he had fallen in love with her.

25

"Happy birthday."

Alexandra looked up from her tea and toast in surprise. The knife holding the apple butter hovered above her plate. She had forgotten about her birthday, forgotten about everything except her newfound happiness with Sutton. Gray Covington was only a day's ride from London, but the estate felt a lifetime away from society and the *ton*. The month since her wedding to Sutton had been the happiest of Alexandra's life. Marriage suited her, and she wondered why she'd once resisted it so fiercely. At least being married to Sutton suited her. Her loss of independence was a small price to pay to belong to the gorgeous man who sat across from her making his way through a plate of eggs and bacon. She awoke everyday in a state of bliss.

"Thank you." She smiled back at him, noting with pleasure the wave of inky black hair that brushed his shoulders. The earring hid in the shining locks, but she could see the tiny figure in her mind's eye. She would never tire of looking at Sutton. It was like having a beautiful painting by Rembrandt or Titian come to life. Albeit one that teased her, argued with her and made love to her with such startling intensity. Alexandra often thought she would die from sheer lust.

"You are most welcome, wife."

"A bit smug, aren't you? How did you find out?" She tried to sound nonchalant, but her heart thudded with fear. Had he written to Mr. Meechum, the Dunforth solicitor, without her knowledge? Had Mr. Meechum told Sutton the Dowager purchased Helmsby Abbey and Alexandra held the deed? She watched her husband carefully, but his expression remained playful.

"I have my ways, Badger."

"Definitely very smug for a peacock." She teased him back as a flood of relief mixed with guilt flooded through her. Alexandra did not yet have the courage to tell him that the Dowager gifted her with Helmsby Abbey upon their marriage. Sutton advanced her funds to take care of the servants there, find them new employment, or bring them to Gray Covington. Alexandra assured him she took care of everything.

It wasn't completely a lie. While Alexandra knew she didn't need the enticement of her estate in Hampshire to marry Sutton, something told her that her husband would not see it that way. Sutton never fully believed she married him for himself. A twisted bit of logic that Alexandra had Jeanette to blame for. Regardless, she needed to tell Sutton the truth.

What if he didn't believe her?

"Pardon, my lord." Zander arrived, carrying a large packet. "The papers, my lord, from London. There is also a note from Lady Miranda." He bowed again to Sutton, then to Alexandra, before marching through the doorway.

Sutton pushed the newspapers aside and tore open his sister's letter. He scanned the fine vellum, squinting a bit as he tried to make out the words before his lips twitched and he broke into an amused chuckle. He tossed the letter to Alexandra. "You're welcome to attempt to read it. My sister's handwriting leaves much to be desired."

"Translate for me." She glanced at the note knowing she would only be able to read every other word. Sometimes she wondered if Miranda was writing in some sort of code.

"It seems that without the protection of her brother, the notorious Satan Reynolds, Miranda is besieged with fortune hunters and other dubious suitors. The Dowager is beside herself and took a cane to one forward baron who tried to steal a kiss from my sister while grandmother wasn't looking. And according to Miranda, the man smells of castor oil which my grandmother finds particularly offensive. Miranda claims the castor oil, and not the attempt at stealing a kiss, is what truly incensed Grandmother. At any rate, she begs us to return as soon as we are able in order to guard her virtue."

"Does she mention Tasterly?"

Sutton scoffed. "Tasterly. What does she see in that man?"

"You should make an effort to know him better. He fears you, and your sister is quite taken with him."

"I do not care for the man. I am sure he has affection for Miranda, likely magnified by the size of her dowry. Tasterly needs to make an excellent match as he has frittered away a large part of his inheritance."

"Your sister is an intelligent woman. If Lord Tasterly is only after her money, Miranda will figure that out on her own."

"It is my duty to protect her." The angelic face took on a stubborn tilt. Sutton was a bit overprotective of his sisters and with good reason. But Miranda chafed under Sutton's restrictions. She would assist her friend when she and Sutton returned to London.

London. She had no desire to ever return. Country living suited her much better. The fear of seeing her uncle or Mr.

Runyon paralyzed her, even though Sutton assured her he took precautions. She also did not want to face society yet.

While the talk of the ruination of Alexandra Dunforth and the circumstances surrounding it died down, the scandal had not disappeared. Sutton and Alexandra had yet to make an appearance in London. This set the tongues wagging in the *ton*. Some said they doubted any marriage took place.

Sutton deftly sliced open another envelope.

Alexandra noticed the spidery hand of the Dowager. She watched his eyes deepen to a dark green, narrowing as he read.

"My stepmother has been busy. Gossiping and gambling with Herbert Reynolds on her arm. She plays the martyr well, telling everyone who will listen about her reduced circumstances." Sutton folded the letter but kept it firmly in his grip.

Reduced circumstances? Sutton had been far more generous to Jeanette than even Alexandra felt necessary. Sutton purchased his stepmother a smaller, fashionable townhouse, staffed to her specifications, and had given her a generous allowance.

"Herbert is covering her debts, it seems."

"Perhaps she cares for him."

The green gaze swung to her. "She cares for no one but Archie. She never has. Jeanette possesses not one redeeming quality."

Alexandra did not contradict her husband. One night, after a particularly delightful dinner, Alexandra made the mistake of asking Sutton about his childhood. She simply wanted to understand. Sutton refused to meet her eyes as he described the depth of his stepmother's manipulation while he was a child. How the emotional abuse intensified the longer Jeanette went without producing a male heir. Of his father's wrenching guilt when he finally realized what was happening. Thank goodness the Dowager had returned to

London at the birth of Miranda or Sutton's view of women would be tinged with his stepmother's poison.

"What could Jeanette possibly gain from marrying Herbert? You've told me that your distant relation is a wealthy landowner who rarely comes to London. He is a country squire. Whatever would Jeanette want with him?"

Sutton gave a choked laugh. "Badger, Herbert is the *only* other male heir to Cambourne. Other than myself. Jeanette covets the Cambourne money and estate above all else. She always has. My father used to say that she married Cambourne, not him." Sutton shot her a wry look. "Why do *you* think," he said softly, "she would bother with Herbert?"

A pit formed in her stomach at the question. "Surely you don't think she would dare harm you?"

"It's of no importance." Sutton gave her one of his most brilliant smiles and waved his hand in the air. The smile didn't reach his eyes. He hid something from her. "Don't you want your birthday gift?"

Would Jeanette actually try to have Sutton murdered? She thought Sutton's stepmother capable of many things, but it never occurred to Alexandra that the woman would be so bold as to try to murder Sutton.

"Badger." Sutton pulled a tiny gilt-wrapped box from his pocket. "No more talk of the wicked witch. Especially not today." He waved the box in front of Alexandra.

"I should like to read what the Dowager has to say for myself." Alexandra made a grab for the Dowager's letter, but Sutton shook his head, and placed the letter out of her reach.

"Nothing to concern yourself with on your birthday."

She moved towards the letter.

He feinted to the right to stop her, but Alexandra was quicker. She slid under his arm and took the letter off the table, darting out of his reach and opening the crisp paper.

'Jeanette has made sure to cast doubt on your marriage. She hints

that the marriage did not occur, and that Alexandra lives at Gray Covington as your mistress. A rumor that Jeanette feeds as she did the gossip that your father did the same with Madeline. Even though the marriage was witnessed and documented, Jeanette still spins her poisonous web. While your sister makes light of it, without your presence in London, Miranda's suitors have been lacking in reputation. Many of her friends decline to call. Please come to Cambourne House and attend several events with your wife at your side.' Alexandra's hand shook.

"We must return, Sutton."

"Gray Covington is close enough to London. We do not need to be there. Do you tire of my company? Do you wish to go to London?"

She placed the letter gently on the table.

"I do not care what the gossips say." He stroked her cheek. "I wished to ruin you." He gave her a lustful look. "I still do. I-"

"Sutton." She placed a hand on his chest. "We have been selfish in allowing Miranda and the Dowager to weather the storm alone. I am not afraid of Jeanette. Odious Oliver has likely eaten himself to death by now. And the *ton* does not scare me. Not even Agnes Dobson. The woman reminds me of an insect."

"Brave little badger." He kissed her softly and handed the box to her. "Open."

Alexandra tugged at the red velvet ribbon atop the box and lifted the lid.

Sutton looked at her expectantly. Smug again.

A beautiful gold locket sat on a bed of red satin. The locket was rectangular and formed so that it looked not so much like a locket, but a tiny golden book. Alexandra picked the locket up by the fine, slim chain.

"It's beautiful. However, did you find such a thing?"

"Look inside." He pressed a kiss to her ear.

Alexandra opened the tiny clasp and gasped in delight which rapidly transformed into giggles. The locket held two tiny miniatures. The left portrait was of a peacock painted in gorgeous blue. The right portrait was of a small, rodent-like creature. She had never seen one, but Alexandra assumed this was a badger. A tear ran unbidden down her cheek even through her laughter. What an idiotic, romantic, ridiculous thing for Sutton to do.

"Do you like it?" He resembled a mischievous schoolboy who has played a prank.

"You are most creative. How did you manage to get a badger to sit for a portrait?" She sniffed and tried to sound tart through the emotion choking her throat.

He wiped the tear from her eye. "I didn't mean for you to cry, Badger." Sutton pulled her around and kissed her possessively and soundly. He nibbled her ear before clasping the chain around her neck. "This is for us and us alone. Our private joke."

The gold felt warm against her skin. Her heart sang. She wondered how he found someone to paint the tiny portraits, and what the artist thought of Sutton's strange request.

His fingers trailed along the chain, then outlined the locket where it lay nestled between her breasts.

"Thank you."

While Sutton never spoke the words, she saw the love for her shining in his eyes. She only prayed it wouldn't fade when she told him about Helmsby Abbey.

❦ 26 ❧

"Tell the Marchioness," Sutton's voice thundered up the stairs, no doubt in some ridiculous attempt to hurry her along, "that we are leaving. With or without her."

Alexandra gave her hair a final pat, frowning as an unrepentant curl tried to sneak out of her careful coiffure. Sadie did wonders with her hair, controlling the tendrils in a lovely, if somewhat severe style. Alexandra gave her reflection a smile. Sutton would detest it.

"You'd best hurry down, my lady." Sadie deftly tucked another curl as Alexandra stood and smoothed her gown. "Lord Cambourne does not like you to keep him waiting. You are lucky that way." Sadie's crush on Sutton had not abated. She was in good company. Maids kept dropping things, spilling wine and tripping, whenever Sutton even looked their way. "Yes, I suppose the time has come. I rather feel like Daniel before the lion's den."

Sadie gave a "harumph." "You've nothing to fear, my lady. Not with Lord Cambourne and the Dowager beside you."

"I suppose," Alexandra answered absently, surveying

Sadie's handiwork in the mirror. Her gown was the color of sapphires, a deep blue that caught and held the light when she moved. Matching gloves, shoes, and a small reticule studded with brilliants completed her ensemble. Sutton had paid the most sought-after dressmaker on Bond Street triple to finish the gown in time for tonight's ball. Even now, an army of seamstresses worked around the clock on the rest of Alexandra's wardrobe.

"You look beautiful, my lady."

Alexandra gave Sadie a small, shy smile. She *felt* beautiful. The gown's color deepened the gray of her eyes and her dark hair contrasted dramatically against the sapphire of the gown. The bodice, cut fashionably low, skimmed the top of her breasts. A diamond necklace studded with sapphires hung around her neck. Diamonds and sapphires twinkled from her ears. The gifts from Sutton were lovely. Reluctantly, Alexandra had taken off her birthday locket for Sadie to clasp the heavier necklace about her throat. The thought of not wearing her locket made Alexandra uneasy.

She smoothed her skirts giving herself one more check in the large, oval mirror.

Sadie opened the door with a flourish and gave her mistress an audacious wink. The Dowager had chosen Alexandra's maid wisely. Once her initial shyness had dissipated, Sadie had proven to be as forthright and opinionated as Alexandra herself.

Sutton waited impatiently at the bottom of the stairs with the Dowager and Miranda. Dressed in formal black, the white of his shirt contrasted sharply with the tan of his skin. The dark hair fell loose, a bit defiantly, to his shoulders. Earlier, Alexandra had heard the Dowager extolling Sutton to tie back his hair with a ribbon for the evening. Sutton refused to do so.

Alexandra's breath caught as she looked at him. Sutton

was simply the most handsome man she had ever seen. And he belonged to her.

He turned as he heard her come down the stairs, his eyes running over her form in appreciation. "I thought to run out to the garden to find you escaping your fate by climbing down the tree outside our rooms, possibly to catch a passing hackney to take you back to Gray Covington."

Alexandra scrunched her nose, appreciating Sutton's attempt to get her to argue with him rather than worry over the Rocheford ball.

"That was my plan, but I could not get the window open. The latch is mounted too high. Sadie refused to bring me a stool."

Miranda laughed. The Dowager snorted.

"Next time I will think to prop a ladder against the house and loosen the latch for you." He took her hand.

She looked into his face, determined not to show her anxiety. It wasn't the ball, exactly, that concerned her. Since their arrival in London, a feeling of doom hovered at the edges of her mind. The Dowager told Alexandra that Archie had not been seen in well over a month. He'd likely returned to the Continent with his tail between his legs. Jeanette was furious at her cousin's desertion. Odious Oliver's townhouse had been sold to pay his debts. Her uncle, as large as he was and hard to miss, disappeared from sight. Miranda thought him in debtor's prison. The only thing left for Alexandra to do was to tell Sutton about Helmsby Abbey. She planned to gently break the news to him tomorrow over tea with the Dowager.

"I'm sorry I kept you all waiting." She held out her hand to Sutton.

"It was worth it." Sutton brought her hand to his lips and brushed it lightly. "You are beautiful, Alex. My beautiful Badger."

The feeling of unease increased. Alexandra put her hand on his arm and tried to tell herself she was being silly. All was well.

❧

"THE MARQUESS AND MARCHIONESS OF CAMBOURNE." THE servant's voice echoed in the ballroom. The *ton* went silent. Dozens of eyes turned to the staircase as Alexandra and Sutton entered.

Alexandra clutched tightly to Sutton's arm. She looked at the sea of faces. Several women eyed her with open hostility, others, jealousy. Caroline Fellowes watched Alexandra with particular menace. The crowd for the most part regarded her with curiosity, as if wondering why a man of Satan Reynolds's ilk would ruin *her* and create a scandal in doing so. Several older matrons huddled near the foot of the stairs opened their fans, so they could whisper behind them unobserved.

Sutton moved forward.

Alexandra froze. A light-headed feeling came over her.

"Buck up, Badger," Sutton whispered out of the side of his mouth. "Lift your chin. Give them your most haughty look. You are a wealthy and powerful marchioness, married to the infamous Satan Reynolds. You should enjoy your notoriety."

Alexandra considered this. If Sutton could withstand years of being gossiped about, she could tolerate this evening. She composed her face into a mask of utter boredom as the Dowager taught her. She barely glanced at Sutton.

"Well, my lord," her tone curt and perfect for the circumstances. "Shall we?"

Sutton chuckled under his breath, guiding her down the stairs as the ballroom broke back into conversation.

❧

DONATA RECLINED IN A COMFORTABLE CHAIR, ALLOWING Lord Wasser to fetch her a glass of punch. The man had to be at least seventy, but he flirted shamelessly with her. She appreciated his efforts. Her gaze ran across the ballroom to the dancing couples. Sutton swirled his tiny bride around the dance floor, practically lifting Alex off of her feet as he turned her.

Alexandra sparkled like a diamond. An errant curl flipped over her shoulder as she laughed up at Sutton. The sight made Donata unbearably happy.

They are right for each other. Her grandson's gaze never left the face of his wife even though at least a dozen women swooned over him tonight, especially that dreadful Caroline Fellowes. He paid them all no heed. Sutton's arms were tight around Alex, holding her to him. The *ton* considered it rude for a husband to dance so many times with his wife, but Donata noted with satisfaction that Sutton seemed loath to let another man touch Alexandra. When Alexandra did dance with another man, Sutton stood grimly on the sidelines. *He is in love with her.*

Donata felt a deep gratitude for whatever fates had led Alexandra to Sutton.

"Your punch, my lady." Lord Wasser tried to make a polite bow, wincing in the process. He put a hand to his back, shooting Donata a look of apology.

Donata laughed. "Sit next to me, you old fool. We are far beyond all that polite nonsense."

Lord Wasser sat and took a sip of his own punch. He touched her hand.

She pretended outrage, swatting him with her fan. Donata was vastly enjoying this evening.

White wheat hair, done up in a complicated coiffure, bobbed through the crowd. The hair, piled high atop a swan-like neck, glittered with diamonds and rubies.

Donata wondered where Jeanette had gotten the jewels. The Cambourne diamonds now belonged to Alexandra.

The regal profile turned and spotted Donata.

A slow, malicious smile spread across Jeanette's perfect features as she made directly for the chairs where Donata and Lord Wasser perched.

A short man, his formal attire ill fitting and disheveled, followed in Jeanette's wake. He huffed and puffed to keep up with her and not spill the two glasses of wine he carried. *Cousin Herbert Reynolds.* Donata suddenly felt ill. Her eyes searched for Sutton.

"Donata." Jeanette's eyes, a glacial blue, pinned Donata to her seat. "What a delight to see you. Let's catch up, shall we?"

She tensed. Jeanette seemed happy. *Much too happy.*

Lord Wasser, sensing the coldness between the two women, bade a hasty excuse to Donata and fled.

Now Donata realized why she'd told Lord Wasser to stop calling on her fifty years ago. He was a coward.

"The delight is all mine," Donata said with false politeness as she faced the evil that was her daughter-in-law.

❦

JEANETTE MADE AN EFFORT TO SEEM SINCERE AS SHE settled herself next to Donata. Not for Donata, she could care less what that old battle-axe thought of her, but for Herbert. Herbert wasn't incredibly smart, but he was infused with the gift of perception that some country folk seemed to possess. It would not do for him to realize Jeanette's true intent. Dull, slow, and prodding, Herbert reminded Jeanette of an ancient tortoise. He worshipped her though and thrived at the slightest bit of attention. He would make an excellent, manageable husband. Jeanette would be the Marchioness of Cambourne again.

Archie promised.

Donata spared a brief glance at Jeanette, focusing her attention on Herbert. "How lovely to see you, Herbert. You so rarely come to London. What brings you to town?"

Damn the old witch. She would have the woman sent out to pasture just as soon as Jeanette attained her rightful position.

"I have been lured by a fair flower." He stammered, looking with adoration at Jeanette.

Herbert's voice irritated Jeanette. High and raspy, he always sounded like a whiney child. Jeanette found it annoying and resolved to tell him to limit his conversation once they were married. He could write her notes or something.

She smiled at Herbert, as if he said the most brilliant witticism. Her eyelashes fluttered, pretending to be taken in by his flattery. "Oh Herbert, you shall spoil me with your sentiments."

Donata coughed and sputtered.

"My lady, are you ill?" Herbert peered at Donata, his concern evident.

"I wonder that the punch hasn't gone bad. I shall be fine, I'm sure." Donata's gaze flicked to Jeanette.

Jeanette grit her teeth. She imagined the old lady screaming as she was forcibly removed from the Cambourne townhouse. The thought made her genuinely happy.

"Is Lord Cambourne here, my lady?" Herbert asked Donata. "I have something I would like to discuss with him."

Good boy, Jeanette thought. She'd told Herbert earlier that Sutton would *adore* hearing about the new threshing technique Herbert employed on his estate. Jeanette didn't have a clue as to what threshing actually entailed, she'd overheard the term from one of the grooms, but Herbert became very excited. He couldn't wait to discuss the topic with Sutton.

She gave her hair a pat and counted the wrinkles on Donata's face. Jeanette had something to discuss with Sutton as well. Something that could give Donata a fit of apoplexy, and thus save Jeanette the trouble of exiling the old woman. She let her glacial gaze roam, stopping when it landed on her stepson. Sutton made his way towards them with the little field mouse clutching his arm. He didn't look at all pleased to see her. Well, she wasn't fond of him either. She pursed her lips and assumed an expectant pose.

Herbert's watery eyes watched her, mesmerized by her actions. The man adored her.

Sutton greeted Herbert politely. He nodded stiffly to Jeanette.

Bastard. Jeanette wished she could strangle him with the diamonds that hung about her neck.

"Herbert, it is wonderful to see you. What brings you to London?" Sutton turned to skewer her with those damned green eyes.

Herbert opened his mouth to reply, but Jeanette stayed him from launching into a recitation of his thresher by brushing her breast against his arm.

Herbert reddened and shut his mouth.

Jeanette supposed she would have to *consummate* their relationship once they married. Her future husband might still be a virgin. That could be amusing for a time. After that she thought sharing a bed with him on an annual basis should be enough.

"Sutton! You look well. Marriage agrees with you." Jeanette shot her hated stepson a brilliant smile.

The field mouse, the cause of so much trouble and Archie's humiliation, dipped her head.

The girl acted as if she were born to the title. How dare

she act the Marchioness. The twit should be *kneeling* in Jeanette's presence. Alexandra was nothing more than an overdressed farm animal.

"My lady, you look well." Composed and polite, the field mouse spoke. Donata likely trained the girl day and night to assume Jeanette's position. Honestly, what had her cousin seen in this girl? Her hair alone was enough to give Jeanette fits. She was sure there was straw in it. Probably a nest of birds, as well.

"I am blissful! Simply blissful. Herbert is keeping me company." Jeanette twittered. "Now where have you two love-birds been? London has missed you." She hoped Sutton and the little mouse enjoyed their sojourn. It was likely the only happiness either one was ever going to have.

"We stayed at Gray Covington." A muscle in Sutton's jaw twitched. He wished to dismiss her and return to the ball. Well, not yet.

"Really? That's odd." Jeanette widened her eyes, so that Sutton wouldn't see the triumphant gleam in them. "I expected that you would have at least taken the time to travel to your estate, Alexandra, Helmsby Abbey. I understand Hampshire is exceedingly lovely this time of year," Jeanette said breathlessly.

Donata gripped her cane. Her hands worried the top of it.

The field mouse stepped back. She paled and looked ready to flee.

"Oh, dear! Have I spoken out of turn?" Jeanette allowed her eyes to widen in surprised apology. "Donata purchased the estate some time ago and gifted it to Alexandra as a wedding gift. I thought it most generous. Oh goodness," her hand flew up against her heart. "Did you not know, Sutton? You shouldn't allow such an oversight to bother you. Clearly your wife is enamored of you." She laughed. "It's not as if Alexandra needed some special inducement to marry you."

Sutton's face turned glacial. He spun on his heel and stalked towards the doors.

The field mouse bolted after him hurrying on her tiny little legs.

Donata's breathing was rapid. Jeanette rather hoped the surprise would kill her. "I guess he wasn't aware. I seem to have truly put my foot in it this time." She took Herbert's arm. "Come, Herbert. I need more wine."

❦

ALEXANDRA FAIRLY SPRINTED TO KEEP UP WITH SUTTON'S longer strides as he wound his way through the ballroom.

"Sutton wait!" she cried.

He never looked back. He jumped into their carriage, leaving the door open.

Panting, Alexandra reached the door. Her husband grabbed her and pulled her into the carriage.

"Sutton. Stop for a moment and listen to me."

He turned and glared at her. Hurt stamped every feature of his angelic face. "Were you *ever* going to tell me? Is this why you agreed to the marriage? Even after ruination you would rather have been a pariah than marry me? My grandmother had to bribe you? I wondered why you never mentioned the estate again, why your beloved retainers never appeared at Gray Covington even though you told me you sent for them."

A million painful needles stabbed her. This was far worse than anything she had imagined. How did Jeanette know? "Sutton, that is not the case. You know that. Your stepmother has twisted things."

"No more lies, Alexandra. Would you have married me if grandmother hadn't sweetened the deal for you?"

Alexandra reached out her hand. "Yes!" She sputtered. "Of course, I would have. Do not allow Jeanette to-"

"She planned this all along. I can see the two of you cooking up your little scheme. She left us in the salon together. She wanted an heir for Cambourne. You wanted that stupid piece of dirt in Hampshire and your merry band of retainers. Hell, you were willing to marry Archie to get it. I suppose in comparison I'm not such a bad bargain."

Tears ran down Alexandra's face. "Sutton, do you hear yourself? Please calm down and we can talk about this. I didn't need Helmsby Abbey to marry you. Your past with Jeanette has poisoned you and-"

"You know I tried to buy it for you," he continued without listening to her. "Meechum told me it had already been sold to a private buyer whose name he couldn't disclose. It was my own grandmother." Sutton's face looked as if it were carved from a block of marble. He looked down his nose at her. "I felt I had failed you by not buying the estate. You let me live with that guilt when all along..." He looked out the window.

"Please let me explain, Sutton." She reached for him again.

He flinched from her touch. He turned back to her. "Tell me this is a misunderstanding. Was the price for your ruination Helmsby Abbey? Tell me I am wrong." Sutton's voice broke. "Please tell me."

"Sutton," she sobbed brokenly. "How could you possibly think such a thing? I love you. Why can't you see that?"

"Damn you," Sutton whispered he knocked on the roof of the carriage.

"Where are you going?" She reached out to him.

The carriage rolled to a stop. Alexandra didn't recognize the street. She had no idea where they were.

"Damn you, Alexandra Dunforth. Why did you have to be

like all the rest?" He jumped out without another glance. "Take the marchioness home." She heard him order the groom.

Alexandra sat frozen as the coach began to move. "I'm not like all the rest," she whispered, but there was no one to hear her.

27

Upon her arrival at Cambourne House Alexandra immediately called for a bath along with a glass of brandy. She stopped crying half way up the stairs. Sutton was behaving like a bloody idiot. It was an emotional, irrational reaction. He would see that after an hour or so.

She hoped.

The Dowager and Miranda burst through the front door of Cambourne House barely half an hour after Alexandra's arrival. Donata was visibly distraught, her face pale and haggard as she angrily railed against Jeanette, completely absolving herself of any blame.

Miranda demanded to know where Sutton was. How could he allow himself to be manipulated by Jeanette? He would come around, Miranda told her. He would be home for breakfast.

Alexandra spent a restless night, listening for his footsteps on the stairs. Exhausted, she finally lapsed into a fitful sleep.

Sutton did not come home. His bed had not been slept in. No note had been sent.

As Alexandra walked into the empty breakfast room, she

took note of the empty space where her husband usually sat.

"Tea, my lady?" Bevins, the Cambourne House butler stood ready with a steaming pot.

"Yes, please."

As the liquid fell into her cup and a mist rose above it, she saw that Bevins quietly picked up the place setting across from her.

Alexandra nibbled at a piece of toast and tried to quell the rising tide of panic in her breast.

Miranda wandered in a few moments later, looked at her brother's empty chair, and took a seat next to Alexandra.

Bevins silently poured her tea.

Miranda sipped at her tea and for the longest time she said nothing. Then Alexandra felt Miranda take her hand. "I shan't leave you, Alex."

A quarter hour ticked by. Alexandra pushed away from the table, prepared to go find Sutton herself, when there was a knock at the breakfast room door.

"My lady." A footman entered and bowed low offering her an envelope on a silver tray. Her named was sprawled across the front in Sutton's bold hand.

"Do you want me to open it?" Miranda asked.

Alexandra shook her head.

"He's a fool, Alexandra, if he can't see that you love him." Miranda's emerald eyes welled with tears. "I cannot fathom his sheer stupidity."

"Nor can I." Alexandra sliced open the envelope, pulling out the cream-colored paper it contained. She read it through twice before the contents sank in. Tears ran down her face as she laid the letter down. "Bloody idiot," she whispered.

"Alexandra?" Worry etched Miranda's face.

"He's gone," Alexandra replied calmly, wiping the tears from her face. "Your brother has accepted the offer of Lord Bishop to lead an expedition. He's gone back to Macao."

28

Alexandra put down the ledger and stretched to get the crick out of her neck. Her back popped as she stretched, the tiny vertebrae snapping into place. She rubbed her eyes. The numbers on the ledger were beginning to blur. She worked day and night, determined to oversee the vast Cambourne empire on her own. She barely succeeded. In the three months since Sutton's departure, or as she called it in her darkest moments, his idiotic abandonment of her, the work had been a balm to her soul. Work kept her from dwelling on Sutton. As she put down her quill her stomach growled.

"Yes, yes. Time for tea." Muttering she reached for the bell-pull when she overheard voices in the hall.

"Her ladyship is not receiving today! Please leave your card, my lord and I'll-"

A large, powerfully built man burst into her study slamming the door against the wall. The watercolor of lilies hanging just to the right of the door dangled dangerously for a second but did not fall to the floor

Tall and muscular, the man's very size dominated the

room. Dark, shaggy brown hair hung over his ears and brushed the top of the elegant coat stretched across the broad shoulders. Some would have called him handsome, except for the bend of his nose, a testament to having it broken more than once. The eyes, of course, were what made Alexandra sit back in her chair and clutch the desk tightly. One eye brown, the other a brilliant, azure blue. She'd read about the condition once, it was genetic and hereditary, sometimes carried in families for centuries. The effect was startling, and slightly demonic. She knew who this man was. She was actually surprised they hadn't met yet since he was one of her husband's dearest friends. Then she remembered something Sutton said before their marriage.

Nick's off on one of his ships, chasing the past else he'd be here to see me wed.

"Lady Alexandra Cambourne?" Her name rumbled out of the giant's chest.

Alexandra stood, walking around the desk with slow deliberation. "Yes. I am Lady Cambourne.

The odd eyes flicked over her, settled on her waistline, then ran back to her face. "Bloody idiot."

Alexandra's hands moved protectively over her abdomen. She swallowed. "Excuse me?"

"Oh, I don't mean you," he growled. "You're not the idiot. You're the Badger."

She swallowed again, somewhat unsettled that he knew Sutton's name for her.

"He doesn't know does he?"

Alexandra gripped the front of the desk. Her waist was still small. Her breasts were a bit fuller but not overly so. How did he know-"

He waved away her look of shock. "I am Nicholas Tremaine, Viscount Lindley." His voice, deep and raspy, sounded as if he'd been drinking whiskey all afternoon. "My apologies for missing the wedding. That was poorly done of me. I had business to attend to in France and only returned a short time ago. You know who I am?"

"Besides being the Devil of Dunbar, you are my husband's closest friend."

"Oh yes, I'm damned and all that." He waved the nickname away, chuckling as he did so. "It's the eyes." He watched her for any sign of discomfort.

Alexandra stood her ground. Her senses told her this man would immediately dismiss her, should she show the slightest fear of him. "Did you come for tea or to frighten me? My husband is also possessed of a ridiculous nickname, my lord."

A great, dark chuckle bubbled out of Viscount Lindley's mouth. He smiled at her, a wry grin that glinted of predatory male. Viscount Lindley possessed a dangerous allure that many women would find appealing.

He held up a leather packet tied tightly with twine.

Alexandra's heart lurched. The packet bore the Cambourne coat of arms.

"Cam was right to choose you." His eyes ran over her hair. "He did say you had the most amazing hair. Pity it's not down. Would have liked to see it." He shrugged. "Ah, well."

Affronted by his casual assessment of her, she replied crisply. "If you are quite finished with your...evaluation of me, I would like to open the packet. I assume it's from Sutton."

"Tart little thing, aren't you?" The full lips gave her a slow smile.

Alexandra stepped back from the look in his eyes. Viscount Lindley could be described as *bewitching*.

He laughed again under his breath as he watched her move away from him. "Oh, don't fret. You're quite safe from me. I'm really quite harmless. I haven't cast a spell in ages."

Alexandra sucked in her breath. How did he know what she was thinking?

He nodded at the packet. "Open it. Don't expect a personal letter, it's simply full of legal documents. Things signed by solicitors. Cam's on one of my ships bound for Macao. He's likely just now settling down around the tip of Africa."

Alexandra raised an eyebrow. "You opened my packet?"

Viscount Lindley ignored her outrage. "If he wants to get a message to you, he will. My ships stop all over the world, exchanging cargo and information. I'm leaving on one myself tonight. Bermuda." His large hand scratched at the whiskers covering his chin.

Viscount Lindley's valet had been remiss. He needed a shave. A pewter ring glinted on his thumb, pitted and worn with age. Scars covered his knuckles.

Alexandra cleared her throat. Had the circumstances been different, and Sutton at her side, she would ply this man with questions. Miranda had given her the history of the Tremaine family one night over dinner and it was quite an interesting tale.

He raised a brow.

Perhaps it was true—the things they said about his family, for the man seemed able to guess her secrets.

"I must leave for Bermuda tonight, even though it now appears that I should not." He pointedly looked at her stomach with worry. "The storm season is approaching. If I do not leave now, I may not have another chance for at least half a year. Things there require my immediate attention." Viscount Lindley looked torn. "Cam has taken measures for your protection, as have I."

"If Lord Cambourne truly cared for the safety of his family, he should not have gone off to Macao to converse with monkeys and traipse all over the Asian peninsula."

"I have to agree with you." He moved forward and took

her hand, startling Alexandra. His hand, large and warm, dwarfed her smaller, chilled one.

Biting her lip, she blinked back tears. How dire were circumstances if the Devil of Dunbar showed her pity?

"Alex, Cam will come back. He should just about now be realizing what an idiot he is. Forgive me for being...somewhat ill-mannered but," Viscount Lindley sighed, "Cam loves you. Terribly. It is not a state he has ever experienced before, which does not excuse his blatant stupidity at leaving. I do not even know what you argued over, but certainly it can be remedied."

Alexandra pulled her hand away, regretting the loss of warmth and the strange feeling of safety Viscount Lindley gave her. "We shall be fine, my lord. *I* will be fine."

"Stubborn." His tone showed approval. "As you wish, Lady Cambourne. I've given instructions to Zander at Gray Covington. You will not return there. Too close to London. You ladies are to retire to Blackburn Heath. The family seat is three days journey from London and damned impenetrable. You will be safe there. The country air would do wonders for your...condition." The suggestion held more of a command than a request. "I have already recommended such to the Dowager."

"I appreciate your concern, my lord. I will take your suggestion to heart."

Viscount Lindley did not like having his regard ignored, but he acquiesced. "It's been a pleasure, Lady Cambourne." He placed his hand on the knob and opened the door, thought better of it and shut it. His dark head swung back, and the odd eyes stabbed her with intensity. "He will come back, Alex. I promise." As he walked out, she heard him mutter, "If I have to shanghai him myself this time."

Viscount Lindley's heavy tread echoed on the parquet floors as he left her. Her legs felt boneless, incapable of holding her up. Cautiously she untied the twine wrapped around the leather packet. Viscount Lindley did not lie. No note addressed to her personally was inside, only a sheaf of legal documents making Alexandra Reynolds, the Marchioness of Cambourne, responsible for all of Cambourne in the absence of her husband, the Marquess.

Alexandra ran her fingers over her stomach as tears trailed down her cheeks. Her heart hurt, as if someone had sliced open her chest at the loss of Sutton. The weight of responsibility that fell on her shoulders nearly made her knees buckle. Sadness and disbelief filled her. If he did come back, it would not be soon.

She put a hand to her mouth, crying silently lest the servants hear her and intrude on her despair. She must be wise now. She'd told no one about the child she carried, not even the Dowager. No one must know. Announcing the impending birth of the heir to Cambourne would put her and her child in grave danger. Jeanette, especially, must not find out.

Jeanette married Herbert Reynolds barely two weeks after Sutton's departure. Jeanette *knew* Sutton would leave. The woman stalked Alexandra's every move, visiting Cambourne House often under the guise of seeing Miranda. The former marchioness would perch, like a vulture, on the edge of the settee and ask after Alexandra's health while pointedly looking at Alexandra's stomach. She would pretend concern and ask after Sutton.

Thoughts of Jeanette brought Alexandra swiftly back to her conversation with Viscount Lindley. She was not brave, nor was she stupid. Jeanette would expect Alexandra to stay close to the Dowager and Miranda. So, she would not.

Alexandra walked over to the desk and dropped the packet next to a lengthy letter with several invoices attached. The letter detailed various renovations Alexandra began last month at Helmsby Abbey. Renovations she would need to oversee personally.

The Cambourne coach would leave by the end of the week for Blackburn Heath, but Alexandra would not be making the entire trip. She was going home.

29

"Hit 'im harder! Bloody fucking toff!"

The Marquess of Cambourne stood his ground and swiped at the blood running from his lip. The crowd, a motley collection of sailors, thieves, and other disreputable characters cheered on their champion. Sutton's opponent was much larger, bald, and powerfully built. He was also stupid and slow, like an enraged bull. Actually, Sutton thought that was the man's name. Bull.

"Take his head off!" someone in the crowd screamed.

"Yes," Sutton mocked Bull, "take my head off."

Bull swung at Sutton.

Sutton bent at the waist, leaning back until he swore his hair brushed the cobbled stones of the alley.

The crowd roared in disapproval as Bull's fist hit nothing but air.

Sutton lurched back up. His fist connected solidly with Bull's jaw and he winced with the pain of contact. It was possible he'd broken a finger.

The big man stumbled back, shaking his head to clear it.

Sutton didn't intend to spend the better part of the

evening fighting for his life in a filthy alley. When the *Perse-phone* docked earlier today in Port Elizabeth, Sutton only meant to find a dark tavern in which to nurse his guilt over leaving Alexandra. He'd needed a distraction.

Well, I've certainly gotten it.

Sutton watched as Bull cracked his knuckles, readying himself to beat Sutton to a pulp. Sweat poured down Sutton's face. How had he gone from an evening of self-recrimination and scotch to this?

I just wanted a drink.

Sutton had sat down at the seedy tavern as the sun began to set and ordered a bottle of the best scotch the establishment provided. He was no stranger to the world of pickpockets, thieves, and sailors that taverns such as the Mermaid's Tail attracted. There were worse establishments in Macao with less friendly clientele. Sutton sought only the refuge of drink, anything to blunt the stupidity of his leaving London.

I allowed Jeanette to drive me from my home. Again.

The betrayal he'd felt upon finding out that Alexandra had kept the truth of Helmsby Abbey from him led Sutton to make a hasty decision. His anger caused him to settle in at White's with a bottle of whiskey. Hurt pushed him to make the irrational choice to join Lord Bishop's expedition.

Alex.

His guilt and shame at not trusting his wife filled him with revulsion. She would not have kept the truth from him without good reason, the good reason being that Alex probably feared he would behave exactly the way he did. The scotch, Sutton thought, would blunt the worst of it.

Unfortunately, Bull eyed him with suspicion the moment Sutton entered the tavern. He didn't care for the cut of Sutton's coat nor did he care for Sutton.

Sutton feinted to the left and spun. Not quick enough. His reactions were dulled by the scotch. Bull caught him on the side of his chin, knocking Sutton sideways. The big man grabbed at his collar, meaning to pull Sutton up to finish the beating.

Sutton shrugged out of his shirt.

Bull roared angrily as he held up the empty white shirt and tossed it to the ground.

"By all that's holy, look at the dragon!" A filthy-looking man with buckteeth and ginger hair pointed at Sutton's back. "Never seen a toff sport such a thing. Any man who can stand the sting of the needle is a fighter."

Sutton saluted the small, ginger-haired man. He had a supporter.

The ginger-haired man began taking odds. He shot Sutton a grin while urging the crowd to bet.

Sutton wondered how much his life was worth in Port Elizabeth. Several pounds, at least.

Bull ran, hitting Sutton square in the stomach and knocking the wind out of him.

The stones of the alley lacerated Sutton's back as he slid across them. His hands tried to grasp something, anything he could use to defend himself, but found only garbage and something squishy Sutton didn't wish to contemplate. Sutton's hand closed over a brick. He closed his eyes into slits, pretending to be too stunned to move.

Bull thundered towards Sutton.

The crowd roared. "Finish him off, Bull!"

Bull grinned. His upper teeth were missing. The big man loomed over Sutton. Bull turned to the crowd. "Always put yer bets on Bull!" He reached towards Sutton's head, meaning to pull him up by his hair.

The brick hit Bull on the side of his temple. Bull looked shocked for an instant before his eyes rolled up into his head and he went down, landing in a pile of refuse.

The crowd stood in silence, shocked at the loss of their

champion. Then the yelling began. A scuffle broke out. A man spit on the unconscious Bull. The ginger-haired man collected his winnings, winking at Sutton in the process.

Sutton backed away from the melee. He pushed aside an urchin who was making for Sutton's discarded shirt and took the cloth from him. The shirt was filthy and torn, but since he had lost his jacket, the shirt was all he had left. Blood trickled down his back, stinging the wounds made by the sharp stones of the alley. A good fight, one with fists, cleared a man's mind.

Alex.

Sutton could imagine the Badger raining punches and kicks upon him. He deserved it. He'd left her. *Abandoned* her. Sutton hoped to God Alex would forgive him.

"I'm a fool," he said as he rounded the corner towards the docks. Ships lined up as far as the eye could see. Port Elizabeth was the last port of call for those rounding the tip of Africa, headed to Asia. The *Persephone* would take on supplies and additional crew before heading first to Madagascar, then on to Macao. The *Persephone*, however, was going to be leaving without Sutton. Lord Bishop would need to lead his own expedition. The idea of wandering through the jungle, cataloging exotic animals and fighting off the natives didn't hold the same appeal for Sutton as it once did. Nor did almost being beaten to death in an alley. He wanted to go home.

Home was Alex.

Another of Nick's ships docked just this morning to take on supplies before heading to England. A stroke of good luck. He approached the captain, a man he'd met previously on the docks in London while in Nick's company. A berth for Sutton was secured with little fanfare.

He planned to approach his prickly Badger carefully. First, he would bribe her with trips to Thrumbadge's. Pleasure her so thoroughly that she would lack the strength to deny him forgiveness. Lastly, he would hold her to his heart and tell her what was in his soul. That he loved her and prayed that she could love him in return. He would never leave England again unless she was at his side. Sutton winced and touched his swollen lip. He would tell the Badger he loved her as he loved nothing else in his life.

As he approached the *Persephone,* a stone rattled on the dock behind him. The back of his neck tingled. Absorbed as he was on thoughts of Alex, he neglected to pay attention to his surroundings, a mistake he hadn't made in years. Someone was following him.

Damn.

He ducked just in time to avoid a blow to the head and the heavy club hit his already bloodied shoulder and back.

The man came back at him from the side swinging a wicked blade.

Sutton pivoted, but his foot slipped on the wet street. The knife nicked his ribs. He spun and kicked, his foot catching the man on his stomach.

The man went down to one knee, trying to catch his breath.

Sutton clenched his fists, ready for his attacker to get up. "Who sent you?"

A shadow fell across Sutton's shoulders as the rough feel of a rope draped around his neck. His assassin had a partner. Immediately he reached up, sticking his fingers between neck and rope, in a desperate attempt to keep from being choked. The heavy cord drew tighter, cutting into his fingers.

Sutton swung from side to side, desperately trying to dislodge the man who stood behind him holding the rope. He swung one arm wide, attempting to strike a blow. His fist hit nothing but air.

The man in front of him stood. "Archie says hello."

The rope continued to cut off his air supply. He saw stars. He saw Alex's face.

Sutton stopped thrashing. The world around him grew dim. The toe of a boot kicked his ribs as he fell to the dock. Hands picked him up and carried him to the water's edge, then flung him in the air. The shock of the icy water made him gasp for breath against the wrench of the rope. His body was pulled rapidly down through dark water.

The assassins had taken no chances. A large weight attached to the other end of the rope hastened his descent into darkness even as he felt the rope loosen. His last conscious thought was of Alex and how incredibly angry she would be with him if he died.

30

Alexandra helped herself to another muffin. Mrs. Cowries adored baking and Alexandra was a willing test subject for her housekeeper's new recipes. These particular muffins were filled with berries and held a hint of vanilla. She liberally applied butter to the still-steaming muffin and turned her attention to the letter on the breakfast table, but not before addressing her swollen stomach.

"Your Aunt Miranda is most upset that we are still here and not at Blackburn Heath." She chuckled and patted the mound again. "Now I fear it is too late. But she's coming to visit."

Miranda and the Dowager still resided at Blackburn Heath. At first shocked that Alexandra would leave them to return to Helmsby Abbey, the Dowager gave into Alexandra's stubbornness. She'd agreed to maintain the charade that Alexandra was at Blackburn Heath, making sure to write to her cronies in the *ton* on a regular basis, certain the gossip would get back to Jeanette. Now that Alexandra admitted she carried the heir to Cambourne, the Dowager and Miranda were determined to bring her to them. Alexandra refused to budge. Now it didn't matter. She was simply too large to travel. Her child would be born at Helmsby Abbey.

She put down Miranda's letter, wobbling a bit as she did so. Her enlarged size amazed Alexandra. Mrs. Cowries suspected twins. But Alexandra claimed her size was due to the enormous amount of food Mrs. Cowries continued to tempt her with. She patted her stomach in contentment. If not for Sutton's abandonment, Alexandra would be blissfully happy.

No letter had ever arrived. Nor had he communicated with the Dowager or his sister. Alexandra assumed her husband communicated with Viscount Lindley, but since the viscount was in Bermuda, she could not ask him.

Alexandra tried not to think of Sutton. Most days she succeeded. The renovations to Helmsby Abbey took nearly every waking moment. When she wasn't supervising the building of the new barn, Alexandra tended to the vast Cambourne estates assisted by an army of solicitors. But at night, Sutton invaded her dreams.

She woke nearly every morning by reaching out to touch the pillow next to her head, disappointed each time that Sutton's dark head did not grace it. Alexandra dreamed of the dragon, its endless tail stretching out as far as she could see. She begged the tail to wind around her and bring her to Sutton. He had to be at the other end. Except he never was.

The baby kicked, interrupting her thoughts. She watched in amazement as her stomach rippled and moved. Closing her eyes, she thought of the child she carried. No matter what happened Alexandra would have this child. Forever. Cherished and loved by her.

While he hadn't known about the child she carried, Sutton made sure that she, the Dowager and his sisters would receive every bit of the Cambourne fortune and estates that was not entailed. Herbert would receive the title and Black-burn Heath but little else should Sutton not return. Alexandra often wondered if Jeanette, immersed in her greed and ambition, and certain of her own intelligence, would think Sutton capable of outsmarting her. Jeanette would be very surprised.

A carriage rolled into the drive of Helmsby Abbey bearing the Cambourne coat of arms. Alexandra's heart caught in her throat. She hurried to the front door, clenching her hands in excitement. She opened the door and rushed out to the drive.

The carriage door swung open and a spill of violet silk followed. "Goodness, Alexandra! You look as if you swallowed the Christmas goose!"

Alexandra felt her face freeze into a smile. She tried not to show her disappointment that the coach contained only Miranda. But she wasn't quick enough.

Dazzling emerald eyes regarded her with regret. "You thought I was Sutton." Miranda murmured something comforting and held Alexandra close.

"I suppose I did. I know it's foolish." Alexandra hugged her friend tightly. "I am so very glad you are here. I've missed you terribly." She pulled back from Miranda's embrace and took her friend's hand. "Not in the least disappointed."

"You are a poor liar, Lady Cambourne. My goodness, what a charming place. And you say there is a library? Oh, I shall adore getting my hands dirty while I help you clean it. I am relieved that your horrid uncle didn't sell your books as he did the furniture."

"Odious Oliver never did see the value in books," Alexandra said wryly.

Miranda waltzed through the large front door and removed her bonnet, tossing it on a side table. Jameson, the aged butler, moved as quickly as he could to catch Miranda's cloak.

"My apologies, my lady." His hand shook as he collected Miranda's things.

Miranda looked over his head at Alexandra. A smile twitched her lips.

"This is Jameson. Jameson, this is Lady Miranda. See that the blue room is made up for her."

Jameson nodded, hurrying away as fast as his aged legs could carry him. When he vanished around a corner, Miranda burst into laughter.

"He is even older than Grandmother. Possibly older than Bevins and he is quite ancient." Miranda looked at Alexandra, all amusement gone from her gaze. "You were right to save them. Because of you they have a home."

"Yes, well," her voice caught, "it has cost me dearly. Though I have no regrets."

Miranda moved forward, but Alexandra waved her away. "It's all right. Women's nerves. The baby." She ran her hands over her stomach.

Miranda looked as if about to mention Sutton, then thought better of it. She smiled brightly. "Yes. The baby. I am full of questions. Does it kick? Do you dream about it? I say that only because I read once that a woman who is *enceinte* will sometimes dream about her child and the dreams come true. And furthermore-"

Alexandra laughed, grateful her friend had chosen a subject Alexandra did not mind discussing. "Miranda, that is quite the most anyone has said to me in quite some time. I must catch my breath."

Miranda giggled, her green eyes bright and so like Sutton's that Alexandra felt a spurt of longing for him.

Miranda cocked her head, her gaze knowing. "He's a dimwit, Alex. I never thought to say such a thing about Sutton. But he has to be addled to have left you." Miranda put her hand to Alexandra's cheek. "He does love you, you know. I saw it that day at Thrumbadge's. My brother is just a bit," she hesitated, "*damaged.*"

Alexandra shook her head. "Miranda, you don't need to tell me."

"You need to understand why he would react the way he did. I'm not excusing Sutton, mind you, only I empathize. I know all about the business between him and Mother. She's a terrible person, my mother." Miranda's lips hardened, and she looked away for a moment. "When I was a child and Sutton just a lad about to go to Eton, my mother used to say things to him. Horrible things. I knew even then she hated him." Miranda shook her head. "Sutton used to moon after Mother. Obeyed her every whim. He was so desperate for her to love him. Hungry for it, in fact. I often wondered why, as she never loved me, and I don't miss it."

Alexandra noted the thread of hurt in Miranda's words and gently placed a hand on her friend's shoulder.

"I am not excusing his behavior, Alex. I just want you to understand that Sutton never allows anyone to see who he really is, but I suspect he allowed you to, and it scared him. Mother saw that. She is an expert at finding a person's weak spot and exploiting it.

"I should have told him, Miranda. About Helmsby Abbey. I knew it was wrong to keep the truth from him."

"Actually, I believe the fault is Grandmother's. She shouldn't have purchased Helmsby Abbey without telling either of you, though it's glorious, by the way."

"I don't blame the Dowager. I blame myself." Alexandra's brow wrinkled. "I should have told him before I married him, but I was-"

"Afraid he would run away? Mother did this to him before. Years ago." She cocked a brow at Alexandra. "But we won't speak of that now." She gave a pointed look at Alexandra's stomach. "I know Grandmother's told you everything. About Elizabeth. In case-"

"Sutton doesn't return." The words hung in the air between them. So, the Dowager had lost hope that her grandson would come back to England. Desolation and emptiness stole over her, and for a moment she allowed herself to wallow in it before pushing it aside. Now was not the time for her to be weak. The lives and well-being of many depended on her. Alexandra lifted her chin, pushing aside her fear. "No matter what," she placed her hand on her stomach, "we shall be fine."

Miranda nodded in approval. "He *will* return, and I look forward to watching him beg your forgiveness. But until then, I am here. I won't leave you."

31

Alexandra walked down the hallway towards her study, ready to do battle with a stack of letters from London and the never-ending ledgers. Miranda received a note yesterday that a special shipment awaited her in the village. Another shipment. Since her sister-in-law's arrival a month ago, Miranda seemed determined to restock the Helmsby Abbey library with every book Thrumbadge's offered. Her eyes took on a special glow of delight as she read the missive and begged Alexandra to come with her, but Alexandra declined. Her condition, she told Miranda, made riding in a carriage very uncomfortable.

Miranda commandeered a groom to take her into the village.

Alexandra waved them off from the porch, Miranda chattering non-stop to Michael, Helmsby Abbey's head groom. She stood on the porch for the longest time until the carriage disappeared from view. The sweetness of the grass caught her nostrils as the sun warmed her face. She was putting off the inevitable. The ledgers.

She walked back into the house and plopped herself down

in the ancient, overstuffed leather chair. Kicking off her slippers, she wiggled her poor feet. They were terribly swollen. Mrs. Cowries soaked them every night, but it didn't seem to help. The size of her stomach certainly gave credence to Mrs. Cowries' theory that Alexandra carried twins.

With one hand resting on the mound of her stomach, Alexandra's other hand picked up a freshly sharpened quill. Her hand hovered over the paper as she glanced towards the study window. The curtains of the study were drawn tight against the late morning sun.

Odd.

The servants opened them every morning, as Alexandra preferred to work with a view of the gardens while she toiled at the large desk. Her ears picked up the sound of heavy breathing. Her neck prickled in fear. Someone was in the room with her, hiding in the dark far corner.

"Hello, niece." Odious Oliver emerged into the dim light and waddled towards her. He looked awful. His skin sagged around his chin and his eyes held a yellow cast. Stains dotted his waistcoat and the elbows of his coat were so worn she could see his shirt through them. The bit of gray hair left on his head hung to his shoulders in greasy strands.

Bile rose in her throat. Her uncle. Here. Dear God, why had he come?

"My, but you've been busy. Renovating this pile of manure, though why you'd bother I'm not sure. Managing Cambourne. But I see you have a vested interest." His bulging eyes took in her swollen form. "That must be the heir to Cambourne. Pity we won't need him. We've found another." He sneered.

Alexandra's heart raced. "Mrs. Cowries! Jameson! Derek!"

Oliver shook his head sadly. "Oh, that won't do any good, my dear. Besides the fact that your servants are so decrepit that they couldn't give you assistance if they tried, I've taken the liberty of locking them in the barn while you were lazed about the porch. Mrs. Cowries in particular was not pleased to see me. Had to put a flour sack over her face to get her to listen. That woman never did like me. Always refused to make me my favorite pudding." Her uncle leaned over the desk, his hands splayed out over the stack of papers. His breath smelled of soured wine and ill humor. "No matter, we're going to set the barn on fire. Warm this place up a bit. Perhaps I'll roast a sausage along with your servants."

Alexandra paled. "Miranda is here. She–"

"She won't be rescuing you." He shook his head at her shocked look. "Don't fret, niece. Her carriage wheel will simply be loosened. How fortunate that my man watching the house overheard her plans to visit the village. She will be delayed. Hours, likely."

"Get out. Get out of my house." Alexandra trembled in anger mixed with a desperate fear. She pointed at her uncle, her finger shaking as she spoke.

Odious Oliver smirked. "You're not in charge, you bossy little twit."

A carriage rolled into the courtyard.

Alexandra looked expectantly towards the door at the sound of the wheels, praying that Miranda had forgotten something and returned.

"Why couldn't you have just married Runyon? Stupid little overeducated bitch."

Alexandra flinched from the hatred in her uncle's voice. She stood, gripping at the desk to steady herself.

"Now things are going to go much harder for you. Exactly what you deserve since you ruined everything." Odious Oliver gave an evil chuckle, his eyes widening with insane merriment as Alexandra flitted from behind the desk. He made as if to grab her and laughed maniacally when she sidestepped out of his touch.

Alexandra needed a weapon, something, anything, to fend

off the monster in front of her. Her eyes spied the letter opener on the desk.

Oliver wagged a bulbous finger at her. "No. Not a good idea, niece. You could slip," his tone became more menacing, "and stab that brat in your belly."

Alexandra moved backwards towards the wall, her eyes continuously searching the room. Cold metal touched the back of her arm. Her grandfather's sword! Eyes never leaving her uncle's face, she slid the sword into the folds of her skirt.

The sound of the front door opening met her ears. Steps sounded down the foyer.

Oliver's face creased in worry. He looked like a terrified walrus. Sweat ran down his sallow cheeks.

"Who is here?" Alexandra grabbed the sword tighter.

"It's a surprise." Odious Oliver regained his composure, but the anxiety is his voice bled through his words. "Speaking of surprises, Alexandra, did I ever tell you what a surprise it was for your aunt, when I returned unexpectedly?"

Alexandra began to shake her head slowly, somehow sensing what her uncle would say.

"She wrote to Mr. Meechum, that dunderhead solicitor, telling him the *entire* Dunforth fortune was to be given to *you*. Did you know that? Ridiculous woman. I was her husband. She even revised her will to revoke my guardianship. I was not pleased." He twirled his mustache into greasy points on each end of his face. "Totally unacceptable."

Alexandra swayed against the wall. Her aunt hadn't lied to her.

"Stupid woman, Eloise. She boasted about changing the will, coughing and choking on her own spittle. She thought I would just go away, fade back to London without a penny to my name. Not bloody likely with the duns beating at my door everyday." His eyes took on a crazed sheen. "The will never made it to Meechum. She barely made a protest when I told her I would take every farthing of the Dunforth money and dispose of you." He cocked his head in thought. "Well, she may have protested. Couldn't hear her through the pillow. I did push it down bloody hard. The woman would simply *not* shut up." He sighed and shrugged as if making a joke. "I needn't have worried anyone would hear. All the servants are quite deaf."

Alexandra clasped the sword tightly and stifled a sob of anguish. He'd *killed* her aunt. He'd *sold* Helmsby Abbey. He'd *traded* her to that depraved cur Archie Runyon to pay his debts.

"You filthy, disgusting..."

"Now, Alexandra, is that anyway to talk to your beloved uncle? Tsk, tsk, your manners are quite lacking." His grin widened, showing the stumps of rotten teeth. But, not at her, at someone who opened the door and entered the study.

"Hello, pigeon."

She nearly fainted dead away. Archie Runyon. Dear God. She still had nightmares about the man. She thought him gone to the Continent. Panic, so profound it threatened to make her black out coursed through her frame.

"Help! Someone, please!" She screamed as loud as she could.

Her uncle shook his head at Archie Runyon. "Silly goose, I've told her they are all locked in the barn. No one can hear her. She's not listening."

Archie Runyon, perfectly dressed in a light blue suit, walked into the study swinging his wolf's-head cane. His glacial blue eyes bored into her. "Shut up, Alexandra, or I will light the barn on fire this instant. *This instant.* I do so enjoy a good fire, and it's quite chilly in Hampshire." He looked around the room, sniffing a bit. "I have to agree, Burke, this is a pile of manure and brick. Disgusting." He put a handkerchief over his nose. "Quite dusty. All these silly books." He waved at the bookcase.

Alexandra pushed herself as close to the wall as she could. *I must not faint.* The baby kicked as if in agreement. No, she must not faint. Her hand slid over the sword, her palms thick with sweat.

Runyon moved further into the room, catching sight of her enlarged waist. "Oh dear, I see that some things have transpired in my absence." He pointed the cane at her stomach. "Pregnant women disgust me. They remind me of cows and farm animals, which I suppose in this setting is appropriate. We shall have to fix that."

"I will kill you if you come near me." She brandished the sword. The weight of the weapon made her hand shake.

"Really? You are going to run me through?" Runyon gave an amused chuckle. "I doubt that. Dear Lord, you are so repulsively large, you can barely move. You've become hysterical. Burke, take the sword from her please, so we can get on with this."

Alexandra looked at the two men wildly. She waved the sword between the two.

Odious Oliver mopped his face with a filthy handkerchief. He shot a look at Alexandra holding the sword. "Look here, I've paid my debt to you Runyon. I told you she didn't show up at Blackburn Heath. I followed Miranda. I told you how to get to Helmsby Abbey. That was our agreement." Her uncle sniffed as if insulted. "Swordfights were not part of the bargain."

"Miranda is unharmed?"

Burke nodded. "One of the carriage wheels has been loosened, but not enough to cause the carriage to tip over. It will simply slow her down."

Archie nodded in approval. "Good. My cousin does not wish her daughter harmed as she could be useful a bit later."

He moved towards the desk, giving a giggle as he watched Alexandra try to lift the sword higher. "Alexandra do put down the sword. You must compose a letter for Miranda. I've no doubt she is familiar with your handwriting. I shall tell you what to say. Your disappearance combined with the horrible news of Cam's death should drop the Dowager like a stone." He laughed evilly. "Never did like the old bitch."

Alexandra paled, clutching the sword tighter. "I don't believe you. Sutton could not be dead." The room spun.

"Oh, I'm quite certain he is." Archie replied. "No body, of course, for a funeral, but when you are wrapped in chains, and thrown into the ocean, well even Cam couldn't avoid his fate."

A sob escaped Alexandra. "Oh my God." She wanted to crumple to the floor and weep until she couldn't feel anymore.

Seeing her bend over, Archie raised his cane at her uncle.

"Damn it, Burke, take the sword, and let's get on with it. She can barely stand she's so overcome with grief."

Odious Oliver approached her cautiously, his eyes narrowed. She could smell the sweat on him. One fat arm reached out.

Alexandra brought the sword up turning it sideways, with every bit of strength she possessed. Rage fueled her as she thought of what these men had done. The blade sliced into her uncle's arm, just below the elbow. She pulled it down, opening the flesh on her uncle's arm to his wrist.

Blood spurted, spraying Alexandra's cheeks.

Her uncle screamed in pain.

"You bitch!" He cried, clutching his heavily bleeding arm. "You burdensome female how dare you strike me!"

Runyon pretended to flick a piece of lint off his shoulder. He adjusted his cuffs. "Do hurry, Burke. I grow weary. She is with child and presents no challenge."

Odious Oliver walked to the fireplace, grabbing the poker. "I should beat you senseless you ungrateful bitch."

"Do not injure her." Runyon commanded. "I don't want her hurt. Yet."

Alexandra raised the sword again, her muscles burning with the effort. The sword shook, her strength failing. Giving a mighty groan, she swung the blade at her uncle again.

Burke batted away the sword with the poker. "How tiresome you are, Alexandra. Horribly overeducated." He pinned the sword with the poker and took the weapon from her easily. He turned triumphantly to Runyon. His cheeks flushed red. His breath came in deep gulps. Apparently, the effort of disarming Alexandra was nearly too much for him.

He threw both sword and poker to the floor. "I kept my part of the bargain, Runyon. You promised me if I brought you here, and helped you, I could sell this place and everything in it. My debt to you forgiven." Her uncle scanned the study. "I wonder how much I can get for all these old books?"

"Oh, *that*. I neglected to inform you that there's been a change of plans. Although, I *am* forgiving your debt to me." Runyon calmly took a pistol out of his breast pocket and cocked it.

Hearing the sound her uncle turned to Runyon, just as Runyon put a bullet between his eyes.

A bright red hole formed in Odious Oliver's forehead. The moonlike face, still dripping sweat, froze in an expression of surprise. His obese form wobbled.

Runyon stepped out of the way. "Oh dear, which way should he fall?"

The study shook as her uncle's body fell facedown on the floor, causing the vase of flowers on Alexandra's desk to shake.

Alexandra screamed.

Runyon approached the body, nudging Burke's form with

his toe. "Don't carry on, pigeon. You hated your uncle. I hated your uncle. He was a disgusting pig who never appreciated you. You should thank me. Now, be a good girl. Come write Miranda a note. I'll tell you exactly what to say." His dipped a quill in the inkwell and held it out.

Alexandra couldn't move. She watched the blood begin to spread over the carpet where her uncle lay. She shook her head.

"Are you worried about Miranda?" He said with false concern. "I promise she won't see a thing." Runyon called over his shoulder, "Bigby?"

A large, thuggish man appeared at the door of the study.

Alexandra shrank back. The man bore a large scar and held a pistol in his belt.

"Put this," he pointed his cane at Burke, "in the barn. Don't set the fire yet. I wish Miss Dunforth to light the flint." Runyon tossed a bag of coins at the man. "Please disappear from Hampshire."

The man nodded and caught the bag of coins. He rolled her uncle neatly in the rug, barely sparing Alexandra a glance. A small trail of blood followed them out.

"Oh dear, you'll have to tidy that up before we leave. Now on to the note."

"Monster. You are a monster." The bile rising in her throat made her choke on every word. "I won't do it. I'd rather die than help you."

"Hmmm. You *will* do so, or I shall cut out that child with this very sword." He pointed to the weapon still lying on the floor. "I studied with a physician once, in France. Did I tell you that? I know just how to do it."

"Not even you would do something so inhuman." Terror for her unborn child paralyzed her.

"Oh, but I would."

"Why are you doing this to me?" The words came out in a

sob as her mind raced for a way to escape the elegantly clad madman standing in her study.

"Because I *can*. Now be a good girl and sit at the desk."

Alexandra moved slowly away from the wall.

"You are an intelligent woman. I appreciate that about you, Alexandra, truly I do. You clearly see that your failure to follow my instructions will result in the demise of the child you carry. Although my cousin herself has never felt that particular inclination to protect her children, she assured me that other women did. As always my darling Jeanette is correct."

Runyon smiled, assured of her defeat. He walked to the window, turning his back on her as if to prove she presented no threat to him. "After you write the letter, you'll mop up this mess. I expect you'll need to pack. I refuse to buy you any clothing while you are in this condition."

Alexandra eyed the weapons still on the floor. The sword was simply too heavy, but the poker was not. "What do I have to do to spare my servant's lives?" Silently, she inched closer to the poker.

Runyon chuckled and rocked on his heels, still staring out the window towards the barn and surrounding fields. "I will let you possibly spare *one* of them." The enjoyment in his voice could not be missed as he taunted her.

She bent and quietly picked up the poker. "Please, all of them. Must I beg? I shall if need be."

"Once we get to Italy, we will get rid of that brat." He informed her. "I'll let the child live, but you must give it away. Perhaps to an orphanage or a workhouse. I hate children. Dirty little buggers."

Alexandra summoned all the strength at her disposal, knowing her life and the life of her child and servants depended on her. With a heave, she swung the poker at the back of Runyon's head. She aimed for his bald spot wishing the blow would split his skull, but the poker was heavier than she thought. Her aim went wild. The blow only grazed the side of his head, but it was enough to bring Runyon to his knees.

He grunted, his hands reaching out to steady himself as he fell. The wolf's-head cane slid from his hands and out of reach.

"Damn you!" He screeched. "Damn you to hell, Alexandra." He touched one hand to the side of his head, holding up his bloody fingertips to her. "Just for that, pigeon, we will light the barn now!"

Alexandra shook her head wildly and ran.

Her feet flew across the back hall of the house. Her only escape was through the small side door leading to the vegetable garden. From there, Alexandra could make her way to the path winding through the woods to the village. Silently she prayed for the safety of her servants. She must not stop even though her lungs already burned with her efforts.

A scream of pure rage followed her out the door. Runyon was on his feet and coming after her.

Alexandra headed for the thick woods. She tripped over a branch, caught herself, and kept moving.

The baby kicked. This time harder.

"Alexandra!" Runyon bellowed. "You've been a bad, bad girl! I'll have to use the whip on you."

He is insane.

Alexandra ran as fast as her swelling form would allow through the thick mat of leaves and underbrush. Her heart shattered with every step she took refusing to believe the poison Runyon uttered. *Sutton cannot be dead. I would feel it. I would know.* Runyan had to be lying.

Please God let it be a lie.

Her dress snagged on a thorn bush and she pulled it free, but a piece of fabric was left behind. Runyon would see it.

But still, she didn't stop. She knew these woods well, had played in them all of her life. Surely, she could lose him. Alexandra ran into a copse and hid among the leaves

Panting, Alexandra held her hand against the bulge of her stomach, willing the child within to cease kicking. A hard pressure had built between her legs as she ran. Sweat poured down her back and between her breasts. The cramp took her by surprise and she sucked in her breath at the pain.

A crash came through the woods, like an angry bear, followed by a scream of triumph. "Not very good at hide and seek, are you? I've found a bit of your dress. Lord, but you are careless!" The footsteps behind her slowed as if he were deciding which way to go.

Alexandra covered her mouth from weeping aloud, more terrified than she had ever been in her life. How was she to survive this? *Sutton. You stupid, impossible Peacock. How could you leave me to face this?* Her arms curved protectively around the child in her womb.

"I have to protect you," she whispered as her hands ran over her stomach. "I will not allow that monster to harm you nor take you from me. You are the heir to Cambourne. I will not let him take us."

How long had Jeanette and Runyon been planning this?

"Come, my pigeon." Runyon cajoled just to her left. "You cannot hope to outrun me Alexandra. Not with your belly full of that bastard's child."

She could hear him beating away the dense grass with his cane. "Come dearest, I assure you Cam *is* dead. There is no way he survived a bludgeoning and a drowning, even the luck of Satan Reynolds must run out eventually. It would break my heart to report that his young widow threw herself into the nearby river, drowning in her grief." He gave a nasty chuckle at his pun.

Desperate fear ripped into her. He was right, she couldn't

outrun him. Her side ached and something wet ran down the inside of her leg. She spied a large hollow log to her left. It looked rotten and filled with vermin, but the log also looked large enough to hide her. Crawling on all fours, she moved towards the log. Spiders and what appeared to be a small snake scattered from the area as she approached.

"Alexandra. Answer me, you stupid bitch!" He slapped the cane against the ground. "I am growing weary of this silly game! I am going to beat you senseless for wasting my morning in such a way. Do you hear me?"

Alexandra inched her way into the log on her side. She ignored the bugs dropping in her hair and the splinters digging into her hands. Pulling her feet in, she concentrated on controlling her breathing. Silently she wept while her body shuddered in shock and terror.

The crunch of a boot sounded just outside the log. The cane swung back and forth, knocking against the rotted wood.

Suddenly a strong hand wrapped itself around her ankle, the fingers digging into her flesh.

"No! God, no!" Frantically she tried to wedge herself deeper into the log. Her face scraped against the interior of the log tearing her skin. Blood rushed down her cheek.

Runyon gave another tug, ripping her hose. "Lord, stuck in there like a pig in a poke."

Alexandra dug at the inside of the log, her fingernails breaking, as she clawed for purchase in the rotten wood. She kicked her feet wildly, hoping to land a blow on his face and was rewarded with a muffled sound of pain.

"I've got you now!" Runyon bellowed in a childish voice, as if she were only toying with him and not fighting for her life. "So predictable in virtually every way. Except for that very disgusting display of wanton behavior with Cam. Public ruination by the biggest rake in the *ton*, was something I did not foresee. You'll be paying for that little episode for quite some time." He pulled her legs, twisting her calves painfully.

Her skirts ripped, sticking to the log. Runyon gave an exasperated sigh and pulled harder. The lower half of Alexandra's body emerged from the log.

"Leave me alone. I shall have you arrested. I know about Elizabeth. Your relationship with Jeanette" Alexandra spat at him. "I know what you did. I'll tell your father." The log shredded beneath her fingertips as she struggled to gain purchase.

"Alexandra you are so terribly unsophisticated. I would venture even backward in some ways. I worship my cousin, and she adores me in return. You will learn to worship her as well. Jeanette and I enjoy the games we play together, we have since we were children. When she visits us in Italy, you will be required to play those games with us."

"Sick." Alexandra hissed. "You are both detestable, horrible creatures. That any mother would allow her daughter to be touched in such a way is revolting...NO!" Alexandra screamed as the lower half of her skirt was ripped off.

Runyon's hand made contact with her nearly naked buttocks. "Do not ever speak of my sweet Jeanette in such a way again. As far as Elizabeth is concerned, I was merely toying with her. Jeanette didn't mind. Robert made such a stink".

"Elizabeth was a child. You monster." She stuck at him with her foot, one shoe coming off. Alexandra felt her hair catching on the log as he pulled her body towards him.

With one great tug from Runyon, Alexandra popped out in a dirty heap of log and leaves. Grabbing her by the hair, he held her up, grunting with the effort. He turned from her stomach in revulsion. "We must get rid of *that* as soon as possible. Good lord you resemble a sow about to sprout piglets. He leered at her breasts. "But there are some benefits

I suppose. Your tits are much larger." He reached out and pinched her swollen nipples. "Delicious."

Alexandra hit him with her hands and slapped at his face, struggling to break free. Tears streaked down her cheeks. "Please," she begged, sounding like a madwoman. "You can do whatever you want to me, but please don't hurt my child. Please!"

"Oh, Alexandra. I don't make deals with naughty little sluts like you! I will do whatever I *wish* to you and your child." His pale gaze fell back to her stomach. "Now what to do with the Spawn of Satan?" His eyes widened as he thumped her belly with his forefinger. "Sounds much like a melon." An insane giggle escaped his lips.

The thud of hooves broke Runyon's ramblings. Someone was coming.

"Alexandra! Alex!" The deep baritone echoed through the quiet woods as the horse slowed.

Runyon poked his head up, sniffing the air as if he were a small fox about to be dispatched by a hound. He shook his head in wonderment.

Alexandra twisted, trying to release herself, shocked at the sound of her husband's voice.

"Unbelievable!" Runyon's face bore a look of frustrated amazement. "How in the *world* did he survive? Jeanette will be livid. Simply livid! You just *cannot* get good help these days. I suppose that if one wants something done correctly, one must do such things oneself." He looked down in disgust at his waistcoat. "And just look what you've done to my waist-coat. Horribly soiled because you refuse to behave." He shook her.

Alexandra raised her hands and pummeled Runyon, all the while screaming as loud as she could. "Here! I'm here Sutton!"

Runyon's ungloved hand shot out and slapped her across the face, making her head snap back.

"Shut up, Alexandra. I am so very tired of listening to you talk." He shook her harder.

Alexandra struggled against the blackness that was stealing over her vision, but she kept screaming, her throat feeling as if it were stripped raw.

A large bay mare galloped towards them, the rider bent low over the animal's neck. It was one of the horses that pulled Miranda's carriage just an hour earlier. The rider's long, dark hair fluttered around his shoulders as he headed straight towards them. The glint of jade sparkled from one ear and his face was contorted with rage.

Alexandra struggled. She smacked at Runyon's hands where he held her, then bent down and bit him hard, on the wrist.

"Bitch." He shook her as a dog does a small animal. "Damn him. *Damn you.*"

Sutton jumped off the horse to grab at Runyon. As he did, her captor threw her back towards the fallen log. Her head connected with the rotted wood and for a moment Alexandra saw stars. A gasp of pain left her lips as another cramp rippled across her mid-section.

The two men tumbled to the ground amid the tall grasses.

Alexandra couldn't see anything except the moving of the grass and muffled grunts of pain. Pushing herself away from the log, she struggled to pull herself upright. A silent prayer escaped her lips as the wolf's-head cane rose high and pummeled the grass.

Sutton grunted in pain.

Runyon turned in a semicircle, the cane held high as if not knowing where to strike. Suddenly the tall grass shifted as if a large snake slithered towards Runyon. A large snapping sound rang through the clearing as some part of Sutton made contact with Runyon's leg, breaking the bone.

Runyon fell.

"You worthless bastard!" Runyon spat. "Now look what you have done! Why aren't you dead? You should be dead!" Runyon whined in a crazed voice as he rolled towards the area where Alexandra sat, weeping in pain and rage.

Sutton stood, looming over Runyon. He spared a glance at Alexandra before looking back down at the man screaming in the grass. "Really Archie, you should be more careful of the loyalty of the men you hire." His booted foot made contact with Runyon as he kicked the injured man. "That's the problem with mercenaries, Archie. They can be bought. Fortunately for me, Viscount Lindley pays far better than you or Jeanette. Once he dispatched your assassins, he saved me and sent you word I was dead." Sutton kicked Runyon again eliciting another yelp of pain.

"He said..." Alexandra stuttered. "Viscount Lindley said he took precautions." Alexandra silently thanked the large, menacing Devil of Dunbar for his foresight. She would thank him much more effusively in person.

"If you move again, I'll kill you." Sutton warned the man lying in the grass. "And I do so wish to kill you."

"Sutton." Alexandra held out shaking arms to her husband. "You're not dead."

Sutton gave Alexandra a half-hearted smile. "I've lived years telling Nick to stop acting like a meddlesome old aunt. Always inserting himself in everyone's business. I will never do so again." He knelt to enfold her in his arms, his eyes widening as he took in her stomach.

Alexandra caught the aroma of cinnamon and horse. And Sutton.

"Jesus." Sutton took a deep gasping breath as if the sight of her caused him pain. "I left you and you were with child. How can you ever forgive me?"

Alexandra shook her head, shaking out twigs and leaves. "You couldn't have known, though that doesn't excuse you."

She sniffed as the tears ran down her cheeks and her heart lifted in joy at the sight of him. "How did you find me?"

"I am the package Miranda went to the village for. I sent word two days ago. She was incredibly frustrated you didn't wish to go with her. Just as we rounded the bend and Helmsby Abbey came into view, the carriage wheel loosened. Then I heard you scream." His voice grew rough. "I took the horse and rode towards the sound."

Alexandra began shaking. "Sutton—"

A shadow loomed behind Sutton.

Runyon stood on one leg, dragging his broken limb behind him. "You...should...not...be...here." Runyon pulled apart the cane, revealing a wicked blade.

Sutton pivoted, but not quickly enough. Runyon's blade flashed in the sunlight before burying itself in Sutton's side. He toppled over, a large bloodstain blooming the fine white lawn of his shirt.

"No!" Alexandra screamed and crawled towards her husband, the pain in her belly growing more intense. Sobs wracked her body along with the tightening of her stomach. She looked down and saw a trickle of blood running down her leg to stain her hose. Was she to lose Sutton and the baby? Alexandra wished nothing so much in that moment but to die, with her husband and child.

Runyon stood unsteadily, a smug look of triumph on his face. He took out a handkerchief and mopped sweat from his brow.

"You see if you want a job done correctly," he pushed back the blonde curls that had fallen over his forehead, "you must do it yourself." Runyon struggled to maintain his stance on his wounded leg. "Now it's just you and I, my little pigeon! We must make haste. We have a barn burning to oversee!"

"No. I'm not going anywhere with you." While Runyon laughed, Alexandra inched toward her husband. Upon reaching Sutton, she cradled his head in her hands as blood from both their wounds mingled and darkened their clothing. "Please don't leave me. I cannot do this without you. I *won't* do it without you. *Please*."

"Love you." The green of his eyes blazed brilliantly on her. "Have forever. Should have told you." His skin took on a grayish hue as his eyes fluttered closed. "I'm sorry, Badger."

"You cannot die. You *cannot*." Alexandra sobbed brokenly.

Runyon hobbled closer. He grunted in pain as he looked down at Sutton and the sobbing Alexandra.

"Dead! Yes! *Finally*!" His insane laughter echoed through the quiet clearing as he reached down to grab her. "Such fun we will have, Alexandra!"

It was the last thing Runyon ever said to her as the sound of a single shot rang out through the quiet woods.

Sunlight filtered over the newly restored gardens of Helmsby Abbey. Alexandra closed her eyes, soaking in the warmth of the sun and the peace of her garden. She rocked back and forth, humming gently to the bundle in her lap. A pair of curious green eyes stared back at her, nearly hidden underneath a thatch of dark, curly hair. Her heart constricted in her chest. "I almost lost you," she whispered to the bundle. The horror of the day in the woods still haunted her. It might forever. Sometimes Alexandra would awake, sweating and shaking as she remembered the way Runyon spun from her, a confused look on his face. The jerk of his body as the force of the pistol ball hit his chest. He'd stood there for a few seconds as if stunned that someone had dared to shoot him, before he crumpled to the ground.

Furiously she wiped at her eyes.

"No more tears, my love. You promised me." Sutton reached across the small space that separated him from her and took her hand, careful not to disturb the infant he held.

The air of the newly restored gardens held a profusion of

roses, the aroma sweet and subtle in the air. Red, yellow, pink, but not a single one white. The roses had been all she could see from her window as she gave birth to the twins, with Miranda holding her hand and Mrs. Cowries bathing her brow.

The poor village doctor, ill equipped to handle Lady Cambourne in labor with twins and the life-threatening wounds of Lord Cambourne, ran back and forth between Alexandra and Sutton's room, scuttling between the two in a frenzy. Dr. Piper had finally relented to Mrs. Cowries and had the village midwife sent for to tend Alexandra.

The old rocking chair creaked as Sutton shifted, grunting with pain.

"Damn."

The wound healed well, but slowly, forcing Sutton to rest instead of rushing back to London. It was just as well for the Cambournes didn't need another scandal and strangling his stepmother would have fed the gossip for years.

Runyon's blade sliced deeply, right through the lower half of the dragon, neatly bisecting the tail. Sutton would have a magnificent scar, but he survived. Runyon's blade, had it struck a few inches to the left would have killed her husband. Another thought that gave Alexandra nightmares.

"Shush, Madeline. Daddy's sorry." Sutton tried unsuccessfully to soothe the fussing bundle that he was now clasping to his chest.

Alexandra could barely see her daughter's mass of dark curls, so swaddled did Sutton have the baby.

"She's safe, my love. Don't hold her so close."

Sutton gave her a solemn look from the depths of his beautiful eyes. "I shall always hold her close to my heart. Both of them. Until I breathe my last." He squeezed her hand. "As I will their mother."

Alexandra squeezed back. "I love you." The words whispered into the breeze and Sutton smiled, a dazzling smile that made her heart flutter.

Bees buzzed, stopping at each flowering rose as happy in the garden as she and Sutton were. Alexandra closed her eyes enjoying the sense of peace and contentment that filled her.

She and Sutton sat in silence, the small snores from the bundles they each cradled the only sound except for the bees. As the sun rose higher in the sky, the click of heels on the old cobblestones disturbed the tranquility of the early morning.

"There you are. Auntie Miranda must say goodbye." Miranda floated over to Alex and pressed a kiss on Robert's downy head. She stood and moved to the bundle Sutton held. "And a kiss for you, my beautiful Madeline." A letter dangled from her gloved hand. "This just arrived from Cousin Herbert, in Yorkshire. You shan't need to worry about Mother again."

Sutton took the letter from his sister, scanning the contents while Alexandra waited patiently.

"Herbert sends his congratulations on the birth of our children as well as an assurance that Jeanette will bother us no more." Sutton said ruefully. "Apparently when Jeanette was confronted with the knowledge that Archie was dead, I was alive, and there was an heir to Cambourne she became hysterical. Violent. She screamed obscenities and blame," he looked at Miranda, "over Archie's death. Herbert had her sedated. She is thought to be insane. He's hired a nurse for her and she does not leave her room."

"She's a prisoner?" Alexandra said softly, not in the least upset by Jeanette's fate. If any woman deserved such it was the former Marchioness of Cambourne.

"Yes," Sutton said. "Herbert promises that she will not be permitted to ever leave his estate. The poor man is despondent as well as furious at the way he has been manipulated. Though I sense, from the tone of his letter, he still loves her. She will have no further contact with any of us, especially Elizabeth."

Miranda squeezed her brother's shoulder. "Well, that's a relief, isn't it? Finally, I may have cakes with my tea and not be told I am going to become stout!" She gave a half-hearted smile.

Alexandra looked up at her friend, wishing there was something to be said to assuage the pain that haunted Miranda. Whatever the depth of her evil, Jeanette was still Miranda's mother, as unfortunate as that was. Jeanette had screamed out her rage at Archie's death in the Cambourne townhouse, cursing Sutton and Alexandra, but especially denouncing Miranda. The servants had heard, quite possibly the neighbors as well. Sutton assured Alexandra that he'd taken care of the matter.

Alexandra was hopeful that would prove to be true.

Noting Alexandra's regard, Miranda smiled brightly and placed her hands on her hips, her eyes full of love as she looked at her niece and nephew. "They aren't quite as upset at my leaving as I expected they should be. It's very disappointing. I suppose with all that eating, burping and sleeping, they are quite busy and will hardly notice I've left."

Alexandra looked up at Miranda. "But I will notice, my dearest friend." How she would miss Miranda, to whom she owed everything.

Miranda bit her lip and her eyes shone with emotion. "I shall eagerly await your return to London. Elizabeth will be coming home from Scotland soon I expect. She is beside herself that she is now an aunt. And to twins."

Sutton shook his head. "Gray Covington, I think, Miranda. Not London. At least not for some time," Sutton stated firmly. "My marchioness prefers life away from the glare of the *ton*. As do I." He shot his sister a look. "Do not return. Stay with us."

"I'll be fine, but Grandmother will expect you and Alexandra for the Season." Miranda frowned, wrinkling her lovely brow. "She says I'm getting long in the tooth and must decide upon some man to marry. It shall be difficult, as I am riddled with scandal." Miranda tried to sound flippant and didn't succeed. "I now have a better understanding of Arabella's view of the *ton*."

Sutton grabbed his sister's hand. "Nick's sister has the disposition of a scorpion which owes more to her unmarried state than her brother's reputation. And I would have you marry for love, Miranda."

A pained look crossed Miranda's features and she shrugged. "Perhaps that is not my fate. And the *ton* doesn't frighten me."

"You are quite brave, Miranda, and much stronger than I." Sutton said quietly.

Miranda bit her lip and looked away. "No, I'm not."

Sutton took his sister's hand and pressed a kiss to her knuckles. "You are." His voice cracked with the depth of his feelings. "I will never be able to express to you my gratitude." He gave a rueful laugh. "Nor will I ever accuse you of nagging me again."

A tear slipped down Miranda's cheek.

"For had you not insisted so firmly, I would never have taught you how to shoot a pistol."

❦

THANK YOU FOR READING SUTTON AND ALEX'S STORY. IF you enjoyed Wicked's Scandal I would greatly appreciate you leaving a review.

Keep reading more of the Wicked's....
Devil of a Duke (Book 2)
My Wicked Earl (Book 3)
Wickedly Yours (Book 4)
Tall, Dark & Wicked (Book 5)

ABOUT THE AUTHOR

Kathleen Ayers has been a hopeful romantic since the tender age of fourteen when she first purchased a copy of Sweet Savage Love at a garage sale while her mother was looking at antique animal planters. Since then she's read hundreds of historical romances and fallen in love dozens of times. In particular she adores handsome, slightly damaged men with a wicked sense of humor. On paper, of course.

Kathleen lives in Houston with her husband, a college aged son who pops in to have his laundry done and two very spoiled dogs.

Sign up for Kathleen's newsletter:
www.kathleenayers.com

Like Kathleen on Facebook
www.facebook.com/kayersauthor

Join Kathleen's Facebook Group
Historically Hot with Kathleen Ayers

Follow Kathleen on Bookbub
bookbub.com/authors/kathleen-ayers

ALSO BY KATHLEEN AYERS

THE WICKEDS

Wicked's Scandal

Devil of a Duke

My Wicked Earl

Wickedly Yours

Tall, Dark & Wicked

Still Wicked

Wicked Again

Made in the USA
Middletown, DE
10 February 2024